Wandering
with Wizards

or
A Muggle Holiday

William Wilkin

Bell Street Publishing, LLC

Published by Bell Street Publishing, LLC,
7360 Middlebrook Cir
Nashville, TN 37221-6545

Copyright © 2018 by Bell Street Publishing, LLC

ISBN: 978-0-9903164-6-6

First Published in the United States,2019

Cover Art: W. Wilkin
Graphic Design: Matthew A. Stone & William Wilkin

Contents

Acknowledgements

I owe an immense debt of gratitude to several people who have contributed substantially to this book's artistic integrity.

There are my two sons, James Wilkin and Matthew Stone.

James and Matthew contributed a number of graphic design suggestions that are incorporated in the cover design and interior of the book.

He exhibited attention to detail and artistic consistency far beyond my capabilities.

My wife, Lou, contributed in both obvious and subtle ways to the completion of the book. She is a Spanish teacher and has extensive experience editing and correcting texts–both student and professional. Any remaining grammatical and spelling errors must not be accounted to her. They proceed from my eccentric ideas about the value of deviating from standards occasionally to accurately portray a state of mind or emotional content. A subtle way that she supported the completion of this book was her endless patience with those eccentric ideas.

In addition, she was willing to endure the many, many times that I worked into the early morning hours pursued by my characters who insisted on telling their stories at the most inconvenient hours.

She has always been emotionally constant in the shifting winds of our lives throughout the long thankless years of the struggle to bring these stories to print.

Bravo Lou!

Preface

For those of you who have not read any of the preceding books, I will warn you that this preface contains spoilers. If you want to learn about the story line to the point where this book begins, you could read the stories in sequence—*In the Realm of the Blind, The Chessmaster, The Spare Wizard,* and *The Ministry Witch and other tales of perfidy.* However, reading the first book by itself would give you a good grounding in the Realm of the Blind.

This story takes place in the universe of the Realm of the Blind where Hogwarts School for Witchcraft and Wizardry exits. It is a residential finishing school for magical youth.

The main character James Wendt is an English Literature Professor and Muggle (non-magical). He has been hired by the Headmaster Albus Dumbledore to bring diversity to the school and the slightest touch of liberal arts education to an institution that is basically a vocational school. Dumbledore has been assassinated by Severus Snape who is now the Headmaster of Hogwarts. Wendt was last seen attempting to flee England to the United States.

Wendt and the Assitant Headmistress Minerva McGonagall are "an item." However, the astronomy Professor Aurora Sinestra seems to have designs on Wendt.

The would-be despot Valdemort has a gang of followers who call themselves Deatheaters. Valdemort was permanently separated from his body but survived as a disembodied spirit. He had recently been gifted a new body and threatens the magical world order as he once had done. He and his followers are determined to enslave the Muggle population. Thus, Muggles like Professor Wendt are on their *persona non grata* list. They have been trying to kill Wendt for several years because of the effrontery of a Muggle in choosing to teach at one of the premier schools of magic.

The magical government of England was led by Minister Fudge who wished to deny the survival of Valdemort. He has recently been replaced by a new Minister of Magic who recognizes the obvious–the return of Valdemort.. Harry Potter is now a wanted man—the number one undesirable. Every relative of Potter is now in danger. They would be used by the Deatheaters to reach Potter. These relatives include his cousin Dudley Dursley, his aunt Petunia Dursley, and his uncle Vernon Dursley.

Other teachers at Hogwarts include Rubeus Haggrid (Professor of Magical Creatures), Severus Snape (formerly Potion-master), and Professor Flitwick (Professor of Charms). Other staff at Hogwarts include the Janitor, Filch; the Librarian, Ms. Pinz; and the Nurse, Madame Pomfrey.

Riding With Wizards

I gazed back through the rear window of the Ford Fiesta as we pulled away from home. I watched as the little house on Privet Drive shrank and shrank. I'd driven away from home many times with my parents. I'd never looked back like I was this time. That was because, of course, I knew that it would be a long time before we saw it again. Just for a moment, a wave of fear ran through me like that first shock that you get when you jump into a pool. You feel it all through you, but it's gone in a moment. The fear was that I might never see #4 Privet Drive again after it disappeared. Privet Drive runs a long distance and gradually curves away to the right. I saw our house shrink so that it looked like every other house on the street. Then I couldn't tell whether it had two stories. Then I wasn't quite sure which house it was. Another wave of panic struck. I had the crazy idea that if I couldn't tell which one it was, #4 would no longer exist.

I convinced myself that I could see it for a very long time after it had finally disappeared for good. Then I turned back to see where we were going. I had never paid much attention to roads and streets, to towns and cities. I knew in a general way where we were—in the suburbs of London. I knew that we were near the M11. I even knew that the street we were driving on now would cross the M11 shortly. It happened, and we got on the M11. I even knew that we were heading North on the M11. I was proud of myself for a minute, knowing where we were and what direction we were going. Then it struck me as it had not before.

I didn't know where we were going.

Another wave of panic struck. It lasted longer. I kept one idea in my head, though. It saw me through that wave. Me Dad knew where we going. He was driving. He had to know where we were going.

It hit me then that I had no idea how long it would be before we would return. I had the idea that it would be like a long holiday. Me parents and I had once traveled to the Azores and spent two whole weeks there. It was the first time that Harry Potter had been away from us for a

3

long time without being in school. That was two years ago. It was like a real holiday for us. We were free of Potter and could do what we really wanted to.

Me dad had been saving up for a family vacation without having to drag <u>him</u> along for years and years, so we could afford to take a good long trip. It was in July. It was off season in the Azores. It was hot, but the beaches were not crowded.

I thought with longing for the old days–not just the days of that trip but even the days with Potter around. We weren't being chased by and traveling with wizards, and we could do pretty much what we wanted.

Of course, when he was around, I could play my little tricks on Potter. I hadn't been able to do that the last couple of years. It had been good, and I hadn't even realized it. Mum is always saying that we don't know it when we've got it good.

One day she was sitting at the kitchen counter gazing off into the distance. I was hungry and wanted something to nosh on. So, I just asked her for something to eat. She swung around and looked like she was going to snap me head off. But she stopped long enough to ask what I wanted. I told her, "a candy bar." That seemed to shock her.

"That was what I was thinking about. One time when your Aunt. . . ." She stopped in mid-word and her mouth dropped.

I just said, "Aunt Marge." I thought she might be going crackers, but she stared at me as though she were seeing me for the first time.

"No. Your Aunt," She said the name slowly as if trying to remember how to say it. "Your Aunt Lily. I had a candy bar, and she wanted part of it." She stopped again, and I thought she would start bawling. She got hold of herself and said, "I didn't want to share it with her. I DIDN'T share it with her." Her voice seemed to break, and she did sigh two or three times. It made me worried. She went on, "I didn't share. I wished and wished that I could go back and do it over, but you never can go back–never."

The look on her face made me think she had lost her best friend. I was still worried about her. I tried to make her feel better, "It was just a candy bar."

She looked at me again as though she'd just realized I was there and said that crazy thing, "You don't know when you've got it good, Popkin. You just don't."

I just stared at her and didn't have the slightest. But I knew now what she meant.

□

Now, Dad was driving feverishly taking bends in the road without slowing down. The wizard and the witch sitting with me in the back seat were

4

shaking with fear but too polite to say anything. I was not feeling all that good myself.

Mum in the front seat would shriek each time we went around a sharp curve and would shout Dad's name every time we approached a slower car.

Dad just said, "I've got it." Then he'd swerve around the car and accelerate on.

I asked him where we were going. He just snarled, "Ask your friends in the back seat."

Their names were Diggle.

The witch said, "It's near Hartlepool, dear. We have a little cottage on the North Sea."

I didn't have the slightest idea what Hartlepool was or what it was like. With that I suddenly realized that I couldn't tell anyone what the witch looked like. I stared at her for the first time. I had never known anyone who looked like her. How can you describe what someone looks like if you've never seen anyone like them before? I suppose it was the strange clothes. She had a tall pointy hat that flopped down like a Santa Claus hat, but not red or white. It looked like it was old. There were something like sparkly sequins on it, but they looked like they were starting to fall off. She was wearing something like a cape, but it fit her tighter than a cape. It was all dark. I couldn't have named a color. Now that I think about it, I don't think that I ever noticed what color her eyes were.

After I'd been staring for a while, she asked me, "Was there something, dear?"

I said, "No. I've just never been to Harlepool before."

She said, "Oh, it's a nice little town. Out of the way, you know."

She fell silent. I knew that must be good. You want someplace out of the way if you were hiding.

I glanced at my watch and was surprised to see that we'd already been gone for nearly three hours. That thought brought on a wave that was almost nausea. I didn't know a lot about England but I knew that you could get almost anywhere on the "M" roads in about six hours. Wherever we were going, we were a lot closer to it than I really wanted.

An idea occurred to me. "Dad, aren't you getting hungry? I'm hungry. Let's stop somewhere."

That was almost a sure-fire thing. Dad has an appetite that's even bigger than mine. Of course, I really wasn't hungry. I was just trying to get us to slow down. Maybe we'd have to spend the night at a hotel. That would be good.

He just looked half way round, and I could see that there was a strange expression on his face as he looked at Mum. She gave a little half-nod and said, "Now, Popkin, we've got to get to the house before it gets dark. We'll just keep driving for a while. Just be patient."

Oh, I was patient. I could wait forever to get to this house we were going to. I just knew that it would be strange. There probably wouldn't be any computer games. I had a horrible thought. What if they didn't have a computer!

The wizard misunderstood me completely. He said, "Now, don't you worry. It won't be long before we're home, and then we'll have a real proper meal for you–lots of fresh vegetables and good brown bread and butter."

"Yeh," I thought, "Just what I want. No hamburgers or chips. No soda."

That little talk did do one good thing for me. It gave me something solid and not spooky to worry about. I was almost feeling good when Dad announced, "We're about half an hour from Hartlepool."

I even was happy when the wizard said, "Our home is closer than Harlepool. Just slow down, and I'll tell you where to get off the A19."

He was right. We pulled up to the little cottage after less than a half hour. It was after 6 PM, but I really wasn't hungry. I made a fuss about wanting to carry bags in for everyone. I wasn't being kind. I just wanted to put off getting settled in as long as possible.

Of course, that couldn't go on forever. I ended up taking all the bags up to our room. It was just one room that Mum and Dad and I had to share! I asked where my room was. Everyone agreed that it was the same room for me, Mum, and Dad.

Dad wasn't really happy about it either, but we were all stuck. There just wasn't another bedroom in the cottage.

After we left our luggage in our one room, we came downstairs to the dining room. At least we weren't eating in the kitchen. Somehow, there was a pot on the stove that was bubbling away. It was a foul looking brownish stuff. I was getting my stomach ready for the miserable taste that was heading for it. I was about to ask Dad if we could go to the restaurant that I'd seen on the road a few miles back when the witch brought the pot into the dining room and put it on the table. Then the smell reached me, and I wasn't so sure. The witch ladled out a big bowlful of it. As I breathed in the smell, I decided that it was worth a try.

I had a spoonful at my mouth when the witch exclaimed, "Mr. Dursley, haven't you forgotten something!"

I looked around wondering who she was talking to. She seemed to be talking to Dad, but she was looking straight at me. I figured she must mean Dad and started to bring the spoonful to my mouth when she said, "Young Man! I say you have completely forgotten something."

6

I looked around and figured that it must be me that she was talking to. I thought a minute and said, "Oh, yes. I didn't use my napkin." I was drawing at straws, but that was apparently not what she was talking about. She did tell me what it was. "You're forgetting grace."

I didn't have an idea what she was talking about, but I figured that I needed to wait for grace–whoever or whatever it was.

Then, the wizard said, after a long, unpleasant silence, "I'll return thanks."

He bowed his head, and I figured that must be the thing to do. So I followed his lead and listened as he said, "Lord, for the grace of food to share and friends to share it with, we are thankful." He was silent then, and I heard the clink of spoons on bowls. I raised my head experimentally and found that everyone else was eating, so I finally put the spoon into my mouth and found the most amazing taste that I'd ever had. It was hot, full of tastes, and seemed to fill my stomach as few meals that I'd had ever did. Of course, that might have had something to do with the three bowls of stew that I had and the mountain of bread that I ate.

The witch seemed to like the appetite that I had for the stew and bread. Now that the meal was over, I asked the obvious question, "What's on the telly tonight?"

The witch and wizard loked at each other in puzzlement. My Dad told me, "I don't think that they have telly, my boy."

I stared in disbelief, but as I thought about it, I realized that I'd not seen a telly anywhere in the house. In despair, I asked, "No telly at all?"

Me Mum just shook her head and said, "I'm afraid not Popkin."

I looked from face to face and asked, "What do we do then?"

That question seemed to cheer up the wizard, "Oh, we have lots of games. Let's see, we have Monopoly and Brooms and Owls. We have Road to Gringotts and Dungeons and Dragons. And, of course, we have tarot cards and ordinary playing cards. OOH! We have Wizard's Chess. What do you like to play?"

I saw a ray of hope. I asked, "Where's your computer? I want to play Dungeons and Dragons." As soon as the words were out of my mouth, I knew I would regret it. He walked to the front closet and opened the door. On a high shelf, there were a stack of boxes. He picked up his wand and said, "accio Dungeons and Dragons."

The box turned out to hold a board, a pair of dice, and a bag of Dragons. At first, I thought they were just tokens, but I could see through the plastic bag that held them that they were moving around. The thought of dealing with tiny dragons that maybe breathed fire was a bit much. I asked, "Do the Dragons, uh . . you know . . . breathe . . . "

The wizard was delighted and said, "Of course, they breathe fire. Delightful." He started to reach into the bag to pull one out.

7

I interrupted him and said, "Oh second thought, I'd just as soon play . . . uh," I thought for a minute. What would be safe? Surely, Monopoly would be OK. "Uh. . . Monopoly. Yeah, Monopoly sounds good."

The wizard seemed disappointed, "Well, that would be fine. Are you sure that you don't want to play Dungeons and Dragons? It's one of my favorites."

"Yes", I thought, "I'll bet it is." I said, "Well, you know, I am a guest."

He nodded somewhat glumly, "Yes, you're right. Monopoly it is."

He sent the box flying back into the closet and "Accio Monopoly." brought out the Monopoly box. The outside looked pretty familiar from a distance, but I wasn't going to assume anything.

A closer examination of the box showed that the familiar man on the lid of the box was wearing a cape and appeared to be riding a broom. In his hand he held a strange ball that looked roughly like a cross between a tennis ball and a bat. I didn't mean to laugh but I did. The unexpected image was that strange.

Dedalus, for that was the wizard's name, had taken the laugh in the wrong way–as he often did when dealing with my family. He seemed to think it was a laugh of recognition. He was saying, "Yes, it's the Quidditch edition–very popular. I picked this one up at the Weasley's in Diagon Alley."

He quickly removed the lid and pulled out the board. The board, at first glance, was very much like any other Monopoly board. However, the pieces were quite another thing. I picked one up and looked at it. It appeared to be a young woman on a broom. She was carrying what appeared to be a soccer ball under her arm. Dedalus smiled and said, "I rather fancy that piece myself when I play. The chasers are the very image of speed. Don't you think, Mr. Dursley?"

I continued to stare at the piece in incomprehension. He seemed to take my silence as a sign of agreement with him and he prattled on, as he pulled one piece after another from the bag. "The Beater, of course. Ah, here's many people's favorite, the Seeker." That piece was a man riding a broom with his right hand extended toward a tennis ball with wings magically suspend in thin air just beyond his hand. "The Keeper. The Referee." He almost lovingly held them. The last seemed to be a woman on broom with a whistle in her mouth. Dedalus was going on, "The Goals." That consisted of three hoops of various sizes resting on poles.

By this time, me Mum and Dad and the witch, Hestia, had joined us. Me Dad exclaimed, "Monopoly, eh. I like a good game of Monopoly."

Dedalus smiled broadly and said, "Pull up chairs. We'll play. This is the Quidditch edition. Which piece do you fancy?"

Dad frowned as he examined them. He finally picked one–the Beater, I think. It looked like a cross between a wizard on a broom and a cricket batsman. I think the bat was what attracted Dad.

Mum chose the Referee. She asked who was going to be the banker. At home, she liked running the bank. Dedalus seemed puzzled, but his wife caught on, "She means the Goblin. Who's going to be the Goblin?"

I was confused and asked what Goblins had to do with bankers. Both Dedalus and Hestia laughed. He said, "Of course, you don't know. Wizarding banks are nearly all run by Goblins. So, the banker in Monopoly is called 'The Goblin'."

At first, Mum didn't seem to want to be called The Goblin, but the attractions of handling money were too much for her. She accepted the role of Goblin. Later–much later–that became a little nickname that me Dad had for me Mum. He would call her "his little Goblin," but now, he was not that excited about her being The Goblin.

I decided to be the Keeper.

The game was played almost exactly like regular Monopoly. Of course, the place names were different. The Go square was just like the standard game, but after that there were differences. For example, they didn't have railroads. They had something they called Port Keys. I guess they have something to do with travel. If you bought all the Port Keys, you could travel directly from one Port Key to another on your turn without rolling the dice if you happened to land on one.

Where the Boardwalk and Park Place were, there was Gringott's and Diagon Alley. The Go To Jail card said, "Go To Azkaban." All the money was something called Galleons.

There was a square for Hogwarts on the same side of the board as Gringott's. On one throw, me Mum landed there. She made a noise that was a little like a funny giggle and a little like a gasp. She said, "Well, who would have guessed that I'd get to Hogwarts." I had absolutely no idea what she was talking about.

I was never lucky at Monopoly, and I was the first to go bankrupt. Me Mum dropped out shortly after that, but she stayed on as The Goblin. Dad was always good at Monopoly. He stayed on until the end when it was just he and Hestia. Hestia had more than half of the properties, but she didn't have much money. Me Dad had loads of money but not an awful lot of property. Dad is crafty and drives a hard bargain, but in the end, Hestia bankrupted him as he was about to go around GO. He's not always a good loser, but this time he was a good sport. He shook hands with her and warned her that he was going to come back for a re-match.

Somehow it was after midnight, and we all were happy to get to bed. Even Dad was not a bad sport about all three of us having to share a room.

At Home with Wizards

That night, I woke up sometime before dawn. I had to use the bathroom. The night before, I was picked to sleep on the little sofa that was against one wall of our bedroom. The other inside wall had a small closet. It was good that we hadn't packed much. We didn't get half our things in that closet as it was. The rest lay in open suitcases spread around the floor as much out of the way as we could manage.

I was too tall by a foot or so for the sofa. So, my feet extended over the side of the sofa. It wasn't easy to sleep, but we were all so tired that I did eventually get to sleep.

I'd never been in me Mum and Dad's bedroom at home at night. Everyone was embarrassed about how we would put on our pajamas. Mum had the right idea, though. She took her nightgown, as she called it, to the ONE bathroom in the house and changed there. She carried back her clothes, grumbling about not having time to do a proper wash-up before bed.

I went next. I was really nervous about carrying me pajamas to the bathroom and about bringing back my clothes and about going to bed in me parents' room and about Dad and Mum being in bed together. I guess I knew that they must sleep together, but it's one thing to know something like that and very different actually watching them both getting into bed, trying not to touch in front of me.

And all this stuff happened with Dad's flashlight being our only light. There wasn't any electricity in the cottage, and the house was lit with oil lamps. When it was time for bed, Mr. Diggle wanted to send a lamp up with us, but Mum was sure that we'd start the house on fire, so we used Dad's flashlight from the car. For about the first five minutes it was kind of exciting. We took turns holding it for each other. The fun didn't last long though. Pretty soon the flashlight got heavy. Finally, Mum took it and put it on a table with the light pointed up so it lit the ceiling, and the ceiling lit everything else–sort of.

Anyway, Mum and Dad got into bed without touching, and then Dad turned off the flashlight. Then, I heard a sort of sloppy sound. I was pretty sure they kissed. They didn't do that much at home, but somehow away from home they held onto each other (when they thought I wasn't looking) and even kissed a lot more.

So, it was plenty dark when I got up to go to the bathroom. I didn't dare try to get the flashlight. I'd have wakened everyone up for sure. I quietly put both feet on the floor, took a couple of steps toward the bedroom door, and tripped over something. I think it was a suitcase. I managed not to scream even though it scared the dickens out of me. I was careful making my way to the door and didn't trip over anything. In the hall, it was even darker, but I followed the wall with my hand and managed to reach the door to the bathroom. I opened it and stepped inside. It was dark, and it seemed a lot larger than I'd remembered. Then, I tripped over a chair that hadn't been there before. I fell and landed on something that was soft. I realized it was a bed! What was a bed doing in the bathroom? It was then that I realized that I was in the Diggle's bedroom, and Dedalus picked up his wand and lit it.

"What in Merlin's beard are you doing in here, boy?"

I could only gasp and say, "Sorry, sorry, sorry." as I walked backed out of the room. I then found the real bathroom and did my business.

All went well on the way back to my room. I opened the door, came in, and took special care to avoid the suitcase from before. Just as I was reaching my sofa, I tripped over a chair. I fell to the floor and bruised my shin, my arm, my jaw, and various other body parts. I shouted, "Oh, shit!"

That woke both me Mum and Dad. He shouted too and turned on his flashlight. The room was flooded with light. I was sprawled on the floor, draped over the upturned wooden chair, and with my rear end pointed up.

Dad asked, "What in the world are you doing?"

All I could say was, "I went to the bathroom."

He angrily asked, "Why didn't you take the flashlight?"

I could only say, "I didn't want to wake anyone up."

"Well, you bloody well did, didn't you?"

All I could say was, "Yessir."

"Well, get to bed, and let's try to get a little sleep with what's left of the night." He glanced at his watch and added, "Sheesh, it's already 4:30."

□

The next day, we were all awakened at 6 AM. It was some sort of bugle. We later learned that it was actually a magical musical instrument that

11

could sound like almost anything. It was brass on one side and wooden on the other. You didn't have to blow into it. You used your wand to sound it.

Dad was the last to wake. He spluttered and then foamed at the mouth. "What the bloody hell was that?"

Dedalus knocked on our door and said, "Breakfast in fifteen."

None of us were in any good mood when we reached the kitchen after fumbling into clothes.

Dedalus was in good spirits though. He asked, "How did you all sleep? Oh, I know that Mr. Dudley had a tough night, but I hope your parents fared better."

Dad just grumbled and muttered, "What's for breakfast?"

What was for breakfast turned out to be scrambled eggs, toast, bacon, marmalade, and orange juice. One thing that I had to admit about living with Wizards. Meals were always good.

When we were nearing the end of breakfast, Dedalus asked THE question that I'd never expected, "Who wants to weed the garden?"

Hestia also had a question, "Who will mow the yard?"

All of us were mystified by these questions. I think we all thought that mowing the yard would be something that was done by magic, and nothing needed to be done by anyone. It turned out that we were wrong.

Hestia explained, "These are all jobs that have to be done by wizards as well as Muggles. You can do some of these jobs with the help of magic, but they all require time and concentration by both Muggles and Wizards."

I looked to Mum in appeal. Surely we were guests and didn't have to do these things!

It turns out that Mum and Dad were agreed about our having to work for our keep.

Dedalus said, "Another thing is that we need to de-gnome-ify the front yard."

I thought, "Remove yard gnomes, ugly plastic figurines. That's got to be easy." So, I raised my hand for that.

Dedalus said, "Thanks. That ought to be a good job for a young strapping lad like yourself."

That comment made me think again about the job. Maybe somehow it wasn't going to be such an easy, wonderful job after all, but I appeared to be stuck with it.

Mum volunteered to help clean up the dishes and dust. Dad was in for weeding the garden and mowing the yard. I was ready to help Dad with the mowing if he was still working on weeding when I finished with the gnomes.

So, Dedalus went with Dad to the garden to get him started. I waited for that to end. It gave me some time to think over the prospects for this

12

stay. No telly. No video games. No phone. No friends. No movies. It was looking to be like a long stay in prison.

Dedalus came and sooner than I hoped. He led me to the front yard. He had us sit down on the porch steps and wait. I said, "I don't see any yard gnomes. What do I need to do?"

Dedalus just said, "Quiet. Be patient."

I was. Sure enough, shortly I saw an ugly little face. Dedalus pointed at it and whispered in my ear, "There's one of the little buggers."

I couldn't believe my eyes. Dedalus slapped his forehead. "Oh, I forgot. You'll be needing gloves."

I was a little afraid to ask why, but I did. "Oh, they don't look it, but they can be pretty fierce when they're riled up. They've got sharp teeth too." He made a sort of claw-like outline with his fingers and snapped the jaws of the claw together a couple of times.

I sighed in dismay while Dedalus took out his wand and said, "accio gnome gloves." Through the open window flew a pair of heavy leather gloves. He caught them and put them on. "I'll demonstrate for you how it's done."

"They're not very smart, but they have a certain low intelligence that serves them well in their stead. You've got to move slowly and deliberately, get into grabbing range, and snag them around their body. Watch out for the teeth."

He stood and stalked the gnome slowly. When he was about a foot away from it, he swiveled rapidly and caught it around the middle. He picked it up, being careful to avoid the head that was swiveling around to try to get its teeth into him. He then slipped his grip down to the legs, swung the thing around one full revolution, and flung it away as far as he could manage.

He came back to me with a large toothy grin on his face and said, "And that's how it's done. Now do you want to give it a go?"

I nodded forlornly and took the gloves that Dedalus offered me. I slowly put them on, making sure that they were snug. I then walked slowly over to where another pair of gnomes had appeared. I got almost a foot away, and the one popped back into its hole. I turned to the other a couple of feet away. That one, I had better luck with, if you call it luck. I managed to get to a foot away. I sprung and managed to catch it around the middle and stood triumphantly. The beastly thing squirmed so hard that he got loose and nicked my wrist as it got away.

"That damn thing bit me!" I almost screamed.

"Yes, laddie, they will do that. Try again."

I thought, "Try again. Try again! You old fool! Why would anyone try that thing again?" But I grimaced and determined to make the next one pay for the other's bite. I snuck up close, got hold of him good, and wasn't quite sure how to proceed. I managed to throw him some distance.

Dedalus said, "You've got to fling them further than that or they'll be back tomorrow."

I stared at him, "Be back! Be back tomorrow! I thought this might discourage them from ever coming back."

"Oh, I told you. They're pretty dumb."

I wondered who was dumb, the one getting thrown, or the one throwing. I had an idea that seemed pretty smart. I asked, "Don't you exterminate them?"

"Oh, no. no. That wouldn't be sporting. You have to give them a chance, don't you?"

I saw no reason to give those buggers a chance, but it wasn't my home, so we'd give them a chance. I caught the next one, slipped him down so that I could pitch him by his legs, and sent him flying so that I thought he was going into orbit.

Dedalus looked at me and said, "Wow. I don't know if that one will be able to find his way back."

I said, "I hope not."

The rest of the morning and into the afternoon was spent de-gnome-ifying. I'd gotten fairly decent by the end, but I was absolutely bushed. I was not giving Dad a hand regardless how hard it was to do what he was doing.

I found that everyone else had finished with their chores before I did. They were enjoying some cold lemonade in the kitchen. I staggered in and gladly accepted a glass without comment. I was far too bushed to comment.

That night, we had another game night. This time we played card games. I already knew a couple of card games. Everyone knew poker, of course. Dedalus and Hestia weren't that interested in poker. That was OK with me.

I also knew hearts. The reason that I knew hearts was that my gang at school liked to play hearts. It wasn't that they liked hearts so much. It was that they liked the significance of the black queen. That lady could make you or break you. My crowd liked to call her "the bitch" and sometimes "the black bitch". They liked to talk about how hearts was mainly about hunting "the black bitch."

I don't need to tell you that when we played hearts with the Daedelus and Hestia, there was no talk of the "bitch". I had never learned spades. Spades is a lot like hearts but the "you know who" has no special significance. I learned that game at the Diggle's that night.

Eventually, I learned several other card games: Cribbage, Euchre, Bridge. I actually had learned Bridge before. Several years ago, my Aunt

14

Marge had wanted to have Mum, Dad, me, and her play Bridge together. She tried and tried to teach us. Mum and Dad got it OK, but I just didn't want to learn it.

I didn't.

□□

The next day, I volunteered for weeding. It seemed like it should be easier than de-gnome-ifying. And, in a way, it was. You mostly got to sit. You just identified weeds and dug them out of the ground. The ground was soft, so it was easy to get them out. The problem, of course, was that you had to identify the weeds and not pull up the crops. It took me a little time to learn that.

The first day at weeding, I'd dug up a lot of plants and was proud of myself–until Dedalus reviewed my work and made me put a third of the plants back in the ground.

Another problem with weeding was that you were constantly bending over. Your back ached like the dickens after a couple of hours until you got your back muscles developed.

One day, we actually got to harvest some crops. I was harvesting carrots. The feeling of accomplishment of actually bringing food to the kitchen was amazing. Then part of it went into a stew, and I felt like all that effort was just disappearing before my eyes.

Hestia noticed my disappointment. When I'd explained why I was disappointed, she told me something. "Dudley, that is the way with all farming. That's why pig farmers don't name their pigs, but, at least with wizards, we can extend the usefulness of our produce. We can multiply our crops. One carrot can turn into a half-dozen, a dozen, or more."

I was astounded. I asked, "Then why do you ever have to farm after you get the first crop?"

She smiled as though she were dealing with a five year-old. "We can duplicate it, but the problem is that that is exactly what we are doing. If you make a duplicate of a five day old carrot, that's what you get–another five day old carrot."

I excitedly asked, "But what if you duplicate a one day old carrot?"

"Then you've got a one day old carrot, and it ages right alongside the original."

That was disgusting. "I thought you could do things with magic?"

She smiled and said, "Certainly we can. But there are limits–as with everything Muggle as well.

"We set aside part of our produce and duplicate it to take to the farmer's market, but as you see, there are limits."

As the days got shorter and the growing season came to an end, the work decreased. I found that I actually ached to be outside and active.

After a day or two of inactivity, I began begging for chores to do. And it wasn't just for the pleasure of physical activity. When you worked a full day, the pleasure of being able to do something for fun was intense. The card nights were some of the best nights that I ever had–even more so than when I played the best video games. Most card games left time for talk, jokes, even silence. They were all more pleasurable than the same things when you hadn't put in a days effort.

So, I started to invent activities outside to wear me out. I walked some, but I began running as well. It had begun as mostly walking supplemented by the occasional sprint. After a while, it became mostly running. Then it was all running!

I ran for a while in the morning, came back, and did what chores there were in the late morning and afternoon. Then ran again in the late afternoon.

We all came to really enjoy the time that we spent together. I never really got to the point of liking Bridge, but there were four for Bridge–two natural teams–the two pairs of married people. I enjoyed just watching the games.

Of course, we played board games too–like Quidditch Monopoly, but there were other board games as well. There was a game that I sort of remembered from long ago, Parchese. There were word games. We played Scrabble some. I had never liked Scrabble because you kind of have to know a lot of words to play it, but Wizard Scrabble had lots of words that neither Mum nor Dad nor I knew. It kind of leveled the competition.

I began to see what I missed by not having relatives who lived close by us. I began to see the time that I'd spent alone on video games as lost time, never to be found again. I even wished that I'd done more with Harry. I guess Mum and Dad never encouraged me to do that, but I wished now that they had.

On Our Own

I had gone for a particularly long run that morning. I had gotten the trick of running on sand, and I made good progress on the beach. It was a beautiful afternoon with clear skies that gradually turned overcast and cool as I ran. That actually worked to my advantage. With the overcast, I could run faster without overheating than in full sun. It was such a wonderful day that I just kept going and going. Finally, I turned back for home so that I wouldn't miss the great meal that I was sure would be on the table shortly after I got back.

As usual, I frequently was able to concentrate on other things. This time, I thought about the chess game that Dad and I had played the previous night. I could see the first moves in my head. He had white and had begun by moving his King's pawn two squares forward. I matched his move. I had decided to match his moves for a while and see where that got us. He moved his Queen's pawn out one square, and I did the same.

As I played through the moves in my head, I could visualize the chess board. In a funny way, it made it easier remembering the moves. Dad had beaten me, and I was trying to figure out where I'd gone wrong. As I puzzled through the game, I lost track of where I was. I suddenly found that I'd reached the end of the beach. It was further than I'd run before. I had to turn around and get back if I didn't want to be late for supper.

I was running hard as I got close to the cottage and was out of breath when I reached the small cliffs that hid the cottage from view from the beach. The trail down to the beach was a couple of hundred yards from the cottage. I started up it. When I reached the top, I couldn't help gasping.

Even in the disappearing light of the setting sun, I could tell that there was something terribly wrong. The back door was off its hinges. Several windows were broken. One was partially open and off one hinge.

I stood frozen by shock. Then the one important thing hit me with a shock like jumping into a cold pool of water! Where were me Mum and Dad? I forgot everything else and ran with all the strength that I could never quite reach when I was running on the beach. I got to the rear door and paused before entering to shout out, "Mum, Dad are you there?"

There was no answer. I leapt across the threshold and ran to the dining room. There was no one there, but the table and every chair was turned over, smashed, and scattered around the room. It was as though some great animal–a bear or lion–had run rampage through the room.

The living room was the same. I walked up the stair, now fearing that I would find some terrible scene of carnage in our bedroom. Now I walked carefully up the stairs. The rapidly darkening skies had made it hard to see little things like broken staircase spindles scattered around. I gingerly walked up the stairs and hesitated at the door to our room. It was completely off its hinges. In the dim light of the bedroom, I could tell that every drawer of the dressers was turned out, and all the clothes in the closet were scattered about. But! There was no sign of anyone. I called again, and only silence answered me.

I sat on my sofa. It was intact anyway. I only then began to wonder what I should do next. Whoever had done this had either found my parents and taken them somewhere or probably hadn't found them. In desperation I looked everywhere for some sign of them. They would perhaps come back hoping that I had returned.

So, should I wait for me Mum and Dad to return, or should I leave. After all, the people who might come back first would be the people who had done all this damage.

After a long while I decided to wait for whoever would return first. I looked around for some sort of weapon in case of the worst. There was nothing but broken furniture and clothes spread about everywhere. Then I saw me Dad's golf clubs in a corner. I walked over and reached into the bag trying to pick the club that would do the most damage if I wanted to swing it with all my might. I finally decided that an iron would be the best. I picked the #9 and swung it a few times. I liked the shorter handle and wicked angled head. I could give someone a good whack with it.

Then, I sat on the sofa waiting for whoever came first. The last light of day had long since disappeared when I heard a door below swing open. I was tempted to call out, but decided that it would be better to let them declare themselves. I got up as soundlessly as I could, walked behind the sofa, and knelt down with my nine iron at the ready.

I heard what seemed like feet on the stairs. My mouth tightened and constricted to a mere line. I'd stopped breathing and prepared to spring as soon as I identified the intruder.

18

A squeaky board just outside our room sounded. I took a deep breath and swore in my head because I didn't want to make a sound. The blasted door made a noise as someone bumped it with a foot. There was some sort of light on the other side of the door. It was not bright enough to reveal whoever was entering the room.

The door was not in the way, but I still couldn't make out the form in the doorway. I decided that I had to attack now if I were ever going to. I leaped over the low sofa, easily clearing the back. I was raising the nine iron like a cricketer would. I began my swing. and the man in the door turned, illuminating his profile.

IT WAS DAD!

My swing had started, and it continued as though my arms were no longer in my control. I was convinced that disaster was striking without any chance of my preventing it.

□

A voice called out something that on reflection I realized later was "Arresto Momentum." At the time, I didn't know what it was. Instead, I realized that my arm stopped swinging. My muscles cramped as they tried to continue the swing against an immovable force.

The next instant, there was a flood of light. I saw me Dad clearly and he saw me as well. He exclaimed, "Where were you! We had to leave so quickly, and you weren't here."

As he was speaking, Mum threw her arms around me and just said, "Oh, Popkin, Popkin, Popkin."

He led me downstairs where I saw the Dingles waiting for us. As soon as we were on the main floor, he said, "Quickly, you must pack! Just one bag apiece. Then we'll leave before the Deatheaters return!"

Dad nodded and said, "Yes. Each of us. One bag. We're not coming back."

So, we all trudged back up the stairs to our room. Mr. Diggle carried his wand high behind us. It was very bright, and we had no trouble seeing everything.

Dad and I pawed through our clothes that were mostly scattered around. I found that my big suitcase was broken, but my backpack wasn't. I started to ask Dad about what we should bring. He just stared and shouted, "Get packing. We don't have time!"

Me Mum was frantically throwing clothes in all direction. Now and then she would pull a dress or pair of slacks out of the pile on the floor and throw it into her overnight bag.

I grabbed a couple of pair of jeans, two shirts, some socks (I wasn't sure that any of them matched). They were stuffed into my backpack with an extra pair of shoes. Dad finished before any of us.

Dedalus rushed us out of the house and away from it. Dad took my arm and pulled me back toward the house. Dedalus turned back to us and urged us on.

Dad said, "Hold it right there. I've got my own idea about how to protect my family. We're parting ways here."

Dedalus smacked his forehead with a hand. "You are being crazy. You don't stand a chance by yourselves."

Dad faced him directly and said, "You couldn't protect us for even a month. I'm going to protect my family on my own!"

I looked Dad in the face and could tell that he was not going to be talked out of this. Dedalus kept trying for a few minutes, but his wife looked over at Mum who shook her head. Then Hestia nodded, walked over to Dedalus, and put her hand on his arm. He looked at her and realized that it was over.

Then he walked over to Dad and held out his hand. Dad took it, and Dedalus said, "If we ever meet again, I'll be surprised. Good luck."

He and Hestia, walked off quickly, their suitcases trailing behind them a foot or so above the ground.

Dad led us quickly back to the small barn where our car was hidden. He threw open the doors, and we quickly loaded our bags into the car. Dad drove the car through the door and onto the country road that ran in front of the cottage.

I asked the obvious question, "What the fuck happened? Where are we going?"

Dad didn't turn. He just muttered, "Not now. Not now."

He drove furiously but not like he had on the way to the cottage. That had been panic. This was hard determination.

After a little while, me Mum asked timidly, "Where ARE we going?"

Dad slowly said, "I've not the foggiest."

We drove in the deep dark of a moonless night. Slowly a light grew in the sky. We were approaching a city. We began to pass scattered houses and then petrol stations and churches and. . . and RESTAURANTS. I asked if we couldn't stop for something to eat.

Dad's face went through various grimaces and finally settled into frown, "Yes, I suppose we should, but I want to get farther before we stop."

Finally, he asked Mum to pick someplace. He did that when he was busy driving. She pointed at a pub, The Crown and Roses, and we pulled into the little car park next to it.

It turned out to be a nice little pub. There were a couple of blokes at the bar arguing friendly-like about the new Premier League teams that had just come up from the Champions. They were trying to decide which would be the most trouble for the local team, the Black Cats.

I ordered fish and chips, and me Mum and Dad ordered the beef stew. With me Dad having a pint in his hand and Mum a glass of wine, with a fire in the hearth, and food on the way, the world seemed a lot different.

I asked what had happened while I was out running.

Dad looked at Mum and her face drooped as she realized it fell to her to tell me about it. She looked down into her glass, as though an answer were there. Then she began.

□□

"It started shortly after lunch. We, Hestia and I, were cleaning up after lunch. I was washing dishes. Every now and then, I looked up from the dishwater to look out the window above the sink.

"One time, I saw a bright white spot in the distance over the seacoast. When I looked up again, it was more than a dot, but I couldn't make out what it was. Then next time I looked up, it seemed to be much closer and looked somewhat like a gull.

"I mentioned to Hestia, 'Look at that crazy gull, heading straight at us.' She was drying the dishes and looked over my shoulder.

"Almost immediately she said, 'That's no gull. I think it's. . .' She didn't finish her sentence. The thing was flying far faster than a gull. In the last second or so, I was sure it would smash through the window.

"It didn't, but it did somehow come through the window and into the kitchen. It looked to me like a large, bright white owl, but it spoke with an English accent.

"It said in sepulchral tones, 'The Ministry has fallen. The Ministry has fallen. Flee your home, Hestia. Flee.' Then it disappeared. I was still trying to understand what it meant, but Hestia didn't hesitate.

"She shouted, 'Dedalus, Dedalus, come here right now.

"There was a distant call of 'We're on our way!' In a moment, your Dad and Dedalus ran into the kitchen.

"Hestia said rapidly, 'Roland's Patronus was just here. He said that the Ministry had fallen, and we have to leave.

"Dedalus asked her to repeat that. She did. He then nodded and said, 'So soon! He's right. We've got to go right away. Where's the boy?'

"Hestia looked at me. All I could say was, 'He's out running. I don't know when he'll be back. It may not be for a couple of hours.'

"Dedalus said, 'We've got to go right now. We'll disapparate someplace and wait a couple of hours to return. With luck, they'll have come and gone and not found anyone at home.

"I immediately objected, 'We can't go without Dudley! We've got to find him!'

"Dedalus grimaced. He said, 'We'll get you three out of here and safe, and I'll come back and fly my broom around to try to find him.' Hestia blanched when he said that, and it didn't make me feel much better.

"We walked outside. Your Dad and I immediately headed for the barn to get to our car, but Dedalus insisted that we walk with him away from the house.

"Your Dad tried to convince them that we could travel faster by car, but finally, Dedalus lost his temper. Then, he just used some kind of magic to make us follow him. It was like we were being pushed from behind by some invisible giant.

"Anyway, we got about a quarter of a mile from the house, and he told Hestia, 'Let's disapparate to the last Quidditch World Cup grounds.'

"Then Hestia held her hand out toward me, and Dedalus extended his to your Dad. He said, 'Take our hands and hold your breath. Many people consider their first disapparation somewhat unpleasant.'

"Your Dad asked what he meant by unpleasant. Dedalus would only smile and shrug. So, we each took a hand, and then the world turned inside out around us. I was sure that I was going to be seriously sick, but after a second or two, it was over. We were on a high hill overlooking a sea. I have no idea which one."

Dad said, "Your Mum doesn't tell it right. I once had a wisdom tooth pulled. It broke and the dentist had to dig around to get it out. It was hurting a good bit, so he shot me with some extra Novocaine. Before he did that he told me that it would hurt a bit. It was the most excruciating thing for about 2 seconds that I had ever experienced–until now."

Mum picked up the story again. "We just dropped down to the ground. We were both that shocked by this disappearing thingee. Anyway, Dedalus did say that he was going to disapparate back and try to find you. He had hardly said that when he seemed to whirl about for a second and then disappeared.

"We waited for a long time. He finally re-appeared, and he looked fagged-out. But he started talking almost right away."

⊡

I disapparated about a mile away from the cottage. I didn't want to take a chance that THEY might spot me. Then I approached slowly. When I got to the place where we just disapparated from, I could see a bit of what was happening in the house. There were flashes of light and bangs and the sound of rending wood–even from that distance. So, I stayed in the cover of some bushes and watched, waiting until they left. They were thorough. Toward the end, they seemed to become frustrated at missing us. Then the real trouble started. I was afraid that they might set the house on fire, but they didn't.

Then, suddenly, several of them stepped out in front and disapparated. I waited a long time to make sure that they hadn't left someone, but there was no sign of anyone. So I slowly approached the house, ready to disapparate at the slightest sign of trouble.

Nothing happened. I reached the house and made a quick inspection. Everything was a mess. I tried to find my broom. I crawled through the debris that seemed to be everywhere–fragments of glass, broken chairs, tables. When I finally did find it, it was broken into many pieces–at least I think that it was the remains of my broom that I found.

I decided that I had to keep searching for the boy. I left the house and headed for the beach. As soon as I was far enough from the protective spells of the house, I disapparated. I was determined to go up the beach northwards at ¼ mile intervals. I saw a few figures on the beach, but none that looked like your son. I made sure that I was not fooled. It seemed to take forever. Finally, it began to get dark and cloudy. I gave up the search, thinking that I would return for all of you and continue the search with help.

Dad took up the story at this point. "We disapparated back to the cottage. Now that we knew what to expect, we were not so disturbed by it, right, Pet?" He looked to her, and she nodded her agreement. He went on, "We landed a good distance back from the cottage and watched it as the last light disappeared from the sky. No one saw anything, so we started to move toward the house. As we approached, it remained as silent as a graveyard." He looked at me a minute, maybe trying to judge my reaction to what he was about to say. Then he said, "We both were rather afraid it would be a graveyard.

"We reached what was left of the front door. Dedalus motioned us to be quiet and took the lead. He opened the door as quietly as he could and stepped over what was left of the door-frame. He then lit his wand somehow and led us through the shambles that was left of his house.

"He stopped at an end-table that was left standing–unharmed. He picked up a photo that was in a frame that was completely intact. He gazed at it a moment and laid it down, face down.

"Then we finished searching the ground floor. I insisted on going up the stairs first. I was terribly afraid of what we might find, but if it were to be your body, I wanted to find it, not a stranger. We tried to walk up the stairs quietly. We couldn't be sure that there wasn't a Deatheater up there. Dedalus followed me closely. I reached the top of the stairs and reached out my hand to the doorframe of our room.

"I took a deep breath and slowly crossed the frame. I stuck my head in, and you nearly knocked it off! I can't tell you how happy I was to see you. You know the rest."

Yes, I did. I said, "You don't know how close you came to having your head knocked off like a golf ball off a tee!"

I was about to say something more when Dad noticed that the barmaid was standing over us with a bill in hand. She asked if we wanted anything more to eat or drink. He pulled his wallet out of his pocket and his American Express out of his wallet. As he started to look at it, he hesitated and then shook his head and handed it over. She took it and was off.

Mum asked what we were going to do next. I hadn't thought about it. I was so engrossed in the story and so hungry that I had no questions. However, it seemed like a really obvious question now that she'd asked it.

Dad said that he'd ask the bar maid about nearby B&B's and hotels. She came back with the receipt. He signed it and asked the question.

She gazed up to the left and blew a strand of hair out of the way of her imaginary vision. After a moment, she said, "Well," drawing out the word, "there is a B&B back toward Hartlepool about ten miles, but they might be full. Anyway, I don't know their phone number. If you're looking for something close. . ." We certainly were. It was late, and I didn't fancy driving around the country for hours looking for a bed. "You could try the Hog and Hound down the road toward Sunderland a mile or so. It's an Inn and is reasonable." She quickly added with a little reddening of her cheeks, "At least I hear it is."

Dad thanked her, and we were off. All three of us watched the road like hawks for any sign of the Hog and Hound. When we finally saw it, we all sighed our relief when we noticed that it had a neon sign out front that was lit and said, "Vacancy."

There was a decent crowd in the bar. Nobody seemed to pay any attention to us. Actually, we had a hard time attracting the attention of somebody. The man we got was the manager. He registered us and apologized that he didn't have a room with an extra bed. He did say, "There's a nice sofa, though. I'll send someone up with some extra blankets and a pillow."

The room was small as was the sofa. I was going to have to let my feet hang out somewhere–over the arm or off the edge, but by this time, I was getting used to crowded rooms. And frankly, we were all so happy to get a room in a small friendly inn that we didn't much care if it was not the most comfortable room we'd ever been in.

There was not even a Telly in the room, but I could not have cared less. There was a table and two chairs. Dad pulled the table up close to the sofa and we sat around the table. He had a sort of council of war in mind.

He started off with the question that was on top of all our minds, "What do we do next?"

Mum–always the most practical–said, "The first thing is to get a good night's sleep. Things will look different in the morning."

I couldn't contain myself any more. Now that the immediate threat seemed gone, I unloaded. "Yeh, now that there aren't Deatheaters on every side, everything's hunky doree, right?"

She started to answer, but Dad interrupted us both, "We're not going to get anywhere if we're bickering all the time. We're going to stay here tonight, but we know we can't stay here forever. Everyone should think about what we do for the long run."

Nobody was happy, but Dad was right. There wasn't anything else to do today. We needed a plan. Nobody had one. He was going on. "Your Mum's right. Let's try to get a night's sleep in and hope for better things tomorrow."

The Times to the Rescue

We ended up spending a couple of days in the inn. We were there long enough to fall into a kind of pattern. We slept in like we were on vacation. We had a late breakfast or maybe it was an early lunch. I took walks in the neighborhood and watched the Telly in the bar. Dad bought a Times of London and the Echo, the local paper. Mum read *the Echo* mostly and Dad, *The Times*.

As a matter of fact, he spent hours at a time reading. He seemed to read every word on every page. I don't know what he was looking for. Maybe he didn't know either.

The thing that we never did was to go anywhere. Even when the proprietor of the inn suggested that we try a local chip shop for lunch, Dad would say that he liked the food in the Inn. We took every meal in the Inn and did it at odd hours when nobody else was in the inn. Dad even asked permission to park in the back of the inn away from its little car park and the street.

One night Mum and I asked about going to see a movie at the local theater. Dad almost blew his top. He pulled us into our room and said in an intense whisper, "I'm trying to keep us out of sight. Don't you realize how dangerous going to the movies can be!"

I tried to say, 'I don't think Wizards go to movies," but I didn't get that out. He just stared me down, and I shut up.

The next day was Sunday. He was pouring over *The Times* as though his life depended on it. That night over a late dinner, he was still reading it when he threw the section that he was reading, the travel section, down on the table and almost shouted, "Ah Hah!"

Both Mum and I stared at it. There was an article about a tour group that was going to have a Jane Austen tour of England. Mum noticed an article about someone who was trying to see a football game in every stadium in the Champions League. She asked, "Do you fancy touring the Premier League stadiums?"

26

Dad just rolled his eyes, "Don't you see it?"

Both Mum and I just stared at the page again. Was there something that we missed? Finally Dad put his finger on an advert on the facing page. It read, "Nowegian Cruise Line Repositioning Cruise." Under the headline, there was a smaller title, "Make the Passage to the Caribbean in Traditional *Style and Elegance*!" The words Style and Elegance were in italics and bolder print.

Mum summed it up pretty well, "Why would we take a cruise. We're not on Holiday!"

Dad smiled a canny smile. "That's the point, isn't it. Who would expect us to take a cruise when we ought to be holed up in some out-of-the-way place?"

The light began to leak in. I thought, "Yes." But then, a question occurred to me, "Dad, what's a repositioning cruise. And when do we get back?"

Dad's smile grew, "A repositioning cruise doesn't return. We don't get back. The cruise leaves a port in the north and travels to a warm area for the winter cruise season. They move the ship so they can keep doing cruises in the winter."

Mum said, "Then do we ever come back?"

"I don't know. Maybe someday the Deatheaters stop looking for us. I suppose when they get Potter. Then nobody cares where we are."

Mum gulped. I didn't know what to think.

She asked the important question, "So what is the plan?"

"I don't have the details yet. There a few things that we have to do. We need to get our money together. We need to make a reservation on the ship. We need . . . " He was apparently lost in thought. I knew better than to try to interrupt him.

That night he gave us orders, "I want to be ready to go early tomorrow. Pack everything tonight. We get up, have a quick breakfast and are on our way."

Neither of us dared to ask exactly where or why. When he is on a roll, it just doesn't pay to interrupt him.

□

The next morning we were up early. Dad had set his alarm for 6 AM. We were packed except our pajamas. We took our bags down to the car. The proprietor thought we were trying to sneak off without paying. He was right behind us staring as Dad finished putting the luggage in the boot.

Dad was a little nervous, "This isn't quite what it looks like."

The proprietor asked, "Just what does it look like?"

Dad just frowned and said, "We just want to get an early start. We're going to have breakfast and settle up."

27

The proprietor frowned deeper and said, "Breakfast isn't until 6:30. Come in and pay up."

We did. Dad again pulled his American Express card from his wallet, stared at it for a bit, and then handed it over. I think the manager expected some problem with it. He held onto it until the charge printed, and Dad had signed it.

I wondered about that, and asked Dad about it over breakfast, "What is it with your credit card. You've been staring at it recently as though you'd never seen one before?"

He took a deep breath, exhaled, and said, "It's just that I'm afraid that someone could track us because we used our credit card." He got his wallet out. He took each of the credit cards inside and broke them in half, one at a time, starting with the American Express.

Mum almost fainted when he broke that one. She exclaimed, "You're not serious. How will we get on without them?"

Dad had a one word answer–cash.

We finished breakfast and, true to his word, paid for it with cash. Outside the inn, walking to our car, Mum asked, "But we don't have that much cash with us do we?"

Dad replied, "We'll stop at the bank and get most of it out of the bank."

We got in the car and started off. I had a question, "Dad, just where are we going?"

He smiled again. "Oh, you'll see."

I did. Eventually. First, we went to a bank branch, though. We had been driving for a couple of hours. I didn't know where we went. If I'm not driving, I don't have any sense of where we are.

□□

We all went into the bank. Dad didn't want us to separate. We sat in the Branch Manager's Office. He insisted on seeing identification before cashing a check that was so large.

He wore a pin-stripe suit and was just this side of being overweight. He was examining Dad's driving license as though it were a rare stamp. "Well, the photo certainly looks like you. Still. Why do you want to take so much money out of your account? You're hardly leaving a hundred pounds in it."

Dad stood his ground. "Well, it's mine. It doesn't matter what I'm going to do with, does it?"

The manager looked down at the photo again, maybe hoping he would discover that my Dad wasn't who he said he was. He looked up again. "Well, you really seem to be who you say you are. I suppose, I can't keep you any longer. But eight thousand pounds is really quite a lot of money just to be carrying around. I hope you know what you're doing."

Dad just smiled and nodded.

The manager asked, "How do you want it? Twenties? A few tens and fives?"

Dad was definite. "Five hundred in tens and the rest in twenties."

Completely defeated, the manager left his office and returned with a large manila envelope. He handed it to Dad who pulled out two rubber-banded stacks of bills. Dad glanced at them, riffled the one with twenties, and nodded.

We left the bank branch, got in the car and drove off. Mum asked Dad, "Where are we going now?"

Dad sighed, "I suppose I have to tell you now. You both have to be ready for what we're going to do next."

I was sitting in the front seat. He turned to me and said, "We're going back home and . . ."

Mum asked, "Are you crazy? It's too dangerous!"

I nodded, but Dad shook his head. "We have to get into our safety deposit box. To do that, we need our key. That is still in our house. So, . . ."

Mum said, "So, we need to go back home."

Dad went on, "Son, I want you to drive the car. You'll drop me off three blocks away from the house and return there in half an hour. If I'm not there. . ."

I interrupted, "But Dad, nothing's going to happen to you."

He continued, "IF I'M NOT THERE, the first time, you'll try two more times. If I'm not there then, you and your Mom will buy tickets on the repositioning cruise and stay away from England."

I looked back at Mum. She just said, "You know your Dad. We've got to do as he says."

The rest of the drive back to Little Whinging was very quiet. We arrived in the late afternoon. Dad drove to the middle of a block, stopped, got out, and handed the keys to me. He handed the manila envelope to Mum and walked off.

I drove away. I was inclined to follow him, but I knew that it was pointless. We drove to a Starbucks. I ordered a latte and Mum a hot tea. We sat glumly and watched the clock. Then, we drove to the meeting place.

Dad wasn't there. I drove away again. We went back to the Starbucks and talked this time. I asked what we did if Dad wasn't there the next time. Mum shook her head. "I don't care what your Dad says. If he doesn't show up, we're going to the house."

We drove back on schedule. No Dad. We nodded to each other, and I drove off but went to our home. We might all die, but we'd die together!

We drove into our drive. It seemed like we'd been gone for a hundred years. Nothing had changed on the street. The yard was overgrown with weeds. But me Mum, who prided herself in having the finest yard on Privet Drive, didn't pay the slightest attention to the yard.

We walked up to the door. Mum went in as bold as brass. I followed, and we didn't see a sign of Dad. We went up stairs, into their room, and found Dad bent over a chest of drawers. He had one drawer out and was examining its underside.

Mum said, "You silly man. It isn't in that chest of drawers. It's in the . . ."

Dad slapped his forehead. "Of course, it's the dresser drawer, isn't it?" Then he went to Mum's dresser, pulled out the second drawer, turned it over, and revealed a small envelope taped to the bottom. He tore it off, and we ran down the stairs and out to the car.

Dad just said, "Drive."

I took the driver's seat and sped off. "Where are we going?"

Dad said, "Watford."

"What are we going to do in Watford!"

I found out. I knew in a rough way how to get to Watford. I arrived on the M25. From there, Dad directed me. We drove past a Tube station, and he had me park in a car park of a Sanesbury. We walked to the Tube station with our luggage.

I suppose I should have known better, but I asked where we were going. Dad answered sensibly, "I could tell you, but it wouldn't mean anything to you. The best I can do is just to show you."

So, we entered the Tube station, bought passes, and waited on the platform for the next train. It arrived, and we boarded. It was getting late, and I was getting hungry, but I decided to wait for the end of the ride to complain. After several stops, we got off. We left the station, and Dad looked around. He took in the streets as if he were a connoisseur tasting a wine for the first time in a long while.

Then he led us off on an East-West street, commenting as he went. "I don't remember if the inn I'm looking for is in this block or the one after. We'll see shortly."

We did see shortly. It was the second block. It was not shabby on the outside, but it looked like the exterior had been the way it was for a very long time. I could barely read the name over the entrance–The Sheepshead. It was a strange name, but what the heck. Dad must have a reason for bringing us here.

We were about to enter when he stopped Mum and me. He said, "OK. We're not going to register as ourselves. We're going to be the Johnson's. We keep our real first names."

Mum, who was always the most practical of us, asked, "Won't they ask for identification?"

Dad's planning shone through, "Not if we pay in advance with cash."

I thought Mum was on to something, but it happened just as Dad predicted. When he took the money out of his wallet, the clerk just smiled and had him sign the register with no inconvenient questions about ID's.

Then we had dinner at the inn and went up to our room. This time, the room was larger but not what I'd call comfortable. There were two beds, a small table and two chairs. There was even a little bathroom with a narrow shower. The table had a TV. We never turned it on the whole time we were there. That was partly because we all had a strange feeling that if we didn't connect with the real world through the TV, then we maybe would fly under the radar.

As soon as we opened our suitcases and began to make ourselves less uncomfortable, Mum started out innocently enough. She asked, "How did you know about this inn? We've never stayed here, I'm sure."

Dad looked from one of us to the other and back as though deciding just what we'd accept. He said, "I stayed here once when the Cisco branch had a training retreat here."

Mum seemed puzzled and then said, "Oh, yes. It was not long after we married. I remember that weekend–sort of. It was our first weekend apart."

Dad just grunted.

Mum seemed satisfied, but I could tell she was puzzling over something. Dad went down to the Lobby, found a copy of *The Times,* and read it. I asked if I could jog in the neighborhood. Dad thought a moment and said, "I think it should be OK, but don't get too far away."

Again, Mum seemed ready to ask something but didn't.

When I got back from my jog, I asked Dad, "What about our car? Can we leave it in the car park all night?"

He just shrugged, "It'll be safe enough."

That seemed strange, but I kept quiet.

The next morning we slept in, got breakfast at the inn, and boarded the Tube for the City. We stopped at a station that I didn't recognize, but when we left the station, I recognized the area. Dad led us to a branch of our bank.

I asked, "I thought we got all our money out of the bank."

He said, "We did. We're here for something else."

It turned out that this branch was where me Mum and Dad had their safety deposit box. The assistant manager checked my Dad's ID and led him into the vault. We watched through the glass door as a clerk turned her key. Then Dad turned his key and opened the box. He took out a small manila envelope and signaled for the manager to let him out. We left the bank and went back to the Tube station.

In a lonely corner there, he opened the envelope and handed each of us our passports. "Keep these on you at all times. Where we're going, you'll need it."

I asked, "Then we go to buy tickets?"

Dad said, "A good idea, but we're going somewhere else first."

We got on a train headed toward the city. We got off several stations down the line. We had to walk a couple of blocks, but it wasn't long before we were entering a brokerage firm. Dad talked to the secretary and got us an appointment with a broker after lunch.

We found a little French restaurant and had the first really good meal since we left the cottage. I asked Dad again about our car. All he would say was, "We're never going back for that car. It's another link to us. We need to leave everything behind."

⊡

We arrived at the brokerage early and waited. I knew that Dad would be doing something with stocks–maybe selling some.

The broker whom we met with didn't know Dad, and we had to go through the ritual of checking ID's.

"Well, Mr. Dursley, what can I do for you and. . ." Here he nodded at us, "your family."

Dad said, "I want to sell most of my stocks and bonds. As a matter of fact, I'd like to sell 80% of them."

The broker just stared at Dad for a full minute. Then he said, "You really mean to sell 80% of your holdings?"

Dad was as calm as I'd ever seen him. "Yes, sir, I do."

The broker seemed to mull that a bit more and asked, "Is there anything about our firm that you don't like? Have we given less than excellent service?"

The corners of Dad's mouth lifted a bit as he said, "You've always been helpful and courteous. I'm quite happy with your service."

The broker's head tilted toward his left shoulder as he said, "Then I don't understand why you want to leave us. Has some other firm offered lower fees or some other inducement?" He hesitated again and then said,

32

"We'd be quite willing to match any reasonable offer you might have received."

The corners lifted a little more, "No, sir. There is no other firm. I just want the money put into my bank account that you normally put payments into."

The broker turned to a computer on his desk and keyed something and said, "That's quite a lot of money. It's really not a good investment to just leave it in your checking account."

Dad seemed to be enjoying this little talk a lot. He answered, "Oh, yes. I'm quite aware of that."

"And you know that you'll have to sell some equities at a loss?"

At that, he actually chuckled. "Oh, yes. I'm afraid that's unavoidable."

The broker seemed to be beside himself, "Do you mind if I ask you what you intend to do with the money?"

Dad seemed ready to burst out laughing, but he managed to say, "I don't mind at all if you ask."

The broker stared for a moment and then said, "Well? What are you going to do?"

Dad answered, "I'm sorry, I just can't tell you."

Then the broker tried one last desperate ploy. "I know. Someone has a no fail, get rich quick scheme. All he needs is a little extra financing, and he'll return three pounds on the shilling. Am I right?"

Dad did break out in laughter. I was a little worried. He usually didn't joke with other businessmen. This time was different. He managed to get out, "Oh, this investment is much more valuable than that."

He pressed on, "Now, how quickly can you sell and get the settlement into my account?"

The broker looked genuinely glum. "Well, if you insist, we can do the sale this afternoon. It won't be until the day after tomorrow that the money will be available in your account."

Dad seemed as though he might actually argue about that but finally said, "That will be quick enough, although I'd double your fee if you could make it available tomorrow."

The broker just shook his head. "Day after tomorrow."

Dad stood and held out his hand. He said, "I really appreciate all the help you've been. The next time that I'm ready to invest again, I'll have you at the top of my list."

The broker had accepted this and just said, "It's always been a pleasure for the firm to deal with you. I hope we can win your business back sometime soon."

Dad nodded and said, "Not half as much as I do." That seemed to mystify the broker, but he didn't say anything more.

We left the brokerage feeling good–all of us. I asked, "What's next?"

Mum asked, "How about going to a matinee. I've been wanting to see the Truman Show."

Dad and I agreed that we wanted to see Armageddon. We compromised. We'd see Armageddon today and the Truman Show tomorrow.

Dad insisted that we sit at the back of the theatre. Neither Mum nor I objected.

After the movie, we went back to the inn. Dinner there was the same as before. The menu didn't change. We were all beginning to get a bit nervous. We'd not been anywhere else as long as we'd been here-except, of course, the wizard's cottage. We trudged up to our room after supper. It was comforting to be in an out-of-the-way inn but after a while the truth that we were in an out-of-the-way inn for a reason sunk in with us.

Nobody slept very well that night. I didn't have any dreams–that I remembered. That made me happy, but the day turned out to be a bright clear day. We went down to breakfast with renewed hope born of a night's rest. Dad borrowed a phone book from the day manager of the inn and searched for something. He apparently found it because he wrote something in the little notebook that he always kept with him. However, he was as secretive as ever.

After breakfast, he bought a *Times* and we read it for a bit in the Lobby of the inn. Then at about 9:30, he announced, "We're off. Follow me."

It turned out that we were off on a fairly long walk. We went at least ten blocks. He kept insisting they were short blocks, and we'd arrive shortly.

As a matter of fact, it wasn't all that long. We entered an office building. He went to the index of offices, found what he wanted, and we took the elevator to the second floor. It turned out that the second floor housed a dentist, a real estate agency, and a travel agency.

It was the travel agency that we were headed for. We entered and discovered that they were just opening. That was good because no other customer was there. It was also bad, because they took their time getting organized, their computers turned on, and their coffee brewed.

Finally, we were escorted to an office of a certified travel agent whose name plate declared her to be Joy Anderson. She had short blonde hair that didn't even reach her shoulders. I guessed that she had to be in her fifties, but it's hard to tell with ladies like Joy. She was smartly dressed and was pretty. I wouldn't have been surprised if she were in her forties or even in her sixties.

Joy got up, greeted us, and offered us coffee or tea, and seats.

None of us were interested in any of it other than the seats. She started with the usual chat that everyone thinks is necessary, but even Mum was not particularly interested. Finally, she got down to business.

"How can I help you reach your travel goals?"

Dad was very up-front. He simply handed her the advert from *The Times* travel section and said, "We want to take this ship when it sails."

Joy smiled, "Good. I like it when clients knows exactly what they want." She read the advert carefully and said, "We work with this cruise line, so it should be no problem if they still have berths."

Then she turned to her computer, and as she keyed rapidly, she said, "I'll just look up this cruise online and see what they have available and prices." As she was still alternately keying and waiting for something to show up on the screen, she continued, "Do you have an idea what kind of stateroom you want?"

Dad said, "It depends on what the prices are."

Joy looked at her screen. "Well, you're in luck, there are a few of every price category available. Now, what price did you have in mind?"

Dad cut to the chase, "OK. Let's be clear. I want a stateroom that can accommodate my wife, son, and me. We would consider two staterooms if it were cheaper to spit us up."

Joy smiled, apparently anticipating that answer. "There are a couple of options. Most staterooms have a small sofa that can become a fold-out bed. The question is how much space do you want to have and how high above the waterline do you want to be."

Dad smiled, "Start quoting prices from the bottom up. I'll tell you when to stop. Include all fees and VAT."

The first price was 2289 pounds for the three of us. It had a full-size bed, a sofa, a table and two chairs. The next was 2799 pounds. It had a Queen bed, a larger sofa, a table and four chairs. Joy was about to quote another price, but Dad interrupted her. "That's enough. That one sounds good."

She wanted to quote one higher price. It had a little balcony. Dad was adamant. He simply said, "No." But he said it with such finality that she stopped and went on to the next point.

"I think I can get you a better deal on a cruise that leaves a week later. You could have the balcony for the price of the one you just took."

Dad was still adamant. "We've got a strict time-table. We need to leave this week.

She stared at him but took a deep breath and went on, "Then, we need to talk about what you want to do when you get to Galveston. We can set up local tours. The Johnson Space Center is there and there's lots of local . . ." She stopped. She could see that Dad had stopped listening.

Dad said, "We'll arrange our own tour after that point."

She sighed and said, "But surely, you want to set up return flights?" She said it resignedly, suspecting the truth that Dad didn't want to do that either.

Dad just shook his head "no" in confirmation.

Joy said, "Well, there are a few last details that we need to handle. Since you're traveling to a foreign country, we'll have to verify that your passports are up to date. Did you happen to bring them?"

Dad nodded and he handed her his passport. Mum and I immediately followed his example. She seemed a little surprised that we were this ready, but she took them and examined them, even comparing our photos to ourselves. She nodded and said, "These seem to be in good order." She handed them back to us.

Then she said, "That only leaves. . ." But before she could finish, Dad interrupted her.

"Would you excuse me for a few minutes? I need to use the WC. Do you know where . . ."

"Oh, yes. There's one on this floor in the middle of the building. Don't rush. I've rarely made a sale this quickly."

Dad left, and we were left to make small talk until he returned. She asked Mum if Dad was always that positive about things.

Mum said, "Oh, he's usually very definite about his ideas."

He really was back in a couple of minutes, looking rather satisfied with himself. He sat and said, "Miss Anderson, you were saying?"

She answered, "The only thing left to do is to arrange for payment." She turned to the keyboard and worked at it for a couple of minutes and then a printer behind her desk started rattling and a piece of paper came off. She handed it to Dad and said, "Here's your statement."

He looked at it a minute and said, "I thought you said it was 2799 pounds, including fees. But this says 2842 pounds."

Joy grimaced, "I said that the number included VAT, but there are always a few fees that can't be calculated until the final contract is written. The difference isn't even 50 pounds."

It was Dad's turn to grimace. "All right. I don't like it, but I suppose I've got to bear it."

Joy seemed to be genuinely sorry to disappoint, but she went on, "How do you want to settle? Check? Credit Card?"

Dad had a surprise for her when he said, "Neither. I want to pay with cash."

Joy stared for a second and said, "Really? You surely don't have that much with you?" She hesitated and perhaps considered the possibility that such an odd customer might just have that much cash on his person. "Do you?"

36

He smiled, "As a matter of fact, I do." His bulging wallet made an appearance at that point. He opened it and began counting out the money.

Joy interrupted him. "Wait a minute. I'm not sure that we can even take cash."

He frowned, and she quickly added, "Wait a moment, I'll check with my manager." She got up and left the room.

In a couple of minutes she was back. "I've checked. We can accept cash, but we only have a very small amount of cash in the office. You'd have to give us exact change. I've asked my manager in to help count. We have to have two employees present when all cash transactions are handled."

Dad continued counting. Shortly, he'd counted out one hundred forty crisp new twenty pound notes. Then he started with smaller bills. He had a tenner, a five, and three ones. He looked over at Mum and asked, "How much cash do you have in your purse."

She was surprised by the question but got out her purse and started counting. She had three fives, and seven ones.

Dad turned to me, "Turn out your pockets, what do you have?"

That surprised me as much as anything that happened on this crazy trip. I didn't understand the first time he said it. It was that unexpected. But on the second time, I had my pockets emptied on Joy's desk. I had a fiver and a few coins. Dad took the fiver and all but four of Mum's ones. He handed them over to Joy. Just then another woman came in whom Joy introduced as Agnes. She had black hair longer than Joy's and seemed to be a little younger. She and Joy counted the money separately and agreed. Joy filled out a receipt for the cash received. She, her boss, and Dad all signed it. They both left the room for a few minutes.

Then Joy returned alone. She went over the contract with Dad. He and Mum signed it. Then Joy worked the computer again, and another set of sheets came out of the printer.

She handed them to Dad. She explained, "This is your receipt for the stateroom. It's named here, and the three of you are named as leasing it for the duration of the trip. This will grant you admittance to the ship. Of course, keep it in a safe place and have it with you when you board.

"Now, the ship leaves port on Friday. You may board and take possession of your stateroom as early as 9 AM, but the ship won't serve lunch. There will be a buffet line available in the mid-afternoon. Most people board in the early afternoon. In any case, you shouldn't wait till after 5 PM to board."

Dad said, "Oh, I think we'll board at nine." Both Mum and I nodded vigorously.

Joy was surprised, "Really? Well, if you want to do that, you should bring along some lunch. They won't have anything for you. Even the gift shop won't be open till they set sail.

"You could have something to eat from the buffet in the afternoon, but I'd really wait for the formal dinner the first night. It's very nice, and they'll go over the important things about sailing at that time. Have any of you sailed before?"

We all shook our heads, no.

"Then, you'll really want to pay close attention at that meal."

We nodded. Then she said, "That's really all." She handed Dad a business card. "Here's my card. It has my direct line and the office number in case some issue arises, but they run these cruises very well. You should have no problems."

Joy rose, and we shook hands all around. She wished us, "Bon Voyage!"

Outside the office, Mum demanded, "What was that with cash! Is that all the cash we have?"

He chuckled, "No. I've got the rest in a money belt under my trousers. That's why I went to the loo. I was getting some money out of the money belt. I just wasn't expecting to need quite that much."

It was past our normal lunch time, so we had a quick lunch and went to see *The Truman Show*. Dad thought it was loopy, but Mum liked it. I think she has a little thing for Jim Carey.

After dinner that night in our room, we were all pretty antsy. We could see that if we just held on for a couple of days, we'd be on the ship and at sea. Somehow, none of us thought about what happened after the cruise ended. Just getting that far seemed such an achievement that we couldn't look beyond it. We all just wanted those couple of days to be past us.

The next morning, we got off to our typical start on the day. But this time, we walked to the nearest tube station and traveled a couple of stops out from the City.

It turned out that we were going to a branch of our bank. We got in and were immediately greeted by a teller who wasn't helping anyone and wanted to help us.

Dad just shook his head and said, "I need to see the branch manager."

We had to wait a while. It was closer to eleven than ten when he was finally free. His name was Edward T. Brooks. He was very friendly. After a little worthless chat, he asked how he could help us.

Dad explained that we wanted to make a rather large withdrawal from our account.

Brooks asked for Dad's ID. Dad gave him his passport. Brooks glanced at the passport photo and Dad and worked the computer at his desk. After a minute, he whistled, "You made quite a deposit overnight. Are you planning on making a down-payment on a house or something?"

Dad smiled and said, "No, I want to withdraw fifty-two thousand pounds."

Brooks' mouth worked for a moment, and he whistled. "You're joking of course?"

Dad just smiled and shook his head, "No."

Brooks started to say, "But that's crazy!" He stopped just as he started to say the "C" word and turned it into, "incredible. You can't mean it!"

"I'm afraid I do."

Brooks fell back in his chair. He seemed to be considering. Then he said, "I think we don't have enough cash in the branch to do that and service our normal business. I think that I can get enough over from another branch to let us fill your order."

Dad started to say that it was alright, but Brooks interrupted, "For that much money, you'll have to fill in a couple of forms anyway. It's good that you brought your passport." He turned to a credenza, opened the upper drawer and began searching for something. After a minute or two, he said, "Ah ha! Here it is."

He'd found a form consisting of several pages. He handed it to Dad and said, "Please fill this out." Dad started to get up. Brooks stopped him. "I have just one question, if you don't mind?"

"Go ahead, the worst I can do is not answer."

"Just what do you want to do with that much cash?"

Dad leaned back and said, "You know, I don't think I've ever had as much fun as I have lately just smiling inscrutably as I don't answer that question."

With that Dad got up and went to a table in an unoccupied cubicle and started filling out the form.

At 2 PM, Brooks came over to our table where Dad was reading *The Times*, I was playing a video game on my gameboy, and Mum was just staring off in the distance. He invited us back to his office.

Brooks said, "We got together your money. We could only assemble 40,000 of it in twenties. The rest is in smaller bills. I'd advise you to count it carefully."

Dad asked, "Why? Shouldn't we trust you?"

"Yes, you should, but if you've counted it carefully, then you can be sure that nothing has gone wrong and you will know that if any of it disappears, it didn't happen here."

Dad nodded wisely.

Brooks went on, "I think that we should make sure that it isn't too obvious that you're walking out with a lot of money. So, I've had it put into my laptop bag. It's not expensive, and I've been meaning to get a new one anyway.

"Are you sure that I can't talk you out of this crazy idea?"

Dad shook his head. Brooks led us to a back room that was empty except for a large table with a bunch of chairs around it. There was a laptop case on the table top. Brooks said, "Take your time and be sure that you've got it all. When you leave, I'd suggest carrying it by it's shoulder strap but with the strap over one shoulder and the bag under the other arm."

Dad thanked him and we started counting the money. I'd never seen so many bills at one time in my life.

We walked out of the bank, trying to look like it was perfectly normal for my Dad to carry an old laptop case over his shoulder, bulging with something.

We reached the street, and Dad seemed to have another second thought. Instead of heading for the Tube, we waited on the sidewalk, and Dad swung his hands wildly whenever a cab drove past. Eventually one stopped.

The cabbie unlocked the door, and we got in. Then he asked, "How are you paying?"

Dad didn't hesitate, "Cash."

The cabbie showed no sign of moving but asked, "Where are we going?"

Dad told him to go to the Tube station near our inn. The cabbie turned around and stared at us. Then he said, "Why don't you just take the Tube here. The station is only a block or two down the road."

Dad's face set in a grim expression. "Do you want the fare or not?"

The cabbie turned around and said, "OK. The fare will be about thirty pounds."

Dad wasn't fazed but just nodded (of course, the cabbie couldn't see that) and said, "No problem."

I wondered how many times he'd heard that and then been stiffed. He didn't seem disturbed, but pulled out from the curb, and we were off.

As we stood near the Tube station, Dad followed the cab with his eyes until it disappeared. Then he said, "Let's go." We walked very briskly to our inn. We got in. Dad tried not to recognize the nods and greetings directed at us. We went up to our room, and he gave a sigh of relief. It was as if we were in some way safer there than in the pub.

He sat us down on the chairs, and he took the bed. He looked back and forth from Mum to me and back. Then he spoke, "From now until we are out to sea–and I mean sea, not the channel-we will be here or in a cab or in our cabin on the ship. We don't go anywhere else for any reason–to eat, to watch the telly, nothing!"

I meekly asked, "What about the loo?"

His mouth curled into a snarl and said, "Yes, the Loo," with his teeth bared.

Mum and I knuckled down and accepted this strict requirement. Dad ordered meals by telephone from the front desk. He tipped the people who brought food to our room generously but "Not too generously."

The next day—the day of our departure—we packed. Dad transferred as much of our money to his money belt as he could. Because of his substantial waist, it was easy to hide a good bit of it. He gave a good bit of it to Mum, and he even gave some to me. I stood gaping at him as he counted out twenty pound notes into my hand.

As he did this he told both Mum and me that we were not to touch any of it without his permission except in extreme emergency.

We were dressed, packed, and standing at the door as he hesitated. He eventually opened his normal wallet and pulled out a twenty pound note that he placed on the dresser. He picked up the pad of paper at the desk and tore a sheet off and wrote, "Thanks for the excellent service." He signed it, Room 234. I thought to myself, "I wonder if the room can afford a tip that large?", but I said nothing.

We walked down to the front desk. Dad handed the single key to Room 234 to the desk clerk and said, "We'll be checking out now."

The Desk clerk looked up in a bored way and said, "Hope you enjoyed your stay, Mr. and Mrs. Johnson." He worked the computer on his side of the desk for a few minutes and then a piece of paper came out of the printer behind him. He handed it to Dad, who glanced over it and said, "Here's our payment. Just keep the change for yourself."

I looked over Dad's shoulder and saw that the total was about 365 pounds. Dad handed over four hundred pounds in twenties. The desk clerk gaped and then quickly opened the till, inserted the bills and withdrew change for himself. "Have a good trip wherever you're going."

Dad just smiled. We left.

I thought that we'd take the Tube to the seaport, but Dad hailed a cab again and gave the cabbie the address. He stared, but Dad said, "If you get us there quickly and don't ask questions, I'll give you a hundred."

The cabbie gaped and perhaps calculated his net earnings after everything was taken into account. Then he nodded silently, and we all got in.

Everyone was carrying his or her own luggage. Dad had been strict about that from the beginning. In case we got separated, everyone had what they needed to keep going. I thought he was overdoing it, but I wasn't about to complain.

It was a long silent ride. No one made a sound. It took over two hours. We arrived at the dock of our ship about 10:30 AM. The cabbie said not a word–especially after receiving five crisp twenty pound notes. He did examine them carefully, but they passed muster.

We walked down the lane toward the port. The cabbie drove off, and we never heard anything of him again–not name, nationality, or even sex, come to think of it. It might have been a she. She didn't help us out. She just waited until it was obvious that we had all our property off her cab and drove off.

It was a long walk to the gangway up into the ship. But for once, none of us were in a hurry.

The Purser

We reached a little booth at the base of the gangway up onto the ship. There were two people there. One was dressed in a white officer's uniform that declared her to be the Purser. The other seemed to be dressed like a porter.

Dad handed the purser our tickets. She looked at them carefully and asked to see our passports. We all produced them, and a quick glance at them satisfied the purser. She handed back tickets and passports and declared, "Welcome aboard the Princess of the Caribbean.

"You're probably the earliest passengers of the day. Please give the porter your things, and he'll see you to your room. His name is Oswald. He'll be your primary contact with the ship during the day. He'll give you a quick tour of the ship on the way to your cabin. If you have any problems or needs, he's your Jonnie-on-the-spot! He carries a pager, and you just have to page the number on your phone." He looked us over and finished, "On behalf of the Princess Line, we wish you the best possible cruise."

Dad just mumbled something and picked up his bag. We followed suit. The porter said, "Please allow me."

Dad held onto his bags. Following suit, we held onto our bags. The Purser said, "Oswald. It's OK." Then she said to us more than to Oswald, "I'm sure they'll give you a generous tip."

I thought to myself, "Fat chance of that."

However, Dad just nodded and said, "If we get along, you'll find that I'm quite generous."

We walked up the gangway and onto the main deck. A short walk took us past a ballroom and a swimming pool. All along the way, the Porter was giving us running commentary about the ship–the location of the gift stores, the pools, the movie theatre, and so on.

Eventually we reached an elevator. The Porter hit the up button, and almost instantly, the doors opened to a spacious elevator. He took us up three floors. We all smiled as the doors opened, and we found there was no one waiting for us.

We exited and were led to a cross hall. We went down it and turned to the right at cabin 3F23. The Porter pulled out a flat plastic card, slipped it into a slot, and we heard a click. The door was then open although we couldn't tell from looking at it.

The porter pointed out the cabin number and our name emblazoned on a neat plastic card, "V. Dursley." He opened the door for us and preceded us in. Inside, he turned on lights, pointed out the Loo, the floor to ceiling window, the telephone, the bed, and a sleeper sofa.

He looked at Dad squarely and asked, "May I unpack you?"

Dad was looking out the window that had been revealed when the Porter had pulled back the drapes. He swung around rapidly and almost lost control of his voice as he exclaimed, "No. You may not!"

The Porter finished by letting us know about the afternoon buffet that was still almost four hours away. He suggested that we walk about the ship familiarizing ourselves with it.

He finished by saying, "Be sure to keep your ticket and passport to hand today. Once we're at sea, you can put those in your safe or in the Purser's safe, which is easily the more secure."

Dad thanked him and almost forgot to tip him, but he caught his *faux pas* just before he made it. He quickly opened his wallet and pulled a twenty pound note out. I think it was the first that came to his hand.

He handed it to the Porter and said, "Could you be sure that we're not bothered the first couple of days? It's been a difficult week, and we just want to get some rest without interference."

The Porter glanced at the note and nodded. He bowed slightly and said almost inaudibly, "You can be perfectly sure of that."

The door closed as the Porter left, and we all just flopped down onto chairs and bed. That only lasted a moment.

Dad leapt up, locked the cabin door, checked the main window to be sure that the drapes were completely closed, took a quick walk around the cabin, and returned to the bed where he had lain, "Remember. No one leaves the cabin until we're well at sea tomorrow."

I had managed through this adventure to keep my silence where silence seemed necessary. But this was too much. I'm afraid that I whined, "But Daaaad. We have to eat. Can't we order from room service?"

Mum had not been wasting her time while we talked. She had a brochure in hand. She said, "Here's the meal schedule. The first meal is in the grand ballroom. There *may* be a light buffet set out there around 3PM. But everyone is expected to put in an appearance at the evening meal at 7PM. The Captain, the Chief Purser, and other Officers will present a PowerPoint review of the ship, the way it works, and other details."

Mum immediately asked, "What is PowerPoint?"

Dad smiled, maybe the first time in days, and said, "It's a fancy slide show. I suppose that we don't want to be conspicuous. We'll attend that."

Mum went on, "Your table will have a ship's officer who will answer questions and help you with any issues after the presentation. Your table is 3F2."

"I laughed," and said, "Hey, that's almost our room number."

No one seemed amused.

□

It turned out that there were a few snacks scattered around the room. There were cookies. There were chocolates on the pillows of the bed. There was a small bowl of individually wrapped mints on the table.

Dad seemed to be struck by indecision while Mum and I unpacked our luggage. Dad sat down and stared at the bed.

After a few minutes, Mum put a hand on his shoulder and asked, "Is there something wrong, dear?"

He looked up and said, "I suppose that we should go to dinner. It would be suspicious if we didn't, but . . . " He trailed off.

I jumped into the conversation, "Well, I sure am going. I'm starved!"

Both Mum and Dad stared at me as if I'd suggested jumping the railing. I said, "Well, it's like you said, people will wonder if we don't show up," but they frowned at me. Then I grabbed a cookie because we still had a couple of hours before dinner. That started a rush by all of us to get as much of the loose food in the cabin as we could find.

At the end, both Dad and I had a hand on the last cookie. We were both grim, but I finally gave in and released my hold.

Then we spent the rest of the afternoon sitting and watching the slow, slow progress of the clock on the wall. Nobody said anything. Nobody did anything. Nobody smiled.

Eventually the time reached 6 PM. We jumped up and rushed to leave the cabin. Dad managed to get control of his emotions first and held the door open for the both of us.

We made our way to the main ballroom and found our table. We were the first there other than the ship's crew member that was assigned to our table. We later learned that every table had a ship's officer. Ours for the night was one of the Pursers.

She introduced herself as Jennifer. She greeted us and gave us a quick review of the program for the night. The Captain would give us a brief welcoming speech. Then, the meal proper would begin. We would be able to have pleasant conversation. If anyone would like to ask questions of the ship's officer who was at their table, they could during the meal.

Over desert and coffee the Executive Officer would present a PowerPoint slide show highlighting the many opportunities of the ship for fun and recreation. He would also present basic safety guidelines.

The Captain's speech had one good thing about it–it was short. So, we were quickly onto the meal. Slowly, the other guests who were seated at our table joined us. We were introduced to the Johnson's (real Johnson's), the Jeffrey's and the Barber's. By the time we began the main course, everyone was with us except for the occupant of 3F24–our neighbor.

Hardly anyone mentioned his absence. We all assumed that he was in his cabin or walking the decks or something.

The desert was unlike anything I'd ever had before. It was baked Alaska–ice cream somehow baked inside a pastry but still solid. I was sure that I'd gone to heaven. I missed some of the Executive Officer's talk about the safety guidelines, but I'd finished desert in time to pick up the slides about the facilities of the ship.

There was the grand ballroom that we were in. It was used for meals like this one. It also had a stage and was used for shows of various sorts. Tonight after dinner, there was going to be a musical review here. I saw Mum's eyes glisten when she heard that. Dad gave a sort of resigned nod, knowing that he'd have to stay with her for this.

There was a small theatre where movies were screened in the afternoon and the evening. They showed everything from old classics up to current movies fresh out of the theatres. Tonight, they were showing a classic—*Charade*—whatever that was about.

After the talk was over, Mum and Dad had decided to stay in the ballroom for the entertainment, but that would not start for half an hour. The ship's officer stayed to answer questions. Dad asked a question immediately. "Jennifer, I noticed that our neighbor from 3F24 didn't show up for dinner. Do you know anything about him?"

She did a double-take and seemed flustered. However, she recovered fairly quickly and said, "Ah hum. I'm not allowed to give out personal information about guests." As she said that her face flushed.

But Dad kept going, "No. I don't want to know personal information. I just was wondering if you knew why he didn't show up for dinner."

Jennifer seemed to relax and said, "Oh, I see. No, I don't. And, as a matter of fact, I'm rather curious about that myself." The subject seemed to hang in the air for a moment. Then one of the Johnson's asked something about the ship—how many passengers there were or something like that.

Dad returned with another question for Jennifer though. "Do you know when we'll be into the Atlantic proper?"

She seemed to be relieved to be getting ordinary questions and replied with professional aplomb, "It will be sometime after midnight. It depends on the weather conditions and currents and so forth, but we will be out of sight of land shortly and into the Atlantic before sunrise for sure."

Dad nodded and seemed a bit relieved himself. She asked him a question in turn, "Are you worried about being on the open ocean, because I can assure you that this ship is utterly safe. I've crossed myself several times and . . ."

Dad interrupted, "That's not it at all. As a matter of fact, I feel a bit safer on the open ocean myself."

She nodded wisely and said to the table in general, "Yes, that's very wise. There's less danger on the open ocean than there is on busy waters like the channel." She didn't return her attention to us, and there were questions from the other guests anyway.

After she left the table when the entertainment started, I decided that I'd try one of the Exercise Rooms. I got up and Dad immediately glared at me, "Where are you going?"

I shrugged and said, "Just to one of the Exercise Rooms."

"Young man, I want you to sit down and." Here his voice dropped, and he almost whispered, "Stay close."

I rolled my eyes and said, "Aw, Dad, I just want to get some exercise in. I haven't done any proper exercise in days and days—not since we left the . . . " Here I dropped my voice, "You Know Whose house."

Mum touched my forearm. "Dear, please just go along with your Dad." Her gaze was almost pleading. There seemed to me to be something more there than just trying to avoid a public argument. I couldn't guess what it might be, but I just had the feeling there was something there. For the time being, I went along with it.

□□

It was not easy to do this because the musical review had lots of music that Mum and Dad would like, but I could hardly stand. I smiled and got through the evening. Then when it was over, we all went back to our room. It was after 10 P. M. but I knew that it was too early to go off on my own even though the Exercise Rooms would be empty at this hour.

We passed 3F24 on the way to our room. Dad stopped for a minute at the door and appeared ready to knock, but he didn't.

Inside our room, we had a little council of war. Mum and Dad sat on the two chairs, and I sat on the sofa. Dad started off, "OK. Tomorrow morning, we can wander around as we like. Personally, I'm going to stay in our cabin as much as possible, except for meals."

I smiled internally at that and said to myself, "Well, that will let me have lots of time out of the cabin." Outwardly, I just smiled.

He went on, "I'd like everyone to be aware of their surroundings at all times. There will be no standing at the rail and gazing off into the distance. Never forget where you are and why we're here."

Mum surprised me by asking, "Why ARE we here?"

Dad stared at her as though a giant turnip was sitting across from him and had just asked the question. He said, "What do you mean, 'why'? We're here because we don't want to be killed by wizards."

She shook her head and said, "I know that! What I mean is, 'Why on a ship?'"

Dad nodded and said, "We're here because this is the last place that wizards would think to look. How do wizards get around, do you suppose?"

Mum shrugged. Then Dad turned to me, "How do you think?"

I thought hard about it and said, "Well, the giant, Haggerd, flew a motorcycle to us." Then another idea hit me. I was sort of excited that I'd thought of a second way wizards travel. "And don't they fly broomsticks?"

Dad said, "Right you are! And don't forget . . ."

I had another idea, so I interrupted Dad, "And didn't they come to visit us once through the fireplace?"

Dad was practically beaming as he looked at me, "Right again! Dudley, you're pretty smart.

"Now, think. Is there a fireplace anywhere in this ship?"

I shrugged but said, "I've not seen one."

"Right again! There aren't any. And being out on the sea, we're . . ."

Here Mum interrupted, "We're far away from land. It would be a long way to fly a broomstick or a motorcycle."

I thought of a question, "Why are you so interested in that bloke in 3F24? What's he to us?"

Dad nodded knowingly, "We've got to keep our eyes open. We've got to be on the lookout for anyone behaving strangely. Our neighbor hasn't shown up for the main meal, and we've not seen him a single time. That's very strange, I say."

I had an idea. "Why don't we just knock on his door and get to know him?"

Dad pondered over that a while. I thought that I'd stumped him, and he was trying to think of an answer. Finally, he said, "I don't want to attract any attention to us. We just want to lie low and stay off everyone else's radar."

That was it for the evening. We took turns showering and then went to bed. It was getting close to midnight when that happened. It was almost time for me to go exploring on the ship.

Breakfast the next day was as wonderful as dinner had been the previous night. We had kippers and eggs of every sort—benedict, poached, fried, boiled, scrambled, omlets, and on and on. I decided that I'd try one each breakfast and see if I ran out of varieties before the cruise was over.

We all went to breakfast together. Dad seemed to want to put off the moment that he released me to wander the ship on my own as long as possible. On the way to the ballroom, we gazed over the side of the ship on the port side to the seemingly endless expanse of water. We seemed to be in a world apart from the one that we'd left less than a day before. The skies were clear with only a few thin high clouds and the sea was calm. We watched a few gulls orbiting the ship until we reached the ballroom.

After a great deal of pestering, Dad finally relented and agreed that we must be on the open sea and that I could wander around freely, but he added, "But we're having all meals together at the advertised time." He shook his finger at me and added, "No browsing the buffet at an odd hour and claiming that is lunch. We all eat together so that we can be sure that we're all safe."

Mum was not so hard-nosed, but as I left to explore the ship, she pulled me aside for a whispered, "You be back at our cabin before noon and before 6 PM. I don't want to have to stop the ship to search for you!"

I started to laugh at that and then re-considered. She might just do that.

The first thing I did was to take a run around the ship. I started off with the idea of running every corridor of every deck. I got off to a good start. However, by the time I'd circled the ship on several levels above the main deck, I slowed to a jog because it was clearly going to be more of a marathon than a sprint. By the time I'd run the circuit of the ship on all levels above the main deck, I decided that it was time to explore more carefully.

I stopped a crewman to ask how to get to the Exercise Room. He scratched his head and said, "I guess the closest is the deck below us toward the bow–that is the front of the ship. It's on the interior. When you get close, there are signs. Just follow them."

It wasn't as easy as he made it sound finding the Exercise Room, but after a wrong turn or two, I found it.

It was smaller than I expected, but it was fully equipped. It had running machines—the fancy kind with heart monitor and timers and electronic display. There were free weights and weight-lifting machines. There were machines that I'd never even seen before.

There was a crew member in charge of the room. That was good and bad. The good part was that you could ask for help if you got stuck. They made sure you didn't hurt yourself accidentally. But that was also the bad part. You couldn't just go to a machine that you'd not used before and figure it out for yourself. If you even looked like you weren't sure about something, they were right there, ready to help. It got to be a bore. I ended up not spending a lot of time in the Exercise Rooms until the cruise was nearly over.

What I ended up doing was to run around the ship a lot. I eventually did reach every deck and corridor that wasn't actually locked.

I got to a door that had a sign that read, "Engine Room: Authorized Personnel ONLY." I tried the door. It was locked.

Above decks, I found that I could go anywhere except into people's cabins. There was one exception. The highest part of the ship had the Captain's Cabin, the Bridge, and the Navigation Room. There probably were other rooms but I never got into them. I found out about the Bridge and other rooms up there much later in the cruise.

I got into a little trouble running in corridors. Every time I did that and ran into a crew member, they would stop me and lecture me about the dangers of running on the ship. Eventually I got tired of being stopped all the time, and I just jogged slowly when I was in corridors.

There were swimming pools, but I was never much for swimming. There were a lot of people lounging around them–including ladies in bikinis. I might have spent more time pool-side if it weren't that all the ladies were ladies–that is, ancient. I bet there wasn't a single teen other than me. I wondered if there were even one woman in her twenties. Above that there's no point in even looking.

I had such a good time jogging the decks that I almost forgot about lunch. When I did realize that it was almost noon, I had to sprint all the way back to our cabin. I entered just about exactly at noon.

Lunch at Sea

Dad didn't see it that way, "Dudders, it's already five after noon. Your Mum almost called out the Royal Marines. You've got to remember what we're doing."

I scratched my head, "Yeh, what is it we're doing?"

He made a face and said in a barely controlled whisper, "We're running away from You-Know-Who!"

"Yeh." I had almost forgotten what we were doing.

Mum asked, "What were YOU doing?"

I shrugged, "I took a jogging tour of the ship. I found an Exercise Room. I did a lot of poking my head in places." I actually hadn't been poking my head into places, but it sounded so lame just to be jogging and going to the Exercise Room that I had to say something.

Dad said, "Well, I did more than that. I looked up an officer and asked where we were."

I wasn't impressed, but I asked, "Yeh. Where are we?"

"Well, for your information, we're two hundred knots west of France."

I wasn't going to give him the satisfaction of asking what a knot was. It didn't matter; he told me anyway. "A knot for your information is about 800 feet more than a mile. We're plenty far from England. For one, I'm breathing a little easier now."

Having gotten that straight, we headed for lunch. Breakfasts were much less formal than lunch or dinner. There wasn't an officer at your table. I don't know where they ate breakfast, but the other two meals they ate with passengers.

This lunch, the officer that ate with us was the Laundry Officer. His name was Pullover or something like that. When he told us that I had a hard time not laughing, but Mum kicked me under the table. When she kicks you under the table, you don't forget it, and you pay attention to what's going on.

Dad asked him how it was determined what officer ate at what table. The Laundry Officer answered that it was random but that eventually all officers–including the captain–would eat with us sometime. There would be repeats too.

That got my Dad interested. He asked, 'Last night, one of the Pursers ate with us. Her name was . . . uh . . .'

The Laundry Officer smiled, "It was Jennifer wasn't it?"

I wondered how he knew, but he answered that immediately. "She's our only female Purser. Also, she's very popular. You were lucky to get her the first night."

Dad agreed. I thought that I felt the first hint of Mum kicking me under the table, but I realized that she was kicking Dad because his eyes bulged out and he coughed. However, he was determined. He asked, "I have a question about another passenger. I would guess a Purser could help me. Is that right?"

The Laundry Officer agreed that the Purser would know something about passengers. He added, "But, you know we take the confidentiality of passengers seriously on this ship. She probably wouldn't be able to answer your questions except very trivial ones.

"As a matter of fact, I could probably answer some questions. As Laundry Officer, I know what each passenger has laundered. We keep very good care of everyone's property."

Dad scratched his chin and said, "I'm just a little curious about a neighbor of ours. He's supposed to sit in that empty chair over there." He indicated Mr. Wendt's chair. "But so far he hasn't been at any of the three meals that we've had on this cruise."

Ensign Pullman seemed bored, but he said, "Oh?"

"No, and we've not seem him come or go from his cabin."

Ensign Paltry shrugged his shoulders about half an inch, "He might be taking his meals in his cabin. You'd be surprised how many people do. Even though we have stabilizers that keep the ship very level almost all of the time, a number of people think that they are sea sick or are likely to become sea sick if they eat in the dining room. They think they're safer in their cabin." He hesitated and added, "And I suppose they are safer from embarrassing themselves if they do become sea sick.

"He may just be one of those. You could knock on his cabin door and introduce yourselves."

My Dad nodded, but I doubted that he intended to. He did ask, "If I wanted to talk with Jennifer, how would I find her?"

Dad's eyes bulged, and he coughed again, so I guess Mum kicked him under the table. Poultry said, "She has an office in the island."

Dad squinted, "Island?"

Pullover grinned and looked like he was about to laugh, "Yes. Sorry. I used to be in the service. I was on an aircraft carrier for a while. That was what we called the tall superstructure where the ship was steered. Here, the *island* is the tallest part of the ship where the Bridge, the Navigation Room, and so forth are. We don't normally let people up into the upper parts of that area, but the Purser's office is easy to reach, and the Pursers normally work there 9 to 5 or so.

"You could go there during normal working hours and probably find her. And, of course, you could just look around at the evening meal. She'll be at someone's table."

At that Dad coughed again. He was not having a good day.

Pullover turned to the other passengers whom he'd been ignoring most of the meal and tried to make conversation.

□

After lunch, I went back to exploring and exercising, but I did stop in at the movie theatre to see what it was like. They were showing a Western movie. It was a comedy that I hadn't seen before. It was called, "Maverick." It seemed like the few other people who were in the theatre either had seen it several times, or it was familiar for some other reasons. People kept laughing just before the funny parts came. Sometimes they would call out a character's name before they were introduced.

Well, it was a funny movie, and I enjoyed watching it. I decided that I'd stick my head in every afternoon to see what was showing.

After the movie was over, it was after 5 PM. I was tired of exercising and exploring, so I decided to go back to our cabin a little early.

I realized that I'd pass 3F24 before I reached our cabin, so I decided that I'd just knock on the door and see what Mr. Wendt looked like. What harm could it do?

When I actually reached the door, I felt a little differently. But I found some courage and tapped lightly on the door. Nothing happened. I tried again, pretty softly, and nothing happened. I decided that one more try would be enough. This time I thought I ought to knock loud enough to actually be heard.

I guess I overdid it, because Dad poked his head out our cabin door and shouted, "Let us have a little peace and . . . " Then he noticed that it was me knocking and whose door I was knocking on. He grabbed me and pulled me inside our cabin.

"What in the world do you think you're doing!" he exclaimed. "He might have answered that knock!"

"Well, that was the idea."

"But we don't want to attract any more attention than we have to!"

Mum was nodding enthusiastically.

"I thought you wanted to know about this guy. Isn't talking to him a good way to find out about him?"

Dad shook his head and said, "No, no, no! I want to know about him. I don't want him to know about us."

"OK. I'll not do it again."

Dad looked around as though he were afraid someone would overhear. "Please don't."

That was the last we heard about 3F24 for a while.

3F24

For the next couple of days, we went through the usual round of things. I exercised in the morning and looked in at the movies in the afternoon. If I didn't like them, I sat out on the deck and got some sun. We were getting ever further south, and the weather kept becoming warmer.

I was in the one of the Exercise Rooms, doing reps on one of the weight machines. There was no one else in the room other than the obligatory exercise staff members. I vaguely noticed the sound of the door opening. I thought nothing of it.

Then I heard a voice that I knew say, "George, why don't you take a break. I'll spell you for a while."

He thanked her and left for someplace. It was at this point that I realized who the voice belonged to. I was almost done with my reps, so I just kept going.

The voice walked over behind me and asked, "Could I talk with you for a minute?"

"Sure. If you can wait a couple of minutes, I'll finish this set that I'm working on."

She replied, "Go on, I'll talk as you finish your set." She then began her story. "The first night at dinner, I sat at your table, and you and your family talked with me a little."

I answered the implied question, "Sure, I remember. So?"

The voice went on, "You and your family seemed curious about the man in 3F24."

"Well, that was mainly me Dad. So?"

"Are you curious enough to want to get into his room?"

"Maybe. If I were, I'd just knock on the door."

She hesitated, "But you haven't have you?"

That was not quite true, but it was certainly true for Dad. I said, "No. I guess not."

"I have knocked on his door several times. There was no answer. I did it during the evening meal. Incidentally, he's not showed up for any has he?"

I grimaced. She didn't notice because she was still behind me. "No, he hasn't."

Then she dropped the bombshell. "How much do you want to get into his room?"

That made me drop the weights. The sound seemed to bounce around the room like the bell ringing in some Dracula thriller. I swung around in my seat. "Just how would we do that?"

Jennifer, the Purser, smiled, "I can get a key that will let us into his room."

I had to laugh, "Well, what do I bring to the gig? Why do you waste your time talking with me? You just waltz up to his room, open the door, and find out what's inside."

She shivered—I swear. Then she said, "I'm more than a little afraid of what I'll find in there."

Now, I might have shivered, "What do you think you'll find in 3F24?"

She started pacing back and forth, "Well, I might find any number of things. I might find a body. If I did, I'd want witnesses to testify that I didn't kill him."

My eyes bugged out, "Come on, not really?"

She swung around and faced back at me, "I don't think that's likely but it's possible. Another thing that I might find in there is someone impersonating Mr. Wendt. That person might not like his privacy interrupted."

I scoffed, "Oh, you're a ship's officer. You could just say that you were investigating something. Maybe his neighbors are complaining about how much noise he makes."

She flashed a brief smile. "I might find Wendt, and he might not recognize me." She said that so low that I wasn't sure that I'd heard it right.

She went on in a normal tone. "I want someone to help me. Do you think that you or your parents might?"

She sounded almost as afraid of what might be in 3F24 as Dad was. With a ship's officer to help, maybe he would be interested. What I said was, "I don't know. The only way to find out would be to come to our cabin tonight after dinner and talk it over with Dad and Mum."

She seemed a bit surprised. "Are you sure that they wouldn't be someplace else—like the movie theatre or the casino?"

It was my turn to flash a brief smile. We weren't venturing out of the cabin any more than we absolutely had to. "Oh, I feel pretty sure about it."

She seemed relieved. She turned to leave. When she reached the door turned back briefly and said, "See you tonight."

□

Over dinner, I mentioned casually, "That Purser, Jennifer, is going to visit us tonight after dinner."

Mum almost needed the Heimlich maneuver. She had been swallowing a mouthful of wine. She spluttered so much that I got some of her wine on my face.

She immediately shot a look at Dad. "What is this about?"

He shrugged. "I don't know anything about it. Why don't you ask the boy. He's the one who knows about it?"

She turned her gaze at me. She was looking daggers at everyone at the moment. "Well?"

I just shook my head and said, "It's something that we'd be better talking about in our cabin."

Mum was clearly not satisfied at that, but if there is something that she doesn't like, it's people who make a fuss in public. I knew that Dad and I would be in for it when we got back to the cabin.

We finished dinner in silence and returned to our cabin silently. When we arrived and had the door shut and locked, Mum turned to Dad again and demanded, "Is this your doing? Is that pretty 'ship's officer' coming because you invited her?"

Dad gave a wild-eyed shrug and just said, "This is the first I've heard of it."

Mum turned to me, "What do you know about it? Why is that . . . that Jennifer coming here tonight?"

I took a chair and said, "It's entirely her idea. And, I think that I should let her tell us her idea."

Mum didn't give up. She's like Aunt Marge's bulldog when it's got a bone. She won't give it up for anything. She kept at me for five or ten minutes trying to pry what I knew out. I have been interrogated by the best headmasters, and I know how to keep my mouth shut when it's in my interest.

Fortunately, it wasn't long before we heard a knock on our door. Mum let Jennifer in. Dad was sitting on the bed. Mum and I were sitting on chairs. Jennifer went to the bed and started to sit down.

Mum shot up and said, "Take my chair. I'll take the bed." She strode over to the bed and Jennifer went to the chair that Mum had just left.

Mum picked up the interrogation that she'd left off earlier. "All right, Ms. Purser, what is this about?"

Jennifer looked around at us and asked me, "You didn't tell them anything?"

I just smiled contentedly and shook my head, "No."

She gave me a dirty look and began, "I gather that we all have some interest in the man in 3F24."

Mum started to object, but Jennifer shook her head and said, "We all were at the same table the first night of the cruise. I know that you are interested in him. Dudley confirmed that."

Both Mum and Dad glared at me, but it was clearly too late to deny it.

Dad said, "OK. Let's suppose we are. What is your interest in him?"

Jennifer said, "Let's trade information. You tell me what your interest is and I'll tell you mine."

Mum answered like a shot out of a gun, "No, we won't tell."

Jennifer shook her head sadly. "It would be better if you did."

No one budged. I thought briefly about opening the bag for Jennifer. I was beginning to like her a little. With Mum's and Dad's attitude, I knew I'd better keep quiet.

Jennifer sighed and said, "We'll do it that way then." She hesitated a minute and then went on. "I want to get into 3F24, and I think you do too. We can work together. What do you say?"

Dad stated asking questions. They were mostly the same as mine, and he got pretty much the same answers.

Sometimes I think Mum and Dad are mind readers—at least each others. Eventually Dad said, "We'll do it." Mum just nodded.

Mum asked how it would work.

Jennifer said, "There are various keys that will open the lock in 3F24. There's a master key that will open all locks anywhere on the ship. The Captain and First Officer have the only ones of those. There are keys that will open any passenger cabin door and almost all public areas in the ship. The head purser has that key. I don't have access to it.

"The cleaning staff are divided by deck and section. Each has a key that will open any door in their area. I will 'borrow' one of the keys from a maid assigned to 3F24. They go off duty at dinner time. I can snatch a key during their dinner, and we can have most of the dinner time before I have to return it."

Dad nodded wisely and said, "Then we have to miss dinner that night."

Jennifer shrugged her yes.

Mum asked her first question in a while, "Then we do it tomorrow?"

Jennifer nodded. "Just don't go to dinner. I'll meet you here, and we can enter 3F24 then. If we are quick, we might be out in time for us all to have dinner."

The next day dragged through as though it would never end. I started in an Exercise Room, but I couldn't concentrate enough to make any progress. I ended by just walking the decks—not even jogging.

We had lunch. Dad suggested that we have a hearty meal in case we ended up without supper. Nobody felt like it though.

The afternoon dragged on endlessly.

The dinner hour struck, and we were all waiting for whatever was on the other side of the door to 3F24. Suddenly, time seemed to fly. There was a knock on our cabin door, and Mum nearly jumped out of her skin. After a timeless moment when no one seemed to want to answer the door, I did.

Of course, it was Jennifer. There were sighs of relief behind me. She looked around at us and said, "Well, let's go."

We walked out into the corridor. It was empty, everyone having gone to dinner. She said, "I think you should knock on the door, Mr. Dursley."

Both Mum and Dad looked at each other and Dad said, "Don't you think it would be better for a ship's officer to knock. You could be investigating our concern." Here Dad looked over at Mum who nodded agreement.

Jennifer's lips squeezed shut, and she said, "All right."

So the four of us walked up to 3F24, and Jennifer knocked on the door rather softly at first. I wondered if Wendt could have heard it. With successive unanswered knocks they became louder. Finally, Jennifer declared in an overly loud voice, "I think we should go in and see if he's all right."

She reached into an inner jacket pocket of her uniform and pulled out a silver plastic rectangle that she inserted into the door lock. It clicked, and the lock released. She stood there frozen on the spot.

Dad said, "Go on in. We're right behind you."

Jennifer turned a whiter shade of English winter pale. She looked back at Mum and Dad. It was clear that they weren't going in with her. Then she looked the question at me.

I shrugged, "OK. I'll go in with you." I'd actually been in situations like this a few times in my former life as a JD. Except for the spooky ideas Jennifer had mentioned, I wouldn't have thought twice about it.

She held out her left hand to me. I took it with my right and pushed the door open rapidly with my left. There was nothing behind the door. We walked in slowly and carefully none-the-less.

What we saw seemed to be a perfectly normal cabin. The layout was just like ours. The bed was made and there were signs of habitation. There were a few odds and ends on the dresser—some coins and a few bills, a portable digital alarm clock, a small photo frame with a picture of a young man and an older woman—maybe his mother.

Jennifer and I ventured through the cabin. I opened the closet and found some shirts and pants hanging along with one suit. Jennifer walked toward the small bathroom. The door was closed.

By this time, Mum and Dad were standing in the doorway, seemingly afraid that something awful would happen if they crossed the door-frame.

Jennifer spoke to me in a tight, controlled voice, "Dudley would you come over here?"

She was standing just outside the bathroom.

I walked over and said, "Yes?"

"Would you open that door?"

It opened outwards. I looked over at Jennifer and said, "Step back— just in case."

She nodded and took a couple of steps back. I touched the doorknob and said, "I'm going to throw this open. Don't be surprised when it happens."

I took a deep breath and counted to three. At the end, I twisted the knob and flung it back. Inside the bathroom there was not enough room to hide anything larger than a bottle of Pepto Bismal in the medicine cabinet. I sighed and said, "OK. The big bad bathroom is open." I walked in and found an electric shaver, a small dopp kit on the sink, and a tooth brush.

Mum and Dad had by this time come into the main room and were standing back from the bathroom.

We all searched the cabin thoroughly. We did a fairly good job of not disturbing things, but the CID would have found our finger prints over everything. No one had thought to wear gloves.

⌗

The whole thing had taken about half an hour. By common consent, we closed the cabin up, trying to leave everything as we had found it.

We had plenty of time to get to the Dining Room and eat, but no one seemed to want to. We sat glumly in our cabin talking over what we'd found.

Jennifer said, "That cabin looked lived in. I didn't think to check the waste basket but it would probably have been empty anyway. The maid would have emptied it shortly before."

Mum asked, "OK. We found nothing. It just occurred to me, why didn't you talk to the maid and see what she knew?"

Jennifer chuckled, "In the first place the maids hardly ever see the people in the cabins they clean. The idea is that they should be invisible. That means that the occupants are invisible to them as well.

"Second, I didn't want anyone to know that I was interested in Wendt. Asking the maid about him would be a dead giveaway."

I said, "Well, you should get that key back to wherever you stole it, and we should think about catching dinner–if any's left. What do we do next?"

Dad cleared his throat and said, "We should keep our eyes open for the elusive Mr. Wendt." He hesitated and said, "Just how would we know him if we saw him?"

Mum said, "Easy. He would be going in or out of 3F24."

I asked, "And if we saw him on deck?"

Jennifer said, "I can tell you what he looked like a number of years ago.

"He was mid to upper twenties. His hair was brown, and it was straight. He wore it sort of medium length. He was around 5 foot ten or eleven. He liked casual clothes. I don't know that I ever saw him in a suit."

Dad walked over to her and asked, "Just what IS your interest in him? Was he your fancy man?"

She just looked up at him without a discernible expression on her face. She shrugged and got up. She walked to the door and turned before opening it. "If anyone learns anything, we'll meet in the Dining Room after lunch each day and exchange information."

With that, she opened the door and left our room.

Dad's Story

Nothing happened for a couple of days. No one had anything to report. Then one day I returned to our cabin about 3:30 PM. I just used my key and walked straight into a flaming argument. Dad was saying, ". . . had wanted to leave you, I'd have done it a long time ago."

Mum looked up at him suddenly. "What do you mean, 'you'd have left long ago?'"

Dad looked flustered. Then both of them noticed that I'd just walked in. They both were frozen for a second, and then I got conflicting orders from the two. Dad told me to leave, and Mum told me to stay. I looked from one to the other. They stared at each other as though they were about to start throwing things. As a matter of fact, Mum picked up a heavy glass tumbler.

I started to back out. That seemed to end the standoff. Dad said, more to me than Mum, "I was just trying to find out more about that Wendt person next door. Jennifer seems to know about him, and she's a Purser. She's supposed to know about him."

Mum said to me, "He was chatting up that Jennifer!"

Mum then picked up her question from before about leaving long ago. Dad looked an appeal at me and then glanced over at Mum and seemed to give up. "OK. Let's talk about that."

Mum told me to leave, but Dad seemed to become determined, "No, the boy should stay. This is a good object lesson."

She gave in, and Dad, who had been standing in a sort of defense stance, plopped down on the bed as though the air had been let out of him. He said, "I guess I have to tell it from the start.

"It all happened before Harry came. It happened before you were born, Dudders. Your Mum and I had not been married more than a year.

"I worked for a different company then. No drill bits. I sold something completely different."

I came into the office bright and early every Monday. That's the only time that I was in the office for sure. That's because every week the salesmen have a meeting with the General Manager. We review how our sales calls went the previous week—how much product we sold, if we found good prospects for future sales, what didn't go well. That was frequently more important than what went well. You can learn lots more from your failures than your successes.

Anyway, the sales meeting went from 9 AM to almost noon most Mondays. I always made a point of getting into the office around 8 AM. I went to my office and prepared for the big meeting. I reviewed the previous week and practiced what I was going to say.

Then I would go to the General Manager's outer office and wait with the rest of the salesmen. Sometimes we'd talk with each other. Sometimes the secretary would talk with us.

The General Manager normally started the sales meeting very promptly at 9 AM. When it ended depended on how the meeting went. After the meeting it was almost time for lunch. Most of us went out to have lunch together at a local pub. They'd go to their offices, drop their papers, and we'd meet at the main entrance.

But one day Betty, the secretary, asked me a question as I left. It had something to do with business, but it started a more general conversation. We talked about how the weekend had been. What we'd done. That sort of thing.

It slowly became a regular thing. I spent so much time talking that I sometimes missed lunch completely.

Betty was not what any man would call a stunning beauty. As a matter of fact her appearance was almost what you would call plain. Most men like women to have long hair, preferably blonde. Betty's was short. It was maybe not quite as short as mine, but really not much longer. When I first met her, it was jet black. However, sometime along the line, she had the top streaked with red, and the rest was not black but was a sort of reddish black shade that defied description. The color seemed to depend on the angle that the light struck it. There were times when I thought it was pure black, and others when it seemed to me to be a dark red, but it never stayed one color very long.

She was short and thin. There were practically no curves to her body. Again, that is hardly what men like, but somehow she had a way of gazing up into your eyes that made you think that you were the only man in the world.

I don't think that she was shamming at all. As we talked, she would start rubbing her forearm slowly, rhythmically. I didn't notice it much at

63

first, but after a few weeks, I began to notice. Eventually she would caress her neck. I didn't really think about it at the time, but I realized eventually that she was doing it unconsciously and that she was at least infatuated with me.

One Monday after the morning meeting, we were talking, and she asked me if I would like to have lunch. I shrugged and said that I'd brought a bag lunch from home. She laughed and said, "No. I meant at a restaurant." Her laugh had a disarming quality to it that would make you think that there was nothing in the world that was truly serious.

I laughed too, and said, "OK". By that time, everyone else had left for lunch. She took me to a little inn that was off the beaten track. We ordered and continued our conversation. She seemed fascinated by my stories of selling on the road. Every little story of getting lost on a back country road or a quaint old inn that I stopped at for lunch on a hot day seemed to excite her interest.

Somehow, the food came, and we barely noticed. The hour flew by, and we'd hardly touched our meals. I quickly paid the tab. We left the inn,. and took a cab to get back to the office as soon as we could.

We entered the building separately. That should have told me something. I should have thought about that, but I didn't.

I had not thought out the consequences of what was happening. The wonder of a new relationship starting seemed to overwhelm my ability to think critically. All I could think about was the next time that we would meet. When I was away on a business trip I could only think of my return and my next chance to see her.

That went on for weeks. Then I realized that I should be more careful about talking with Betty in the office. The first Monday morning after that realization was hard. She didn't understand it.

I arrived at the moment that the morning meeting was to start. She shot me a look full of hurt and longing all at the same moment.

I was the last to enter the boss's office. I'd timed it so that I would be. That gave me about 10 seconds alone with her to more mime than speak, "See you at lunch as usual."

Her eyes shot me a look that said that I'd better have a good explanation for my behavior. I agreed internally. I'd better have a good story to tell.

We met as usual at our favorite pub. I made sure that I was there first. I didn't want her to walk in, glance around, not see me, and leave immediately.

She did walk in, glanced around, saw me, and came to OUR table. We'd begun to think of it as OUR table because we always chose that table if it were available. After a while the owner of the pub began to make sure it was open on Monday lunches.

She sat in a huff and started in on me, "What in the world were you playing at? I always look forward the whole weekend to talking to you on Monday morning! It's the only time I can see you."

I looked around, afraid that someone would hear us, and immediately regretted it. She knew exactly what I was doing. I tried to turn that gesture into an asset.

"Look, Bet, we're being way too obvious about the way we feel about each other."

She was sullen. She said the words in a sort of whine. "Why? Are you ashamed of me?"

"No. No. I. . . well, it could get really sticky if we are found out before . . ." I trailed off. I hoped that she wouldn't notice that I hadn't finished the thought, but she did.

She turned a bit brighter and said hopefully, "Before what? Do you have something in mind?"

I really didn't. I had no idea what I could possibly be preparing for. I just sort of hoped that we could go on indefinitely in this deception that we were doing. I realized that everyone was being deceived–us hardly less than Pet. So, I didn't have anything to say. It didn't seem to matter though. It seemed like the indefinite possibility of a something that we were preparing for seemed to be enough for Betty.

We gradually regained our normal joy at being together, and by the time we headed back for the office, we agreed that we'd be much more careful about how we talked to each other in the office. It was to be strictly business.

□□

Then one Thursday, something strange happened. I went to my Thursday sales appointment. When I entered the reception area, it was immediately obvious that something unusual was going on. The receptionist was standing, talking to a number of people.

I listened in on the conversation, and it immediately was obvious why. They were talking about the ambulance which had just left the parking lot. As I thought about it, I remembered hearing a siren in the distance as I pulled into the parking lot. It appeared that the owner of the company had fainted and couldn't be wakened. My appointment was with the owner.

I didn't want to interrupt as the Vice President of the company got things calmed down, and people went back to work. Eventually, I approached the Vice President whom I'd met once before and re-introduced myself.

He was obviously distracted and shook his head to clear his mind. Then he asked, "Did you say that you were Durwood Verby?"

"No, sir, it's Vernon Dursely. I know that this is a difficult time for you, but I had an appointment with Mr. Higginbothom. It was a sales call."

The Vice President, whose name I couldn't quite remember, was still bothered. He paced over to the receptionist and asked her, "When was Durnon's appointment with Higginsbothom this morning?"

She had returned to placid efficiency and checked her appointment book. She replied, "It was to be at 9 A.M."

He looked around distractedly and then turned to me, "What were you going to meet about?"

"I was going to present Widgets International's new line of Thimble Control circuits. We have made very great strides in . . .", but he was obviously not listening, so I said, "Why don't I make a new appointment sometime next week?"

He shook his head as though he were trying to understand what a widget was, but he managed to say, "Yes. Yes. Make an appointment with Doris. Somebody will be able to help you."

I left as quietly as I could. As I walked out to my car, a thought occurred to me—could I move my Friday appointment up to this afternoon and get home early? After getting in the car, I called the offices of the Belinger Corporation. I got the secretary on the line and asked about moving up the appointment. She put me on hold, and after what seemed like a half hour she was back on. She said that if I could make lunch, I could talk with Mr. Belinger, and if he were interested, maybe we could make it a long lunch hour.

I was ecstatic! I could win back a day. I could get home on Friday, maybe Friday morning.

The meeting happened. I had to bend a few traffic laws to make it to the restaurant by noon, but I actually walked in just as he was being seated. I joined him. We had some talk about the unfortunate owner of the business that I'd just visited. Belinger knew what he wanted from the menu. He ate there most work days. He didn't even glance at the menu. I glanced and picked out my usual lunch. It was nothing special—bangers and mash. There probably isn't a pub or restaurant in the U.K. that won't serve it to you even if it's not on their menu.

Belinger noticed how I ordered. He commented, "You order quite decidedly for someone who's never been in this restaurant."

I shrugged, "Well, when you know what you want, it's easy."

He nodded. "Yes, it's easy. I know what I want from Widgets International." And he proceeded to tell me what it was. He was crazy, of course. No one in their right mind would try to put their supplier out of business by demanding such low prices, but it was only an opening salvo. We dickered through our digestion. It was a long lunch indeed. At least three times toward the end of the meal, Belinger's phone rang, he picked it up, glanced at it, and closed it again.

I had made a good sale, and I was proud! I was more than proud, I wanted to celebrate. There was just one little problem—there was no one around to celebrate with.

I went back to my car and made notes for Betty to type up a sales contract. As I finished, I decided that I had to call her right away to tell the boss that I'd run out of sales calls to make, and I'd be on my way home. I could probably be back in town by early evening.

I got her on the first ring. She answered with her efficient secretary voice, but when she heard mine, she immediately switched to her intimate voice, "What's up, Vernie?"

I was tempted to remind her not to use my nickname at the office, but I was too excited to break the mood. "Oh, some good news and some bad news. I'll give you the bad first.

"My sales call today was rushed to the hospital just before I got there. There was no one to talk to, so I was left at sixes and nines."

She made a consoling murmur, and then I said, "But the good news is great. I decided to try to reschedule my Friday for this afternoon. At first it looked like no go, but then the secretary got me a lunch meeting with him. It was tremendous! I made a great deal. The boss may not like how much of a price concession I had to give him, but it really is a big order, and I think there will be more to come later!"

She asked very casually, "Well, what are you going to do tomorrow?"

I hadn't really thought that far, but I did then, "Well, I guess I'll come home tonight. I can get into town by seven if I push it a little. Goodness knows I pushed it to make that lunch meeting in time."

Betty paused and then said, "Well, let me talk to the boss and see what he wants you to do. I'll put you on hold if that's all right?"

"Sure, sure. Maybe he'll have someone he'd like me to see tomorrow before I come in."

She said, "Um hum." I could almost see her nodding slowly as she said that. Then the line went dead as she put me on hold. When she came back on, she said, "The boss is fine with you coming in tonight. We can work in the office to get that big contract written up right. . ." She hesitated then, and I wondered if the call had dropped.

When I heard her speak again, her voice was different. It wasn't her business efficient voice or even the intimate voice. I'd not heard it often enough to know what she was thinking about. She spoke carefully and slowly when she finally did speak.

"I was just thinking. If you really could get into town by seven, then we might do a little celebration of your success. Nothing big, you know, just a quiet little dinner in our favorite pub."

It was my turn to think. There was a rush in my chest, and I felt light-headed. I knew that it had nothing to do with being a great salesman. I had to work at keeping my voice nonchalant as I said, "That sounds like it could be fun. Sure." My voice might not be shaking, but I felt like all the muscles in my body were.

She said, "You could tell your wife that you will be home really late tonight. You know, too bad so sad." I could hear the merriment in her voice as she pronounced that judgment.

I swallowed hard and barely got out, "Sounds good."

Then she declared that she had to get back to work and that she'd see me for dinner.

I called home and told Pet about my good and bad luck. She wasn't nearly so excited as Betty although she seemed glad that I'd be home a day early.

Then I came around to reality and realized that I'd have to get on the road and get moving really quickly. The drive was both pleasant and harrowing.

It was pleasant because I really wanted to see Betty and talk about my good luck today! Observing the weather and the road conditions was pleasant. How would they affect my travel time? Estimating when I'd arrive was pleasant as long as I thought that I'd make it to the pub by 7 P.M. It was harrowing when I began to realize that I'd almost certainly arrive late. How long before seven should I call if I couldn't make it within a few minutes of seven?

In the end, I was driving like a maniac, taking all sorts of chances, spinning around roundabouts at over fifty MPH. I almost hit an ambulance in one of them. I somehow reached the outskirts of the suburb where our office and the pub were with fifteen minutes to spare, but I had to find a parking place and still walk to the pub.

I reached the pub and drove past. I glanced and saw a car pull out from the curb and thought that God was smiling on me. However, another car pulled into the spot before I could reach it. I circled the block and still there was no parking spot. I drove a larger circle on the streets and found a parking spot. It was a long walk from the pub. I glanced at my watch and saw that I had only three minutes.

I got out of the car and started sprinting toward the pub. Maybe I could still make it. I rounded a corner and glanced at my watch. I wasn't going to make it in time. Maybe I'd get there within five minutes. I picked up my pace and arrived at the entrance to the pub about 6 minutes after seven. I was huffing and puffing as I entered the pub. A quick glance around showed that there were no tables available. Betty wasn't sitting at any.

I went to the hostess and asked to be put on the wait list. She nodded and asked my name. That stopped me dead in my tracks. I pretended to be out of breath and catching it up as I thought. Did I really want to give her my real name? Maybe more important had Betty already got on the wait list and maybe was in the loo while I was out here.

So, I asked, "Is there a Betty Cummings on the wait list?"

The hostess asked, "Is that your fancy lady?"

I opened my mouth and turned it into a gasp for air as though I still needed to catch breath. After a deep breath, I said, "I'm supposed to meet her here. I'd not want to get on the wait list if she's already on it."

The hostess smiled knowingly, "No, she's not–by that name anyway."

I grimaced internally and said, "Then put me on the list." I turned to go to the bar to wait, but the waitress stopped me.

"Wait here now. What name should I put on the list?"

I smiled because the idea of a fake name occurred to me, "Bishop. Just Bishop."

"All right, Mr. Bishop. You can wait at the bar, and I'll call you when your table is ready."

I turned again toward the bar, but I wasn't finished. She asked, "Oh, yes. How many for the table?"

"Just the two."

She smiled knowingly again and said, "Just the two, then."

I got to the bar and ordered a whiskey on ice—lots of whiskey, not much ice. About five minutes after that, I saw Betty waltz through the entrance–at least, it seemed like a waltz to me. She glanced around and started to go to the hostess but noticed me at the bar.

She came over to the stool next to me and said, "Then you're on the list?"

I nodded. She smiled and said, "Be a dear and order me a sidecar."

I was happy to do that. After I'd finished, she started talking a mile a minute, "I was so bothered about being late, but I should have known that you'd be here and have a table requested. I just love sidecars, but I never order them for lunch. I'm afraid I'll not be up to my usual standard of efficiency. Have you ever had one?"

The sidecar came, or I think that she'd have kept up the stream of happy comment. She was obviously keyed up, and I wondered how she could be as excited as I was. She took a deep swallow and sighed appreciatively. Then she seemed about to continue her commentary when the hostess came over and put her hand on my arm.

"Didn't you hear me call your name?"

I didn't have time to answer because Betty spoke rapidly, "Oh, no. We didn't. We were just talking away like we had all the time in the world." She turned to me and said, "Let's go!"

We were seated and glanced at the menu. I'd not seen the dinner menu before so I stuck my nose into it, trying to figure out something that I would like. The waitress came over and looked at us for a moment, "I see that you've already got drinks. Do you know what you want off the menu?"

I shook my head and asked for a little time. Betty just said, "Vernon will order for me." With that she gave my arm a little squeeze, "Won't you dear?"

I smiled a silly wide smile and nodded. Then I went back to the menu to puzzle it out. I saw something on the menu and caught the waitress before she got out of range, "Are the oysters any good?"

She smiled, "They're fresh from the coast this morning."

"Then we'll have an order as an appetizer." The waitress nodded and hurried off.

Betty giggled and said, "You naughty boy." Why that should make me naughty didn't occur to me just then, but she seemed to have slipped off a shoe because her foot caressed the inside of my shin.

I really have practically no idea what happened during the dinner. Certainly, I talked about my lucky coupe. Certainly, Betty gazed admiringly up into my eyes. Certainly I tried a boxcar or was it a sidecar–whatever it was that she was drinking.

What is certainly true was that we suddenly discovered that it was almost 10 PM. Betty was the one who discovered it. She said, "You know, it's really too late for you to return home–especially with alcohol on your breath."

I realized that she was right and was beginning to think my way through that fine mess. Betty was Johnny-on-the-spot. Almost without a hesitation, she coyly said, "You know what we could do?"

I shook my head dumbly, "No. I don't."

"Well," she drew that word out as though she were thinking about it as she spoke. Later events proved that it wasn't a case of impromptu thought. "We could stay here the night. I'll bet that they've got at least one room available for the night."

I was taking a swallow of sidecar as she said that, and I almost choked. But, I also felt the heart in my chest beat wildly. I said, "But you don't have any clothes for tomorrow do you?"

She surprised me by saying, "Well, I always keep a change of clothes in the office–you know, just in case."

I was shocked, but I was also getting very excited. "Well, I'll check to see if they have a room."

Betty just smiled, "Well, actually, I did check and made a reservation–you know," I had an idea what I knew, so I joined her in the refrain, "just in case."

She smiled broadly. "A girl can't be too careful."

I smiled too, "You know, I don't think that was the sort of thing that they mean when they say, 'A girl can't be too careful.'"

"I'll go out and call home and make up some excuse."

"Why don't you just call from the table?"

I didn't want to tell her the real reason—I was scared and didn't want to show it in front of her. So, I just said, "Oh, I've got my reasons."

Betty stretched her arms and said, "Don't be long. You know, I'm getting pretty sleepy." Then she did a very decent imitation of a yawn.

I went outside the pub and pushed the speed dial button for home on my cell. After several rings, Pet answered, "Who is it?"

"It's me, Pet. Listen, It's a long story, but I finished my calls today and was trying to get home tonight. I didn't think it would be this late, but I had a flat, and I've put the spare on. I'm bushed ,and I'll stay here. I'll see you after work tomorrow. I'll be in the office."

She shot back, "Where are you staying? What's their number?"

I had to think fast again. It wasn't that easy with those sidecars in me, but I said, "I just finished with the tire. I don't know where I'll stay. I'll just pick a likely looking place on the way. By then you'll be asleep. If anything more happens, I'll get in touch right away."

She wasn't happy about it, but I think she was mainly concerned that I find a safe place to stay quickly. We finished the call with the little terms of endearment that always finish our calls. I brought my suitcase with me.

I went back in and found that Betty had already left the table and was getting the room key. After that, we walked up the stairs. She commented, "I had them put the tab on your room bill."

I agreed, "Good idea."

Then as we rounded a corner of the stairs, she took my hand and dragged it, saying, "Race you to our room!" So we ended running up the stairs to the second floor. We found our room, and after I unlocked the door, she stood sort of leaning on me. It just was so obviously a good idea to pick her slight form up and carry her into our room that I did it without any hints. She was wearing that broad smile that seemed to be permanently part of her face. I kicked the door shut and she said, "Just lock it, will you."

I tossed her on the bed and locked the door. I gazed down at her. Somehow her short black hair draped over her right forehead was amazingly attractive. I was frozen for a moment by the vision. Then, I lay beside her on my side and kissed her.

Somehow, she opened her mouth wider than I would have believed possible. She was actually laughing into my mouth. Then something more material was entering my mouth, and I found that the experience of having her tongue caressing mine was also beyond my belief. I was fascinated by the experience and we continued for quite some time.

71

In the mean time, my hand flowed down her back slowly. She was wearing her silk blouse still, but I felt her back through it as though the blouse were made of nothing more substantial than the veritable ether.

The idea had occurred to me at some point that I could caress and then kiss, and then lick every square inch of her body. I made a halfhearted attempt to consummate that sterling idea.

There was just one little problem. Long before I got very far on that program Betty had discovered that I had risen to the occasion and was completely ready for the program of satisfying her desires. So I did.

I had no idea how many times I satisfied her desire. It could have been three or four. In my ecstasy, I might have overestimated my powers, but eventually we both fell asleep. I was wakened sometime late in the night by the cold. Betty was thoroughly asleep, and I didn't wake her as I put on my pajamas.

Later, an alarm woke me. I glanced at my wrist and saw that it was sometime around six in the morning. It was still dark, but Betty was up and doing something. I managed to mutter, "Why so early?"

She laughed, "Some of us have to work."

I mumbled something and she asked, "What?"

"But why 6 AM!"

She laughed again, "You probably can dress in 15 minutes, but I have to do makeup and get to work early so that I can change in the lady's loo before anyone gets into the office."

I drifted back to sleep. When I finally woke up it was 7:45. There was nothing left of Betty—no sign that she'd been there other than a faint hint of her perfume. Otherwise I might not have believed that the night had been real.

I would be late on a normal day, but I wasn't exactly expected in the office today, so I could stretch things a little. Nevertheless, I rushed through dressing and shaving. I gave up the idea of bathing and just hoped on the powers of deodorant. I drove quickly to the office and went directly to my cubical. My neighbor noticed my presence and sauntered into my cubical.

"Well, you look like you've had quite a night."

I glanced at myself in the little mirror that I keep on the wall. I did look pretty disheveled. I had a ready explanation though. "I had a great day yesterday. I made a big sale with more coming after."

Robert laughed and said, "I suppose you were doing a little celebration last night." He chuckled again and added, "I suppose the wife wasn't there either?"

I nodded. He punched me on the shoulder and said, "Good to see that there's a married man who knows how to celebrate once in a while."

I just nodded.

I worked most of the morning on my notes for the contract that we needed written up. Before lunch I was ready to turn it over to Betty. That was a meeting that I was not looking forward to.

I got my courage up, and then it failed. I decided it would be better to bring it by her desk after lunch than before.

⛛

My intuition was correct. When I entered the anteroom to the boss's office that was her post, I found that her face lit up like a Christmas tree when I arrived. She said, "I was wondering when you'd be around."

She continued, "I've been expecting you for quite some time. It's about time if you expect me to get that contract out today. You're barely in time." She chuckled, "I might have to put some overtime in and I might need your help." She winked at me once with both eyes.

That wink scared me to death. In it I saw a future where we would have to carve out little chunks of time here and there. We'd find excuses to meet while I was traveling. Probably I'd claim that my road trip would keep me out so late that I'd spend Friday night on the road. Of course, I'd have to be careful to choose weeks when I was far from London for the little side excursions.

The idea was terribly exciting. Having a secret love life, especially with the dark beauty that Betty was, was intensely exciting. Even just thinking about it forced me to show my excitement in a way that caused Betty to show appreciation. My mouth went dry, and I tried to say something.

Betty was in better command of herself. She just smiled slyly and said, "Perhaps not after work today. It is Friday, after all."

I nodded mutely and hobbled back to my cube. I was ruined for the rest of the afternoon. At least, I'd been able to get some real work in during the morning hours, but now, just the sight of Betty had my blood roiling. I could hardly find my own desk and log onto my computer. I worked on the only thing that I could manage—filling in expense reports to get reimbursements. I had the deuce of a time doing even that automatic process. I misfiled a couple of lunch tabs as dinner tabs and had to redo the whole report.

Thank God it was Friday. If this had been a Monday, I'd have been cooked for the week. Honestly, I didn't know if I were already cooked for the next week. How could I have lunch with Betty on Monday and work that afternoon? How could I concentrate on sales calls? I might be constantly thinking of the next time I would be with her.

That night, when I got home, Pet was especially affectionate. You'd think that I'd been gone for a month. She wanted to know all about my adventure: how long did it take me to change the tire, where did I stay the night, how long did it take me to get to work in the morning. She commented on how rumpled I look and wondered if I'd slept well.

It was surprisingly easy to answer her questions, once I'd got past the first one. I hesitated trying to figure out how long it should have taken to change tires. I decided that one hour was a safe length of time. Then, the rest fell into place. I stayed in a little roadside pub that had a few rooms. It was something like the Red Lion. I'd filed the bill on my expense report. No I didn't think that there'd be any problem about reimbursement. I'd gotten up early. I'd had an awful night's sleep. I'd hardly slept at all. I was in by 9 AM.

"Well, Vern, you must have flown low to get to the office by then."

I almost laughed at how easy the questions were getting. "You bet. It was still dark, and there wasn't a lot of traffic. I took at least one roundabout at 60."

Pet looked concerned, "Well, I hope they realize at the office just how dedicated you are."

I nodded. I was sure that at least one person in the office knew how dedicated I was.

That weekend there were plenty of chores to keep me busy, and thank God there were. Every moment when I wasn't occupied I was thinking of that unbelievable night with Betty. I found myself chuckling at odd moments with the thought of how wildly exuberant we'd been.

At one of those Pet asked me what was so funny. I thought a moment and said, "Well, it's just ironic. One man's tragedy is another man's luck."

She looked at me quizzically, and I quickly told her the story of the collapse of one of the people I had an appointment with and his trip to the hospital. That had opened up an opportunity for me to make a great sale.

She nodded and said, "You should find out if he's still in the hospital and send him flowers or something."

I nodded dully. Just then my cell phone rang. I picked it up. I didn't recognize the number, and it wasn't in my contacts in the phone. I immediately realized who it was when I heard her voice. "How is my favorite French tongue."

I gasped and said, "Good. Listen, I'm here at home pottering around with the missus. Can we have this discussion later?"

I could hear the pout in her voice. "You are so cruel. Can we get something on this weekend?"

I thought a moment and said, "That would be really hard."

"Oh, I know you're really hard by now." The embarrassing thing was that I was getting hard. "But maybe we could do something Monday night before you leave."

I thought fast, "Maybe. Let's talk at lunch."

She excitedly said, "Wonderful. Lunch on Monday! See you soon!" She hung up.

Pet asked, "What in the world was that?"

"Oh, it was the office. There was a question, but I put them off till Monday."

"Well, I would think so! Do they think they own you body and soul?" Pet was washing the dishes, and she threw the dirty dishrag into the suds. She was that disgusted.

I said ruefully under my breath, "You know, sometimes I think she does."

Pet asked what I'd said. I answered, "Oh, I just said they do sometimes act like they own me body and soul."

She said something expressing her disgust and went on with the dishes.

That next Monday, I had decided that I would go in to the boss's anteroom at the normal time—not early, not just before the meeting and try to talk with Betty the way we normally did.

It was a good plan. It almost worked as I hoped. I arrived and we had a nearly normal conversation like the old times. She apparently had the same idea. However, toward the end, she asked casually, "Where do you end up the week on Friday?"

I gulped hard and tried to maintain my composure, "I'm in one of the London suburbs. I don't remember which off hand." And it was true.

She said, "Nice. That way you can get home quickly." By this time, the meeting was about to start. Everyone else had entered the boss's office. Betty touched my wrist and ran her hand up along my forearm slowly, while saying, "You could get back in time for supper?"

An electric thrill went through my body, but I said, "Might be. We won't know until Friday."

She smiled her heart-melting smile at me. It was not visible to anyone in the office, but I felt the full force. I couldn't help smiling moronically back. Oh, I was lost!

The rest of the day went normally–even lunch. Betty asked me to give her a call on Thursday night to plan "something nice" on Friday. The first day on the road went well too, but on Wednesday night, my cell rang. I immediately saw that it was Betty.

After some affectionate banter she told me that she was dying to see me on Friday. Maybe we could have an early dinner at our favorite pub. Visions of her undressed leapt to my head, and I tried to calculate if we could manage it two weeks in a row. I was non-committal and would only say that I would move heaven and earth to make it happen. That night I would have.

The next morning in the cold light of dawn after a largely sleepless night trying to get her out of my thoughts, a realization struck me.

I would either end up divorcing Pet, or I would have to escape the eyes of Betty. That morning I was on the road for an hour before I arrived at my first appointment of the day. During that hour, I made a plan. I would start a crash program of getting a new job. Half measures would not work. I couldn't simply walk away from Betty. She knew way too much about me —not just my habits, likes and dislikes. She knew how to turn my mind's eye to scenes of bed.

As I drove, half automatically, I planned my campaign. All the companies that I sold to were manufacturers themselves and had sales teams of their own. I already knew them pretty well. Which were good to work for, which were OK, and which were hell holes. I knew a couple of Sales Managers of them. I was much more familiar with the buying teams, but I'd met a Sales Manager or two. Come to think of it, hadn't at least one of them felt me out about working for them? I thought so, but I couldn't remember which it had been.

This very week, on Friday, I had a meeting at one of my favorite companies. Yes, I'd sound out the Sales Manager there for sure. The next week, there were at least a couple who might be open to a little poaching of a good salesman.

So, as the drive progressed, I plotted out my campaign. One this week, probably three next week, who knew how many the week after? That thought sent a chill down my spine. God, I hoped it didn't go beyond three weeks. Could I last that long?

It made all the difference in the world having that decision made and a plan in motion. The sales calls this day went particularly well. It makes a difference if your head is in the right place when you walk into that Buying Manager's Office.

That night I had almost forgotten my troubles when the phone rang. As I picked up the phone, I reflected that it couldn't be Pet. She never called this late when I was on the road.

It was Betty. She was pretty high. Whether she'd been drinking or it was just the excitement of this illicit relationship, I couldn't tell.

She spoke slowly and seductively but with an intensity that came through her voice very clearly. "Are you in your jammies? Or maybe you always sleep the way you did a week ago."

76

I caught my breath. "Jammies."

"Well, I was lying all undressed on my bed wondering what you were doing. Then it occurred to me that maybe just listening to my voice might get a 'rise'," with that she chuckled in a very un-girlish way, "out of you."

The truth was that I could feel my implement of joy rising to the occasion.

Once I had made a sales call on a Yank who was over here on a temporary assignment with IBM. He was on the fast track to the top of the management pyramid. On the fast track, you have to do a lot of moving and put in a stint at all sorts of places. He was the Buying Manager briefly for the CICS team here. It was funny, he pronounced the letters individually. All the English employees pronounced it like a football, "kicks". Anyway, he had this strange glove mounted in a frame over his desk. It was really thick and padded. It had only a couple of slots for fingers. Just to make conversation, I asked him what the glove was for.

He glanced over his shoulder and said, "Oh, that glove. I was a catcher," he quickly amplified, "a baseball catcher when I was in college at MIT. That, my friend, is known in the trade as one of the implements of ignorance."

I didn't know anything about baseball at the time, so I asked him how many implements there were. He answered, "Oh, there are four. There's the glove, a padded thing that covers your torso and parts of your thighs, there's the shin guards, and finally, there's the mask."

I couldn't help laughing. "The mask? Is there something about the game that requires that no one recognize you?"

He laughed in his turn, "Oh, you have to understand that the mask doesn't keep you from being recognized. Quite the opposite, it keeps your face safe so that your friends will recognize you."

I gulped, "Is baseball a very dangerous game then?"

"Like any sport, all players can get hurt, but the catcher is especially prone to it. The catcher has to sit on his haunches and catch balls that are thrown at him upwards of 100 miles per hour. That's why you need a padded glove. Some catchers add a little more padding inside the palm of the glove and still come away with their hand smarting."

He reflected a moment and then added, "Then too, if a ball gets out of control, as it tends to with spitball pitchers, the idea is that rather than dodge the ball as any sensible person would, the catcher sometimes has to block it with his body and keep control of it that way."

I must have gulped again, because he smiled and said, "It's really not as dangerous as I make it sound. I came away with both my eyes, my nose, both ears. What more do you want?"

Anyway, that flashed through my mind. Betty noticed and asked, "Am I boring you?"

"No, ma'am. Actually I was distracted by a part of my body that just grew to twice its size."

She hummed appreciatively. She then said, "I know that you can't appreciate it, but I've got my legs spread wider than you can possibly imagine."

I gulped. The gulp had a lot in common with the gulp that I made when I'd been talking with the IBMer. I said, "I can't talk with you another second. I won't get a minute's worth of sleep if you say one more word."

"Maybe you could just drive down to my flat right now."

"That does it. I have to hang up. I've got to work tomorrow." I did hang up.

The next day, I was in the office of the Grunnings Corporation. I'd made my sales call. I had two very good reasons for making a good impression. First, I wanted to make a sale to the company. Second, I wanted to sell myself as an excellent salesman.

As I left the Buying Manager's Office, I stopped at his admin assistant and asked if she could see if the Sales Manager were free for a few minutes.

She looked at me quizzically, but picked up the phone and dialed a three digit number. She spoke into the receiver and said, "Marge, yes, it's Tam. Might your boss have fifteen minutes to talk with a salesman standing in front of my desk?"

She kept holding the phone and not speaking, so I guessed that she had been put on hold. She nodded her head and said, "It's Vernon Dudley from International Widgets." Then she fell silent again.

After a while she just said, "Thanks. See you at lunch." Then she hung up and turned to me. "You can have ten minutes from right now. The manager is Paul Rand. His office is at the opposite end of this hall. Now, go!"

I went. I don't think it took me a minute to get there. I was a little short of breath and said to the Admin when I went in, "I'm. . . "

She interrupted me. "You're Vernon Dursely. Go right in."

I did. I'd met Rand a couple of times in the Buying Manager's Office and maybe even been introduced once. He had been watching the door. "You have eight minutes. I have a hard stop then. Go."

I took a deep breath to center myself and said, "To start with, this has to be confidential."

He nodded slowly and said, "Not an unusual request. Sure."

I still hadn't sat, so I took a chair and began, "I'm a damn good salesman. I know your product line pretty well. I've been selling to you for a couple of years.

"Ask your buying group. They know me. They know I'm straight. I don't sell vapor products. I just wouldn't. That's one of the reasons I want to sell for you. You've got good products. I can stand up and sell them without a second thought."

Despite the lack of time, he looked at me for what must have been a full minute. Then he said, "OK. You told me one of the reasons you want to work for me. That's not the main one. Let's hear more."

I was ready. I'd been practicing my elevator speech since yesterday. "I know enough about you to know that you're a good boss to work for. This company is a good company to work for. You're located close to London and closer to my home than International."

He nodded again, "I get that. But that's not your main reason. If you want me to buy, you've got to bring your main reason."

I took a deep breath. I glanced at the clock reflected in the glass of Rand's window. I had maybe a minute left.

"It's the real reason that I don't want you to let anyone know that I've come to you. It's International. The environment has changed."

He nodded again. He glanced at his clock too. Then he asked me, "Can you join me for lunch? I don't have time to go into that now."

I thought. I could make my next appointment a quickee. They were an old reliable. It was almost just a formality that I made a sales call. I nodded. "Sure, I can make my next call and be back by lunchtime."

"Good. Meet me here. There's a good fish and chip shop that I eat at on Fridays."

When I returned, there was indeed a fish and chips shop. It was a small hole in the wall with maybe eight or ten tables and a long line of people waiting.

Rand said, "You can see that it is really good food. Look at the lines." We were standing at the back of one. He came directly to the point. "Why do you want to leave International—really?"

I knew that I would have to face that question, and I'd thought about a variety of reasons. Whatever I said had to be basically true, but just how much of the truth did I have to tell? Did I simply say that there was someone that I had to work with, but I simply couldn't get along with? Did I hint at harassment? Maybe I could claim that there was someone who stood in the way of my advancement?

In the end, I'd decided on my answer and I gave it decidedly, "There is someone with whom I have to work, but we have a personal conflict that we can't resolve."

I knew what the next question would be. "How do I know that that won't happen here if I hire you?"

Here, at least, I could answer fully openly and honestly, "I know this company. I know a lot of the staff. I know there's no one who would be a problem."

We had reached the end of the line. Rand ordered for us and paid for us. There were a couple of tables unoccupied. He chose one and sat. He commented, "There's always a few tables open. Almost everyone does take-away and eats elsewhere."

Looking around at the shabby surroundings, I said, "I wonder why?"

He went on, "I see why you want this to be confidential. You don't want to generate more trouble at your work. I'll tell you. I like you. I wouldn't mind hiring you. BUT, I'll have to convince upper management that we can use another salesman. I'll also have to convince myself that you won't do this with one of our customers a year or two down the line."

I had been eating the fish. They were good. Luckily my mouth was full. It gave me a minute to think before I answered. "You know that I can't guarantee that. No one could. All I can say is that I'll do my best to live up to your trust."

He sort of shook his head in a way that was neither positive or negative, "I suppose I can't ask for any more."

"Thanks for seeing me. I really appreciate that."

We finished our lunch, and we got up to leave. We shook. I said, "You were right about the fish. They're worth having to eat in this dive." I turned to go, and then I thought of one last point. "Oh, one other thing. Of course, you're not the only person that I'm going to approach."

"Yeh, I figured. Good luck."

We parted, and I went to my last appointment of the day.

I got home on schedule. I then had to make a decision. I didn't have any warning. Pet asked me when I arrived in time for a late supper with her, "Was it a good trip?"

That simple question forced me to confront a problem that I'd put off in the hurried excitement about choosing companies to apply to and what my elevator speech was going to be. The biggest question that I'd avoided like the plague over the last couple of days was when did I tell Pet that I was trying to change jobs. One look at her told me the answer to that question. It had to be now.

"Well, Petunia," With that one word I realized I'd telegraphed to her that it was going to be a serious discussion. I never used her full given name unless it were truly serious. She seemed stricken. She sat on the sofa, and I joined her and took her hand.

She spoke before I could go on. "Is it really that serious?"

I nodded and said, "Judge for yourself. I said that it had been a good week, and it has been. The best part of it is that I talked with the Sales

Manager of the Grunning Corporation about joining his sales staff . . ." I didn't finish the sentence because Pet gasped.

"Then you're fired!"

I almost laughed. "Oh, no. no. Nothing like that. I've just decided that I want to move on to another company. That sort of thing happens all the time."

"But, but, why didn't you say before?" She stopped a full minute and seemed to be examining the consequences. "Dear, there has to be something that's happened that could cause this. You seemed to be so happy until—well, until now."

I had to make a snap decision about what to tell Pet. I temporized to gain time. I said, "Pet, I'm going to get a glass of port. Would you like something?"

That distracted her for a moment, "Oh, I'll have a gin and tonic."

I went to the kitchen and mixed her drink and poured mine as I thought feverishly. I decided on the tack that I would take when we sat and I started to explain. "Pet, you're right. There is something that's come up recently."

Pet, who had been sitting, stood suddenly and exclaimed, "I knew it must be. What is it? Is you boss a pill?" Then she gasped, "Has something happened and we need money? Are they paying you enough?"

I shook my head, "No. It's nothing like that."

She lowered herself back into her chair and asked, "What is it then?"

Before I could speak, she answered her own question, "It's one of your mates, another salesman. Something's gone wrong, hasn't it?"

I was glad that she had come up with that idea herself. It made it easier. I answered, "That's it, really. There's a promotion coming up and one of the other sales reps has been doing everything possible to sabotage my chances.

"The boss's secretary. . . " I didn't even have to finish the sentence. Pet jumped to the conclusion that another salesman was seducing the boss's secretary to get inside information and preference for the promotion.

I just gave the slightest nod, and she exulted, "Well, I'll show that cheater that he can't do that to you. I'll. . ."

I interrupted her. I certainly didn't want her starting a war, especially since there was no one to go to war with. "Look Petunia. I'll have none of that. He may be using underhanded tricks, but I'll not have you stooping to that level. That's why I decided to go elsewhere."

She was on her feet again. "I won't have you run off by that kind of trick."

I interrupted her again. It was important to head her off. "Mrs. Petunia Dursley, you listen to me."

That got her attention. I don't think that I'd ever used her full name when talking to her. Her mouth dropped open, and she plopped down into her seat. I went on, "I will not have you doing any such thing. I mean it." I paused for emphasis. "I've made up my mind, and I'll not change it. I'm leaving International, and that's all there is to it. I don't want you meddling in this. I'm not kidding. If you did anything like that, it would be as much as asking for a divorce."

She gasped. "You can't mean it!"

"I do. If you can't follow my lead on my job, then what has become of our marriage vows?"

She actually looked contrite. I'd hardly ever seen that expression on her face as she bent her head as though she were considering her feet. The squeak of a voice was something I'd never heard before, "Yes, dear. If you really want me to just support your decision, of course I will."

I gave a sigh of relief. It was one disaster averted, and who knew how many left to go?

The rest of the weekend was one in which I was constantly on tenterhooks. I didn't think Pet would have a change of heart, but who knew for sure? Also, I was afraid that Betty might call me.

Somehow I got through the weekend.

The next week was easier than the weekend. My time was pretty much programmed, and I only had to follow the pattern for the work week. I stopped in at the normal time to talk with Betty. We kept it pretty low key —just the usual sort of questions. Did you do anything special? Did you go to that new movie from the States? Wasn't the weather dreadful?

Just before I was to go in, she touched my arm and smiled the broadest, sunniest smile I'd ever seen in my life. Then, she said one word with a low intensity that made me worry, "Lunch."

I nodded agreement, and she whirled around in her swivel chair to face the door.

That lunch almost sunk me. We went to our usual pub. She arrived first. When I arrived, she'd already been and was sitting at the bar. She'd ordered us both sidecars. When I sat, she put a hand around my neck and drew my ear near to her mouth. She said only one word, "Upstairs." She got up, and I followed her. She'd already got a key and she trotted up the stairs. When we reached the top, I was already prepared for what was to follow.

Before she unlocked the door, she opened her mouth, and I thought she was going to swallow mine. She giggled when she felt my preparation. We were inside, and I was ripping her clothes off her lithe body. It wasn't the best love-making we'd done. We were both in too much of a hurry, but as we dressed afterwards she laughed at the fact that my body was still ready for more. "You'd better get yourself under control before we get back."

I could only nod.

I had four possible companies singled out to approach about a job. The first was on Wednesday. The Sales Manager was non-committal. He seemed interested in getting my resume. I had updated my resume over the weekend. Pet had helped. I thought it was pretty good. The Sales Manager just glanced at it and set it on his desk, "Well, I'll give it a good look, and I'll let you know what I think."'

The next day, I had two companies that I thought were good prospects. The second one was like my first prospect that week–generally positive but just barely. All he would say was, "Let me have a copy of your resume, and we'll be back with you." He didn't even take the resume. He had me give it to his Admin.

The last of the week seemed even worse. I only had a couple of minutes with the Sales Manager. He sent me to Human Resources. My disappointment must have shown on my face. He said, "They do all the hiring decisions and they're not bad blokes."

I was directed to H.R. by the Admin, and I trudged in without any real hopes. The Admin had me take a seat, and she took my resume into the office of their recruiter. I waited nearly half an hour and was on the point of leaving when the Admin's phone rang and after a moment's discussion that was almost all on the other side of the connection, the Admin motioned me to follow her. She led me through a door that led into a large room with half a dozen cubicles. The outside wall of the room was all offices. There were no windows. I followed the Admin to a door that had a name on it, "Director of Recruiting, Lorena Breitbar."

When we arrived, the Admin opened the door from the outside and said, "Ms. Breitbar will see you now."

I entered and found myself facing a tall, thin brunette. Her hair was pulled back into some kind of knot that was quite complex. She was wearing a light grey suit and had her hand extended toward me. I took it and began to introduce myself. She shook her head no and said, "That won't be necessary. I've been looking at your resume. Please sit."

I did, and she offered me a bottled water. I declined with thanks. She just nodded and began, "I like what I see. You have a very good reputation here. I did a quick check with the head of buying. He likes you a lot. He thinks you might fit in fairly well.

"I just have one problem. We really don't have a position at the moment. I want you to be the first person that we interview when we do have a position."

My face sagged. She noticed and said, "That may not be so far in the future as you might think. We're acquiring another company and I think we'll need more sales staff when we start selling their products.

"Of course, I can't tell you what company. We expect the transaction to complete next week. As soon as that happens, my mouth is watering to get hold of their personnel files to decide which employees we'll keep, but between you and me, I think that their sales staff is weak, and they are underpriced.

She looked down at her desk as if trying to find something. Her lips pursed. I'd seen that many times before on sales calls. Usually then, it was trying to make that final decision about whether or not to buy, and sometimes, how much to buy.

She looked up and said, "I probably really shouldn't say this, but I wouldn't be surprised if their problem is the Sales Manager. I could see you fitting in that role."

She hastened to add, "You understand that this is certainly NOT a promise, and we may well keep the Sales Manager. In the end, there might not even be a place for you on the staff at all."

I quickly nodded, "Oh, of course, that is well understood, but might I ask how quickly you expect to be in a position to talk more definitely about that?"

She pursed her lips again, but maintained eye contact. She seemed to know that I might be in a hurry. When she spoke it was very slowly and with caution, "Now, you realize that this is very much speculation. Let's say that I get access to personnel files next week, and we start review immediately of all their staff. I expect that most will be easy keeps, but we would consider seriously before deciding to let someone go. Let's say mid-next-month as a guess."

I didn't control my face again, and my disappointment showed through. I regained control as quickly as I could, but she had caught it. She said, "Now, I'm inclined to prioritize consideration of the sales staff. It might be the early third of the month."

I smiled. I could see that we'd reached the end of the interview. She had picked up my resume and put it in a file folder. So, I took the initiative, "It's been a pleasure speaking with you. Thanks very much for the opportunity. I hope you have a good day."

She smiled broadly as well and stood. We shook hands, and she wished me good luck.

The rest of the sales calls were routine, and I got home on Friday in time for dinner. Pet had fixed one of my favorite meals–Yorkshire pudding, roast beef, and mash. There were some veggies on the side.

As usual she saved talk about the week until I'd gotten well into the meal. I went straight to the chase. "I talked with a recruiter at a company that I have as a client."

Pet broke in, "Who?" She was sitting on the edge of her chair and had dropped her fork with a morsel of meat still on it.

I smiled broadly, "Oh it would be unethical for me to tell you what company because they revealed some insider information to me, but I can tell you that she talked about the possibility of my being a Sales Manager."

At first, it was as though she hadn't heard my words. Then she clapped her hands together briefly. "Oh, well done! Will we have to move?" Her mind had already given me the post and was thinking of domestic issues.

"It's too early to talk about that. If I'm considered, it won't be for a month at least."

That deflated Pet a bit, but she perked up again and talked about what was going on in her circle of friends.

The weekend went well. With two strong possibilities of jobs in hand, I felt a lot better, but I still had my list of companies for next week to apply for a job.

There was just the one snag on the weekend. On Sunday afternoon, the phone rang. I was feeling so good that I called out to Pet, who was in the back yard, "I've got it."

I lifted the receiver and was shocked to hear Betty's voice. "I know that I shouldn't call you at home, but I just couldn't wait until tomorrow. I've got to know how your sales trip went."

I checked that Pet was firmly ensconced in the garden, and I gave Betty a brief resume of the trip, excluding of course, the job interviews. She was bubbling over with excitement, and I thought that she wouldn't have heard if I'd said that a meteor had landed in the back yard. She was talking about going to see a movie. I think it was *Kramer vs Kramer*. I chuckled to myself as she was speaking. At the office in the sales room, we call that "Crymore vs. Crymore". I personally liked *Apocalypse Now*.

Anyway, she eventually ended her discussion, and I prepared to say goodbye. She had another topic, though. Before she could start, I noticed some movement out of the corner of my eye. Pet was coming in. As a matter of fact, she might have heard my last words. I finished the conversation by saying, "My wife just walked in. I've got to hang up. See you at work tomorrow." That might have seemed a dangerous ending, but it really wasn't because I was ready to answer Pet's inevitable question.

"Who was that dear?"

"Oh, it was work."

She clucked her tongue and asked, "Doesn't your boss ever let you alone?"

I just shrugged. She went on, "I can see why you want to get out of there."

I smiled and said, "Oh, it's not awful, but you're right. I do want to move on as soon as I can."

The next day at work, there was the usual ordeal, or was the pleasure so intense that it was actually a joy? I don't know even now. The usual chit-chat at Betty's desk before the morning meeting was always pleasurable. Now, it had become intense. There was the secret shared joy at seeing each other, the occasional secret caress that lasted only a second or two but which we both knew was charged with something more like fire than comfort, and there was that oh so casual "see you later", which promised so much more than a glance at a distance. It was particularly wrenching for me because I had the secret within a secret that I was working as hard as I could to insure that there wouldn't be a "later." This day seemed like any other to both of us. We met as usual at the usual pub. This day Betty got there before I did. She stood at the door on the outside. When I arrived, she closed with me and kissed me with mouth wide open. It was just a few seconds, but it caught my breath. For the rest of the lunch, we seemed to be living within a spell. I had suspended my disbelief in our relationship as a fiery short-term pleasure, and the vision of a forever seized me.

We got back to the office as usual. I went to my cubicle to call and set up appointments for the week. In the midst of that, I received a phone call. The voice at the other end said, "Mr. Dursley, will you hold for Mr. Rand of Grunnings?"

I gulped. "Yes, ma'am."

In a few seconds the line clicked, and Rand was speaking. "Mr. Dursely, I have good news for you. I've spoken with upper management, and they agree with me that you will be a valuable addition to my team and that I should immediately make you a job offer before anyone else discovers what a find you are."

I gasped. Then I collected my wits and said, "That's wonderful, but you're sure that there's no chance of a change of mind?"

I could almost see his face on the other end of the line, "Absolutely none!"

I continued to hold my breath as I considered. After a moment, Rand asked with a bit of trouble audible in his voice, "Are you still on?"

I got hold of myself and made the decision. "Yes, sir. I am. I just didn't expect news so quickly. Well, sir. I'm your man."

There was relief in the next words, "Great. How soon can you start?"

The rest of the questions were easy, "First thing next week."

"Great! You know our offices. Come round in a day or two to sign the employment contract."

"Can I do that tomorrow?"

"It won't be quite ready then. How about Wednesday morning?"

"Fine."

"Just come up to my office. It won't take long. Oh, and drop by bright and early Monday morning, and I'll take you down to Personnel. That will be all right?"

In a daze I said, "Certainly."

"Be seeing you soon, then." Then he rung off.

I leaned back and started to think about priorities for this week. Certainly first was to let my boss know. I didn't fancy having to go in and tell him that, but it had to be done and right now. I picked up the phone to call his office when I sensed someone standing over my shoulder. I looked up and saw that it was the occupant of my neighboring cube. He asked, "Sounds like something big came up? A big sale?"

I smiled broadly, 'Yes. I just closed a big sale. Maybe the biggest of my career."

His smile was not quite so wide as mine, "Care to share details?"

"Not just yet. I've not got it absolutely sewn up, but it should be by the weekend."

He left, and I made the call that I'd started before my neighbor appeared. Betty answered, of course. There was nothing but pure pleasure when she recognized my voice, "Ooooh! Back in touch so soon?"

This was going to be pure hell. I tried to make my voice bright, "Yes. I've really got to see the boss this afternoon. Is there any way you can fit me in?"

She hesitated and then came back. "There's no room on his schedule, but I'll see what I can do for you." She emphasized the "you". Then she went on, "I'll give you a call when I have something." She finished with a cheery, "Be seeing you!"

I rung off and started to think about preparing for that meeting. I'd have to suggest some re-arrangement of work assignments to cover my territories. The boss might not like my suggestions, but I wanted to be ready with them. I also started re-organizing my personal things so that I could clear them out quickly. I started putting some into my brief case.

The call from Betty did come around 3:30. Betty had succeeded in clearing a half hour from the boss schedule at 4:30. I started making notes of the points that I wanted to make with him.

4:20 came way too quickly. I walked down to his office and entered the outer room. Betty flashed a smile that would have melted an iceberg and said, "He'll see you right away. It's the end of the day. Maybe you could walk me to the tube station." It was a statement not a question.

I nodded and opened the door. Inside, the boss was sitting behind his desk, but he rose rapidly and came around to shake my hand, "What can I do for my favorite salesman today?"

I think it was not hyperbole. He wouldn't have said it if it weren't true. I grimaced. This was going to be hard, but like any difficult sales call, the quicker you get to it, the better. For sure, this was going to be a sales call. There were things I wanted, so I needed to be prepared to negotiate for them. He motioned me to sit.

I started immediately I was in the chair. He interrupted me to ask if I wanted something to drink. I simply shook my head no. I started in, "I've got some bad news."

He asked, "And some good news, I trust?"

"Well, it's pretty much bad news. I've decided to take another job. I just accepted the offer, and I start first thing next week. I'm happy to give you my enthusiastic service this week in lieu of two weeks notice. It will be on the house. I don't want paid for this."

His mouth had dropped open for a moment and then closed. He seemed to be considering what to say. I know that it's critical to give people time to think, and I was happy to give him as much time as I could. Finally he said, "That's definite?"

I nodded.

He went on, "What is it? Money? Do you want your own office? Someone offend you?"

At that I gave an involuntary laugh that I choked off quickly. He went on, "If it's money, I can do a good raise for you and maybe even a performance bonus." He stopped and seemed to be studying me for a minute. "That's not it, is it?"

I shook my head.

He thought for another minute and said, "It's somebody here, isn't it?"

I tried not to react, but he nodded slowly, considering. "Not one of the salesmen."

You've heard of light bulbs going off. You could actually see that happen in his face. He smiled and even chuckled. "I know. It's Betty, isn't it? You two have been thick as thieves lately. You're leaving because of her." It was a statement. I didn't nod or do anything to confirm his guess, but he was convinced.

He said, "You know, I could get her transferred. She could go to . . . oh . . . say the continental buying unit. She might like to be in Paris."

I just shook my head. He nodded, "So, it's that bad is it." It wasn't a question, just a statement of fact. "OK. I'll hate to lose you, but I guess I've not got much say in it."

While I seemed to have the advantage, I went on. "Sir, I really mean it about giving you the best week you've ever had out of me, but I've got a favor to ask." He nodded assent, and I went on, "I'd like you to keep it a secret until I'm gone. I'll drop the sales report off on Saturday."

He nodded dully. "Sure, I don't blame you. I'd ask for confidentiality if I were in your shoes. Give the Human Resources girl a call tomorrow. She may be willing to come in Saturday morning to let you sign papers and turn in your keys. We'll make Saturday your last day so that you can come into the offices and not get nabbed for trespassing." He chuckled as something seemed to occur to him. "I don't know if she'll let you give us this week for free. That'll be between you and her."

I nodded and volunteered to give him some suggestions for splitting up my territory until they replaced me. The boss was quite good about it. He listened to my ideas and pretty much agreed. Then I got up to leave.

He asked, "Would you like me to go with you? It might save you some embarrassment."

I shook my head, "No, I kind of agreed to walk Betty to the Tube. I'll keep that promise."

"OK. It's your funeral if she worms it out of you. She's pretty good at that, you know."

She didn't worm it out of me. She was just so happy to be walking in public with me that she didn't care what I'd been talking about with the boss. I stopped at my desk to pick up my brief case. Everyone was gone. We did walk to the Tube, but she insisted on stopping at "our" pub for a drink. I agreed.

She was ebullient when we sat down at "our" table. She even insisted on ordering something special. "How about a bottle of champagne? I have a feeling that something special happened in the boss's office. Something to celebrate?"

I agreed. It was our last time together (I hoped). I opened the bottle and filled our glasses. She said that this was just a little foretaste of what would come before very long when she'd be wearing a special ring. I raised my glass and said, "To the next time that we're together."

She giggled as she drank from her glass. It was both sad and somehow re-invigorating to see her so happy. We finished our glasses, and I insisted that I had to get along. She was sorry that we had to leave the unfinished bottle.

We left the pub, and she hung on my arm, resting her head on my shoulder from time to time as we walked to the station.

We arrived. She flung her arms around my neck and gave me a kiss that I will probably never forget. Her final words to me as she went down the stairs to the Tube were, "I've never been happier in my life. I don't think I will ever be happier again." I tried to force my mouth into some sort of smile. I have no idea if I succeeded or not.

The next day, I was off in the car to my first appointment. I'd decided that I wouldn't tell Pet about our good luck until I'd actually signed the employment contract.

The day was extraordinary for sales. I only saw two firms, but both went amazingly well. Maybe it really would be my best sales week ever. I had most of my deep worries behind me—just. I had my new job, I'd said goodbye to my . . . At that thought, I mentally gulped. I'd said goodbye to my mistress. I'd never thought of her in those terms, but today, now, I did. I guess she wasn't my mistress until yesterday. Before, I'd really thought of her deep down as my lover who might really be my wife someday. I shivered a moment at the thought of how close to the abyss I'd come. I might not have escaped yet, but I was a whole lot better than I'd been a couple of weeks before.

The next day was another really good day on the road. I'd stopped by Grunnings and signed the employment contract. Rand and I shared a quick glass of Dewars Black Label and I'd moved on. At noon, I called in to the Human Resources girl back in my office and we talked briefly. She was not particularly happy at the idea of coming in to work Saturday morning, but she admitted that in HR as she called it, there were lots of unusual things that you had to do. She reminded me that one of those was firing people. That was the only negative part of the day.

I gave Pet a call at 8:00. I expected it to be a really fun call. I was in at Grunnings, and all was right with the world. When I reached her, she had just finished dinner. I began on a happy note, "Pet, don't fix dinner Friday. I'll be a little late, but let's go out to dinner–someplace fancy. Maybe that Italian restaurant that you like in town."

She was surprised and then began to think about it. She began slowly and as she went along got faster, louder, and higher, ending by almost shrieking, "You've got a new job! Can I congratulate the new Sales Manager?"

That was not quite the reaction that I'd expected. I had to say in an almost embarrassed tone, "Well, I'm not Sales Manager yet, but you just wait. . . "

I didn't get to finish what I was saying because Pet broke in with the exclamation, "But I thought that you were being considered for Sales Manager. What happened!"

I couldn't see her face, but I was pretty sure I knew what it looked like, and it wasn't smiling. I composed myself and answered, "It is a great opportunity at a very good company. The Sales Manager likes me, and I think there are good opportunities for advancement . . ."

Again I was cut off by Pet. "Oh, I understand all of that, but you have a chance to go directly into a manager position. Why ever didn't you wait to see if that would open up?"

I decided to stretch the truth a little, "Pet, this was a take it or leave it offer. The other job might come in a couple of weeks or a couple of months or never. I want to move on. This was the opportunity, and a bloody good one to boot." I was beginning to get a little hot under the collar myself. I'd gone through a lot so far for our marriage. I wasn't going to change course just to get a better position that might or might not ever come!

She was still mad. I didn't have to hear her voice to tell. The sound of her breathing made that clear. I decided that we'd reached an impasse and weren't going to get any further. So I broke the silence by saying, "I'm still looking forward to dinner out Friday night."

She grudgingly admitted that she was too. So we hung up, and that was it for the night.

The next day was another good day. I was determined to do my absolute best before the end. There was still the nagging conversation from the previous night to get around. I was sure that if I could navigate the weekend without getting into a major row, I'd be OK.

On Friday, I had my last sales call for International and started the drive home. I'd have to work really late after I got home to put together my sales report, invoices, and recommendations for future efforts. As a matter of fact, I'd probably have to work through the night so that I could turn in my keys, ID badge, and everything the next morning. I gritted my teeth to the task and hurried to get home as quickly as possible. I got home and we took the Tube to the theatre district where our favorite Italian restaurant was. We were fairly quiet on the ride. At least, Pet wasn't still overtly angry.

We arrived. After we were seated and I removed Pet's coat, I saw that she was wearing a new dress. I asked her about it, "Is that a new dress you're wearing?"

She smiled slyly, "You noticed, did you?"

"How could I avoid noticing? I don't think I've seen that much lovely leg in a long time."

She smiled—almost involuntarily—and said, "I wanted to celebrate properly. This is a big day for you."

I agreed and found that my gaze kept straying to her legs. She noticed it as well. At one point, she chided me, "I'm up here," when I had been staring for a particularly long time.

We got home, and we both joked about being ready for bed already. I'd forgotten all my good intentions about working sales reports. I quickly found myself helping her out of her very short skirt and helping myself into her.

I set the alarm on my watch for 4 AM just before I drifted off to sleep. It almost didn't wake me. I struggled up and went to the dining room table to spread out my order forms and report templates to work through all the paperwork before the morning was over.

Pet was up and working on breakfast humming all the time. What was she so happy about? I supposed that it must be about the amazing sex that we'd had the previous night.

She didn't complain about my covering the dining room table with paper or with my gobbling down breakfast from a plate on my knees. I'd finished everything, but it was already 10 AM. I had to get dressed quickly and off to the office.

I carefully packed my papers in my briefcase after removing the things I'd brought from the Office. There was another thing that I wanted to do this morning—finish packing my personal belongings.

I arrived at the Ofice in half an hour. The first thing that I did was to go to the Boss's Office and put everything in his inbox. There was a lot, but I managed to get it to fit. I made sure that something already in the box was on top. I didn't want Betty to be tempted to do something.

With that thought, I took it all out and ran it through the copier so that I would have a back up—just in case. I returned it all to the inbox. With that I glanced into the waste basket next to the copier. I saw pieces of what appeared to be a picture. I was afraid that I knew who was in the picture, but I pulled out the pieces and worked them together. It was a picture of me. I tried to remember where it could have been taken. Then I realized that it had been part of a photo of the sales team that had been taken at a football outing that we'd all gone to as a group thing. The photo had been cut out of the group photo and apparently copied at a larger size–wallet size.

The pieced together shards of the photo showed that a black marker had been used to X through my face. I reflected on it. Apparently, the boss had announced my resignation before the close of business yesterday. That closed off one part of my life.

Then I went down to the HR girl's office. She was working on something at her desk. She noticed me and said, "Well, you took your time getting here."

"I'm sorry. I wanted to leave my final reports in the office before I turned in my keys."

She sniffed, "Well turn them in and your ID badge. We've got a lot of papers for you to sign before I give you your final paycheck."

I shook my head. "I said that I didn't want to be paid for the last week."

She looked me directly in the eyes for the first time since I'd entered the room. "Too bad. You're going to take that with you. You know that you are a lot better off than Betty."

My mouth must have dropped open because she said, "Oh, yes. Betty and I are friends. She told me about how you treated her. Get these things signed and get out." She handed papers across her desk to me, but it was clear that she'd much rather have been throwing them at me. ". . . This is a non-compete agreement. Your signature acknowledges it. There's a release you give us from all responsibility for damages to property that you haven't reported yet." She droned on and on as I signed. I was afraid to stop and read them. They all looked to be standard documents.

When I'd finished, she said, "Get out. I can't stand seeing your face."

I said, "I've still got a few personal things in my cube. Would you let me in so I can clear it out?"

She snarled, "I suppose. Come on, don't waste any more of my time."

She led me down to the large room where the sales team had their cubes. She unlocked the door and accompanied me to my office. I'd left a cardboard box there on Monday so that I could load my things into it. I had cleared a lot of things out of the desk drawers before I left, but I'd not removed things from the desktop so that it wouldn't look like I'd cleared out. I opened desk drawers just to be sure. There were a few things in them. I'd forgotten that I kept a bottle of Scotch in one of the drawers. It was still intact. I put it in the box and surrounded it with some papers from the drawers.

I took the personal things from the desktop. A couple of pictures—one of Pet, one of my Mum and Dad and my sister Marge when we were all much younger—went into the box. I had a fancy desk set that I took. There were a few things that I didn't bother with. I left a pad of personalized paper, the kind that says, "from the desk of . . . " There were a couple of sales award plaques on the walls of the cube that I loaded, and then I was done. My career of eight years with International Widgets fit into one medium cardboard box.

I turned rapidly around scanning the environment for anything I might have missed. When I finished it the HR girl said, "That's enough reminiscing. Get out before I have security help you."

I was polite. "Thanks. I'm sorry for the trouble I caused you coming in on your weekend."

She just sneered, "You should be."

I walked slowly out of the office, scanning the surroundings as though I could memorize years of experiences as I went. We reached the Main Entrance. The HR girl opened the door for me, and I walked out into the sunlight.

I took my time driving home. I even drove around the building once as a sort of victory lap. Then, I headed for home.

The Captain's Cabin

Dad had finished his story. He ended by looking at me and saying, "It was about nine months later that you were born. I can't prove it, but I think that you were conceived on that Friday night." He had been looking directly at Mum through the whole story until then.

When he finished Mum stood up and looked from one to the other of us. I could tell that her anger had passed from mere disgust to the point where she couldn't say a word.

Finally, she said, "And you expect that to make it all right!"

Dad didn't say anything. He just gazed at her placidly. She began pacing back and forth. I was braced for the explosion. When it came, it wasn't nuclear as I'd expected. Instead it was a cold fury. "You will never speak to me when we're alone. You will never eat with me again. We will go to meals here at different times. I will not sit with you at the same table. You will never look at me again! You will not sleep in the bed here. If Dudley will let you sleep on the sofa that is his decision."

Mum had made her position crystal clear. I said nothing. I didn't want to invoke the nuclear option.

That night Dad had insisted on using a spare pillow, and the spare blankets in the closet to make his bed on the floor. I didn't object.

The next morning, Mum was up early and had apparently gone to breakfast early. I guess that showed me which side of the bread my butter was on. Dad and I went to breakfast together, and it was almost as quiet as though Mum had been there with us. Our fellow passengers were all gaily breakfasting while our meal was more like a fast.

I spent most of that day and the next exercising. I worked out in the gym and did lots of jogging on the deck. The weather was beautiful. When I wasn't exercising, I was standing at a railing gazing out on the endless sea.

The next night Dad had fixed a better bed with some cushions from deck chairs, but I'm sure he wasn't much more comfortable. The pattern of meals was pretty well laid out. Mum went early. We went late except for the evening meal.

On the second day in purgatory, Dad announced that he was going to eat dinner early. Mum didn't acknowledge hearing, but when the two of us left, she made no objection.

We arrived at our table and were surprised to find that on each of our plates—including Mum's—was a small white envelope. I opened mine and read, "Mr. Dudley Dursely, the captain requests and requires your presence in his cabin this evening at eight PM. The Purser, Jennifer Waters, will accompany you to the Captain's Cabin. Please be prepared for her arrival at your cabin at quarter to eight. Yours, Captain Burton."

I looked over at Dad. He shrugged. He didn't have any idea what it was about. I, however, had been escorted to the Head's office on more than a few occasions. This had way too much of that feel about it for my tastes.

Dad and I discussed the options. We agreed that we'd be better off if we stayed until Mum arrived and talked over the situation so that we'd all be ready for the interview in the Captains Cabin.

We took our time with the meal. That was something that we'd not been able to do the last couple of days. Eventually Mum arrived and openly stared at us. She asked, "I'm surprised to see you two." That fixed it. I was definitely included with Dad.

Although he could have answered under her ban, he left it to me. I said, "Mum, there's a letter for you at your place setting. I think you should look at it before we say anything more."

She apparently hadn't noticed it. She looked at the plate and pulled her chair out to sit. She picked up the envelope and handled it almost reverentially. It was made of good quality paper. She seemed almost hesitant to open it—like she didn't want to ruin the purity of the unopened envelope. Finally she did though.

A glance at the letter caused her whole expression to change. It lit up with joy. She said, "Oh, my. THE CAPTAIN'S CABIN." She said it that way—all capitalized. "This is marvelous." For the moment she seemed to have overlooked the technicality that we were ALL invited—even Dad. She murmured something like, "How wonderful! What an Honor!"

Dad and I glanced at each other. I think he had tumbled to the fact that it might not be quite the honor that Mum seemed to think it was. There was nothing that either of us dared to do, though. I sure wasn't going to break Mum's bubble any sooner than it had to be.

Dad ventured, "We'll go back to the cabin and dress for this. See you there."

Mum just nodded absently, still staring at the letter.

We left and searched the closet of the cabin for our suits.

96

Mum arrived at 7:15 and dressed quickly but efficiently. We were all seated waiting for the arrival of Purser Waters at 7:45. When that hour arrived, there was a knock at the door. It was Waters.

She was absolutely silent through the long walk up to the Captains Cabin. Mum was going on and on about the honor. Apparently no one, including Waters, wanted to break the spell she was under.

It struck me that Waters was taking her time about getting us there. When we arrived at the elevator that would take us up into the "island," she even let a group of other people on ahead of us. Thus we ended riding up by ourselves. She used a key to unlock the elevator to reach the level labeled "BRIDGE."

We arrived, and she led us down a short corridor to a plain door. She opened it and led us in. The room was like a very small dining room. It had a table that would seat eight (cramped) or six. The walls had photos of various cruise ships. I suppose they were all owned by the company that owned this ship. At the far end was a cabinet with plates, silver, and so forth on display. On one side of the table were a small sink and a liquor cabinet above it.

There was one person in the room when we arrived. He looked like a waiter. That was exactly what he turned out to be. He opened a door at the other end of the room, and the Captain entered through it. The waiter pulled his chair at the far end of the table. He sat and said, "Please be seated."

We all found seats. Mum insisted on being at his left hand. Jennifer sat beside her. Dad insisted that I sit at the Captain's right hand. I think he wanted to be as far away from the Captain as he could manage. That was me as well.

When we were all seated the Captain said, "I am Captain Thomas Burton." Mum was about to introduce us, but he quickly said, "I am aware that you, madam, are Mrs. Vernon Dursely. That this is your husband. Your son, Dudley." He indicated me. He finished with Jennifer, "And, of course, I'm very aware that this is the Purser J. Waters."

We all nodded silently. Mum was still pretty excited but also awed enough to maintain silence. He turned to the waiter and said, "Albert, I'll have a glass of filtered water. See what these people will have."

The waiter turned to Mum, who asked for a glass of red wine. Jennifer asked for a glass of filtered water. Dad asked for a glass of whiskey. I started to say, "I'd like a coke and rum. . ." Mum's gaze cut me off before I said "rum".

Albert efficiently delivered the water to the Captain, then Mum's wine to her. He gave Jennifer the glass of water with the bottle partially emptied. Dad got his whiskey. I got my Coke in a glass and the chilled can. Then he surprised me by leaving the room.

At that point, I knew that we were in for it. I sipped on the Coke while it was still possible to enjoy it. There was lots of ice and not much room left for the Coke.

The Captain said, "The reason that you've been summoned here is that I need to deal with a situation that all you four have caused. I will start with the Dursely's. When I'm finished with them, you, Ms. Waters, will come next."

Finally, Mum began to get the drift of what was happening. She almost choked on the wine that she was sipping. But she managed to croak, "Situation?"

He rested his chin on his hands joined together as for prayer. He took a deep breath as though preparing for a sprint. Then he seemed to have resolved his internal question or problem and sat up straight and began.

"It's important for me to make clear what my position is. I, as the captain of this ship, am the closest thing there is to an absolute monarch while we are on the open seas. I can do virtually anything, give any order, and my word is absolute law. That's the way maritime law is.

"Now, let's get down to this situation. You four are guilty of breaking in to the cabin of another passenger. We don't know for sure whether or not you took any of his property."

Dad surprised me by saying indignantly, "We are English citizens! We have the right to see a lawyer!"

The Captain didn't seem surprised or even troubled. Instead he calmly said, "You have not been listening carefully Mr. Dursley. There is no law on this ship other than me. Whatever I say it is, it is.

"Now, you will find that I am not unreasonable. As a matter of fact, right now, I'm being very reasonable. We know that you four invaded another passenger's cabin and . . ."

That sent Mum over the top. "You do not know that! How do you know that!" You could see the lines stand out around her lips. She was ready for a fight. I happened to glance over at Jennifer. Her mouth was wide open in surprise. She quickly sunk back in her chair as if to say that she didn't know any of us—especially this crazy woman.

The Captain turned his gaze directly at me Mum, "You really have not been listening. I will say this only one time. I have the power to send you," he paused and then looked at the rest of us, "to the brig right now, throw away the key, and turn you over to British authorities in the port of Galveston, and never think of you again. As a matter of fact, that's what the book would say that I ought to do."

Mum's eyes opened wide. She had clearly never been in a place like this before. I had. I knew that she was handling it all wrong. I tried once to signal her with my eyes, but she was completely impervious to reason. Finally, she sat back in her chair. She seemed to be weighing the situation.

"Yes, Madam, we know with absolute certainty that you entered the cabin of James Wendt. We know the precise time. We know how long you were in the cabin." He then named the date and times. "We have security cameras in all halls. We have the tapes. Don't trifle with me. I can make it very uncomfortable for you four." He paused and leaned forward. "Don't tempt me."

Her mouth dropped open, and I think that for the first time the fact that she might end up in jail struck her as a reality. He turned to the rest of us. "That, of course, goes for all of you."

I was pretty darn sure that the rest of us had the idea from the start.

The Captain leaned back again and said, "You may well be wondering why I've waited so long to call you in. Well, it's because I am very reasonable. I don't automatically assume that someone breaking into another's room is an attempt at larceny or even necessarily an unjustified act. So, I did some research on you all. Even you, Jennifer.

"What I found puzzled me. The Dursleys are all upstanding citizens." He reflected a moment, "Well, Mr. Dudley Dursley has a few black marks against him, but nothing in the same realm with grand larceny or piracy."

We all looked up in surprise at that last word. The Captain went on, "Yes, if I really wanted to press the definition, what you did could be considered an act of piracy.

"Now, I have no intention of charging you with piracy, but I have three possible courses in front of me.

"First, I could take the worst construction of all this and assume that you might have taken something, send you all to the brig, and have your cabins and personal effects searched thoroughly. And when I say thoroughly, I mean that we wouldn't stop at taking things apart."

Mum gasped at that. Dad seemed troubled. I was expecting something like that, so I wasn't particularly troubled—at least more than I was already. Jennifer was just glum.

The Captain went on, "The second thing that I could do is say to myself, 'These people are basically good decent people. Maybe they had a decent reason for what they did.' If I assumed that, I could have you confined to your quarters until the end of the trip. You would be served meals there. When you disembarked, your effects would be searched and I'd turn you over to the authorities in America and wash my hands of the whole affair.

"There is a third thing that I could do. I could find out what your reasons were, and if I thought they were reasonable, maybe. . ." He paused and then continued, "Maybe have a quick search of your quarters made and not turn you over to authorities at all. I would still require you to remain in your quarters except for meals. I would let you disembark as though nothing had happened shipboard."

I surprised everyone by asking a question, "Would you report what we said to anyone?"

He actually smiled at me, "No, young man, I would not. I would rather not have to file paperwork and get involved with civilian law officials myself."

I nodded. We all looked at each other and then another surprising thing happened. Jennifer jumped up and declared, "I did it because I think there's something bad happened to Jim Wendt. I used to be his lover." Then she added in a low voice that maybe only I heard, "sort of."

The Captain turned his attention to her and said, "I told you, I'd deal with you after the Dursleys." He then turned to the rest of us, "Were any of you his lover?"

We all shook our heads. Then the Captain asked, "You have nothing to say in your defense?"

I surprised people again, "I do."

He turned his attention to me, "Well, go ahead, young man."

I had been here before. I knew that you wanted to tell as much of the truth as you possibly could. I'd been thinking about what I would say. I was glad that the Captain didn't know much about questioning people. You did it separately to look for inconsistencies. I thought I could tell the story including the little lies better than anyone else, so I started.

"Well, we are trying to get away from terrorists." Everyone stared at me with disbelief in each and every eye—especially Jennifer's. But I went on, "We're trying our best to keep our presence on the ship a secret." I hesitated, "You can check how we paid for our tickets. We paid with cash, not a check or credit card."

The Captain surprised me. He nodded and said, "I checked. I wondered about that. It was the one thing that rang false about you people." He paused again, "But, terrorists?"

I went on, "Oh, yes. We have a cousin who . . . well. . . he got mixed up with some queer people. Some of them were real honest to goodness terrorists. They kill people and torture them and everything."

The Captain nodded, "Yeh. I saw that. You have a cousin, Harold Potter."

Dad interrupted, "It's Harry. Just Harry."

The Captain gave him a look that silenced him in a second. Then he said, "Go on."

"Harry rubbed some of these people the wrong way. They came looking for him. Harry's friends—the good ones—helped us get away before they came looking for us. These terrorists wanted to find us so that they could force us to tell where Harry is."

"Do you know where he is?"

I shook my head and went on. "We stayed with them for a couple of weeks, but the terrorists somehow found us. We had to flee. This thing— this cruise was a last minute crazy idea for getting away from the terrorists.

"Then we got on board and things seemed to go fine for a while but there's this guy in the room next to us. Only he's never there. He never shows up at meals. We never see him on deck. We went to Jennifer and asked her what she knew about him. She'd never seen him. We were worried that he might be one of these terrorists trying to get at us.

"When we talked with Jennifer, she couldn't believe that he was a terrorist but she was even more worried than we were that something had happened to him. We made a plan to check out his cabin. We did it, but we didn't find anything. Or really, we found everything—everything that ought to be there."

The Captain asked, "So, you believed he was a terrorist and Ms. Waters believed he was a good guy or at least not a terrorist. This is sort of a strange alliance, isn't it?"

I wasn't sure what the word alliance meant, but I thought I had the gist. I said casually, "Well, we used her. I admit it. She got us into the cabin. That was all we cared about."

The Captain gave a quick glance at Jennifer. I guess it was to see her reaction. She didn't object anyway.

The Captain turned back to me, "And just what did you expect to find in that cabin?"

Here, Dad gave an answer, "We wanted to see if there was any sign he was staying there—you know, rumpled clothes, bed unmade. AND I hoped that we'd find his passport. Get an idea what he looked like. Maybe he had been watching us for days, and we just didn't know it."

Mum added meekly, "I wanted to find out where he was from."

The Captain looked at me again. He had a gaze that seemed to look right through you. He was doing that thing again. "What did YOU think you might find?"

I looked around the room as though looking for guidance, but I was actually quickly considering what I might say. I sure wasn't going to tell the truth. That is, that I wanted to see if he had a wand. I tried to think of a way of saying that without seeming to. I finally settled for, "I guess I thought there might be a weapon."

Captain Burton looked to me again. "What kind of a weapon were you expecting—gun, knife, bomb, something else. Were you expecting something exotic?"

I hope he didn't see in my eyes the panic that he was getting close to the truth. I just shook my head. "Yeh, any of those, I guess."

There was a long gap in which there was utter silence. The Captain for the first time seemed truly puzzled. Finally, he said, "Well, I wasn't going to go into this, but I think I have to."

"I have never seen Mr. Wendt myself. When I arrived at the ship before sailing, the head Purser—obviously not you, Jennifer—came to me with this." He pulled from an inside pocket an envelope. He reached into the envelope and pulled out a sheet of paper. It was folded, and the only things that were visible were the letterhead, the date, and the person to whom it was addressed. He went on, "Do you know what this said?"

He didn't insult our intelligence by waiting for an answer. "First of all, the Purser told me that I wasn't to open it until we were in international waters.

"I waited until we were out of the English Channel. When I opened it, I found that the letter said that MI6 had come on board ship about a day before sailing. They had brought the luggage of a passenger. He would not board the ship before we sailed or ever. His luggage would be unpacked and put into the stateroom. No one was to know that he wasn't on board. We were to do everything we could to hide the truth.

"When we arrived in Corpus Christi, MI6 would board and remove his property.

"Now, you see why I suspected that you were not ordinary thieves."

Somebody sobbed. I looked around and found that it was Jennifer. She asked through tears, "Is he still alive?"

For the first time the Captain looked like he might be a real human being. He shook his head, "I don't know. This is the sort of thing that I suppose people do when they want others to think that someone is alive when . . . he isn't."

She sobbed again. "Who would have thought that that simple, kind man would have enemies like this who would want him dead?"

The Captain turned official again, "All right. Dursleys, here's what you're going to do. You're going to stay in your cabin except to go to meals."

I interrupted again, "What about me? I'd like to keep using the fitness facilities."

He looked at me, evaluating, I guess. He said, "Well, can I see your passport?"

I handed it over. He nodded. "I thought so. You're technically a minor. I'm going to give you a break. You can use the gym as much as you like. But I swear if any of you are out of your room for the rest of the cruise for anything but meals and exercise, you'll be in the brig, and I might just forget that you're down there.

"Second, you're not to discuss Mr. Wendt or his cabin or his presence on this ship with anyone outside this room. Is that clear?"

We all nodded.

"Any questions?"

No one had any. He went on, "Then you're dismissed. I hope you enjoy the rest of the cruise."

We all got up and started to leave, but the Captain said, "Oh, not you Ms. Waters. Please keep your seat."

The rest of us left. When we were outside, Mum sidled over to Dad and took his hand in hers.

Jennifer's Story

We exited the Bridge and took the elevator to the main deck. Apparently, you didn't need a key to leave one of the special decks by elevator, only enter it.

When we reached our cabin, Mum released Dad's hand, and none of us talked for the rest of the evening. We just got ready for bed and made the best night of it that we could.

The next morning was business as usual for us. We went to breakfast separately. I then went to the gym. I worked weights and did the elliptical and stationary bike. I then went on a jog along the jogging path that went along the main deck.

Again, lunch was just Dad and me. I went to a different gym in the afternoon. By now, I was pretty worn down, but I was not going to go back to the cabin until I absolutely had to. So, I did a walking tour of the jogging path.

I have to admit that I stopped frequently and just gazed out over the sea when the path went next to a railing. It was while I was standing at one of these places that I was surprised to hear someone behind me say, "What are you doing above deck?"

Startled, I looked around and saw a member of the staff standing behind me. I was so surprised that I just said, "Duh."

He replied, "You're supposed to be in your cabin when you're not in an Exercise Room."

He didn't know whom he was dealing with. I had practiced law in far too many Headmasters Offices to be put off by this whelp. I said, "I don't think you heard the Captain's order clearly." I didn't give him time to reply but plunged ahead. "He ordered that I could spend as much time as I wanted working out on any of the ship's exercise facilities."

The staff member, whose nameplate said Thomas R, begged to differ, "Yes, well the deck isn't any exercise facility."

I smiled complacently as only one can do who has the facts of the case clearly on his side. I said, "Look down at my feet. Where are they?"

He looked down reluctantly, perhaps expecting some practical joke. But he did see the lines of the jogging path. "So, you say that you're using the jogging path because you happen to be standing on it?"

"I am using it. Just because they call it a jogging path doesn't mean that you can't exercise by walking it."

Thomas R. grimaced and said, "I don't see you walking."

I smiled complacently again, "I'm walking. I'm just slow walking it. Walkers all along the path stop to admire the view."

He grudgingly admitted it and went on about his duties. I also went on with my walking, pausing only infrequently. By the late afternoon I'd had as much exercise as I could stand and returned to the cabin.

I spent some time on the sofa just resting my eyes but the exercise that I'd been doing raised a keen appetite. I was getting ready to go with Dad for dinner when Mum said, "I think the Dursleys have to stick together at this time. I'll go with you."

Both Dad and I welcomed that decision. We all went to dinner together. By the time we got there, it was well into the dinner hour. There was one couple who left our table just as we arrived.

The meal was, as always, superb. I was leaning back wondering what would come forth for desert when I heard a familiar voice behind me. "May I join you?"

□

It was Jennifer. By this time, the only ones who were left at the table were the four of us and an elderly gentleman who looked around at us and said, "It looks like I'm intruding in a private party. Please excuse me. I'm going over to the ice cream sundae bar. I'll take my treat back to my cabin. Thank you for the privilege of dinning with you."

We all waved him goodbye, and Jennifer sat down next to Mum. Dad asked her, "Are you sure that you should be sitting with us. The Captain seemed pretty definite about our not talking with anyone."

She smiled, "Yes. It's OK. After all, he just said that we shouldn't talk with anyone outside our company that night. We were all there, so it's OK.

"While we're talking about it, let me tell you that things didn't go all that badly for me. He would have been perfectly within his rights to fire me on the spot and kick me off ship at Gakveston and even prefer charges there.

"But, what he actually did was to give me a severe dressing-down and cautioned me about anything of the kind again. He didn't even put it on my personnel record."

105

I commented that it was kind of him to be that generous. She agreed. Then she went on with a different topic. "I have a question for you."

Dad shrugged, "Go ahead."

"No, I mean a question for your son. Dudley, when you answered the Captain's question about what you expected to find in Jim's cabin, you said a weapon. He had a feeling that you had something unusual in mind. I think he was right. What were you thinking about?"

I looked at Mum and Dad, but they had no guidance for me. I shrugged and said, trying to feel out how accepting she would be about truly unusual weapons, "I could tell you, but I think that you'd just think that I was crazy."

She stared directly in my eyes, which was pretty darn difficult to endure, her being a pretty, older woman. She said, "Try me."

I got the feeling that she would not think I was crazy, so I went on. Before I could, she held up a hand and said, "Wait. I'll show you a magic trick. " She opened her purse and extracted a moleskin notebook. She pulled out a pencil, wrote one word on a page, tore it out, folded it, and handed it to Mum. Then she said, "Go ahead."

"I was thinking wand."

She smiled grimly and said, "I knew you were going to say that." Then she pointed at Mum who opened the folded sheet and showed us what Jennifer had written. It was the word, "Wand."

I had a moment when the hairs on my body seemed to stand on end. I asked, "How did you know that?"

She looked at the three of us and said, "If Jim were involved, it almost had to be magic. From the first date, we had strange things happen around him. I don't say that he caused them. As a matter of fact, I'm sure that he didn't, but they just seemed to happen."

I was fascinated to know what she would think was a strange thing, especially on a first date. So, I asked, "If I can be nosy, what was the strange thing that happened on your first date?"

She almost laughed but caught herself. "Well, we were out walking on a complete whim—absolutely unplanned—that evening. Suddenly, an envelope dropped out of the air and landed on Jim's head. I glanced up in time to see what looked like a large bird flying away."

All of us were watching her without the slightest reaction. She looked disappointed, "Well don't you think that is strange?"

Dad answered, "I can't tell you the number of those letters that we got when Harry was first with us." He chuckled and added, "They were literally flying out the fireplace at one point." He straightened up his face. "But you're right that is strange."

Jennifer was the one who ended up surprised. "You mean to say that you know about those things."

Mum just nodded.

"Then. . ." Whatever Jennifer was thinking she never finished. A tear formed in her eyes. "I want to tell you something that I've never told anyone—not me Mum, not Dad, not any boy friend."

Mum patted her hand, and she went on, "I told you that he was my lover. It would have been more honest to say that I was in love with him, but I thought that he never really loved me. But now, seeing you lot running away from these magical folk makes me think that I had him all wrong.

"You see, he went to work at this really strange school in Northern Scotland."

Dad interrupted, "Hogwarts School of Witchcraft and Wizardry."

She stared at him and said with real force, "He would never even tell me the name of the school." Then she went on, "I guess I see why now. At the time, I thought he had some guilty secret."

She gulped and said, "He just kept getting stranger and stranger. Then one day, I just said, 'Shove it, I'm not going to have any more of this crazy stuff.'

"And that was it. For a long, long time I couldn't get him out of my head. I started putting two and two together and getting four or forty or four thousand. I fantasized what had driven him away. At one point, I was convinced that it was a magical school, and some witch had cast a spell on him, used a love potion, whatever.

"Now, seeing you, I think that he was trying to protect me from the sort of thing that's been happening to you. I think he never stopped loving me." The anguish she was feeling came through her voice.

Mum patted her hand again and said, "Now, Now," and after a minute she added, "I think you never did stop loving him."

Her tears were flowing now, one at a time, like raindrops of a soft spring shower. She looked up and asked, "Do you think he's still alive?"

I completely understood her now. I tried to think of something to say to help her escape her pain. I finally said, "Well, let me say that even though you're older." At this, Mum kicked me under the table on the shin. So, I corrected, "Even though you're more mature than I am, I can totally not understand how he could ever give you up."

She gave an effort at a smile and then looked around, noticing that there was hardly anyone left in the ballroom. She got up and said, "Well, I don't want you to get in trouble. I'll see you around, and if I can ever give you any assistance, please ask."

Dad said, "Well, you know that we have some contacts in the wizarding world. If we ever learn anything out about this Wendt, we'll get in touch."

107

She thanked us and left the ballroom by a different exit than we had to take to get back to our cabin. On the way back, Mum took Dad's arm in hers and said, "It makes you realize what you've got doesn't it. I don't think I'll ever take a good man for granted again." With that she sort of leaned on him, and I decided that Dad wouldn't be sleeping on the floor that night.

□□

The next day, we all had a jolly breakfast together, and I was preparing to leave for the gym when there was an announcement that came over the public address system. It said that the ship was going to make an unscheduled stop at a small unnamed island where all passengers were invited to board a ship's boat to travel to the island for a picnic lunch. Mum was downcast. "I long to lunch on a tropical island. It would set me up for life," she moaned.

Dad was the realist. "Well, you might as well not go wishing for what we can't have. The Captain was ever so specific about that. Let's go up to our cabin."

Just then, there was an oh-so familiar voice behind me. Why was it always behind me? "Mr. Dursley."

I answered instinctively, "Yes." As did my Dad. I turned and found Jennifer close behind me.

She said, "The Captain's compliments. He wants you to know that you are welcome to go ashore."

I looked at her in complete puzzlement. She explained, "He feels that the restrictions that he placed on you only apply to the ship. You are free to go if you wish."

There was general pleasure at that declaration. I asked her if she were going to be among those going ashore.

"Oh, no. I have duties here that I have to do. Please feel free to go. Just don't discuss 'you know who'."

Dad assured her that we wouldn't. He then asked me if I were going. "No. A little island with a few palm trees and sandwiches. That is not for me. But you and Mum go and enjoy yourselves. I'll be doing my usual exercise routine."

Mum was disappointed that I wasn't going, but I reminded her that I was not going to be around the house much longer, and she had better get used to it. That set her on a weepy course.

I did go to the gym as usual and did some jogging. I noticed the ship's boats being deployed and thought that Mum and Dad would be boarding shortly.

I saw them pull away from the ship with the first set of passengers. I knew there would be at least one more trip because there were still people lined up. I continued my jog and returned to the gym for some cool down stretches before lunch.

After leaving the gym,I walked slowly toward the ballroom for lunch. I wasn't in a hurry because I'd have to wait perhaps a half hour before the earliest lunch was set out. I stopped and gazed at the island in the distance. As I'd thought, it was not much more than a hill with a few palm trees. The last boatload had just landed.

As I gazed, I noticed a moderate-sized cloud in the distance. It seemed to be growing even as I watched it. As a matter of fact it was growing very rapidly and seemed to be approaching rapidly. I was sure that it would reach us in minutes. I looked around the deck and saw no crew or indeed anyone who seemed to be concerned. My Mum and Dad were on that island. I ran to find some crew member. I headed for the elevator to the Bridge. On the way there, a crew member stopped me.

"Aren't you supposed to be in the gym or your cabin?"

I stared, not believing my ears. I shouted, "Do you not see that storm headed this way?" By this time the sky was definitely darker.

He nodded. "Right, you need to get to your cabin right now. The captain will be making an announcement any minute now, BUT you get to your cabin."

Just then the public address system sounded and somebody's voice came on, not the Captain, saying, "Attention all passengers. There is a squall that has just blown up. It's headed this way and will arrive in a few minutes. Go immediately to your cabin. Once inside, secure all loose objects, placing them in drawers or your closet. I repeat, Attention . . ." The message repeated.

I demanded of the crew member, "What about the people on that island?"

He grimaced, "They'll be all right. We'll pick them up as soon as the squall has blown over. Now, you get to your cabin and don't keep me from my duties."

I could see a lost cause. I left, heading in the general direction of our cabin. As I went, I looked around desperately hoping to see something that could help in this situation. There were life boats. I briefly thought about releasing one and trying to go over to the island to rescue my parents. However, before I could act, the storm had reached us. I was struck by a wave of rain and strong wind. The deck tilted up, and I stumbled and hit the deck and the wall that supported the next deck.

I tried to scramble to my feet, but I slid on the slippery deck. I kept trying to get up. Then the ship tilted the other way. I was sliding toward the railing. That convinced me that I'd better get indoors somewhere.

I made it to a door and fought my way indoors against the tilt of the deck, the wind, the rain, and the loose junk that was rolling around. There was a bucket that had escaped from someone cleaning the deck that almost knocked me down.

I did get inside. The going was easier there. I didn't have to contend with the wind, the rain, or loose junk. Just handling the swaying deck was enough all by itself. I eventually reached our deck and the door to our cabin.

I opened the door and found that there were things rolling and sliding around in our cabin. There was everything—a hairbrush, a pillow was caught in a corner, a variety of pencils and pens. Then I saw the broken glass that was quickly migrating all over the place. Shit! That guy was right about getting to the cabin.

I thought I'd help Mum and Dad. Now, I saw that, at least for the moment, I could hardly help myself. I was down to making a list of all the stuff that needed to be cleaned up after the ship stopped rocking like a crazy hobby horse.

So, I just put my back to a wall and waited the storm out. It wasn't very long I suppose, but it was the worst half hour that I'd ever spent. When the storm blew over, I got up and started picking up all the mess. The contents of our waste basket were everywhere. I got them back into the waste basket and then started adding the broken things. Finding all the shards of glass was time-consuming and disturbing. How could I be sure that I'd gotten it all?

Next, I started putting all the things that weren't broken back where they belonged or at least in a reasonable place.

By the time that I'd finished that, I was ready to go out and see what was going on with the survivors on the island. However, just then, my parents dragged into the room. They were soaked to the bones. I was standing there dumbfounded that they'd already gotten back.

Dad said, "You were pretty smart not to come over to the island with us."

I came out of my surprise and asked, "What was it like?"

Mum said, "Just awful! We had hardly started on the canapes when this storm blew over us. ALL the food was ruined. My sun dress is . . . well you can see what's left of it."

I hadn't noticed until then, but it was soaked and it clung to Mum's form like. . . well . . . like . . . it . . . wasn't . . . there . . . at . . . all. Her short hair was plastered down on her skull. The effect was striking. If she'd tried to look seductive, she'd have had a hard time bettering how she looked right now.

I immediately turned away and pretended to be looking for something. My eyes landed on the waste basket. I pretended to be engrossed by it. I picked it up and said, "One or more of the glasses broke and were flying around the room. I think I got them all, but you'd better be careful. I'm going to take this to somewhere I can throw it away before another wave hits us, and they're scattered around everywhere."

I left the room as quickly as I could. Outside, there were still lots of signs of the chaos we'd just gone through. The deck chairs were scattered around, there was loose paper everywhere. Near the pool, there was more water on the deck than in the pool. I noticed a crew member and hurried over to her. I asked, "Where can I dump this? There's broken glass in it."

She was obviously unhappy about having one more thing to do. She just looked around as if hoping someone else would appear whom I could be dumped on. Seeing no one, she said, "I'll take you to the trash room."

She led me off quickly—almost at a jog. We went down a couple of decks, and she pointed off down the corridor we were in, "At the T turn right. The garbage room is clearly labeled. Now, I've got to get back to my duties." She then hurried off.

I found the room and started back for the cabin, but I decided that for several reasons it would be good if I took my time. For one thing, I really wanted to give Mum time to get a shower and get into dry clothes. I didn't care that much about Dad. Then too, this was an opportunity for me to see parts of the ship that I'd never see otherwise. If I ran into a crew member who questioned my right to be there, I could pretty honestly claim that I'd gotten lost after cleaning up my cabin. So, I enthusiastically set off to see as much of the ship as I could.

I figured that I could get away with going down a level safely but probably not farther. I was still carrying the empty trash can and I thought I must look pretty funny. As I went walking randomly through that lower deck, I eventually ran into the last office that I wanted to see. It was the Security Office. It had a window in the door. I tried to look as innocent as I could and walked casually past it.

As much as I wanted to I didn't glance in. Down the corridor was another door with a window in it. The glass was re-enforced. It had a label beside it—Brig. Just then, someone behind me said, "Sir."

Startled, I whirled around to see a crewman with a side-arm in a holster on his belt. He asked very politely, "Are you lost? Can I help you find your way to the main deck?"

I smiled, "Yes. I was just emptying some broken glass from our cabin."

The officer nodded. "Yes, you turned the wrong way when you left the trash compactor. Let me show you up to the main deck?"

He directed me and followed me. We quickly found stairs that led up several levels to the main deck. As we parted, he smiled but said in a stern voice, "Be careful the next time you're touring below decks. It's easy to get turned around."

"Yes, sir."

When I got back to our cabin, I found Mum and Dad sitting on the sofa, prim and proper. Assessing the situation, I said, "I'll just leave the waste basket and go exercise." They both smiled me out the door.

The Bridge

The next couple of days were boring compared with everything before. We were in the Caribbean, and it was summer. The heat was sweltering during the day, but the nights cooled fairly quickly. I continued my exercise regime. I don't know what my parents did during the days in their cabin. I didn't ask, and they didn't tell.

The night before we arrived at Galveston, we went to dinner as usual —together. At our places at table there were little envelopes much as there had been several days before. We sat and stared at them for a while, afraid to even touch them before Dad said, "How bad could it be?"

He picked up his and slit it open with one of the knives at his place setting. He unfolded the note and read aloud, "Mr. Dursley, the Captain requests and requires your presence in his cabin immediately after dinner. Cordially, Captain Burton."

I asked the obvious question, "We know how to get there, but we don't have a key to the elevator." Neither Mum nor Dad had an answer to that question, but we were not going to worry about it.

As we were well into the main course, a ship's officer hurried to our table and sat in the officer's place. "Sorry I'm late. I had some last minute duties." It was Jennifer. She went on, "I'll be taking you up to the Captain's suite after your meal."

There were several other passengers at table. They were all appropriately impressed. One of them, an older blonde who looked quite good enough for anyone's taste, sitting next to Dad said, "How exciting. Please tell us what happens before the night is over."

I had no idea how she expected Dad to find her to relay that information, but Dad didn't even deign to answer. Instead he lavished all the more attention on Mum.

After we'd finished, we stayed at table, apparently waiting for the rest of the passengers to leave the table. As soon as the last left, Jennifer rose and signaled for us to follow her.

This time, we knew the route and really didn't need her guidance, but she led anyway.

We arrived in the small dining room. It was just as it had been before, including Albert waiting for us. As before, when we were all in place, he opened the door at the back, and the Captain entered. He invited us to sit.

I say it was all as before, but that is not quite accurate. This time Mum and Dad sat on the same side of the table. I think they were holding hands beneath the table. Jennifer sat on the other side of the table with me. I sat on the Captain's right hand as before.

This time, Albert read off to each of us, in order, our drink orders, waiting for confirmation on each. The only change was that Mum decided to have a white wine. He efficiently produced them as before and left the room.

The Captain said, "This is heading toward being a bad habit. I have a letter here that I just received this afternoon by email from my home office." He pulled a folded sheet of paper from inside his jacket. "You may all read this yourself. It's short and to the point." He handed it to Dad who was sitting next to him on his left.

Dad glanced at it and then looked more carefully. He then handed it to Mum. She read it carefully from the first and handed it across to Jennifer.

Jennifer hardly glanced at it and handed it to me. It read, "Captain Burton, when you arrive in port, you are required to postpone the departure of the passengers named Dursley for several hours." That was all, except for the signature of the President of the Cruise line.

When I'd finished it and handed it back to the Captain, he said, "I've never received such a memo in my career. I'm sure that you've noticed that it has no reason for detaining you. There are no agents who will meet you—not agents of the Line, of the British Embassy, of MI6, of the American Federal Bureau of Investigation—no one. I can only conclude that someone is intended to meet you, and that no one on the Line is to know who they are or their purpose in meeting you."

He paused a moment as if trying to decide how to get a bad taste out of his mouth—whether to spit it out directly or rinse his mouth or try to swallow it. Then he went on, "That deduction—that the Cruise Line wants to wash its hands of you and whatever will happen to you—is repugnant. It suggests that you have reason to fear that meeting whomever you will meet."

Dad immediately asked, "Why did you invite us here then? What will you do?"

Burton seemed to turn on a dime. His next words were like a tour guide's. "Please come with me. I want to show you the Bridge."

He stood and preceded us out the door that we'd entered. He motioned us to follow him down the short corridor to a door that had a keypad next to it. He blocked our view of the keypad and apparently entered a code. The door clicked, and he pulled it open. "Please follow me into the Bridge. You'll have to crowd together. The Bridge is not designed for tours."

We did crowd in together. I'm pretty sure that it was Jennifer who was behind me. I swear that I felt a hand pat one of my buns.

The Captain addressed one of the men who sat on fancy chairs in front of some sort of electronic console. More than half of the room was made of clear glass that gave a great view of the sea ahead of us. The room itself was dark except for lights on the consoles and video monitors above the glass that showed views of the ship and sea behind. The glass was so clear that I could see bright stars near the horizon.

"Mr. Cravits, we are having a little tour of the Bridge for the benefit of our guests." He then turned back to us. "Mr. Cravits is the Helmsman. He steers the ship and controls power from the engines. He normally uses the rudder to steer the ship, but it is quite possible to steer the ship with the engines alone." Cravits' smile was visible reflected in the glass.

"Mr. Storms is the navigator, and he doubles as communications officer. Actually, the position of navigator is almost obsolete. With GPS satellites and computer dead reckoning, there is almost no need for the traditional use of compasses, chronometers, sextants. However, he is skilled with those as well.

"As a matter of fact, the ship has computer-based autopilot and radar collision avoidance, so it is quite possible to do most of a cruise with no one on the Bridge." He added, "The computers will do away with all of us, will they not, Mr. Storms?"

He responded, "Whatever the Captain says, sir."

The Captain said, "As a little demonstration. Let me pose a question to Mr. Storms.

"Mr. Storms, when will we arrive in Galveston Port?"

Storms quickly replied, "Sir, we will arrive in port at six hundred hours Central Daylight Time the day after tomorrow. We've had to throttle back a little to make that time. The sun rises at zero five fifty hours CDT that day."

The Captain went on, "Let me pose a little problem for you two. First, Mr. Cravits, when does the Customs Office close in Galveston this time of year?"

Cravits must have known that by heart because he immediately answered, "Twenty-One Hundred hours local time, sir."

The Captain then turned to Storm, "Suppose we wanted to arrive at seventeen hundred hours CDT tomorrow, what throttle setting would be required?"

Storms immediately answered, "Yes sir. I'll have that estimate for you in a moment." He had begun keying into his keyboard as he was speaking.

In about a minute he provided the answer, "We'd need to set the throttle at 90%."

The Captain directed the next question to Cravits, "Mr. Cravits, is that setting feasible and safe?"

Cravits replied, "Sir, the sea is calm, and no storms are forecast on our course for tomorrow. The engines have no exception conditions at the moment. Yes, sir, that setting is feasible."

In the extreme quiet of the Bridge, the Captain's next word was quiet but quite easy to hear and understand, "Execute."

The Helmsman didn't do what I expected—keying into a computer console. Instead he pressed forward two things that looked more like automobile gear shift levers than anything else. As he did that, he said, "Yes, sir."

There was no surge, no feeling of added speed. I was disappointed.

The Captain turned to face the door and said, "Excuse me." We made room for him. He reached the door and opened it. "Please return to my Conference Room."

So that was where we had met him. We left the Bridge and the Captain was about to, when the Helmsman asked, "Sir, do you have any orders for us?"

The Captain simply replied, "No, carry on."

□

We returned to the Conference Room and resumed our seats. The Captain took a sip of water and said, "Ms. Waters, I have instructions for you."

"Yes, sir."

"Tomorrow, as soon as we enter Galveston Bay, you are to proceed to the cabin of the Dursleys and begin postponing their departure from the ship. You will do this by conducting them and their possessions to the nearest gangway by which they will depart the ship. You will remain with them, and you will detain them for three hours. Note, not a second longer."

Jennifer stared at him and asked, "Sir, just when does the clock begin on the three hours?"

The Captain looked shocked, "Why, Ms. Waters, the moment that we enter the Bay. Do you understand?"

She nodded, almost enthusiastically, "Yes, sir, I do understand."

The Captain stood, as did we all, and said severely, "I wish that I could say that it has been a pleasure having you on-board, but I regret to say that I cannot. You cannot be off this ship soon enough for my tastes."

Then he added, "I wish you all Godspeed." He then shook all our hands—except Jennifer's.

We left the Bridge level, and as we rode down in the elevator, Jennifer said, "I am off duty. I suggest that you invite me to your cabin for pleasant conversation."

Dad did. What happened when we arrived at the cabin was not exactly pleasant conversation. Mum and Dad sat together on the sofa. I offered the desk chair to Jennifer. She declined with thanks and sat on the bed instead. Jennifer gave the place on the bed next to her the slightest pat, and I sat beside her.

Dad asked if she wanted something to drink. She declined and directly began, "OK. You will be packed and ready to leave no later than 4 PM tomorrow, right?"

We all nodded.

"Good. Then you need to do some thinking about what you will do after getting through US Customs. What did you have planned?"

Dad answered. He said that we had planned to rent a car. We'd spend a day or two touring Galveston and then go on a driving tour of the Western US ending in the State of Washington. He'd not shared any of that with Mum or me. He tends to be a little secretive as his recent story revealed, but this was unusual.

Jennifer nodded throughout the discussion. Then she began, "It isn't an awful plan. I suppose that you're not paying for anything with check or credit card."

Dad quickly answered, "Oh, no. I'm that smart anyway."

Jennifer looked at all of us. "OK. Here's my suggested plan for you. You can take it, leave it, use as much of it as you like. I don't want to know what you decide to do.

"First, as you say, only pay with cash—for everything. Second, don't rent a car. You can only pay with cash if you rent locally. Even then, they may require a credit card.

"You could take a bus from here. You can be anonymous on a bus, pay with cash, get on and off where you like. But I don't think I'd do that if I were you either."

We all stared at her. Mum asked, "Should we walk, then."

Jennifer smiled—the first time this night. "No, no. That would attract attention too. If you want to get to the Northwest of the United States, I'd go by boat."

Dad immediately shot back, "Surely you don't mean by cruise line?"

Jennifer's smile stuck, "No. Not a lot of people know that shipping lines frequently offer inexpensive passage on their freight-carrying ships. Galveston is a good place to find such ships. There are several shipping lines here."

I asked, "How do we do that"

"You go down to the docks. Take a cab. They will know the offices of all the shipping lines. Of course, pay with cash. Ask them if they carry passengers. Tell them where you want to go. They may not offer that service or not to where you want to go. Even if they do offer your destination, you may have to wait longer than you want to for a berth.

"If they have something you like, pay with cash for your passage and give them the least amount of information you can. They will certainly want to see some identification. Your passports would be fine."

I asked, "How does that help us. We could go by bus and not have to give them anything about us."

Jennifer nodded but said, "Even so, anyone following you would expect you to use buses. They might not even think of the possibility of going on a freighter."

Dad agreed but asked, "What if there isn't anything soon enough for us?"

Jennifer shrugged, "Then you've got to use buses, but even then, I'd use a mixed set of transportation. For example, take a bus to Los Angeles and switch to train up the coast. If you don't like the train, stop every day or two and stay overnight. Then take another bus."

Dad agreed, "That sounds like a good idea. Is there any other advice you have for us?"

She shook her head. "I don't do this for a living, so you'll probably soon be better than I am. Good luck. I'll be back here around 4 PM—just to make sure you're ready."

She left. By this time, it was close to our normal bed time anyway, so we started to get ready for bed. Dad interrupted us and said, "Let's just sleep in our clothes tonight, just in case."

Mum was dumbfounded, "What are we going to do in the middle of the sea—take a lifeboat? I could never get to sleep in a dress."

Finally, we agreed it would be all right to wear pajamas. However, none of us got much sleep that night.

□□

The next morning, we were up with the sun, invincibly awake. I decided to go exercise. The Gym was open 24 hours, and I could always jog. So, I spent the morning exercising. I didn't even feel like breakfast. I don't know if Mum and Dad had breakfast. I doubt it. In the afternoon, I could no longer distract myself with exercise, so I just went back to our cabin. Of course, Mum and Dad were there and had already finished packing. The only things that were visible that didn't belong to the ship were my parents luggage and my things that were spread around as they had been last night.

Mum hugged me and demanded, "Where have you been! We've been so worried!"

I shrugged, "Where else could I be? I was in the gym."

She just fluttered her hands and said, "OOooooh."

I started packing. We had at least three hours before Jennifer would show up, so I was not going to be in a hurry. In a half hour I was packed. I'd have been packed in ten if Mum hadn't kept interrupting me with suggestions on how to fold and pack my clothes.

Then what did we do? We alternatively sat and paced. It was a lot more distracting to pace than to try to sit. I kept from glancing at my watch as long as I could. Then finally I alternated between the ship's clock on the wall and my watch.

Then a miracle happened. There was a knock on the cabin door. We'd been expecting it, waiting for it, hoping for it, but when it finally came, it surprised us. I jumped to the door and opened it. It was Jennifer. She was actually a little early. It was hardly 3:30.

She said, "Come with me."

We walked out with our luggage. Mum asked, "Isn't this early?"

She just led us out on the deck and looked off the side of the ship. She pointed at a point of land and said, "I declare us in the bay." With that she pushed a button on her watch.

I asked her what she'd just done. It turned out that her watch, though a lady's watch, worked more like a man's digital. It had a countdown timer. She showed me that we had 2:59:32 left until we could leave the ship.

She helped us carry our luggage down a couple of levels to the side of the ship. This was where the gangway would be. She pointed over the rail at a small boat approaching the ship. "Do you know what that is?"

I couldn't resist the temptation and said, "A boat?"

She laughed, "No. It's the harbor pilot coming to guide the ship into our dock."

Having just been on the Bridge and seen the helmsman, I asked, "Isn't that the helmsman's job?"

"No, he handles that job between ports, but inside ports, there are narrow channels and sometimes tricky currents. The harbor pilot knows all about that and knows how to maneuver large ships in tight spaces."

I laughed, "You win." We watched as the boat left the side of the ship and eventually saw that the ship was turning. We watched the progress of the ship up the channel and turn to back into a dock. I had to admire the way the pilot got the ship into place. I was surprised to see that it was almost 7 PM when it was in place.

Then some crewmen came up to where we were standing. They were grumbling about having to put down the gangway so quickly. They noticed us standing there with our luggage and became very silent. It was now almost 7:30 PM. Jennifer pointed down to the end of the dock and said, "When you reach the end of the dock, turn right and keep going. Before long you'll find the Customs office. They're not expecting you, but they'll help you."

We all looked at each other for a long minute, and she said, "Good Luck! I don't know if we'll ever meet again, but if we don't I wish you all the best. And if you learn anything about Jim Wendt, please get in touch. You should be able to reach me through the cruise line."

We wished her the best and good luck finding Wendt. Dad held his hand out to her to shake. She walked right past it and gave him a hug. Then we all hugged her. I was the last. When I did, she planted a wet kiss on the cheek facing away from Mum and Dad. I was surprised but tried not to react.

We walked down the gang plank and waved when we reached the bottom. Then we hurried down the dock and on to the Customs Office. It was easy to locate.

Inside, there was a large room with several stations where people could put their luggage and officials could examine them. There were a couple of officers there. They seemed to be busy with people who didn't have luggage or anything.

Dad went up to one and asked where people went to get their passports stamped. The official just said, "Go to the end of the line and we'll get to you."

There wasn't much of a line, but it seemed like each person took lots of time. It turns out that they were from freighters and they were arranging for inspection of cargos to be left or picked up at the port.

It was after 8:30 before our turn came. The official had apparently had a long day. He just asked, "Where are you coming from?"

We answered. He gave a cursory glance at our luggage and asked if we had anything to declare. We apparently didn't have the form that we needed to fill out. He handed us some and was patient waiting for us to fill them out. After we did, he glanced at the form. "Here for tourism?"

We agreed that we were. Then he asked a non-standard question. "Why were you in such a hurry to get off the boat?"

That had Mum and Dad stumped. I'd been in this kind of situation before and answered calmly, "We just were in a hurry to see the country."

He stamped our passports, and we were out of the office as quickly as we could. Once completely out of the dock area, we looked for a cab. Miraculously, we found one.

Dad was ready for this. When the cabbie asked us where we were going, Dad said, "Take us to a good hotel in the tourist district."

We arrived at a well-lit street with several hotels on it. The cabbie dropped us at the most imposing. Dad paid the cabbie with British pounds.

The cabbie argued a little about wanting dollars, but Dad convinced him that pounds were worth more and he'd pay him one for one pounds per dollar.

Dad led us into that hotel. I asked, "Isn't this a little too swank and obvious. That cabbie knows we came here."

"Right you are, me boy, but we're not staying here. They have a Concierge. He can help us change some pounds for dollars."

He did. The Business Office of the hotel could change some currency for us, and they suggested a bank nearby where we could convert larger amounts. He also asked, "But wouldn't it be easier to use your credit card to withdraw some US dollars?"

Dad smiled, "I don't trust credit cards, especially in foreign parts."

The man stared at Dad and watched us as we left. From the business office, we walked out on the street and then down the street. I don't know what Dad's criteria were for picking a hotel, but he seemed to have one. It didn't take us long to find one that satisfied him.

We checked in, went up to our room, and relaxed for the first time in a couple of days.

⊡

The next day, we went down to the hotel coffee shop and had a leisurely breakfast. That is, Mum and I had a leisurely breakfast. Dad excused himself and said that we should stay in the coffee shop until he got back. That was Dad, secretive to the last. It was almost an hour before he was back. When he did return, he paid the check with US dollars. He'd apparently visited the bank that had been recommended to us. We then went up to our rooms and packed.

Mum was dumbfounded. "We just got here, what are we doing?"

"We're going someplace where we'll be less conspicuous."

We could only shrug and follow him.

We checked out and found a cab. Dad told him to go the nearest Howard Johnson's. We went. Dad paid with US dollars again. We walked in, and Dad gave us a little coaching. "We're the Howards from Saint Louis, Missouri. You're Janet. I'm Paul. And," He looked at me and said, "You're Thomas."

This was getting silly, but I asked, "Can I be Robert?"

Dad shrugged, "Sure."

We registered under those names. Dad pulled out a credit card and offered it at the front desk. I ogled him, but he seemed to be oblivious. We went up to our room.

When we got there, Mum asked me, "Will you ask him, or do you want me to?"

"Ask me what?"

I obliged, "I thought we weren't using credit cards."

Dad smiled, "I didn't use a credit card."

"But I saw you with my own eyes."

Dad shook his head, "You saw me use a gift card. After I changed a big chunk of pounds for dollars, I bought a couple of VISA gift cards with lots of money on them. We'll be less conspicuous if we use something that looks a lot like a regular credit card than cash all the time."

I nodded. "Not a bad idea," I thought.

Now we were set up. In the afternoon, Dad took a cab to the dock area to look for passage. That day he went to two shipping offices and struck out both times.

Over the next couple of days he visited all the shipping lines. By the time he was done, he'd found a ship under Panamanian registry that was going to Japan, but along the way, it was going to pick up and deliver cargo at a couple of western US ports. The only bad thing was that it wasn't leaving for nearly a week.

With that news, I decided to revert to my normal habit of plentiful exercise, which I'd given up so far while in the States. The hotel had a small poorly equipped Exercise Room (at least by cruise ship standards) and an outdoor pool. I did my best with what was there. I ran the major streets around the hotel.

The second day after we had our passage, Dad decided that we needed to act a little more like tourists than we were. This was despite Jennifer's warning against that. So over the next few days we went to the beach. It was apparently just recovering from an oil spill a number of years ago. We also went to the Johnson Space Center. It was hard to believe that anybody went to the moon and landed in such dinky little spacecraft. Even after bulking up and losing a fair amount of weight, I don't think I'd have fit in any of the spacecraft that we saw there.

We also went to a strange amusement park—Moody Gardens. The pyramids were crazy. There was a neat boardwalk like the one at Brighton Beach. It was actually fun for a change.

It had been almost like a vacation. These were the first days that seemed that way—even counting the days on the cruise ship. Eventually, the day that our ship would sail arrived.

We got our things together, and Dad went down to the front desk to settle up the bill. I carried the luggage. It somehow seemed to get lighter and lighter as our travels went on. We reached the ground floor as Dad had finished with the front desk. We stepped outside and found that the cab that Dad had called for from our room had arrived.

We were in, and Dad gave the cabbie an address on the waterfront. We drove away, and I looked back, wondering if I'd ever see Galveston, Texas again. We reached the end of the block and were just turning when I saw something very strange happening in front of our hotel. There was a shimmer in the air that seemed to turn into two or three figures wearing something like capes. I gasped as it occurred to me what they might be.

I turned back to see where we were going. I would have said something right then and there, but what could I say in the hearing of the cabbie?

The cab ride lasted seemingly forever. Finally we pulled up to the end of a dock. We got out, Dad paid the cabbie, and he set off at a good pace. I caught him up and said, "Dad!"

He was determined to get on board as quickly as he could. I had to agree, but I wanted him to hear what I had to say.

I repeated my plea for him to listen and reached and grabbed his arm.

"What is it Dudders? We're in a hurry."

"I think I saw a couple of wizards."

Dad stopped dead in his traces. "What did you say?"

"I said that I was looking back as we were driving away from the Howard Johnson's and I think I saw a couple of wizards dispapparate."

He stared at me uncomprehendingly, "Did you say that you saw a wizard disappear?"

"No. No. There were more than one and they disapparated. They appeared out of nowhere. Harry told me about disapparating once. It means that they suddenly appear out of nowhere from somewhere far away."

Dad was still trying to make it out. "They suddenly disappeared from nowhere and then went somewhere far away?"

"NO. They appeared out of thin air at the Howard Johnsons just after we left."

Then, he got it. His eyes bugged out. He took a deep breath. Then he asked, "Did they see us?"

"I don't think so. I think they were entering the hotel."

Dad shook his head. "We'll talk about this after we're on-board. We've got to get on the ship and away from here. Come on, you lot."

We walked down the dock beside a large ship. It wasn't as large as the cruise liner, but it was big. The deck was stacked high with trailers like you see on the road, but they were stacked like matchboxes. I whistled despite myself. Somehow the sheer size and scope of this ship seemed indomitable. It was encouraging to see that something that was not magical could show such power.

We reached the front of the ship and could finally get a look at the name of the ship—The Maersk Toledo.

In the distance was a small figure that at first I didn't realize was a man. He was standing beside a small gangway up into the ship. We approached him and eventually got close enough to see what he looked like—a balding, pudgy, man wearing a suit and tie. When we got close enough to speak conveniently, he said, "Mr. Dursley?" a little uncertainly.

Dad smiled broadly, held out his hand and nodded vigorously, as he said, "Yes! Yes!"

We closed and shook hands all around. The man said, "I'm the Purser of the Maersk Toledo. My name is John Peters. Please come on board. We're close to sailing."

He led us up the gangway. When we reached the top, he turned to us and said, "Let's go to your cabin and drop off your things and then we can take a little tour of the ship—at least the parts that you're allowed to be on."

We went up one deck from the main deck. It had half a dozen cabins. We were in cabin 6. We (actually I) tossed our bags in the room, and we went for a tour.

We went two decks lower where there were lots of important things. There was the mess where we would have meals. There was the laundry room. We were allowed to use it any time–except when the ship's laundry was being done. The rooms were painted gray. They were as drab as you can imagine.

The Purser explained about the mess. "The hours for meals are listed outside the mess on the bulletin board. The menu for the current week is listed there as well. The mess, as you can see, has soda and candy vending machines.

"You'll mess with the crew."

I laughed. I knew what he meant, but the use of the word, "mess", was a lot different than at my school.

He went on, "The cook and his mate normally have some snacks out off official hours, but it's strictly first come / first served. And the cook can even decide not to put anything out. Beyond that, you can have anything to eat that you can beg from the cook. It's always a good idea to be on good terms with the cook.

"Also, off duty crew sometimes come here to play cards and other games. I think there used to be a couple of crew who played chess regularly, but I don't think anyone has used the ship's chess set in a while."

Then, there was—to my great surprise—an Exercise Room. It was also the rec-room. It had some free weights along one wall and a stationary bike and an elliptical exercise machine. I didn't know whether to cry because it was so much less than even the Howard Johnson's Exercise Room had been or to thank God that there was one at all.

I asked the Purser about jogging. That dumbfounded him. Then I asked if I could jog around the main deck. He pursed his lips and said, "I'll have to talk with the Captain about that, but I think it would be OK. You have to understand that it would be completely at your own risk. People sometimes fall overboard," he hesitated and then went on, "Well, that's mainly during storms, but we can't be responsible for anything that happens on the main deck by way of accidents."

Great, I thought. But we were quickly moving on. We went one deck above our cabin. It had a Conference Room, something labeled, "Surgery", and a couple of cabins assigned to ship's officers, like the Execute Officer.

I asked about the Surgery. Peters answered, "No, we don't normally do surgery here, but accidents do happen on working ships and sometimes a cut or gash or worse has to be sewn up. Usually, it's like a Doctor's office. People get sick, and our medical doctor prescribes medicine.

Peters then looked around a little desperately as though he were looking for something else to talk about. I provided him something. I asked, "What do you do? We were on a cruise liner once. It seemed like the Pursers just were gofers when a guest wanted something unusual."

Peters laughed, "I suppose that was part of their duties on a cruise line, but I'm in charge of supplies for running the ship—everything from food for the cook to medical supplies for the doctor to filling the vending machines to ordering DVD's for the Rec Room."

He then went on. "Now, I have to go do some of those duties. You may walk around freely on the decks that I've taken you through. Please don't go elsewhere except maybe Mr. Dursley might have permission to jog on the main deck.

"You're invited to the Conference Room this evening for dinner with the Captain. Don't get used to that honor. It will probably be the last time that that will happen. Otherwise, you're on your own in the mess with the crew. He expects you at 7 PM sharp. Now, I have to go. I hope you enjoy the cruise with us. You'll be passing through some very scenic country when we go through the Panama Canal. And of course, your final destination, San Francisco should be very interesting." With that we'd seen the last of the Purser until dinner.

We went down to our cabin and unpacked. As soon as I'd done that I went to the Exercise Room. While we'd been talking with the purser, we'd shoved off from the dock and were well out into the bay headed for open sea. I looked around the room and thought about my options. I didn't want to do free weights without a spotter. That would never have been a problem on the cruise ship. There was always someone there to spot you. That left the stationary bike and the elliptical. I just didn't feel like the elliptical, so I was for the bike. After doing about 15 miles, I glanced at my watch and saw that it was almost 6 PM. I headed up to our cabin for a shower and change of clothes. I was sure that we'd be wearing suits for the Captain.

I was not disappointed. As I showered, I laughed about the last time that we'd been invited to the Captain's Conference Room. This would surely be different. Mum made sure we were as presentable as we'd been in quite a long time.

We arrived at the Captain's Conference Room at five minutes to 7 PM. Spot on 7 PM, the door was opened, and we walked in. The Conference Room had seats for a dozen. The Captain was standing at the head of the table. There were several other officers in place on one side of the table. We were introduced to them. They were the Purser (whom we'd already met), the Execute Officer, the Ship's Doctor, and the Navigator-Communications Officer.

The meal was served by the Cook's mate. It was really quite good. There was a green salad followed by tomato basil soup followed by a ragout of beef. The desert was ice cream with hot fudge.

There was little talk during the meal, but when we reached desert, the Captain did some explaining. "You are welcome on board our ship. You needed to meet the officers that you'll be dealing with. If you run across problems, your first resource should be the Purser. If you have medical problems, of course, the Doctor is always on call but let me warn you, don't abuse the privilege of having him available. If there are problems that neither of these officers can resolve, there's the Executive Officer. Mr. Green is quite capable."

He paused and looked in turn at all of us, "The two main problems on board a ship are fires and serious storms. In these cases, the warning klaxons will sound. Every man on ship has a duty station in these cases. That includes you. Your duty station will be by the lifeboats at the rear of the ship." He turned to the Purser. "Make sure they know where those are located and the fastest routes to them."

The Purser responded with a crisp, "Yes, sir."

The Captain changed pace and said, "So, any questions?"

There were none. Then the captain suggested that we finish our wonderful ice cream sundaes and retire for the night.

The next couple of days went well for me. I typically got up early and did some jogging on the main deck. I ran between the containers stacked high and looking like the canyons of the American West. Breakfast was not bad on the ship. Actually it was usually the best meal. The serving line had bacon——crispy but not greasy, sausage, eggs that were not rubbery, oatmeal, and more.

There was just one thing about breakfast that was not pleasant. There was a crew member who ate by himself. I'm sure that I caught him out of the corner of my eye occasionally staring at me when I wasn't looking. He sometimes was in the mess for other meals, but he seemed to always be there when I was at breakfast.

One day I was up and running shortly before sunrise. I stopped at a railing to watch the blood red sun lift above the low cloud deck in the distance. The sea was calm and looked like an endless speckled chessboard extending forever.

That day I followed my usual routine and went into the rec-room to exercise. I didn't have anyone there to spot me, so I didn't use the free weights other than the hand weights, But this time, there was someone using the hand weights. Now, I couldn't even use them. So, I walked reluctantly over to the stationary bike and started to get on.

A voice asked, "Do you use the free weights?"

I turned and saw that the crewman with the hand weights was talking to me. I smiled ruefully, "When I have a chance. There's never anyone to spot me."

He laughed, "A common complaint. I'll tell you what. If you spot me, I'll spot you."

I gladly replied, "You bet!"

So, we spotted each other. It turned out that the reason that the rec-room was rarely used by crewmen was pretty reasonable. They mostly had jobs that required strength. They were in pretty good shape just through their jobs. They mostly wanted to get away from using their muscles, not use them more.

My new friend answered my obvious question, "Why do you use the weights?"

He didn't answer immediately. At that point he was trying to clean and jerk a weight that I'd never have tried in my wildest dreams. After dropping the weight he said, "I find it relaxing. It lets me think. I can release my frustrations while I'm lifting."

Besides making it safe for me to do the free weights, this crewman, Matt Soames, was a decent coach. He gave me some pointers and even encouragement. If I'd been on the ship for a couple of months, I think I might have worked myself up to the weights that he was doing.

The next day after I met Soames, we approached land. The Purser visited us during dinner that night and talked about the Canal Zone. He told us that we would be anchored off the Port of Cristobal and that the crew would have shore leave. He suggested that we might want to do some sight-seeing while we were there and also at the other end of the Canal at Balboa and Panama City. Dad and Mum were interested, so I decided that I would go along for the ride.

While we were talking over dinner, I noticed that strange crewman who seemed to pay a lot of attention to me. I mentioned it to the Purser. He glanced over at the man that I had pointed out and said, "I don't know about him. We picked him up in the Dominican Republic. He's a good hand, but he keeps pretty much to himself. I don't think he has any friends."

He reflected for a couple of minutes as we ate. "You know, most sailors are kind of superstitious. I wouldn't pay any attention to him."

I wasn't all that relieved, and Mum had a hard time keeping herself from glancing over at him now and then.

We set anchor the next day and took the ship's boat with several crew members to the land. We breezed through customs. They hardly glanced at our passports as they stamped them. The Customs Official asked Dad if we were there for business or pleasure. He replied, "Definitely not business." Outside, we found a cab. Mum had taken four semesters of Spanish when she was in college, and she kept enough to tell the cabbie, that we wanted to do some sight-seeing. He immediately offered to hire himself to us for the whole day. He offered to drive us to all the sights worth seeing and give us a tour to remember for the rest of our lives. At least that was Mum's translation.

He actually did give us a good tour. We drove through the city and up into the hills. We stopped at a cathedral, which was very scenic. We reached the Pacific shore that had a beautiful park extending along it for miles. To my surprise, there were tall buildings—more actually than in London, it seemed.

For dinner, we went to a cantina that he claimed had the best Panamanian cuisine in the city. The meal went pretty well until the main entrees arrived. Mine was spicy but not unbearable. Dad's was what Mum called, "Muy Caliente!" She had stuck with something mild. Dad ended up drinking three beers and about a gallon of water before he was through.

Although the cabbie tried to get us to stay to see the night lights of the city, Dad just needed to get somewhere so he could lie down near the head (see I picked up some sailor talk) until his throat stopped burning. So, we went back to the ship. As it ended up, we had to wait for the rest of the crew to arrive to take us over in the ship's boat anyway.

The next day we raised the anchor and began the passage through the canal. We went up a river and before long had reached some locks. It was the most beautiful part of the trip. We went between lush banks of the river with hills and mountains in the distance.

I thought that the locks must have huge pumps that pump water into the lock to raise the ship, but I was amazed to find that the locks worked differently. It was the easiest! You sailed into the lock. They closed the gate behind you, and then, water flowed in from the other side of the lock. It raised you up to the level of the river beyond, they opened the gates ahead of you, and then you sailed on.

Our ship was almost as wide as the locks. Standing at the railing, I almost thought that I could reach out and touch the side of the lock. As a matter of fact, at the first lock, Mum and Dad were there with me watching the process. I actually reached out to touch the wall of the lock but Mum grabbed my arm and pulled it back. She said, "Don't you dare!"

I agreed, promising myself silently that I would do it later when she wasn't around.

Later we reached a place where the river widened out, and there were lots of islands. It was strange, unlike any other lake or river that I'd been on. Of course, I'd not been in many lakes. Once, we'd gone to the Lake country, but the lakes there were nothing like this. They were long and thin. This lake was wide. There weren't any islands in the Lake County lakes. Here there were many, and they were large.

We'd have gotten through the canal in a day except that there were so many other ships that wanted to go through. We all had to line up like cars in a traffic jam all trying to get through a one lane street. We ended up having to drop anchor in front of the final set of locks before we reached the Pacific Ocean.

While we were stuck there waiting for our turn to go through the lock, I went down to the mess and bought a bottle of water out of the machine. I sat on a table so that I could see the card game that was going on the next table over. It was a six player game. It had tricks. I tried to figure out what it might be. Maybe it was hearts. Anyway, as I sat there trying to figure out the rules of the game that seemed to be insane, I noticed the crewman who seemed to be taking a lot of interest in me. He was sitting on the table on the other side of the game watching intently. But it was me whom he was watching. Just then, the players of the game took a break and went looking for some food. One of them was my friend who spotted me. He came over and sat beside me. "Do you know the game?"

"No."

"Would you like to learn?"

I was about to say maybe, but I glanced up and noticed him staring at me. I changed the subject of our talk, "Do you know what that guy has against me?"

He glanced over and back, "You mean, Tomas?"

"I guess so. I don't know his name."

"What makes you think he has something against you?"

"He's always staring at me."

My spotter shrugged and said, "Go ask him. His English isn't great, but he should be able to understand you. You should be able to understand him. He's not a bad guy. He just mostly keeps to himself."

I decided to try. I walked around the table and sat beside him. His eyes never left me as I approached. I said, "My name's Dudley. They tell me you are Tomas."

He nodded. Just nodded, nothing more.

I asked, "Why do you stare at me."

He didn't seem to understand, so I tried again. This time I went slower. Still nothing. Then I tried sign language. I pointed at him and said, "You." Then I pointed two fingers at his eyes and then turned them to a single finger pointing at me and said, "Look at me." I couldn't figure a sign for "Why", so I just said the word.

He got it that time. He spoke clearly and slowly. He must have been used to talking that way. I understood well enough. "Bad man. Look for you. Far away. Come close."

My jaw dropped, and my eyes must have been as wide as pie plates. I got up and walked away. My spotter stopped me. "What did he say? You look like you'd seen a ghost."

I nodded. I think I did. I hadn't stopped and kept walking. I had to think. I circled the deck a couple of times as I thought. It seemed like there wasn't much that I could do other than go talk to Dad and Mum. I went up to our cabin.

Mum asked how my exercise had gone when I entered our cabin. "Bad."

She clucked her tongue. "Well, it'll go better next time."

I said, "I don't think so." I turned to Dad, who was reading a magazine at the little desk that we had in our cabin. "Dad, come over here. We've got to talk."

He rolled his eyes and came over to sit on the bed next to Mum. I said, "There's a guy on the ship who's been watching me a lot."

Mum immediately jumped up, "Did he try to get you to do something?"

I almost laughed, "No. No. Nothing like that. I just walked up to him and asked him what the deal was that he was watching me so much. I'll tell you what he said." Then I quoted him exactly. Dad's face fell, and Mum slipped back onto the bed. I asked, "What do we do?"

Dad stood and paced around the room. "Well, we could tell the Captain, but I don't think it would make any difference. What could he do? Maybe forbid him to look at you, but the trouble's already happened." He kept pacing.

Mum said, "He must be a wizard. We're lost."

I said, "Oh, Mum, if he wanted to do us harm, he'd get in touch with You-Know-Who. He wouldn't have told me that."

Mum was puzzled, "Who is You Know Who?" Then she gasped and just said, "Oh."

Dad stopped pacing and faced us, "Well, there's nothing we can do till we reach land. Maybe we'd better get off right away the next time we land in a port, not wait for San Francisco."

I shrugged. "Maybe. Who knows what the right thing to do is?"

On that cheery note we finished the day. Tomas was not in the mess when we went down for dinner. I was happy of that. The next morning, we raised anchor and went through the last locks on the way to the Pacific.

The day went pretty well until the afternoon. I was about to go down to take a run around the deck when there was a knock at the door. We were all a bit jumpy, but we opened the door and discovered the Purser. He just stuck his head in the door and said, "Oh, good. You're all here. The Captain would like to see you in the Conference Room right now."

He took us up, although we hardly needed a guide. He knocked on the door. The captain invited us in. The Purser opened the door, let us in first, and then closed the door behind us.

I think we three must have looked pretty sad. The Captain was seated, and there was no one else in the room. He nodded his head over toward the sideboard where there were a number of bottles, a bowl of ice, and some glasses, "Help yourselves."

None of us were enthusiastic, but we all found something to our tastes. I picked up a can of Coke, filled the glass with ice, added some Coke, and reached for a bottle of rum. Dad frowned at me and then said, "Oh, go ahead. I think we'll all need something stronger than Coke. But if you're going to put something in that Coke, better the Johnie Walker than that rum."

I shrugged and set down the rum and opened the Johnie Walker. I added a generous portion to the Coke, and we all sat down.

The Captain looked around at us and commented, "You look like you're expecting the worst."

Dad just shrugged, "Go ahead."

He did. "There's a problem with the crew." He stopped and thought a minute.

"Before I go into that, I ought to give you some information about ships and sailors. We're a superstitious lot—even the best of us. On land, I'm as enlightened as anyone. I believe in Science and rational thought.

131

"But once you get on the seas, things change. You are somewhere that the forces of nature so overwhelm you that even the best people look anywhere for a port in a storm—so to speak. I've seen seas that were higher than the mast of this ship. You really understand just how small you are when that happens. Anyway, I've got my superstitions.

"Everyone has their own superstitions. But sometimes one crewman can infect others with his superstition. When that happens there can be trouble. A Captain has to stay on top of that. He has to keep it from running away.

"Now, there's a crewman on this ship who has a superstition about one of you—about the young man." I was taking a sip of the Johnie Walker and Coke drink when he said that. I nearly choked on that burning concoction.

The Captain didn't pay any attention to my troubles but went on, "It seems that he's convinced a lot of the crew that you are being pursued by something bad." He stopped and thought a moment. "Do you know the story of Jonah in the Bible."

I was stuck. Dad was puzzled as well. Mum asked, "Does that have something to do with a big fish?"

The Captain nodded. Then it hit me, "You mean Jonah and the Whale."

"Yes. Do you know the story?"

I said, "Yeh. Somehow Jonah got swallowed by the whale. Then. . ." I couldn't remember the rest of it.

The Captain just said, "Let me refresh your memory." He picked up a small leather bound book, opened it at a bookmark, and read,

> "Then the LORD sent a great wind on the sea, and such a violent storm arose that the ship threatened to break up. [5] All the sailors were afraid and each cried out to his own god. And they threw the cargo into the sea to lighten the ship.
> But Jonah had gone below deck, where he lay down and fell into a deep sleep. [6] The captain went to him and said, "How can you sleep? Get up and call on your god! Maybe he will take notice of us so that we will not perish."
> [7] Then the sailors said to each other, "Come, let us cast lots to find out who is responsible for this calamity." They cast lots and the lot fell on Jonah. [8] So they asked him, "Tell us, who is responsible for making all this trouble for us? What kind of work do you do? Where do you come from? What is your country? From what people are you?"

⁹ He answered, "I am a Hebrew and I worship the LORD, the God of heaven, who made the sea and the dry land."

¹⁰ This terrified them and they asked, "What have you done?" (They knew he was running away from the LORD, because he had already told them so.)

¹¹ The sea was getting rougher and rougher. So they asked him, "What should we do to you to make the sea calm down for us?"

¹² "Pick me up and throw me into the sea," he replied, "and it will become calm. I know that it is my fault that this great storm has come upon you."

¹³ Instead, the men did their best to row back to land. But they could not, for the sea grew even wilder than before. ¹⁴ Then they cried out to the LORD, "Please, LORD, do not let us die for taking this man's life. Do not hold us accountable for killing an innocent man, for you, LORD, have done as you pleased." ¹⁵ Then they took Jonah and threw him overboard, and the raging sea grew calm.

Dad asked, "Are you saying that you're going to throw Dudley overboard?"

"No, I'm showing you the sort of thinking that goes on in crews that get infected with the same superstition.

"However, I was thinking seriously of taking Jonah's crew's original idea. I was actually thinking of stopping at Puerto Valiarte and dropping you three off there."

Mum was shocked. "You wouldn't. Maroon us in Mexico!"

The Captain answered, "It's a resort town, for goodness sake. You can sit on the beach sipping margaritas while you wait to catch the next plane to SF. BUT, I didn't say I was going to do that. I'd get in trouble with Maersk. That would be a detour and would cost us at least a day. That would cost the line real money."

Dad asked, "Well, what are you going to do then?"

"I've been thinking about this. I have something that I'd like you to do. Understand, I really, really want you to do it. You will stay in your cabin. You won't go out for exercise. You won't go out for meals. The Purser will bring your meals to you. You won't show your face until you get off the ship."

Mum asked, "Where would that be?"

The Captain didn't answer that. Instead, he stood and motioned us to follow him. We went out into the passageway and followed him toward the front of the ship. He stopped at a door that had a sign above it reading, BRIDGE. I turned to Dad and said, "90%."

The Captain must have good hearing. He asked, "What did you say?"

I stayed cool and just said, "Private joke."

We entered the Bridge. The Captain gave a speech that was remarkably like that on the cruise ship. He asked when the ship would arrive at Long Beach. The Helmsman said, "Seventeen Hundred the day after tomorrow."

The Captain asked if we could make it by zero five hundred tomorrow. The navigator got out a calculator and started working. The Bridge was not nearly as fancy as the one on the cruise ship. There was a big radar screen and a couple of monitors showing views on the sides of the ship and the rear, but that was about it.

The Navigator came back with his answer, "We'd have to go to 95% power starting now. I'll check with Engineering to see if that's OK."

The Captain answered, "Make 95% and if the Engineer has a problem, let me know."

The Captain led us back to his Conference Room, and we all were seated again. Then he asked me, "What was this little joke?"

I had been used to getting questioned about smart-alecky remarks that I'd made and had practice in coming up with good explanations, "Well, you know the movie, Red October?"

The Captain said, "Sure. Preposterous premise but good adventure story. We watch it a fair amount on this ship. It's in the library. Go ahead."

"Well, you remember the Russian attack sub commander asked his Engineer if they can get 105% power?"

"Sure. That's what you were thinking of?"

"Yes, sir."

He harrumphed and then turned to Mum, "To answer your question, I want you to get off at Long Beach. It's a suburb of Los Angeles—the heart of civilization. Maersk won't refund the price of your ticket."

Dad was starting to object, but the Captain beat him, "But, the ship has contingency funds. I'll dip into those to reimburse your travel expenses to San Francisco by plane."

Dad objected, "But what about for a hotel overnight?"

The Captain frowned, "There are flights at least every hour from LA to San Francisco. You won't have to overnight anywhere."

The Captain was tired of dickering with us. He just said, "The Purser will bring your dinner to your cabin tonight. Get going."

We did. Of course, Dad had no interest in taking a plane to San Francisco. We would have to present passports and that would be a problem. We'd be on the grid.

We managed the next 24 hours quite nicely. The Purser brought the best meals of the voyage to us. At 4 PM, the next day, the Purser came to fetch us to board the ship's boat. The Captain wasn't even letting us wait until he'd docked.

We reached the Custom's Office by 5 PM. The US Customs Officer who "helped" us was really a stickler for detail. He made us open all our luggage. He practically unpacked them, looking for who knew what?

Finally, he interviewed each of us. Why were we there? For tourism? Why come in on a freighter from Galveston? We could have gotten here much faster. It was on a lark. We'd never traveled by freighter.

How long would we stay?

Dad was precise. "We are flying back to England from San Francisco in one week."

The agent was still suspicious but he could find nothing suspicious— other than the fact that we didn't even have cell phones. He asked Dad about that.

"Simple, I want this to be a real vacation. I don't want to be called every ten minutes from the office."

"What is the office?"

Dad snapped back, "Grunning Fasteners."

Finally the agent let us go. As soon as we hit the street, Dad got us a cab and asked for the nearest HoJo. We'd begun calling Howard Johnson's that. Everyone seemed to know what we were talking about.

After the cab dropped us off, I asked, "Where to now?"

Dad looked tired, "We're just going to stay here."

We checked in and took our luggage up to our room. There was an International House of Pancakes across the street. We decided to eat there. While we were waiting for our pancakes, I asked Dad, "Have you ever heard of the IHOP?"

He shrugged, "No."

"Me neither, How can they be international."

He just said, "Marketing."

It wasn't awful, but Mum's pancakes are definitely better. The sausage wasn't bad though. After dinner, Mum and Dad returned to the HoJo, but I decided to jog through the neighborhood. It looked safe, and I didn't want to miss another day's exercise.

By the time I got back, everyone was bushed, and we decided to make it an early night. We might as well, there was nothing to do. The TV was as junky here as back home.

Riding the Rails

We got up the next morning, had a decent shower, a real step up from on the Maersk Toledo. It seemed like we might just have a decent day. The weather was really pleasant. The temperature was upper sixties and not supposed to get much above eighty.

We had breakfast again across the street. The breakfast pancakes were definitely better than the dinner ones. Back at the HoJo, Dad made a phone call. The half of the conversation that Mum and I could hear didn't sound promising.

He was talking about travel from Los Angeles to Seattle. He said that he didn't want to make reservations. Finally, the conversation ended this way:

"OK. 10:10 AM from LAX. I've got it. We can just get there, I think."

He hung up the phone and said, "Get packed. We're going as quickly as possible."

I was not satisfied, "But isn't LAX an airport? I thought we weren't flying."

Dad was throwing clothes into his suitcase and only said, "No time to argue, get packed and we're off."

Mum and I packed almost as fast as Dad, even though she was a lot more careful about folding things before packing. We ran down the stairs rather than wait for the lift. Dad was at the front desk in a bound and called over his shoulder, "Hail a cab."

I'd seen that done enough to have gotten the general idea. I had a cab and was loading our luggage in when Dad bounded out of the HoJo and slid into the cab, saying to the cabbie, "LAX. If you get us there by nine thirty, I'll double your fare."

That cabbie made his cab fly. We held onto seat-belts and anything that was secure so that we wouldn't be tossed from side to side of the cab. I started to ask why we were flying, but Dad gave me such a look that I shut up immediately.

We were getting close to the airport at 9:27. The cabbie asked which terminal. Dad simply said, "The train terminal."

The cabbie said, "Shit." We did a U-turn in the street and headed off in a different direction. We arrived at the Union terminal at 9:31, but Dad gave him the promised tip and I think then some.

We quickly unloaded the cab and ran into the terminal. We were all getting to be decent athletes on this trip. The building was not very imposing, but the lines were short. Dad quickly bought us tickets. He had to use some of his store of pounds. I guess the tickets were more expensive than he expected. We hurried out to the train and boarded.

Dad asked where the sleeper car was. It turned out to be at the end of the train. Mum and I looked at each other in surprise. She asked, "Do we have a sleeping compartment?"

Dad just smiled and nodded. Mum asked if we needed a sleeper. He said, "Well, it takes about a day and a half to get there. We'll be happy to have these beds before the trip is over."

Actually, I was happy to have the sleeper compartment right away. The idea of being in a private compartment was really nice. I didn't like the idea of being out in the open on seats. For the most part we stayed in the compartment. But, we occasionally walked through the train.

There was a diner car. We decided to eat one meal in the diner car after we saw the prices. For later meals when we stopped at a station we would get off, buy fast food, and get back on the train. However, that first day, we did everything on the train.

When we arrived in San Francisco, we got off the train and bought some breakfast items—individual serving size juice and cereal boxes. There was a stop in the late morning. We bought some lunch items. In the late afternoon, we stopped at Portland, OR. We got some fast food for dinner.

There were gorgeous views of the ocean and mountains on the trip. I'd never slept on a moving train before. The experience was extremely restful. The monotonous clacking of the wheels on the rails was great for being lulled to sleep.

We arrived in Seattle a little before midnight. There were cabs waiting for the train. As usual we asked for a nearby HoJo. We didn't get there until after midnight. We slept in and stayed there the next night.

I was beginning to wonder what the next step would be. I was pretty sure that we would move to another place, but would it be in Seattle, or would we move further again?

During the day, I used the Exercise Room and did some jogging. The one thing that I half-way expected that we would do, we didn't. There was no tourist activity.

137

The next day, as I expected, we moved on. The cab took us to a place that externally looked something like the HoJo that we had left but there were differences. Oh, were there differences.

In the first place, it looked like somebody had bought a motel and converted it from a place for tourists and business people. It was converted to a place that people would stay for a long time.

The room layout was pretty much standard for all the motels we'd stayed in. There were two queen-sized beds. There was the bathroom. There was a small desk and chair. There was a TV. All that fit as normal. But there were additional things. There was a very small kitchenette complete with refrigerator, small stove and oven, sink and cabinets.

It's not unusual to find a small refrigerator and a kitchen sink and microwave in a motel. However, this kitchenette had much larger versions of all of those things plus much more storage over the oven and stove. Clearly, people could (and I later discovered did) stay there for quite a long time at a stretch.

Then there was the security. Most motels have security. This place had much more. If you got into the small lobby it was because you were a guest or invited. The security was probably at least due to the neighborhood, but more about that later.

There were the guests. The people seemed not to be tourists or business people at all. They looked like people who had local jobs. There were whole families. They had that casual look. I don't mean casual like a family vacationing. I mean that casual look like a family living at home. There's a difference. It's hard to describe, but you would know it if you saw it.

All this has to do with the interior of the place. Then there was the exterior. The neighborhood had gangs. I know gangs. I had a small one myself. There were all the things that show that there were gangs and nasty gangs at that. There was the gang-related graffiti. Again, it's hard to describe, but once you've seen (or made it), there's no mistaking it. Of course, the neighborhood was on the edge of an old industrial area. It was run down, and it didn't look like it was getting up anytime soon.

You add all those things up, and it equals a mystery. Dad has always been secretive, revealing only what he had to, but I couldn't believe that this was where we were headed all along. If it wasn't, then why aren't we moving along?

These questions haunted me for several days. They were tougher than any days we'd had so far. There was no Exercise Room where we were. The neighborhood was not one that I felt like running in except at noon in full sunshine. Even then, I wasn't excited to do it.

This was depressing. I wanted to ask Dad what was going to happen, but he always has a plan. I didn't want to hurt his feelings. I was pretty sure that we were going on to the next step soon.

It turned out to be later than Mum or I hoped. Day after day dragged on. It began to look like we were going to be stuck here indefinitely.

On the fifth night at the Value Place, we were having dinner around the little desk/dinner table. We had moved the table over to one of the beds when we had dinner. Mum sat on the desk chair. Dad and I sat on the bed. The whole meal had gone on in silence.

What was really happening was that Mum and I both were trying to build up the courage to ask about the future. She opened her mouth and began to say something when Dad held up a hand and said, "Wait. I have something to say."

Mum and I were more than happy to let Dad do the talking. He started slowly, feeling his way to what he wanted to say. "I know that we've been having a few hard days here. I'm sure that you're disappointed with where we've landed. You want to know what's next."

I just wanted to know that there was a "next", but I nodded enthusiastically.

He went on. "First I want you to know that I had a plan. It was a good plan. It started when Harry told me about 'Who do you know'."

I interrupted him, "I think it's 'You know who'."

It showed how depressed Dad was that he hardly heard my interruption. He just said, "Yes. Yes. Anyway, Harry wanted us to go with that wizard couple."

I interrupted again, "Yeh, you just couldn't make up your mind."

Dad looked at me searchingly for a moment and then said, "Oh, I knew what we ought to do. I just couldn't find the courage to do it. To leave everything we knew. To leave what had always been safe for us."

I interrupted again, "But you did find the courage, and now we've done a hundred things that we wouldn't have had the courage for already."

Dad nodded. "Yes. I accepted Harry's plan. But then it failed and I had to invent my own plan. It was good plan."

Mum said, "Sure it was. It . . . got . . . us . . . here."

Dad went on, "You see I thought that one of two things would happen. Harry told me that both he and 'you know who' couldn't both survive. One of them would have to die."

He stopped and turned his head for a minute. I wondered if he might be afraid that he was beginning to cry. Then he turned back and wiped his face with his handkerchief. "I thought that it would be Harry who would die. 'You know who' is just stronger, smarter, older. I just didn't think he'd survive for long. When the Deatheaters found us, I was sure that it was because Harry was dead. But now, we know that they're still trying to find us. Harry must still be alive.

"Anyway, I thought it didn't matter a lot who won." With that, Mum gasped, but Dad went on, "If Harry did, then the Deatheaters wouldn't be after us, of course. But even if 'you know who' won, it wouldn't be that bad for us. They're only hunting us because of Harry. With Harry gone, they don't have any reason to keep after us. We'd just be ordinary Muggles. Being a Muggle wouldn't be that great, but at least, they wouldn't be going after us in particular.

"Whichever way it went, I thought it would be over quickly, so my plan was just to go as far away as I could. We went as secretly as we could. I thought that by now, it would be over. I don't know. Maybe it is. But now, I've got to think longer term. Who knows? Maybe it might go months more. Maybe a year more!

"We have to make our money last. So, I picked the cheapest place to live that I could find."

As I listened to Dad talk, I realized that he'd run out of ideas. There wasn't a "next" thing. This was it. I'm sure Mum got that too.

An idea was forming in my head. It was one that I couldn't believe that I was having, but I finally just had to blurt it out. "Dad, we don't have to be stuck in this dump just because we only have so much money. I can go out and get a job. There must be something I can do."

Mum joined in, "Sure. I can work too. We're not finished."

The worry lines that marked Dad's face relaxed some. "That's a nice idea, but we're in the States. We're not in England. They'll want identification and social insecurity cards and things like that. We don't have any of them."

He stopped, and his head turned so that one ear was higher than the other like he was listening for something. He gave a little chuckle. "But maybe there is something we can do."

He spoke slowly as though the idea were forming in his head as he spoke, "We do have British passports. We could cross the border into Canada. I'll bet we could work there without any problem. What do you think?"

It was so surprising to hear Dad ask my opinion of something that I was shocked into silence. Then I said, "Sure. That's a great idea. Where's the nearest city in Canada?"

Dad answered, "Vancouver, British Columbia. We ought to be able to get there easily. I'll bet there's a bus that will take us there."

Mum nodded enthusiastically. Mum was so excited that she started packing already. Dad called Greyhound to find when the next bus was leaving. There was one in the afternoon. Even though we had two days left on the week that Dad had paid for us to stay there, in less than a quarter hour, we were packed and headed down to the entrance. Dad had also called for a cab and we were on our way to downtown Seattle before we knew it.

I reflected that we had gotten really good at packing and unpacking. I said as much in the cab. Dad agreed but added, "Too good if you ask me."

We boarded the bus and after a couple of hours, we thought that we'd arrived in Vancouver, because the bus pulled off the freeway and we were clearly in a city, but it turned out that we were stopping for US and Canadian Customs.

The US Customs agent was efficient and quick. He said conversationally, "I see you entered the country in Long Beach and have traveled up the coast. Did you enjoy the tour?"

Dad agreed that we had. The agent stamped the exit visa and said that he hoped we'd return sometime. We agreed that we'd like to.

The Canadian official was friendly too. He asked if we were here for business or pleasure. Dad surprised him by saying, "Well, actually, we're thinking of settling here. We're hoping for a change from England."

I thought to myself, "Yeh, it would be nice for a change not to be chased around England by blokes with wands trying to kill you."

After the surprise wore off, the agent gave us some advice. "Well, you can stay here indefinitely because you're British citizens, and you can get jobs, but if you really want to stay, I'd suggest that you get a regular work permit and start to apply for Canadian citizenship."

Dad nodded thoughtfully and said that we probably would. Then we got back on the bus with the rest of the passengers and continued the short distance on to the Greyhound station in Vancouver.

Dad broke the normal mode by looking for a different hotel than HoJo. It was a Best Western. We registered for a couple of days. The next morning, we had a surprisingly good breakfast in the Hotel. Dad bought a couple of newspapers and we started searching the want adverts.

Mum had the easiest time. She had noticed that the restaurant next to the hotel had a "help wanted" sign in the window. It turned out that they were looking for a waitress. The wage wasn't great but she got tips and really made a substantial contribution to our fund.

Dad converted the US dollars that we had to Canadian dollars along with some British pounds. He was looking for a sales job. He said that he didn't hope for a posh job like he used to have at Grunnings, but any place where he could use his sales skills would be great. It was slower for him finding a job, but he did get one in a couple of days at a shoe store.

In the mean time, we had moved again. Dad had found a residence inn near the hospital district. There were several hospitals close together. One of them specialized in treating cancer. Friends and family needed a reasonably priced place that they could stay while their relatives were being treated.

The place he found was superficially like the Value Place back in Seattle, but it was significantly nicer. It was nicer in lots of small ways. The kitchenette was better laid out. The refrigerator worked better. The place actually had a small Exercise Room for goodness sake!

It was more expensive than the Value Place but not as expensive as the HoJo's that we'd stayed in. Besides the nicer rooms, the fellow people who lived there were a better group. The management provided a hot cooked meal three nights a week, for goodness sake! They provided breakfast. It was like heaven compared with where we had been.

The neighborhood was strange. I mean that it was a mixture. There were some nice homes in the area and some rather poor homes. There was a Laundromat nearby. A lot of times we used it rather than the one in our place. There were always machines open, and they worked faster than the ones in the extended stay.

□

I had the hardest time finding a place to work. However, one day, I was reading the want adverts, and this came to my attention"

    Janitorial Assistant wanted. Part-time position. Must have good upper body strength. No previous experience required. Reply to box 7B.

For some reason that appealed to me. It's hard to figure why. When I'd been in school, I'd been the curse of janitors. Maybe I thought I owed them something.

I sent my reply in and one day, our phone at the extended stay rang. In all our travels, we'd never received a call on the phone in our hotels. I was almost afraid to answer it. Mum did.

She was shocked to hear that I was the one wanted. I took the receiver. The voice on the other end asked if I were still interested in the position of janitorial assistant.

"I certainly am."

"Then can you come to our school tomorrow morning for an interview?"

I agreed that I could. She told me the name of the school and the location. She said to report to the principal's office when I got there. She also warned me that there was a metal detector at the entrance and that I shouldn't bring any knives "or such-like."

I nodded and agreed to be there at 10 AM. No knives or "such-like". That told me a lot about the school. I'd never been in a school quite as bad as that, but there definitely had been gangs at one or two. Bloody Hell! I'd had a little gang myself.

That night over the dinner table, we had a discussion about dressing for the interview. Mum's preference were for me to wear my suit. Dad's thought was that the right dress was a step up from the typical work wear that an employee would wear to work. That was a pretty low bar. We finally decided that dress slacks and a dress shirt would be good. Mum pushed for a tie, but I held firm.

Since I would have to travel to work by bus, I decided that I'd not take a cab to work. I called the city transit company and found the bus routes to take. Fortunately, I'd only have to transfer once. The route that came closest to us was a major one since it also served the hospitals. The cross route was not so major, but I could get to work in less than 45 minutes if I timed it right. The next morning I was up bright and early, did a jog, had breakfast, and was off to the school.

The bus system was on time. I arrived at the school about 25 minutes early. The neighborhood didn't look great. So, I decided to take a quick walking tour. There were signs of gang activity. Apparently some gang called the Kryps.

The school itself was in pretty good shape, but the grounds were surrounded by a high fence. I wondered whether it was to keep the Kryps out or in. There was indeed a metal detector at the main entrance. There was a police officer there.

He looked me up and down and asked, "Are you a new student? I've not seen you here before." He also looked my clothes up and down. He added in a conspiratorial voice, "I wouldn't wear that to school again." I guessed I must look like a student. I was only a year out of school myself.

I smiled, "No, sir. I won't. How do I find the Principal's Office?"

He directed me straight down the hall and then right at the intersection. I didn't have any problem finding the office. I entered, and the secretary glanced at me. Then she said, "Sit. The principal has a meeting at 10 but then he'll deal with you."

I started to say, "Ma'am, I'm Principal Roberts 10 o'clock appointment." I didn't get past "I'm." She said, "You'll just have to wait."

I almost laughed, but I knew that would only make things worse. I just said, "I'm Mr. Dursley."

She seemed not to be listening. Instead, she said, "Please wait your turn."

I got up and walked over in front of her and said, "I'm Dudley Dursley."

That made her gasp. All she could say was, "Really?" Then she glanced at her watch to see that it was two minutes to 10. She got up and walked to the Principal's door, opened it, stuck her head in, and said, "Mr. Dursley is here."

She turned back and said, "Please go in."

Inside, I found that Principals in Canada had offices almost indistinguishable from Headmasters in the UK. There was an old leather sofa, a couple of wooden chairs, one battered red leather chair, a large desk piled with paperwork.

Principal Roberts looked up, blinked a couple of times, and said, "I thought that Mr. Dursley was here."

I nodded. "I am Mr. Dursley."

"But you're young enough to be a student here."

I smiled, "I am young, but I've graduated, and I'm looking for a job."

Roberts was still suspicious. He asked to see my identification. I handed him my passport. He studied it carefully including the pages of visas.

"Well, Mr. Dursley, you may be young, but you've been around. I see that you are an adult, though only a few months past your eighteenth. Why do you want to work for me rather than go to college?"

I smiled an innocent smile and said, "Well, I've not been a great student. I'm not ready for college. I may never be."

"But why work as a janitor?"

I actually laughed, "Well, it's a job that I think I can handle. And then too, I've spent the last dozen years in school. I think I know my way around schools pretty well."

That made him laugh. Then he became serious again, "Do you realize that this high school is in a neighborhood that has a good bit of gang activity?"

I nodded, "Sure, I noticed some gang graffiti on the way in."

"And you still want to work here?"

I shrugged. "Yeh, my school back in England had some gang activity. I know my way around."

He nodded and then asked, "I see that you're from Little Whinging." He pronounced the name whining.

"That's Whinging with a hard G. Yes, that's right."

"You're a long way from there. What brings you to the far end of Canada?"

I could answer that with no hesitation, "My parents. They decided to move away from home, and I wanted to come with them. We've always been close."

"Then why did your parents come here?"

I scratched my chin to gain a little time to think. Then I said, "Well, my parents got involved with a bad crowd in England, and they want to start a new life."

I thought that Roberts would laugh again, but he got control of himself and apologized. "I'm sorry. That's a story I hear a lot but rarely about parents. Would you be willing to share what the 'bad crowd' was?"

144

I thought a minute trying to think of some group that would make sense to Roberts. Then, I hit on an idea. "Well, sir. I really shouldn't speak for them, but I'm pretty sure it's a terrorist group."

He looked at me hard, "You mean like Irish separatists?"

I tried not to show any reaction but said, "It could be."

Roberts went on, "Well, I wish you all luck. Now, about this job. You'll be doing standard janitorial duties. When the school term starts we get a lot of damage to the school. You know, graffiti, broken windows, that sort of thing. We need extra help to keep the school in good repair. Frankly, I've been trying to find someone for the last month, but when they see this school, they just walk out of the office or don't even walk in. Are you sure that you want to work here?"

I shrugged, "Yes. I'll work hard. I know what I'm getting into—maybe better than you do."

"Well, can you start tomorrow?"

"Yes."

The Principal took me to the Janitor. He was a crusty old man with thin gray hair. He was thin and wore wire-rimmed glasses. He was tall— taller than me.

He and I had a sort of immediate affinity. I would have recognized him as a school janitor anywhere—if I met him in a mall or on the bus. He recognized in me a recent graduate from a school and a trouble-maker.

After the Principal left us to get acquainted, the janitor made his position clear, "My name's John Preston, but to you, I'm Mr. Preston. Is that understood?"

"Yes, sir."

He looked me up and down and said, "I know your kind. You may be dressed up today, but I would recognize you anywhere. You're a trouble-maker, just like those punks who mess up my school," I now knew who REALLY owned the school. He went on, "These Krypt punks are always painting their stupid brags on the walls of MY SCHOOL.

"Well, let me tell you. Your job is to help me. What I want you to do is this here: Clean the restrooms. I guessed you'd call them WC's, and clean up the graffiti. Is that clear?"

"Yes, sir. I hope we can do something about that graffiti."

He looked at me suspiciously. Then he said, "You be here bright and early at 7:30 AM. You'll work till 2:30. You get a lunch hour. Understood?"

"Yes, sir."

He showed me around and gave me a set of keys that apparently were the assistant janitor's set. He warned me about losing them. I'd have to pay for their replacement. One of them opened the back door which was next to the Janitor's Office. He almost always came into the school that way. Then he took me back to the Principal's Office.

At the Principal's Office, I filled out an official employment application. I then filled out a bunch of paperwork for the Personnel Office. I didn't have a checking account, but I'd be paid by check anyway. Maybe I'd use the first wages to open an account.

I left the school mid-afternoon. On the way home, I saw a military surplus store. I got off the bus at the next stop and went back. I'd decided that at this school I needed a little extra protection—like a knife. I bought a sheath for the knife as well. I could strap the knife under my jeans. The knife itself was a beauty. It was serrated and had a no-slip hand grip.

That night was one of the three nights a week that dinner was provided. We picked up our plates of food and went outside on a little patio to eat. It was still reasonably warm ,and I wanted a little more privacy than we would have in the lounge area.

We talked about work. It was a strange conversation. Back in Little Whinging, at dinner, Dad would talk a little about work. Somehow what he did did not seem to have a lot to do with us. Mum would talk about her garden. I would make a point of not talking about school.

Today was completely different. When Dad talked about work, he'd tell about the silly woman who wanted a shoe that was the same size as she had worn as an 18 yr-old. Mum talked about the lunch hour backing up and how she couldn't stop moving for a single minute.

"Those customers! They want me to fill their coffee cup every time they take a sip. They sit in their booth the whole noon hour no matter how many people are backed up. And tippers! You'd think they'd never heard of it."

Then they turned to me. I shrugged, "I got the job."

Mum shrieked with delight. Dad pounded me on the back. You'd think that I'd gotten admitted to Oxford. I said, "Look, being Janitor's assistant is not exactly rocket science."

Mum cooed, "But it's our little Dudder's first real job!"

I told them about the less fun parts of the job—cleaning the loos, painting over graffiti. They were as pleased as punch.

Then I talked about the neighborhood. It was not great. The graffiti was gang graffiti. That changed the tone of the conversation.

Mum wanted me to think seriously about getting a different job. Dad took me aside after dinner and assured me that I didn't have to be courageous about it. It was completely OK to resign and get another job.

I was determined to stay with the job. That sort of soured the mood for the rest of the night, but I had to be to bed early if I were going to get up in time to get to work at 7:30.

When I boarded the bus, it was pitch black. The bus was empty except for the driver and an old lady.

I arrived at school at 7:15. I walked around to the janitor's entrance and used my key to get in.

The Janitor's Revenge

I arrived at school at 7:15. I walked around to the janitor's entrance and used my key to get in. Mr. Preston was there drinking a cup of coffee. He motioned me to take a seat opposite him. "How about a cup, Mr. Dursley?"

I nodded. He poured me a cup from a small tin coffee pot that was on a small electric burner on a table behind his desk. I learned when I was very young to drink hot tea but I never got the taste for coffee. It was rarely drunk in our home, and I never saw the need for it. Now I did.

I took a careful sip. That, at least, I had learned from drinking tea. That was lucky. It was scalding hot. I had a hard time resisting the impulse to scream. Preston asked if I wanted sugar or cream.

I declined with thanks. And it was just as well. He added some "cream" to his coffee from an old nasty cardboard jar of instant "cream".

After we "enjoyed" our cup of coffee, Preston took me on a tour of the school. He showed me where the supply cabinets were, where the loos were, where the gym was, and where all the entrances were.

Then we went to a supply cabinet and loaded a small cart with cleaning supplies. He gave me my marching orders: Go clean all the loos.

I asked, "Even the girls'?"

"Especially the girls'. They are nastier by far than the boys. You wouldn't believe the things that I find in there."

I thanked Preston and set off as he went back into his office. I suppose he was having more "coffee" and "cream".

The first couple of loos were miserable times, but I got used to it. The first time I went into a girls' loo I said I was coming in to clean in a normal voice. I went in to discover a girl applying makeup in front of a mirror. We both were shocked into silence for about ten seconds. Then she screamed, and I backed out rapidly with many "Sorry's." I tripped over my cleaning cart right in the middle of the door. She had a good laugh out of that.

The day finally came to an end. Before it was over, I'd cleaned all the loos twice. I'd scrubbed away at some graffiti in chalk and could barely stomach to eat the lunch that Mum had packed for me the previous night.

The dinner table that night was a much subdued place compared with the previous night. I didn't have any exciting news from work, and neither did anyone else, but it was good to have work that you could have news about.

The next couple of days were the same, and then the blessed weekend arrived. I was up late. I went down to the Exercise Room and exercised to my heart's content. I was paid weekly. It was wonderful to have some pocket money that I'd earned myself. It turned out that Dad had opened a checking account. He cashed my paycheck for me. Most of it went into the account, but I could do things like go to the movies without my parents!

□

Of course, Monday came with astounding speed. I was back to the old grind. The old grind. I now knew in great detail what made it a grind. One day in that week, I was cleaning a boys loo when I caught a boy smoking. When I was in school, I did that occasionally myself. But when he saw me, he immediately ground it out on a urinal and was about to toss it in the urinal when I shouted, "Don't."

Of course, that didn't make any difference to him. He went ahead. I was infuriated. "Do you know how nasty it is cleaning those out of there!"

The kid didn't care. That just put me over the top, "If I ever see you do that again, I'll make you put that stub back in your mouth."

He started to make a smart-Alec comment when he saw the expression on my face and shut up immediately. Somehow, I always had a talent for communicating my intent without a word. This time was no exception.

The kid said, "OK. OK. I get the idea. Such a grouch! I suppose that you're going to tell me about getting cancer."

I smiled wickedly, "I don't care if you get lung cancer and end up coughing up your lungs in a bloody mess. Just don't ever think of doing it in MY LOO." I suddenly realized that I had taken possession of all the loos in the school. Just like Preston owned the school, I owned the loos in the school. It was a strange realization. It was scary too. I suddenly realized what it was with adults–teachers, secretaries, and (yes) janitors.

That night at home over dinner, I told the story. Neither Mum nor Dad seemed surprised or angry. Dad just said that I was maturing nicely. Mum actually seemed to be proud although she didn't say anything.

The rest of the week went fine. I didn't catch any more smokers in the loos. As a matter of fact, I saw a lot fewer cigarette butts in the boys' loos, but the girls' seemed to be just the same.

There was one thing that happened Friday afternoon that was bad. I had almost finished my shift. There was still some school going, but I was just about to finish. I was walking down a flight of stairs, and as I turned the corner, I saw a kid writing graffiti on the wall of the stair well. To make things worse, he was using a spray paint can. You saw spray paint graffiti outside the school and on school sidewalks some, but never inside.

I shouted at the kid, "You, STOP!"

He didn't. That tripped the switch for me. I was going to have to clean that up and NOW after the end of my day. It would be hard too, because it was paint.

I took the stairs two at a time to him and grabbed him. I didn't use any real force, but it surprised him terribly. He fell over backwards and almost pulled me down the stairs. He hit the bottom of the stairs with a thud.

I came down and helped him get up. He was really shaken. I decided this was a good time to remind him not to do graffiti in the school. There was hysteria in his eyes while he said, "You'd better not mess with the Kryps. We'll get back at you for this."

I helped him up and said, "Good. You're a Kryp. Tell your buddies that we don't tolerate graffiti in school."

He looked more scared than anything else, so I decided to add a little bit to the fear level. I said, "This is nothing. I can hurt you ways that don't show on the surface.

"Now, let's get you to the school nurse."

It took a little time to find her. When we did, she was about to leave too. She was clearly unhappy. She checked him out as I explained that he'd tripped down the stairs while spray-painting graffiti. He tried to tell her that I was responsible for the fall. She was having none of it. She said, "Even if he did and I really doubt he did, you had it coming."

This little act of support surprised me and made me smile at her spunk.

It turned out that there were no broken bones and only bruises. The nurse filled out an incident report about the injury. No one was to fault and the student had minor scrapes and abrasions.

I had to go back and get the paint remover and work on the graffiti. The paint remover was something called methyl chloride. It was about the nastiest stuff I'd ever run across. It burned your hands and made you cough. I bet it causes cancer too.

□□

The weekend was typical. We caught up on chores–washing clothes, grocery shopping, and so forth. Sunday was our real day of rest. One of the things we got into a habit of doing was looking at the job listings in the

Sunday paper. We were always hoping to find something better except maybe for Dad. He thought that he might get a promotion shortly.

Besides being practical, it turned into a form of entertainment as well. We started noticing funny adverts. One time Dad noticed an advert for a "fit model."

He asked, "What in the world is a fit model?"

Mum knew right off the get go. "A fit model is used by department stores to make sure that clothes from the manufacturer is the right size.

"What size are they looking for?"

Dad replied, "A perfect 6P, whatever that is."

Mum answered instantly, "It's a size of women's clothing. The P stands for petite. A 6P is pretty rare."

Dad made the mistake of asking Mum, "What size are you?"

Mum snapped, "None of your business unless you're buying me clothes."

Dad shuddered, and that was the end of that conversation.

That particular weekend, I found another funny advert. I saw it and had to laugh. Dad asked, "What have you got?"

I controlled my laughter and said, "This is rich. Listen."

> Owner of a rustic fishing lodge in Northwest Ontario seeking a couple to maintain the lodge during the off season. The successful applicant must be willing to live for five months completely out of touch with the outside world. He must be able to maintain two stroke gasoline engines. He must have basic handyman skills. Other requirements. If interested, reply to box 5D."

Dad said, "You know this sounds a little like an old movie that came out a year or so before you were born."

I jumped in, "To me, it sounds a lot like a movie that came out a year or two ago." Then, we both said in unison, "The Shining."

Mum had apparently never heard of it. So, Dad filled her in, "It's a movie based on a book by Stephen King."

She shuddered, "You mean that man who writes all of those horror movies?"

Dad answered, "Yes. But he's a really good author. The reason that he can write such horrifying books is that he has deep insight into the human soul."

I said, "Dad let me tell the story." He was agreeable, so I did. "The main character is a kid, maybe ten or eleven years old who is psychic. His dad is a writer who has a really hard time getting his stuff published. Anyway, as a day job he agrees to be the winter caretaker for a resort in Wyoming."

Dad interrupted here, "I think it was Utah."

151

"Yeh, yeh. Whichever it was, it's way back in the mountains, and once the winter sets in, and the snow starts falling, it's almost impossible to get to it. So, the owners of the resort always hire someone to take care of the building and grounds in the fall until the spring."

"This writer gets the job. He, his wife, and his kid travel there. At first, everything goes fine except for one thing. The kid, who is sort of psychic, begins getting these visions of things that start out not so spooky but keep getting stranger.

I hesitated for effect, "You see the thing is that the resort was built on top of some sacred Indian burial ground or something. All sorts of bad things have happened over the years at the resort, but they're always covered up. Then in the winter all these ghosts come back to haunt the people who are the caretakers."

"Anyway, both the dad and the son are susceptible to these ghosts. They drive the dad crazy. He kills the mum, but the kid gets away."

Mum shuddered again. "Why in the world anyone would want to watch that kind of story is beyond me."

Dad said, "You see how this could be kind of like us—Dad, Mum, kid. They go to this resort to be caretakers for the winter."

Mum said, "Don't you ever think that I'd do that."

We moved on to other things.

⌗

The new week at work came and things went fairly well the first day or two, but then when I was walking to catch my bus, I had this creepy feeling that I was being watched. I took a quick look around and didn't see anyone, but I couldn't shake the feeling. The next day, I was called into the Principal's Office. I thought to myself, "This is it. I'm about to be sacked."

This time when I entered the office, the secretary recognized me. She invited me to sit and went into the Principal's office. Then she invited me in for my meeting.

Roberts stood and offered his hand to shake. I took that as a good sign. I sat. He offered something to drink. "I don't suppose you have tea?"

"I'm afraid not, but we do have coffee and bottled water."

I still hadn't gotten the hang of coffee despite have a couple of cups of it with Preston every day. So, I declined with thanks. I did ask him what I could do for him.

He stretched and leaned back apparently considering the ceiling. Then he asked himself the question, "How to begin?" I didn't have an answer for him, so I waited patiently.

"Well, when you entered the room, I guess I could have greeted you as the King of Restrooms. What do you say to that?"

152

I was dumbfounded. "Frankly, I don't know. I've never heard that nickname. Where did it come from?"

Roberts looked at me hard and then said, "I see that you really don't know about that nickname. Very well, it's easy to explain.

"First, let me say that I have my sources of grapevine information among the students. You don't have to know how, but they are normally very accurate.

"My snitches, not just one, tell me that you have a reputation. You're known for being very possessive about the restrooms and have been known to chew out a student or two who violates their sanctity.

"Furthermore, you are known to have been involved with an incident involving graffiti inside the school. My source, the school nurse, assures me that you were not responsible for the minor injuries suffered by the offender."

He paused to see if I had any comment. I had been in this position enough times to know that the best policy is to wait for charges, if any come, before commenting. So, I waited impassively.

The principal went on, "The official policy of this school and indeed the Board of Education is that it is wrong to use corporeal punishment."

I interrupted, "Corporational?"

"No, Corporeal. It means physical like pushing a student down the stairs. Now, I'm not suggesting that you might have done something like that."

I promptly said, "I didn't."

"Ah, just so." He steepled his hands and said, 'Well, it's very important that no witness see such an act of corporeal punishment. Do you understand?"

Of course, I understood. I was being issued a caution as they do in football, but I was pretty sure that the principal didn't really object to such methods, just that they not be provable. To be sure of that, I asked, "Well, Mr. Roberts, are you saying that I should be very careful not to use corporeal punishment with students?"

He grimaced, "Well, that's not exactly what I said."

I smiled, "Then, your real concern is that I be careful that no use of corporeal punishment be provable."

His grimaced changed and his lips inclined slightly upward at the corners. "That would be one way of interpreting what I said. It is perhaps not the best way of interpretation, but it is 'good enough for government work' as the saying goes."

I hadn't heard that expression before but I definitely got the drift. We parted company in good spirits. I went back to my primary assignment and had to admit that the restrooms were easier to clean than they had been at the beginning.

I generally ate by myself in the cafeteria at lunch, but lately people—mainly teachers—had been stopping by to say hello, introduce themselves, and even occasionally eat with me. I wondered if that might have something to do with my reputation.

On the down side, I still sometimes felt like I was being watched as I walked to the bus stop on my way home.

On Friday afternoons, I tended to stay a little late to finish cleaning chores before the weekend. This particular week, Friday was no exception. I actually left work a little after the students did.

This time, the feeling of being watched was so intense that I turned to see if I were being followed. I was. There were five of , and they all were students, all seniors or juniors.

I turned fully around and slowly walked backwards keeping my eyes on them. They almost immediately stopped. The one who was clearly the leader spoke, "Well, if it isn't the Queen of the Toilets."

I immediately knelt without taking my eyes off the group. One smart-alec commented that I seemed to be putting myself in position to service them in some indecent way. I didn't say anything. Instead, I rapidly and expertly drew my knife from my calf sheath. I stood and began walking determinedly toward the leader.

The other four walked around me, forming a rough circle. I can't understand how, but somehow, I was sure that I could follow their movements without seeing them.

I didn't change my pace at all. The leader backed a pace or two and said, "Wait. We haven't done anything to you."

I continued my slow walk toward him. I sensed one of the gang approaching me from behind. I turned my head rapidly and said, "Boo!"

He was startled back a pace. The leader who'd backed off another pace or two went on, "Do you know who we are?"

I said without hesitation, "Crips." I emphasized the slight difference between the name as they pronounced it and the common slang for the disabled. I didn't stop walking.

I had been staring intensely at him the whole time. I hope that he got the idea that he would be the first to go down in the event of a fight and maybe that I was about to start that fight myself on my own terms.

He said, "We don't have to have a Rumble here."

I belligerently asked, "Why not?" I still came forward.

"I might want you in my gang."

"I'm sure you would."

"You'd make a good soldier."

I laughed at that.

He came back, "I mean Lieutenant." Meanwhile the kid beside him sharply turned on him but the leader silenced him with a motion of his left hand.

I kept walking. I noticed that the leader's expression relaxed a bit, and I realized that another gang member was approaching from the left. I looked over my left shoulder and stuck out my tongue at him. I could see that it had startled him even as I turned my head back to the leader.

The leader tried one last ploy, "Do a truce?"

I nodded slowly. I sensed one of them approach directly from my back. I went to the ground and swept my right leg around, catching his leg and knocking him over backwards. I was immediately up, and my knife was ready for action. No one did anything.

I quickly scanned around to assess exactly where everyone was and said, "A truce it is. My turf is the school. You can have the rest." I stared directly at the leader with a ferocity that I'd never felt before. He actually cringed back instinctively. I went on, "If the truce doesn't hold, I won't be rumbling."

The leader seemed to understand. I added, "And, don't think you can catch me with my guard down. I know that you've been watching me— where, and when."

He actually bought that load of crap.

He just shook his head.

I nodded and turned my back on him. Walking the rest of the way to the bus stop without looking back was probably the bravest thing that I'd ever done. Of course, I'd never done a lot of brave things in my life.

Somehow, I was sure that I wasn't being watched or followed. I had the idea that I would know if I were. That was the spookiest thing of that day.

I missed my normal bus and so got home later than usual. When I walked into our efficiency apartment, there was no meal on the table. I was pretty sure that Mum and Dad hadn't eaten, so what was going on?

Dad was beaming. Mum didn't look all that happy. Dad explained. "We're going out to dinner tonight. We have good news."

Mum said, "Well, your Dad calls it good news."

Dad went on, pleased as punch, "We've got an interview for that caretaker job!"

I had to think a minute to realize what he was talking about. Then I remembered about the help wanted advert. "Of course," I mused to myself, "Dad actually applied for that."

But for now, everyone was pretty happy to be going out to dinner to celebrate. We went to a small Italian restaurant near our efficiency. We'd eaten there once before. As a matter of fact, it had been our only meal out since we'd moved into the efficiency.

The restaurant had no gourmet treats. It was simple, wholesome, and good food. One of their specialties was serving the meal family style if all at the table agreed to the same dishes. We ordered that way. We had minestrone soup, cheese lasagna, and a Caesar salad. Each was served in a large dish. We helped ourselves to them at will. They were all served at the same time. I suppose the salad, minestrone, and even the lasagna was made in advance.

The meal was not as elaborate or maybe even as good as many of the meals that we'd eaten on our exile. It was certainly not as good as any meal we ate on the cruise liner. It was probably not even as good as the meal that we had with the captain of the freighter or the diner car meal on the train. To us that night, it was food of the gods. We'd not eaten out in weeks and this Italian restaurant did serve good food and plenty of it.

We all went home satisfied and slept well that night despite what was coming the next day—even Mum.

The next day our appointment was downtown with someone whose office was in the fourteenth floor of an office building. It turned out to occupy the entire 14th floor and even the floor below it. We had to sign in at the Reception Desk on the Main Floor because most of the offices were closed on Saturday. We were expected.

We had taken a cab to the address because we didn't want any chance of a problem getting there on time.

The whole floor was occupied by the office of "Rubinek, Tertovsky, and Floyd, Property Management, LLC." There was a Reception Desk just outside the elevator. No one was sitting there, but there was a sign-in sheet. On it was a list of appointments, the office number, and the name of the person occupying the office. Our appointment was with Tom Enigma. I commented about the strange name.

Dad replied, "Oh, I don't think Tom is such a strange name." He was in that good a mood. Mum wasn't. We found the office and knocked on the door. We were about ten minutes early. There hadn't been an appointment for Enigma before ours. Indeed, when he asked us in through the door, we found the room was empty besides him.

He motioned us to chairs. Three were drawn up close to the desk, two yellow, and one red leather. Dad got the leather chair. When we were seated, he invited us to have coffee, tea, or water. I took water. Dad and Mum took tea. Our host had coffee. There was an insulated carafe of hot coffee and one of hot water for tea. There were half a dozen bottles of filtered water and a small ice chest with ice. There were insulated Styrofoam cups for any of the beverages.

We settled again. Enigma opened a drawer of his desk and drew out four pocket folders. He gave each of us one and kept one for himself. Then he began.

"First, I should tell you about our business because you will technically be employees of this company even though you would be hired to be caretakers for one of the properties of our client.

"This is a company that spans Canada. We have offices similar to this in Montreal, Toronto, Edmonton, and now just opened in Windsor as well as here. We manage property of all sorts, including the building we're in, all the way down to small resorts. We think we are the premier property management company of Canada.

"Now let me tell you something about the resort itself. Please open your folder and get the brochure out." He modeled that action, holding the brochure up so that we could see the front of his as well as ours. The cover of the brochure had a photo of the sort you see on Telly adverts a good bit when they're advertising resorts. You could see that the view was from a wide veranda of a building that looked out on a peaceful lake at sunset. There were a few red clouds on the horizon. There was a large boat dock with several boats tied up to it on the lake. The only text that I took in was the name of the resort, Ludlow Fishing Resort.

Enigma was smiling broadly as he turned pages and recited from memory what the interior pages reported, "Ludlow Fishing Resort is a luxury fishing resort near the boarder of northern Manitoba and northwest Ontario.

"It is renowned for its spectacular lakes and streams. Whether your bent lies toward course fishing with fly and tackle, or boat fishing or fishing from the shore, you will find the delights of taking your limit in the week that you are at Ludlow are unexcelled elsewhere.

"The accommodations range from four star in the Lodge to rustic or even primitive in the dozen cabins that all front on the main lake." Here Enigma stopped to point on the photo on the front and said, "You can't see the cabins well in this photo, but you can see the boat dock in front of each cabin."

Then he went on with the sales pitch. "But you don't have to touch a fishing rod to thoroughly enjoy your vacation at Ludlows. There are scenic views in front of very window. There are dozens of miles of hiking trails. You can canoe through the lakes and streams.

"In addition, the resort is always host to interesting people. There are card tournaments, nature talks, and of course, 400 channel cable TV for those who insist on keeping up with events in the 'real' world."

"At Ludlows you can be cut off from all the troubles and cares of your everyday life. There is no phone service or cell phone towers, but for those who absolutely have to be in touch with home, there are satellite phones available."

Enigma had paused, and I said, "I bet most of those things don't go on during the winter."

Enigma wasn't in the least phased, "Quite right. Let me tell you what the duties of the caretaker are."

Mum wasn't buying so far. She asked, "Aren't you going to ask us about our qualifications first?"

"No, ma'am, I save that for the end. You see, most people decide this job is not for them after hearing about the duties and responsibilities."

Dad said, "Go ahead."

"Well, first, let me describe what the brochures don't tell you unless you read them thoroughly. The resort is more than 100 miles from the nearest road and more like 200 miles from the nearest hospital."

Mum interrupted, "How do people get there. And more important how do they get out."

Enigma nodded, "Yes. During the tourist season there are two ways to get in—seaplane that can land on the lakes while they're liquid. The other is helicopter. In the winter, there are also two ways—helicopter and snowmobile."

Mum commented, "It's sounding more and more like the Stanley Hotel."

Enigma took it in stride, "I see you've read Stephen King's novel."

Mum shook her head. Enigma returned, "Or seen the movie. By the way, I prefer the original Stanley Kubrick version."

Mum shook her head again.

"Well, however you learned about it, this is not the Stanley Hotel. There are no ghosts. No one has died at the Lodge either during the tourist season or during the winter."

Mum was like a dog that would not give up worrying its bone, "Well, why are you recruiting here so far from the Lodge? Can't you find anyone locally to take the job?"

Enigma showed a little impatience, "Ma'am, let me finish telling you about it, and you'll see why it is difficult recruiting for this job."

He went on. "So, you have to fly in. Ideally that would be at the end of October, but frequently, the lake is not ice-covered until sometime in November.

"The Lodge has electric power, but not from the power grid. It has two gasoline powered generators. One is sufficient to power the grounds but the second is a backup. Heat is supplied by an oil furnace forced air system in the Lodge. The cabins are of two sorts—primitive and rustic. The primitive don't need to be heated in the winter. They have no electrical systems or showers or even toilets. They are low maintenance.

"The rustic cabins are rustic in name only. They have all the comforts of home—electric power, central heating, satellite TV, and so forth. They have showers, hot water, etc. They have to be kept warm—not hot—say 55 degrees Fahrenheit. There are half a dozen of them as well.

"The Lodge has a dozen luxurious rooms for guests and as many simple rooms for the staff. The Lodge has to be kept warmer, because you'll be living there—IF, of course, you get the job.

"In the winter, the temperatures stay below freezing from October until the end of March. The lakes are frozen from early to mid November through early April. At least one electric generator has to be kept running almost continuously so that the oil-fired furnace and the electric blower keep running and keep the Lodge heated. Of course, it's important to have light and warm water and keep the refrigerators running.

"So, you see that it's important for you to be able to keep gasoline engines running. Can you do that?"

Dad then revealed something of which I never had the slightest clue. He said, "When I was a youth, I owned a Harley. I maintained it myself, including tuning and the occasional ring job."

Enigma nodded and smiled. "Sounds good. The caretaker has to repair other things as well. Windows break, wiring sometimes breaks, small fires start. By the way, fires are the greatest danger during the winter. Smoke detectors have to be kept working."

Mum asked, "What about the furnace, can't that break?"

"In theory yes. But in practice, it's very reliable. We have it inspected in October every year, and every least problem is fixed. The furnace has never failed for the fifty plus years that the Lodge has been in existence."

Mum persisted, "Well, let's just say that the furnace fails this one winter."

Dad added, "Or something else happens."

Enigma said, "There are three satellite phones at the lodge. All are checked when you arrive. They are battery powered. There are battery powered chargers that are continuously kept charged. If something happens that you can't handle, you call the emergency number. It's always monitored. A helicopter will be dispatched to you within 24 hours—basically at the next sunrise.

"But, here's a question about your ability to do this job."

He stood up and crossed the room for more coffee. "OK. Suppose that you hit this situation. It's in January, the temperature is 35 below zero. The furnace breaks down—nothing you can fix. What do you do?"

Dad scratched his chin, "Well, I get on the satellite phone right away and ask for evac."

Enigma nodded, "It's going to get really cold in the Lodge soon. And then, you . . ."

Dad thought a minute. "I get wood off the woodpile and start a fire in the Lodge's fireplace."

Enigma nodded again, "There's not much firewood on the pile. And then, you . . ."

Dad was getting the hang of this, "I get the chainsaw out of the shed and cut down a pine tree. I use the pine cones and small branches as kindling."

Enigma smiled. "Do you still want to be caretakers?"

Amazingly, Mum didn't say anything. Dad said, "We'll think about it. How much time do we have?"

Enigma smiled again, "I haven't offered the job to you yet. You're not the only applicant. By the way, don't you want to know how much we're paying?"

Mum was the one to ask, "Sure? How much per hour?"

"Well, it's an all or nothing job. We're paying 100,000 dollars Canadian."

Mum was struck dumb. Dad looked as cool as a cucumber. I tried to keep my cool, too.

Enigma was going on to add that, of course, room and board were provided. We'd get complementary satellite Telly. We'd be allowed to make satellite phone calls—an hour apiece each week. I laughed to myself about that. How many people would we call? We were hoping that no one in the world believed that we were alive. Just whom would we call?

The answer was that we had very few people that we really were close to. Mum's Mum and Dad had died a number of years ago. Her only sister, Lilly, whom she almost never talked about had died not long after Harry, my cousin, was born. Harry's Dad had died about the same time. Dad's sister, aunt Marge, was the one person that I could think of that we'd probably call, but even telling her that we were alive would be dangerous for her and for us.

Enigma talked about the recreation opportunities that we'd have. We could go snowmobiling on the snowmobiles that the Lodge had. We could go ice fishing. There were skis for cross-country skiing. We could enjoy the rec-room with its championship quality pool table and ping pong. I laughed to myself again. I'd never even heard of snowmobiles before we'd arrived in Canada, and I'd probably not have heard about them if we didn't sometimes watch the telly.

Dad asked, "Do you have any hunting equipment—you know, like rifles, shotguns?"

Enigma was not particularly surprised, but his answer was a bit scary, in a way. "There won't be hunting equipment or weapons at the Lodge. You should have no need for them."

160

Then, he mentioned that the resort had a fully equipped Exercise Room.

Enigma told us that he'd get in touch when they'd decided on a candidate. Then, we could still refuse if we wanted to.

We went back home. The rest of the weekend was a letdown after coming so close. On Sunday we played our old game of looking for weird job adverts, but our hearts weren't in it really.

The week went on as usual. We went to work and had meals and slept. I kept my head on straight as I went to and from work. Mum complained about the customers who threw around quarter tips as though they were manhole covers. By the next week we had thrown the idea of going to northern Canada out with the rotten tomatoes. We were sitting around the dinner table one night, and I asked Dad, "Why did you want to take this job anyway?"

Mum agreed that it seemed like a crazy idea.

He chuckled, "Can you think of a better place to hide from the Deatheaters?"

"Do you think that they still have a chance of catching up with us?" Mum asked.

"I wouldn't put it past them."

So, it was a real surprise when the next night, the phone rang in our efficiency. That phone never rang, and we were happy about that. Mum picked it up.

The side of the conversation that we could hear was brief and didn't do us any good. She said, "Yes. . . I think so, I'll have to talk with the boys. . . We'll give you a call tomorrow."

I asked, "Well, give. What is it?"

She could be exasperating when she was feeling playful, "Guess."

Dad said, "They don't want you to come into work tomorrow?"

She laughed, "You can do better than that."

I guessed it, "It was Enigma. They're offering us the job?"

"Bingo."

That forced us to think hard. Did we really want the job? Mum had promised them a decision by tomorrow, so we had a hard talk. We sat around the dinner table and gave the advantages and disadvantages one at a time. We came up with the usual ones that you can think of.

It's a dangerous job. The pay is great. We could go stir crazy. We could go blind from staring at nothing but snow for six months in a row. The Deatheaters would never find us there. It would be an adventure we'd never forget. It would get us out of our ho-hum jobs.

In the end, we drew straws. Dad broke two straws. One piece was long. One was short. He put them in his hands and spun them by rubbing his hands together until no one knew which was which. Dad wanted Mum to draw the straw. She refused. He tried to cajole her, threaten her, but she wouldn't. I had to draw the straw. It was long. That meant that we would not take the job.

We all looked from one to the other. The disappointment was evident in both Mum and Dad's faces. I suppose it must have been in mine as well. That was what finally persuaded us. Having a decision made it clear to us what we really wanted. As scared as we were of such a big leap into the unknown, we really wanted to do it.

There was lots to do before we could leave. Dad, Mum, and I all had to submit our resignations. It was not easy for me. I'd never had a job before and now, after only a few weeks, I'd have to leave it. I got advice from Dad. He helped me write a letter of resignation. I said that a better position had come up. I had to ask to be let go early because I couldn't give the school two weeks notice.

I took the letter in the morning to the Principle's Office. I couldn't quite get up the courage to hand it to him in person, so I left it with his personal assistant. She glanced at the envelope and immediately figured it out. "You're leaving, aren't you?"

I figured that I could get out of the office before anyone knew. I figured wrong. "Yes, I am."

She asked me why. I was honest, "I got a better job."

She sighed. "I think Mr. Roberts actually liked you."

Then I went looking for the head janitor. He was especially hard to find. He was in the auditorium up in the Sound and Lighting Room. I don't know what he was doing, but he was sitting on a chair with his feet up on the sound board up there. When I opened the door, he came to his feet like a scalded cat.

When he saw who it was, he relaxed. "Oh, it's you. What do you want?"

I didn't say anything for a minute. Then, somehow he figured it out, "You're leaving aren't you?"

I nodded.

"Well, I suppose it was inevitable. You're way too good to stay here long. No graffiti; clean restrooms. It was like magic."

I gulped at that. He noticed. He gave me a queer look and asked, "It wasn't magic was it?"

I gave him a reproachful look and said, "You've got to be kidding me."

He nodded. Then he held out his hand, "Well, wherever you go, I wish you good luck."

I thanked him and told him that I'd work the rest of the day. But in the end, I couldn't keep that promise. The principle sent for me at lunch. When I got to his office, he was in his outer office. He told his assistant, "I'm going to take a long lunch. Things can wait until I get back."

We went to a Chinese restaurant, and he actually tried to convince me to stay. He offered me a promotion. I could take my old boss's job.

I couldn't believe it, and I told him so. "I wouldn't do that. He's the best boss I've ever had. You need to keep him." Of course, he was the only boss I'd ever had, and I suppose Roberts knew that because he laughed.

"Well, Dursley, I thought we had the gang problem here licked, and now you're gone. It's back to the bad old days without you."

I agreed with him and wished him good luck. When we were done, he sent me to Personnel, where I filled out some paperwork and turned in my ID and my keys. Then, I was done.

I took a final walk around the halls on my way out of the building. It took a lot longer than I thought it would, but I was out of the building for the last time before school let out. I didn't look back as I walked for the bus stop.

The next day, Mum and I had quit, but Dad still hadn't. It's hard to make that kind of a change. It's hard to go into your boss and say that you're leaving, but he did his part, and we were free.

We still had quite a lot to do. We went into the management company's office and filled out forms. We kept the bank account in Vancouver to accept our money.

We got a list of things that we'd need for the job. Mostly it was clothes. We needed at least one serious parka and a lesser coat that I would have considered serious back in England. We needed insulated work boots and sweaters and warm socks. We needed gloves. They sent us to an outfitters for most of the things.

They also challenged us to think about all the things that we need for everyday life for six months. The basic necessities were provided by the Lodge. There would be food, water, laundry detergent. But there wouldn't be soap, shampoo, razor blades, special foods that we liked, deodorant, cologne, and so on and so on.

This was getting to be a rather expensive job–at least to start.

And then there would have to be an extra suitcase for each of us to carry these things. We assembled everything from the lists of absolute necessities that we'd gotten and of nice-to-haves. In addition, we got a few extra things. Mum likes to read, so she bought several books. Dad couldn't think of anything beyond the lists that he wanted.

I had a hard time. I had a handheld video game system and a few video games for it. I puzzled whether I should buy a few extra games that I had wanted over the years to have. And in thinking about what I would get, I realized that I had changed. I hadn't picked up that game system in weeks. I hadn't even thought about it. Would I really need those games to while away the inevitable long hours when we didn't have work, when it was too awful outside to go out, and when we were bored with the telly.

I reached deep into my suitcase to find the game system. It was a hard decision, but I solved that question. I took a coin out of my pocket, flipped it, and called it in the air. Heads, I'd take the system, and tails, I'd not.

It came up tails. The rush of relief that ran through my body was amazing to me. I really didn't want to take it. I picked it up and was about to throw it in the trash when I had a different idea. I walked down to the lobby of our hotel. I walked up to the desk and asked the lady there, "It's getting close to Christmas. Does the Salvation Army or someone collect used toys for kids?"

She smiled, "Sure."

"Would you mind throwing this in when they come around?"

She seemed puzzled. I answered her unasked question, "I won't be around to do it myself."

That seemed to shock her a little, so I said, "Don't worry, I don't think anything drastic is going to happen. I just want to do this before I forget it."

She agreed to.

The one point of contention came up when we were planning to travel to Manitoba where we would catch the sea-plane that would take us to the resort. The management company assumed that we would be taking a flight and wanted to buy the tickets. We wanted to go by train.

We almost had a battle over it. They couldn't understand why we didn't want to fly. We had reasons. We had good reasons. None of them were true, of course.

Mum was afraid of flying. That's why we'd taken a boat to the US. Dad wanted to see the Canadian Rockies from a train. He'd read about that. I loved traveling by train. Then, thinking of Harry, I made up a real whopper. "I went to a public school and always traveled there by train. I loved that train trip. It was the last freedom before school started, and it was the beginning of summer holiday. I really want to go by train."

Of course, the real reason was that we could travel anonymously that way. We won the battle, but we had to pay for the tickets ourselves, which was just fine with us!

We just managed to get everything together and ready to go in time to catch the Thursday transcontinental. It left in the early evening. We had to lose a week's worth of rent, but that was OK. It was far less than the fare to Winnipeg.

I couldn't believe that we had managed to get everything packed in the two suitcases apiece that we had. Of course, we had to wear our heavy parkas to make room for everything else. We must have made an odd sight boarding the train, dressed for the sub-arctic while the temperature in Vancouver was still in the low fifties during the day. We had a sleeper but between the three of us and our luggage that we felt that we couldn't trust to the baggage car, it was a pretty crowded compartment. Of course, we spent a lot of our time out of the cabin. But that first night, we went to bed shortly after the train left.

I walked the entire length of the train to get an idea of what we had available to us. The very last car had a sort of observation deck at the end. I stood there watching the miles disappear behind us. Every mile made me feel a little bit safer, a little bit farther from danger. It was a clear night, and the stars burned coolly in the sky. When I walked back along the train to our cabin, re-entering the warm, lighted interior of the train, I felt more comfortable than I had since our sailing days. I realized that while we were in motion, traveling, I always felt safer, and in truth, I think we were safer. When we were stationary, we felt to me like a sitting target waiting for some marksman to place us in the cross-hairs of his gun sight.

That night I slept well, warm, safe, with the clacking of the rails to comfort me.

We were up and moving at a lazy 8 AM. There was a diner car. We found that most of the people who were going to breakfast in it already had. We had a leisurely but simple breakfast and watched the miles of mountains and valleys disappear toward the rear. The rest of the day, we rolled through the seemingly endless mountains. They were snow-capped and remote. I sometimes wondered if the Ludlow Lodge would be as barren and cold as they in winter.

The second night I slept as soundly as I ever did. We had breakfast the second time in the diner. It was almost beginning to seem normal. We had lunch and dinner in the train stations along the way.

It was more boring crossing the great plains of western Canada on the second day, but we still felt time passing far too quickly.

Almost exactly two days after leaving Vancouver, we arrived in Winnipeg. It was late at night and dark. We put together our luggage an hour before arriving. We were ready to leave the cabin the moment the train was completely stopped. I stood at the door. When the train stopped, I opened the door, stepped half-way out of the cabin and froze in place.

Dad bumped into me from behind. I pushed back in and closed the door from behind. I put my finger to my lips and whispered, "Quiet."

Dad whispered, "What is it?"

"I think there is a Deatheater in the corridor."

Dad's face went pale, and he asked, "How?"

I just shook my head. I went to the window and drew the curtains. Time passed. I looked up and down the corridor. The original Deatheater had disappeared but there was another there that I suspected. I pulled back in and shook my head.

Dad whispered, "We have to get off soon. They're boarding passengers."

I nodded and thought. There was a knock on the door. We all shuddered. The knock was repeated. I had no choice. I opened it.

There was an elderly couple there with a porter. He said, "I'm sorry old man, I think this is our compartment."

I opened my mouth to say something, but I could find nothing to say. Dad stepped into the breach and said, "I'm sorry, we've not quite got our things ready to go. Would you please give us a couple of minutes."

The old man said, "No problem. No problem."

I closed the door and Mum looked out from behind the curtain. "I don't think there's anyone out there." I pushed past her and looked my self.

I agreed. "Let's go. Quickly."

I opened the door, and we quickly left the compartment. Dad gave the old couple our sincere apologies while Mum and I walked as quickly as we could to the exit. I stuck my head out. All was still clear. Dad had caught up with us. We walked out, and I suddenly had a sense that someone was looking for me. I took Mum's hand and said to both Mum and Dad, "We've got to hide. Follow me."

I led them behind a wall. There I felt safe from eyes. I breathed a sigh of relief as the train pulled away from the station. Somehow I was sure that the Deatheaters were on the train.

It was late Saturday night, and we considered ourselves lucky to already have reservations at the Charter House hotel that was nearby. We could almost have walked there, but it was late, and we were tired. We took a cab.

The next morning, Sunday, we had on our own. Monday, we would be picked up at the hotel and taken to the general aviation airport where we would fly to Ludlow Lodge.

That Sunday, we tried to find something to do, but we ended up being stuck with walking downtown Winnipeg and looking for restaurants where we could eat lunch and dinner.

Ludlow Fishing Resort

We were waiting at the curbside at 8:30 AM when a black SUV drove up, and a man got out of the back. He asked Dad, "Mr. Dursley?"

"Yes. Are you here to pick us up."

A nod, and we were loading our bags into the back of the SUV. It was a quick drive to the airport. We all were beginning to get cold feet, and I was not excited about getting into a small plane that had big floats instead of wheels.

We loaded our luggage into the cargo hold of the seaplane. Mum and Dad sat in the back. I sat up in the cockpit with the pilot. He'd offered me to either fly in the passenger compartment or the cockpit. I'd chosen the cockpit.

Of course, I'd flown in airplanes before, but I was in for a big surprise when the plane took off. We rose into the air so fast that I couldn't see the ground—only the blue sky. I was afraid that I would lose my stomach somewhere on the way up to the point where the ground was too far away to pick out individual people.

We flew over a lake so large that for a short while I couldn't see any shoreline. I knew that our lake couldn't be that one. As a matter of fact, we flew on for quite a long time. I'd gotten bored of watching endless miles of small and large lakes pass under us. As a matter of fact, when the bottom dropped out of my stomach, and we started a steep drop, I had forgotten that I had been trying to guess which lake was ours.

As the lake came closer and closer, and our speed seemed to be way too fast to land without flipping the plane over, I began to wonder if I was going to survive the day. The thought of having come all this way and avoided the Deatheaters so long only to be killed by a crazy pilot seemed too, too funny.

We landed. We touched down. We didn't flip. The speed dropped off quickly, and the pilot used the engine to direct us to what looked like a very large log cabin. As we got closer, it became clear that everything was larger than it appeared from the air. The "log cabin" was actually a three story building with balconies on the second and third floor. The lake was a lot bigger than I thought at first.

The seaplane pulled up beside the main dock in front of the Lodge. I opened the door on my side of the plane, and I stepped down on the pontoon and from there to the dock. There was a portable set of stairs that someone on the ground rolled up to the passenger compartment. He walked up the few steps and opened the door. Mum and Dad came out. Dad was carrying a couple of suitcases. I climbed up into the passenger cabin and took several more in hand. Mum got the last one.

With the help of the ground crew, we managed to carry all of the luggage up to the cabin in one trip. When we entered the Lodge, we found another man behind the front desk. He had a book turned around to face us. It was the guest register. He asked us to sign it. We did.

It turned out that the man behind the desk was the representative of the property management company—the closest we were going to get to the owner of the Lodge. His name was Bishop. He invited us to choose a room to stay in. We could take our pick of all of them. We picked one that had a view out over the lake and had a door that opened on the balcony on the second floor.

He suggested that we take our luggage up to the room and that we come down at 1 PM for a late lunch. Of course, it was more than a suggestion.

We came down to a lunch that was delivered in the dinning room. It could have seated more than one hundred, but today, there were a couple of tables put together to seat the eight of us.

Going around the table to my left was Stoddard, the pilot who had flown us up here. Then came Tarver who was an HVAC man. I later learned that HVAC meant Heating, Ventilating, Air Conditioning. He had come here to inspect, repair, and certify the heating plant before we took over the Lodge. I later considered him the most important of the group.

On around the table was Smithers who was the expert on gasoline engines, electricity, and all things run by electricity. Next to him was the plumber, Jones. He also was inspecting and repairing.

Finally, next to Dad was Bishop. He introduced everyone. There was one other person who didn't have a seat at the table. He was the cook. He was the only person of the group who actually worked at the Lodge during the summer. He was having lunch in the kitchen, I supposed.

Bishop laid out the plan for the next couple of days. It was to be a busy time. We were to receive a crash course in maintaining the Lodge and other buildings.

He began explaining the agenda, "This afternoon, you will spend with Tarver who is here to check out the furnace and ventilation systems in the

Lodge and the rustic cabins. He's really done, but he'll give you a detailed rundown of that."

Then Bishop introduced Smithers. We would spend the entire next day with him. "There are a large variety of gasoline engines employed in different ways at the Lodge. They too are very important to your survival. I understand that you have a good working knowledge of gasoline engines, Mr. Dursley?"

Dad's "yes" was much less confident than when he'd answered that question in the interview.

Then Bishop turned to Jones, the plumber. "Mr. Jones will go over the plumbing with you. He'll sit in at the end of Smithers' time because their areas of interest overlap, but he'll have you exclusively the day after tomorrow. After lunch tomorrow, the cook will give you a tour of his demesne.

"The property that you haven't already covered and emergency procedures is my area. We'll finish the next day, have lunch, and we'll fly back to Winnipeg that afternoon."

That gave us three days and nights with the experts until we were on our own. It seemed like a lot of time, but my experience with the school back in Vancouver made me wonder if it would be enough. It had taken me a while to learn all about janitoring that school.

We finished the meal without much more conversation. It was really quiet. We didn't feel like talking about things in front of strangers, and I suppose they didn't feel much more like it than we did. We might have made polite conversation as my Mum calls it, but we'd be having lots of conversation very shortly. Everyone seemed satisfied to complete the scrumptious lunch in silence. I'll have to say that the people who stayed at the Lodge ate well if this were any sign.

After lunch, we went off with the HVAC man. He took us into the basement of the Lodge. He showed us the furnace, explained how it worked on a simplified level and then gave us the important things to know about it. The most important things were what we could fix ourselves and what we couldn't. We could restart the pilot light. It wasn't like the pilot light in the gas stove at home. It was electronic. It basically came down to restarting the simple electronics that controlled it. You turned off the power, let it sit for sixty seconds, and then turned it back on. If it didn't start, we could try it a couple of more times. If that didn't work, then we'd have to bail, but he finished with the encouraging word that it was really reliable, he checked it, blah, blah, blah. . .

He showed us the pipe from the fuel tank that was buried in the ground just outside the Lodge. It had a valve. You had to make sure that the valve was open. Big surprise. As time went on, I learned that an awful lot of things were buried underground to protect them from the intense cold that sometimes struck here.

The next thing that he showed us was the exhaust. You had to be very careful to be sure that it didn't leak or get corroded. He'd just checked that, so we were OK.

Then there was the heat exchanger and the blower that forced the hot air throughout the Lodge. The blower was, of course, an electric motor and the electrician would talk with us more about that. However, he had some important points to make. The blower was controlled by the electronics. In an emergency, you could override that and just force it to blow all the time.

He took us up to our room and pointed out the thermostat. It controlled temperature in the room by controlling how much the vent into the room was open. As with the blower, you could override the control and force the vent to always be open or closed.

Then, he gave us a little quiz. We had to go back to the basement and stop and restart the electronic pilot light. I was a little uncertain, but Dad had picked it up right away.

Then we went to one of the rustic cabins. Rustic! He showed us the electric heaters buried in the baseboards of the rooms. That was it. I guess he figured he had to because it was the heater for the cabin, and he was the HVAC guy.

I asked him, "What about the primate cabins?"

He laughed. "Sure, let's go take a look." He then led us around the edge of the lake to those cabins. We came to the first one and went in. It was a much simpler design. It had one large room with a sofa, that turned out to be a fold-out. It had a table, chairs, and so forth. It had a fireplace. It didn't have running water or a lot of the other necessities that I assumed everyone had. Interestingly, it did have electricity, a refrigerator, lights, and, of all things, a TV. My surprise must have shown on my face. Then Tarver explained.

"This is for people who want to experience life on the frontier in the 1800's. Of course, they didn't have refrigerators or TV's."

After that quick tour of life on the frontier, we went back to the Lodge. It was by then dark. There were lampposts along the way that I'd not noticed before. I didn't see any wires, so they must have been buried.

We all met for dinner. There was more talk than before. My Mum and Dad and I had lots to talk about with nearly everyone around the table.

□

That night, we discovered just how luxurious the room we were in was. We'd not had time to explore it before. The bathroom was all tile except

170

for the counter that appeared to be marble. It had two sinks. The shower/tub had built-in non-slip coating. The shower head had more settings than I could believe. The "room" didn't have a bed. It had a large sofa, a tiny kitchenette area with refrigerator, microwave, sink and a counter with a couple of bar stools. There was a very large Telly. Between it and the sofa was a coffee table. It hit me then. The sofa was a fold-out. Where did I sleep?

Mum was examining the kitchenette when Dad opened a door to what I supposed would be a closet. He whistled and said, "Hello, hello, hello. What have we here?"

What we had there was a bedroom with a bed that was the largest that I'd ever seen. There was a door into what I again supposed to be a closet. I walked over to it and said, "I'll bet we've got a walk-in closet here–a big one."

I opened the door and was more surprised than Dad had been. There was a truly giant bed–larger than any I'd ever seen. And there was a good-sized Telly and another door leading off to what surely must be a walk-in closet. I commented, "I know who's this is going to be."

Dad surprised me though. He said, "No you don't. It's yours."

I was as surprised as I'd ever been, "But surely you want this."

He replied, "No I DO NOT. I want to be closer to the W.C. This is all yours."

Just to be sure, I walked over to the door and opened it. It led into a small loo. It had a commode, a sink, a mirror, a couple of small shelves for storage. "Wow!" I thought, "the best of both worlds."

We went to bed. I turned on the Telly in my room just to see what I could get. The on-screen channel guide seemed to have hundreds of channels. I searched around a little and found a BBC news channel. Of course, it was the very early morning over there. I listened for a little while and was truly discouraged. The number of unexplained deaths and unexplained disasters was awful. One of the most bizarre was a story about a small office building that had been the scene of some sort of battle between rival gangs. There was video of the interior that showed room after room the walls of which were riddled with bullet holes. There was even one large room that had seemed to have had a good-sized explosion happen in it. I turned the Telly off and tried to get some sleep.

The next day was a full day with Smithers. I had no idea there were so many gasoline powered engines lying about. There were very small tools with gasoline engines. We started in the large tool building and workshop. There were at least three or four chain saws. There were a couple of lawn mowers. There were three "weed-eaters". At least that was what I thought Smithers called them. There were four ice borers for cutting holes in the ice for ice fishing. There were three snowmobiles.

Smithers showed us them all and talked about the very small ones with two-stroke engines that needed a mixture of gas and oil to run properly. Dad knew about them, and I'd, at least, heard of them. All of the tools were that sort.

The snowmobiles were very much like Dad's old motorcycle. He'd not owned one in a long while, but he seemed to pick up on what Smithers had to say really quickly.

I asked an obvious question. "There's lots of cold weather stuff here. You don't expect us to use much of it. Why are there so many snowmobiles?"

Smithers laughed, "Not for you. That's for sure. The owner likes to bring folks up here in the winter for some sports. They fly up by helicopter and the caretakers put them up and provide rooms and meals and so forth. They usually don't stay more than a week and lately he doesn't do it much."

Mum's mouth formed a large "O". Smithers said, "Didn't they tell you about those excursions? Well, don't worry. I don't expect them up this year."

Dad asked another question, "Well, one winter sport that I don't see any equipment for is hunting. Are there no rifles or shotguns?"

Smithers said, "You'll have to ask the man from management about that."

Dad nodded, and I knew from the set of his jaw that he intended to.

The finale of the tour and the thing that we spent the entire afternoon on was what Smithers called "Motor-Generators". There were two of them. They were housed in their own out-buildings. We went to one and got a thorough tour. These were large gasoline-powered motors. Instead of the drive shaft turning wheels like on a car, the drive shaft of these motors turned the armature of a generator. Gasoline was fed into the engine through a fuel line that went out of the building to a large storage tank that was flat to the ground.

Smithers told us about backups. "There's another motor generator in another building just like this one on the other side of the Lodge."

Dad started to ask if the same tank fed it. But Smithers interrupted him, "Another tank, just like that one. That way if some disaster happens–like a fire and explosion, you've got a second generator just waiting to go."

He then showed us the circuit breaker box at the Lodge where the power lines from both generators came together and could be switched.

He went on, "You've got to do basic maintenance on them. You change the oil on a regular basis, check the voltage output, check fluid levels, switch the output when you do that maintenance. You switch the circuit breaker off, turn off the engine that you're going to work on, start the other engine, switch its circuit breaker on, and then do maintenance on the first.

"You let the second engine run until its maintenance interval comes, and then you repeat."

Then he made us go through the entire drill. We did all those things. I thought we were going to miss supper, but we finished and were back indoors before the meal was over.

Smithers said that he'd done a tune-up of the engines and checked all the parts for wear. We weren't done for the day yet, though. He took us back to the generator building. Next to that building was a small shed. We got inside and found that it had a trap door that led down into a sort of basement. It was pretty small. There was an electric pump there. It provided water pressure for the Lodge and the "rustic" cabins.

The water came from a deep pipe that went well out into the lake. The water was very pure and didn't need treatment. The pipes were laid very deep so that there was no chance that they would freeze. They entered the buildings underground and never got anywhere near the surface. That was why it was important to keep the temperature well above freezing in all the cabins.

The plumber was along with us now. He claimed that the electric motors that pumped the water were extremely reliable and didn't need maintenance at all. Just in case, there was another pump house just like this one next to the other generator building.

We then went to one of the cabins. Smithers showed us the circuit breaker there and the major electric appliances. There was a water heater and, of course, the refrigerator, stove, oven, and electric heat. Except for electric heat and water heater the appliances were unimportant.

We got back to the Lodge happy to just fall in bed and instantly to sleep.

□□

The next day, our time was quick with the plumber. Almost all of the pipes were buried deep in the land or in the lake or in the walls. He just showed us the two water heaters in the Lodge and the access points for fixtures. I thought we might get the rest of the morning off when he finished, but he ended his tour in the kitchen. Our next tour began there as soon as the plumber finished. The cook first showed us with pride his kingdom. There was a walk-in refrigerator/freezer that I couldn't believe. You could have fed an army with what was stored there. Of course, it had to feed us for six months. Outside, he showed us the preparation tables, the grills, the ovens, and so forth.

His face became very stern when he finished the tour. "Now, I expect this place to be as spotless and clean as when I leave it with you. That is understood?" He didn't have much of an accent but I thought he might have been German. Anyway, he demonstrated some of the equipment by letting us watch him prepare lunch. We were having a salmon salad with freshly baked French bread. He took us to a section of the basement that was completely separate from the heating section. There was a wine cellar there. He pointed at a small section. "That's where we keep the house whites and reds. You may use those while I'm gone."

The meal was great, but he made us clean up afterwards. I think he wanted to be sure that we knew something about kitchens and cleanliness before he was finished.

Again, we finished ahead of schedule, and I was hoping for a little break. However, Bishop came to us shortly after we re-appeared from the kitchen.

He pretended to be surprised, but I'm sure that he expected us to be at least a little early. "We might as well get your tour with me on the way. Besides, if you were still with the cook when it got close to supper, he'd probably make you work."

This part of the tour was both easier than the rest but also a little scary. We walked into the Lodge manager's office. He had us sit in front of the desk while he sat behind it. He turned to bookshelves behind the desk and pulled out a large loose-leaf notebook. Then he said, "Before I show you this, please look at the other notebooks on the shelves. They contain the operation manuals for all the appliances and motors and pumps and so forth that we've got here. I don't think you'll need any of them, but just in case, there're there."

He then surprised me by getting up and walking over to a credenza on the side. On top of it were the three strangest telephones that I'd ever seen. He picked up the handset of one and said, "Each of these is a satellite phone. You can use them to call anywhere in the world. They're expensive to use, but you're authorized to use them for an hour each week to call whomever you like. If you use more time than that, we'll charge you.

"The cradles are the chargers. They can hold a charge for a week and will give you six hours of talk time per charge. Just keep them in the chargers whenever you're not using them. It's better to use them in this office, but of course, you might have to use them someplace else in case you need advice fixing something. Don't hesitate to use them for that. It won't be charged against your time."

He then handed the phone to Dad. "It works just like an ordinary cell phone. Go ahead and call someone. I want to make sure that you can use it."

This seemed to present a problem for Dad. I knew what it was. He didn't want to take a chance giving away our identity or location. It took a couple of minutes of thought but he placed a call. The end of the conversation that we heard was like this:

"Hello. This is Vernon Dursley." There was a lengthy pause. "Yes, I just wanted to know if I might get my job back when I return." There was another pause. "Sure. No problem. I'll keep in touch."

Dad returned it, but Bishop handed it to me. "Go yourself."

I hadn't expected that, but I had someone that I would have liked to call. I never got his phone number though. Instead I called the school. The Administrative Assistant answered. I told her that I wanted to speak with the janitor. She said that he wasn't available, but could she take a message. I answered, "No. Just tell him that an old friend called." I then hung up.

The phone went to Mum next. She should have expected it, but she apparently didn't. She refused to call anyone.

Bishop shrugged, "I guess two of you are enough, but I'd really recommend that you all be sure that you know how to use those phones. They're your only contact with the outside world. If something serious happened here, you'd need to use one of those."

Mum asked, "What do you mean, 'serious?'"

Bishop grimaced, "I'm glad you brought the topic up. I'll go through a few examples.

"Say that one of the motor-generators stops working. What do you do?"

Dad said, "I'd try to figure out what was wrong."

Bishop asked, "Is that the first thing you would do?"

It didn't take him long to answer, "No. I'd start the other generator."

Bishop pursued that, "What if you couldn't get it started?"

I said, "I'd use the phone to call . . ." I was stuck. I didn't know whom to call.

Bishop seemed pleased. "Yes, that's exactly right. That's what this notebook is for." He opened it and turned it so that it was facing us. "This book has all the problems that we can think of that could happen and what to do in case they do. The very first page has the two phone numbers that are emergency numbers for our management company.

"Also, they're on a label on the back of the satellite phones. There are sections in the notebook for each important system and things that might go wrong. The best responses for each is listed and what to do if that doesn't work. At the end of most of them is the final resort—use the satellite phone."

He riffled through the many pages. At the end he said, "Of course, we hope that you won't have to use the phone, but if you reach the point where you really feel stuck, use the phone.

"By the way, if you run into something that's not in the book, write up what you did and what you suggest doing so the next person can benefit by your intelligence." Then he closed the book.

Then we started a tour of the building. It was a large rambling structure. There were the real luxury suites at the front of the building on the upper floors. Below them were the common areas—lobby, lounge, dining room, and so forth. Behind the front rooms were the kitchen, the offices, and the staff's quarters. On wings to the left and right were additional rooms.

He began discussing normal day-to-day operations. "You've got schedules for maintenance things. Please stick to them. Of course, you will clean your own room and keep all the rooms clean and presentable. I'd like you to leave all the Guest Rooms except yours unopened—except for cleaning and inspections. Leave the common areas alone as well. The one exception would be the recreation room. You may use the pool table and ping pong tables and games. Just be respectful of them.

"Please eat meals either in the kitchen or your rooms. Of course, feel free to use the satellite TV. We have office computers but no internet access. Sorry. If we did, I wouldn't mind your using one to keep track of what's going on in the world, but we don't, so don't. You should be able to get all the news that you can stand from the satellite TV.

"Of course, as I said, you may use the satellite phone on a limited basis to keep in touch with your family and friends." Fat chance, I thought.

He showed us the fire extinguishers and smoke detectors. Keeping them maintained was one of the most important jobs in his view.

We finished in time for dinner.

Around the dinner table, the mood was varied. Everyone who was leaving the next day seemed in great spirits. We were not so much in good spirits. I think Mum, Dad, and I were just realizing that in less than twenty-four hours, we'd be here by ourselves. That was a sobering thought.

Bishop took up the topic of the schedule for the next day. "We seem to have finished a bit ahead of schedule. So, I think we'll dispense with lunch tomorrow. We'll have breakfast. If the Dursleys think of any last minute questions for us overnight, we'll handle them over breakfast, and if necessary, we'll go out and inspect things to answer questions. I think though that we'll not have any trouble getting off in time to arrive back in Winnipeg by noonish. Would you agree Stoddard?"

Stoddard rubbed his chin in thought. "Oh, I'd not want to promise anything, but if we get off fairly soon after breakfast, I'd say noon to one, depending."

That seemed to seal our fate. We'd hardly said two words during dinner. Now, we separated to our various rooms. With every step, it became clearer that this was indeed, "it." When I went to bed, I wished that I'd not go to sleep right away. I wanted to relish being in this huge Lodge with someone else in addition to Mum and Dad.

⬓

Somehow, I did fall asleep and sooner than I wanted to. Breakfast was superb. It was as though the cook wanted to have one last flourish before he left his sparkling, beautiful kitchen for the next six months.

There were eggs benedict, crepes, French toast, pancakes as light and fluffy as I'd had anywhere, freshly squeezed orange juice (how he managed that I had no idea), coffee, tea, muffins, and I don't know what all else.

I'd been wracking my brains trying to come up with some question to delay the dreaded moment when the plane would take off a few minutes later. Dad and Mum were both hemming and hawing. I'm sure they had the same thought in mind.

We helped with luggage down to the seaplane. There wasn't much of it, but we wanted any excuse to let us stay close to them as long as possible.

At the last minute, Dad did come up with a question. "Mr. Bishop, I just wanted to ask a question."

Bishop seemed a bit unhappy that he'd been delayed a few minutes. "Yes, what can I help you with?"

Dad asked, "There's lots of winter sports equipment here–fishing gear, skis, snowmobiles, and who knows what else."

Bishop impatiently asked, "Yes, and your question?"

"Well, I asked why no hunting gear–no rifles, no shotguns, nothing– why not? No one seemed to know why."

Bishop seemed to be relieved that it was an answer he could give quickly, "It's simple. The owners aren't hunters themselves—though they enjoy fishing, obviously. They actually don't like having weapons about. If a guest wants to bring a rifle or shotgun to do some hunting, he may, provided that he has a hunting license and can prove that he knows what he's doing."

Bishop turned, but he wasn't done yet. Dad asked, "One other thing then."

Bishop responded with a curt, "Yes?"

"Polar bears are dangerous and do live around here. How do we deal with them if one shows up?"

Bishop actually seemed relieved, "That's actually simple. You stay out of their way. You let them go wherever they want to.

177

"If you had a rifle or a shotgun, unless you were a good hunter, you'd probably just end up getting yourself killed or maimed." He actually seemed interested in this question, "There's a story—and I believe it—about a group of soldiers in Alaska being out on patrol in a jeep. They were armed with standard issue M-16's. That's a small caliber weapon, incidentally. They ran across a polar bear and tried to kill it. They only made it mad and it mauled them.

"Take my advice. Polar bears are like the proverbial eight hundred pound gorilla. What do you feed it for breakfast?" He paused.

Dad asked, "I don't know. What?"

Bishop laughed. It wasn't full of mirth. "Anything it wants." With that he whirled quickly and joined his companions who had already boarded the seaplane. As he entered, he shouted over his shoulder, "Good luck. See you in the Spring."

Mum just muttered, "I hope."

We stayed on the dock, watching the seaplane taxi out from the dock, accelerate, leap into the sky, and after banking, slowly disappear to the south.

As we stood there gazing off into the skies, Dad started to say something but hesitated. Then he said, "Do you know what today is?"

It had been a busy few days, getting ready to travel, then actually traveling to Winipeg, and finally reaching the Lodge. However, I'd not completely lost track of time. I said, "Sure, it's Saturday, so?"

Dad said, "No, I mean the day of the month."

That I had lost track of, but I knew that it was sometime late in October. I said so.

Dad corrected me, "It's the thirty-first of October."

Mum's mouth just formed a large "O" but she didn't say anything.

I said a single word, "Halloween."

Dad nodded and said, "Bad Karma."

Mum just nodded.

The Long Dark of Moriah

When it was thoroughly out of sight, we turned and headed back to the Lodge. We entered and Mum said, "Let's see what the cook left for us to clean up. The best way to get over the dumps is to get working."

She coaxed Dad and me into the kitchen. It was the worst that I'd ever seen a kitchen be. Mum commented, "I guess that the cook figures that busy hands are not bored."

The next couple of weeks were ones that proved that just because Ludlow's was about the same latitude as Newcastle, it didn't mean that they were at all alike. While this time of year in Newcastle would be cool—even cold, it wasn't anything remotely like the winter that settled in at Ludlows.

Before that happened, we had a couple of cold rainy days. On one of them, I was going out the front door of the Lodge on my way down to the nearest "rustic" cabin. I reached the edge of the porch and was about to step down when I slipped on a wet spot, my feet going out from under me. I went down like a load of bricks. I was lucky that I'd been turning because the door had just opened. I came down on my shoulder rather than my head. I don't know what would have happened if I'd come down on my head. After that, we were all very careful with those steps.

We hadn't seen the sunny side of freezing in many days AND there was lots of snow. I couldn't prove that the lake was frozen over or not. I knew the shoreline was frozen.

It was a chore just to get ready to go outside. We were so happy that we had the serious parkas from that outfitters that I actually began to look at that coat as my favorite clothes. Inside, we kept the temperature well into the seventies for a couple of weeks, but then as we got used to the cold, it just seemed better to have it a bit cooler. Going outside wasn't such a shock.

By the time Christmas arrived, we were in better spirits. We thought that we'd reached the worst of winter (surely it couldn't get colder). We celebrated by watching a marathon of Christmas movies from the satellite and playing games. The week between Christmas and New Years we watched the many Premier League games that happen then.

After the New Year, we had to get back to real work. Mum had been doing the cleaning and most of the cooking and seemed satisfied with that. Dad and I did the mechanical maintenance. We also helped cleanup from meals. We inspected all the cabins every other day or so—even the primitive ones.

One day, we decided that we should start the small gasoline engines. We went into the tool building, and when we saw the snowmobiles, we both had the same idea. I said it out loud, "Dad, do you think we can try out a snowmobile??"

He agreed, and we began working to set it up to run. Dad was sure that he should have no problems because of his motorcycle experience.

We got one of the snowmobiles out of the building and fueled it. After several unsuccessful tries to start it, Dad decided to adjust the choke. We eventually did get it going. Then we had the question. Who went first?

I ended up letting him have the first go. It turned out not to be bad driving it. The main problem was avoiding going too fast. We didn't have a lot of open space to practice on.

I had the idea that fixed that. I asked Dad, "Do you think the lake is frozen over?"

We agreed that it must be, but neither of us was anxious to try it out. We ended up driving the snowmobile out to the edge of the lake and edging on, always alert for cracks or other signs of unstable ice. Nothing happened. We ventured farther and farther out onto the ice. In the end, we decided the whole lake must be frozen solid.

After that, we did a lot of snowmobiling. It was Dad's and my favorite form of recreation. It was cold. If you were going above 20 MPH, the wind chill was something fierce—even in our serious winter gear. We eventually drove pretty far away from the Lodge. It drove Mum crazy to see us drive out beyond her sight.

The limiting factor was the amount of daylight we had. With fewer than five hours a day, you couldn't do a lot of snowmobiling and get your work done too.

Coming from England, we were used to short daylight in the winter, but it didn't make us any happier none the less.

One day in late January, we had decided to find the next lake to the west. We had found maps and had decided to explore as much of the Ludlow property on snowmobiles as we could.

That day, we sort of overextended ourselves. The route to the lake was rougher than it looked on the map, and we took a wrong turn once or twice. We did reach the lake though. At least we thought we had. It was covered with ice and a lot of snow. Was it really a lake or just a large clearing? Anyway, we were obviously getting pretty late in the day, so we turned back and went as quickly as we could manage. Before we'd gotten half-way back, we both knew that we'd not get there before sunset.

We knew that the snowmobiles had headlights, but we sure wanted to have sunlight to navigate by. The sun had just set, but there was still a fair amount of light in the sky when we reached a point that we were sure that we recognized. I was sure that we could navigate from there by headlight.

Still the light was completely gone from the sky when we reached the last rise before home. We pulled up to the top of the ridge. I was leading. I stopped to get a good look at the Lodge before going on.

As I watched, it seemed that there was something wrong. There was nothing that I could immediately identify. Dad, behind me, shouted, "What's the problem?"

I answered in an urgent but low voice. "There's something wrong. Turn off your motor."

He did and got off. He came up beside me and asked, "What is it."

"I'm not sure. But I know there's something funny."

Dad stared along with me. He had brought along a pair of binoculars from the tool building. He scanned the area around the Lodge. Then I realized what it was. "Dad, do you see smoke coming out the chimney?"

He said, "Sure, but . . ." Then it hit him. We never had a fire in the fireplace. "Do you suppose your Mum lit that fire?"

"I don't think so."

"Yeh, I agree." Then he gasped. "I just saw someone walk across one of the windows in the front of the Lodge. I'm sure it wasn't your Mum."

My heart had been racing, and now it felt like the snowmobile engine that I'd just been riding, "What do we do?"

Dad scanned the area around the Lodge. "I don't see a helicopter. And I'm sure that we'd have heard it if it had flown anywhere near where we were. Who in the world. . ."

At that moment, we both knew who it had to be. "Deatheaters."

Dad cursed, "Bloody Hell. What can we do?"

I asked, "How much longer do you think we can stay out here unprotected?" I was getting seriously cold already now that we weren't sitting on a hot snowmobile engine.

Dad's answer was, "Let's go into one of the motor-generator buildings and think."

I couldn't think of anything better, so we left the snowmobiles and walked as quietly as we could down the slight slope toward the Lodge. We stayed on the edge of stands of trees as much as we could. After a long, slow, cold slog, we reached the building.

Inside, at least, it was warm, and we had light. The building didn't have windows, so we weren't too worried about using the light.

I asked Dad what his plan was. He just said, "Don't have one yet. You have any ideas?"

I just shook my head. We sat and thought. Gradually little half-formed ideas came to mind. We mentioned them and put them aside as we thought. There were a few things that kept coming up. Turn off the power to the Lodge. Without light or heat, the Deatheaters would not find it so appetizing waiting us out.

We didn't know what they knew, but they could probably get Mum to pretty easily tell them what she knew. Fortunately, it wasn't very much. We went out exploring. We hadn't returned. We never returned after dark. What they would do with that information we didn't know.

Another idea was that we should get them out in the dark and cold. We knew the ground around the Lodge like the backs of our hand. They didn't —we hoped.

We didn't have weapons other than hammers and shovels and tools. Could we use them somehow?

Dad had an idea that seemed pretty good, "If we could get to one of those satellite phones, we could call for help."

I thought about it for a bit then spoke, "Well, there's a couple of difficulties, but the really killing one is this. What kind of help do we call for?"

Dad grimaced, "Yeh, I was just thinking about that. If we say that we have terrorists who've taken over the Lodge, please send the Royal Canadian Mounted Police—well, what would they do?"

I nodded, "Yeh, they'd think that we had gone crackerbox. What do you call it in the winter?"

"Yeh, Cabin Fever."

"Right. So they send a doctors and nurses. Maybe they evacuate us and maybe not."

Then a thought occurred to me. "Do you remember when I slipped on the front porch?"

Dad nodded with a smile, "Sure, I do. You nearly brained yourself. It turned out OK, but for a minute, I was scared to death that we'd be taking you out in a body bag."

"Yeh. Me too. This might be the time to take somebody out in a body bag."

Dad frowned at that, "There's a couple of problems. Like how do we get them to hit just the right spot on that porch with the slick board?"

An answer hit me, "Maybe we don't have to. If we spread water over the porch, what would happen?"

Dad nodded, "It would freeze and be as slippery as Hell. What do the Canadians up here call it at night? Black ice?"

"You bet. Then we just have to lure them out."

Dad said, "The tough part might be keeping them from coming out until we're ready. You know, the hill goes straight down from the porch. If there was a path of black ice from the porch straight down to the lake, they might break through the ice, and that could be it."

I shook my head. "That ice is as thick as the deck of the dock. It'd never break through."

"Unless we helped it." Dad was rubbing his hands together, and it wasn't just to keep them warm.

"How?"

He turned to the back of the tool shed. "Don't we have some ice borers here?"

I nodded. Then we began to plan seriously. We'd first take buckets of water from one of the cabins up to the porch and pour them out, covering the front of the porch and the hill down to the lake. Then, we'd take the ice borers down to the dock and start drilling holes. We'd have pick axes along to help widen the bore holes.

We assembled our tools and took them down to the lake. Then we went to the nearest cabin with running water and found a couple of buckets. That was probably the hardest thing of the whole adventure. After finding them, we filled them with water and started carrying water up the hill to the Lodge.

That was scary. We were both afraid that a Deatheater would look out a window and see us. They didn't. It took a long time doing that, but we had nothing but time.

Finally, we had worked our way down to the lake. We arrived and had a hard time starting the first borer, but Dad can be determined if he's anything. Finally, the gasoline engine caught, and he adjusted the choke so that it wasn't in danger of dying. We had never drilled into ice before. The first time Dad tried it, it nearly knocked him over. So, we both held it and managed to get it going into the ice. It was HARD keeping it drilling straight down.

It made a racket, and we were sure that the Deatheaters would be out by the time we'd finished the first hole. They weren't. We then started working on another hole nearby. That was quieter as we got better control of the borer. We did two more holes and then set to work with the pick axes to break up the ice between the holes.

Just then there was light that appeared over my shoulder. I turned, and Dad, who was faced that direction, said, "It looks like we don't have to figure out how to coax out the Deatheaters."

Silhouetted in the light of the open door was a figure. I watched him take a step, and suddenly his feet flew into the air and something small seemed to fly out of a hand. There was a loud clunk and several smaller clunks, and the figure slid down the hillside gaining speed as it went.

It suddenly occurred to me that it might knock one of us into the water. I pulled Dad out of the way just in time as the body hit the dock, caromed off, and landed at the edge of the hole that we'd bored in the ice.

We looked at each other with the realization that we had a choice. A wordless conversation went on between us. The point was whether we would push the Deatheater, who might still be alive, into the freezing water of the hole or not. Dad's eyes like mine showed mixed emotions about what to do. We came to a decision. Both of us used our pick ax to push the body toward the edge. It didn't have to go very far before the weight of the body dragged the rest in.

Dad said, "Do we wait to see if he tries to get out?"

I answered, "Yes, but he won't climb out. If he does anything, he'll disapparate somewhere."

Meanwhile someone closed the door of the Lodge. I commented, "I guess that solves the question of whether there's more than one of them."

Dad started to say something when the door opened a crack and someone called out, "Frank! Frank, what's going on?"

I looked to Dad. Without the light of the door, I could hardly see him. He whispered, "Let him wonder a while what happened."

We didn't have to wait very long. Whoever was up there in the Lodge opened the door a crack and shouted out, "Whoever's out there. You'd better tell me what happened to Frank and do it right now!"

Dad grabbed my arm and dragged me up toward the "rustic" cabins. He whispered, "Let's get into the trees. Out of sight."

The voice shouted, "You'd better come out and show yourselves. I've got Mrs. Dursley, and I've got no reason to keep her alive without Frank!" The voice sounded confident.

I could feel more than see Dad nod slowly. I didn't have the slightest idea why he would be satisfied with the situation, but he spoke. "Well, you know what? We've got Frank."

The response was a little less confident, "You can't have him!! He'd turn you into toads!"

This time I smiled and whispered to Dad, "Tell him we've got his wand."

Dad chuckled and was the one with the confident voice, "Guess what! We've got his wand." He said the last in a sort of irritating sing-song voice that would have driven me crazy if I'd been up there in the Lodge.

There was silence for a while. Dad whispered to me, "I think there's a bull horn in the tool shed. If we're going to be doing a lot of talking long distance, I'd like to not have to shout so much."

I pointlessly nodded and headed up to the shed. Dad was right. There was a bull horn. I tested the battery. It worked well enough though I don't think it would last all night if it had to. I had a flashlight, but on the way back down, I wanted to use it as little as possible. There was a trail to the cabins. I could follow it from memory and feel pretty much, but every now and then I turned it on to be sure of my path.

While I was returning, the voice, which seemed to be amplified itself somehow, was booming out, "I don't care about Frank. Do you care about your precious wife-ee?"

I got the bull horn to Dad. He thanked me. Then, he said, "Well, do you really want to go back to 'You Know Who' and have to tell him that you and your big bad Deatheaters managed to kidnap one measly Muggle and a woman at that?" His voice boomed out with the bull horn almost as much as the Deatheater's had.

The Deatheater responded, "I'll take you all in. It's mighty cold out there. You'll not last very long!"

Dad whispered to me, "Go up and cut the circuit breaker to the Lodge. We'll see how he likes it without heat or light."

I said, "Yes. Sir!"

While I was on my way, Dad answered, saying, "Oh, we've dressed for the cold. We're actually comfortable. You, on the other hand, may not find you're so well off when the lights and heat turn off!"

He had drawn out his comments, and I rushed up the trail that by now, I hardly needed any light to follow. Shortly after he finished talking, I was able to flip the main circuit breaker, and all the lights went out. The furnace had been going, and it also went silent. I almost ran back to where Dad was.

When I arrived, he whispered, "Good work!"

The Deatheater answered though. There was a flickering light coming from the Lodge's lobby where the big fireplace was. Then, the Deatheater mocked us, "Oh, we're quite toasty in here. How are you doing?"

Dad came right back, "Oh, we're fine. We'll see just how long you're toasty." He turned to me and whispered, "Do you think you can put a rock or something through one of those windows?

I smiled even though Dad couldn't see it, "Don't you think I've put the occasional rock through a school window?"

I couldn't see Dad's face, but he said, "Good." A little uncertainly.

I went to find a likely rock or two. As soon as I'd found a couple, I moved closer to the Lodge. The first toss was off-target, but I hadn't bowled in quite a while. The next found one of the windows in the Lobby.

But after a minute, something really strange happened. The window pane seemed to fall up and re-assemble in the window. I tried another rock. The same thing happened. I tried a third. It didn't do any better. So, I retreated back to Dad.

When I reached him, he whispered, "Good try. I guess their magic repairs the windows as fast as you break them. Don't worry. Their fire will burn down, and they'll have to go out for firewood."

There was a big stack of firewood on the porch in front of the Lodge. Dad nudged my arm and said, "Let's go up to the cabins. They're not hot but they're warm enough."

We did that and waited for events to unfold. Another advantage of being in a cabin was that we could talk in a normal voice. Dad and I took off the outer layer of coats and sat in front of the window that looked out on the lake, waiting to see what would happen.

□

It seemed like a long time, but eventually the door opened, and someone came out. Dad had his binoculars up and commented, "He's getting some firewood. . . He's close to the ice. . ." But then he was indoors again. He came out again. This time, he dropped one of the big pieces of firewood, and rather than picking it up, he skirted around it. His foot hit the ice, and it went out from under him. He was down and slowly going down the hill.

We quickly put our coats on and ran out of the cabin. I couldn't tell if he were trying to regain his feet or whether the flailing was just random motion. He slowly spun around as he reached the lake. He went across the lake and reached our hole. He seemed to teeter on the brink as we arrived and went in.

Meanwhile, the door of the Lodge slammed shut, and we heard a scream of rage and hatred from the cabin.

We had reached the lake's edge and decided that there was nothing left but to go back to our post at the edge of the trees. We had barely reached that spot before a voice that we recognized—barely—said, "You come here right now, or I'll kill your wife."

I couldn't believe Dad. He waited a full minute. I asked him, "What are you doing?"

Dad said with a smile on his lips that I couldn't see but that I knew was there, none-the-less. "I've got a lot of experience negotiating. We're not finished yet." And then he said, "Do you want your men back?"

The voice came back, "You've killed them."

Dad, as calm as ever I'd seen him, said, "Do you want them back?"

There was no reply. Then, the voice said, "Come up here, and we'll work a deal."

Dad said, "You come out in the open. We'll deal face to face or not at all."

"You come here."

Dad was relentless, "The only way that we all get out of this is for us to deal fairly. You're lost. You've lost two men. Even if you get all of us—and you won't—you'll have to go back and tell your boss that you lost two big, powerful wizards to three Muggles and one of them a woman. What do you think will happen to you?"

There was a long pause. Then the voice returned, tired and resigned to something bad, "What kind of deal can you offer that I could trust."

Dad's smile was broad, "Something for all of us."

The voice said, "Yeh, what?"

Dad said, "Simple. But I have to see your face. I won't know if you're telling the truth if I don't see your face."

There was a long, long pause. "You have to be in the open too."

"I will be. We both come out in the light—you on the porch, me on the hill."

There was another long pause, then the voice said, "OK. But make it quick. It's cold out there."

Dad said, "OK. You open the door. I walk to the edge of the light. You walk out of the door and I come closer. Then we talk."

The door opened. Dad went out into the edge of the light. You could just make out his figure. Then the Deatheater walked out on the porch, just over the door sill. He said, "What's your fancy deal?"

Dad came closer and started to talk, "You go back. There are others searching for us. You just say that you couldn't find us either. If you bring any or all of us back, you'll have lots of explaining to do. If you go back alone, you just say that the other two gave up. The cowards that they were, they ran off because they failed. You'll just be one among many who searched for us and didn't find us."

Then the Deatheater smiled and started to raise his wand.

I had come up as quietly as I could to the side of the house and stuck my head around the edge. As the Deatheater raised his wand, I stepped up to the porch. He started to laugh. I tackled him low, and his legs went out from under him. There was a flash of green light from his wand that went over Dad's head. The Deatheater was on his knees. He whirled and tried to regain his feet, but they went out from under him. He came down hard on his head, slipped down over the edge of the porch, and started sliding slowly down the hill. Dad and I went after him, being careful to avoid the iced part of the hill. He hit the ice and slid a little but stopped before the hole.

It was already starting to freeze over, but there would be no problem getting him in. He was still unconscious or maybe dead. I saw that he still had his wand in his hand. I bent down, pulled the wand from his hand, and broke it over his body. Then Dad and I shoved him in the hole in the ice.

We stayed there for about ten minutes—until we were sure that he wasn't going to come back to attack us. Then we carefully mounted the hill to the Lodge. We brought our pick axes—just in case.

We weren't absolutely sure that there wasn't another Deatheater inside. We went around to the back entrance and used our key to get in. I opened the door as quietly as I could. We came in and walked, pick ax in hand, through the many rooms— the kitchen, the Exercise Room, on and on. We didn't dare turn the power back on. Every room was opened, flinging the door wide and waiting for reaction before entering. Then we closed the door, turned on our flashlights, and searched.

Eventually, we'd finished everything but the Lobby. We'd not seen a sign of Mum. We only whispered when absolutely necessary, and neither of us mentioned Mum.

There were still embers in the fire burning red and cool. The whole Lodge had begun cooling. It would have taken a long time for it to have gotten uncomfortably cool. Luckily neither we nor the Deatheaters had realized that.

We entered the Lobby sure that if there were a Deatheater left, we'd find him there. At first, we couldn't see anyone. We turned on our flashlights and searched. We found Mum.

She was lying on a sofa, with her back turned to the room. Both Dad and I were scared of what we might find if we touched her. Dad did. There was no reaction.

Dad swiftly turned her over so that her face was up. I couldn't see any signs of life. Dad put his ear to her mouth and sighed. "She's breathing."

We tried waking her, but nothing roused her.

Dad asked me to turn the power back on and see if I could get the furnace going again. It wasn't uncomfortably cold, but there was a draft down the chimney that was cool.

It was easy turning the circuit breaker on. Lights immediately turned on. I went into the basement and went to work on the furnace. I'd only started it once, and that was under the watchful eye of the HVAC man. It took several tries, but it finally fired up. The blower motor started, and I was happy to go up to the main floor with a success.

I found Dad rubbing Mum's hands, trying to wake her. I came over to take her other hand. I found that it was as stiff as a board. A fear struck my heart, "Are you sure she's alive?"

"Yeh. She's just hard as a rock, but she's breathing, and I can even feel a pulse in her temple."

After a few minutes with no change, I asked, "Do you think we should call for help."

Dad nodded and said, "I'll go do it."

At that moment, I saw her eyes flutter slightly. "Wait, Dad. I think she just moved."

He leaped over a chair getting to her. She was motionless for another minute or so, and then an eyelid fluttered again. Dad clapped me on the back and said, "Go make some coffee!"

I ran to the kitchen and fumbled through making a pot of coffee. I tried a little before taking it in to Dad. It was hot and thick. It tasted a lot like mud, but it was coffee.

In the Lobby, I found that Mum was sitting up. She still seemed a lot more petrified than alive, but her body was no longer stiff. Dad took the cup of coffee that I offered and put it to Mum's lips and tipped a little into her mouth.

She spluttered and coughed and said, "What is that stuff–some kind of home remedy."

I said, "It's coffee."

Dad took a sip and spit it out. "I'll make some real coffee. You stay here with Mum and keep her talking."

Between Dad's coffee, which was a lot better than mine, and our encouragement, she was up and walking a little. We then had a council of war. It was decided that Mum needed proper rest and a good breakfast in the morning. Also, we needed to get that porch cleared of ice and a rug or something nailed from the door to the steps down from the porch so that nobody else would get killed. Then over breakfast, we could talk further.

Dad went back to the tool shed to see if there were any rock salt or something to de-ice the porch and the slide that we'd created down to the lake. I helped Mum up the stairs to our room. She insisted that I not leave until Dad was back.

We heard hammering, and I guessed that Dad had nailed something to the porch.

We went to bed. Nobody took off their clothes. We were all exhausted, in shock, and who knew what else. The next morning, we were awakened by daylight. We still had probably gotten less than eight hours of sleep, but we couldn't stay abed.

Mum was feeling well enough that she insisted on making us breakfast. It was a proper English breakfast. It had lots of sausage, eggs, ham, toast, marmalade, juice, and coffee. I even had some coffee.

When we'd removed the edge off our hunger, Dad started the discussion. We wanted to know what had happened to Mum, and Mum wanted to know what we'd done. She'd been conscious the whole time that we'd been fighting the battle of Ludlow's Resort as we called it, but she couldn't see anything because she'd been turned away from the action. All she could do was hear the exchanged shouts.

Dad and I told her our story. She shuddered when she heard about what we'd done with the Deatheaters. We were surprised, but she said, "That was awful. You killed them all!"

I exclaimed, "Well, we didn't have that much choice. They'd have killed us—eventually. They'd have tortured us, used us to blackmail Harry, and then they'd have killed us."

Dad agreed, "I'm afraid so. At the end, the leader of the Deatheaters tried to kill me."

I was surprised. I thought that he'd just been going to petrify him like he'd done Mum. But Dad disagreed, "No, Dudders, didn't you hear what spell he was saying at the end just as you tackled him. It was a right sound tackle too. Maybe you should have played Ruggers."

I admitted that I hadn't heard it.

Dad said, "He'd used that "Ever Cadaver" or whatever that spell is. I don't rightly remember it, but it was something like that. It's the killing spell. I heard them using it back near Sunderland when we barely escaped them."

Mum gasped.

Then Dad asked Mum if she could tell her story. She took a big breath and began.

□□

I was sweeping the Lobby. I heard a knock at the main door. It surprised me. I couldn't imagine either of you lot knocking, but who else could it be? I went to the door, opened it, and saw a flash of red light. I saw that it wasn't you and tried to turn and run, but what happened was that I suddenly couldn't move a muscle. I slowly tipped over and fell to the floor. It was lucky that I landed on my side. I hate to think what would have happened if I'd landed on my nose. Anyway, that was all that I saw of the Deatheaters. They picked me up and carried me to the sofa. They put me there the way you found me, so I couldn't see a thing that went on from then until you turned me over, but I heard lots.

They came a little after noon. After they dumped me on the couch, I lay there and didn't hear a word or a sound. It drove me crazy. It got dark outside, and there still wasn't a word. I began to wonder where you lot were, but I sort of hoped that you wouldn't come back. I was that afraid for you.

I suppose the Deatheaters were searching the Lodge for you. Finally, I began to hear then talking. They'd come into the Lobby. They turned on the lights, and they started to argue about getting something to eat. There was a leader, whose name was Ivy or something like that. He insisted that another Deatheater named Frank fix them something to eat. Frank finally gave in and went to the kitchen to find something. He came back. He'd made some sandwiches and some coffee.

The other two, Ivy and George complained about the sandwiches. Frank told them that they could fix the next meal if they were so much better at it.

They started wondering where Vernon was. They didn't seem to know about Dudders, thank goodness. Anyway, they were starting to get impatient. They had a little argument over whether to unfreeze me or not. Before that was over, they decided to start a fire in the fireplace.

I heard a pile of logs go into the fireplace and suddenly I heard a whoosh as they all seemed to catch on fire at once. That was the first moment that I had some hope. I hoped that one of you would notice the fire in the fireplace and realize that I hadn't started it.

Anyway, it was burning quickly. I felt the heat on my back and wondered if they might have caught something else on fire.

Then after a long time, I heard a machine. I know what a snowmobile sounds like, and I knew that it wasn't that. I thought and thought.

At one point, I wondered if it might have been a helicopter. Maybe one of you had taken a satellite phone with you, you'd called the RCMP, and they'd called in the Royal Marines. Briefly, I had an image of helicopters landing and Royal Marines in camouflage coming out. They broke down the door and shot the Deatheaters before they could raise a wand.

But, of course, that didn't happen. Instead the motors stopped. No Royal Marines. No RCMP. Only an odd clanging like hammers on anvils.

That set the Deatheaters off. They wondered what the noise was and prepared an ambush for you when you came in the main door. Of course, you didn't. Then there was a little argument about what to do next. Ivy decided that Frank would go out and investigate. He wasn't anxious to do it—at least alone, but the boss ridiculed him. He said, "What? Are you afraid of one bloody Muggle who probably doesn't have the slightest idea that you're around?"

Frank agreed to go out. He opened the door and there was this thud. George called out, "Frank, shut the frigging door. Do you want to let all the cold air in the world in?"

There was no answer. Then, George shut the door muttering about growing up in a barn. There was no sound for a good while. The leader then went to the door and called out to Frank. There wasn't any answer. Of course, Ivy started talking to you.

He and George started arguing about what to do. You didn't help them any by talking about "You Know Who". George was all for disapparating with me and getting their reward.

Ivy wasn't buying it. He said things like, "Do you mean that you're scared by one bloody Muggle?"

191

George said "Maybe we should ask Frank about that."

Ivy wasn't buying it. He argued, "You want to go back to the Dark Lord and tell him that we could only bring back one Muggle woman—because you were afraid?"

That shut George up—for a while. Of course, you kept nagging them, and then you shut off the lights. If they didn't jump out of their skins, I don't know what they did.

I so much wanted to shout out, "My man and my boy are coming for you," but I couldn't. I was frozen stiff, and I would have cried if I could force a tear out of my eyes.

Breaking those windows kind of spooked them too. Finally, as the fire was burning down, Ivy sent George out for firewood. Didn't they have a row over that? George insisted that Ivy go out for firewood. I think they drew swords over that but nothing happened. Finally, George went out. Ivy insisted that he get lots of firewood—enough for the whole night and into the next day too.

George finally agreed to get three loads, and that was it. He went out and came back in. Then he went out the second time, but he didn't come back in.

Ivy panicked. You know how desperate he sounded. He was worse in here, I'm sure. I'd have given a year off my life to tell that Ivy that you lot were going to get him for sure.

Anyway, he went out to bargain with you. I heard some kind of scuffle and then nothing for the longest time. I figured that you'd have run in if you'd gotten Ivy. I was afraid all of you were dead, and I'd slowly starve to death or more likely freeze to death slowly.

But of course, you finally showed up, turned on the lights, got the furnace going, and got some hot coffee into me.

⊟

Mum finished her story by asking, "Now what?"Dad rubbed his jaw and thought, "Well. . . I think that we have to decide whether we need to be rescued from here."

We talked about that for some time. Of course, we were all afraid that in a day or two the Deatheaters' buddies would show up wondering what had happened to their friends. On the other hand, there was the problem of what we would tell the rescuers about why we needed to be rescued.

Was it because we had been attacked by terrorists, and we were afraid their buddies were going to come to get us? That approach had so many problems in it that none of us wanted to do that.

Maybe, we could just claim that we were stir crazy. Of course, the problem there was that eventually, the lake would melt, and the bodies would surface. We'd be assumed to have been guilty of the deaths. Of course, that was true, but we didn't want anyone to come to that conclusion.

We discussed at some lengths alternatives for dealing with the bodies. Eventually, we decided that we ought to pull them out of the lake as soon as possible. In the bitter cold, they'd not decay, and we could come up with a good plan before doing anything further.

So, the next thing that Dad and I did was take our pick axes down to the lake. The surface was frozen over–just as you'd expect in this arctic cold. However, it had not frozen enough to require using the ice borer. The pick axes sufficed to break the surface. We fished around with them and eventually snared one after another of the bodies. We pulled the bodies up to the tree line near the "rustic cabins". We had had a good day's work getting those things out of the lake and dragging them up to the trees. Somehow neither Dad nor I wanted to leave them where we could see them easily from the Lodge.

We got back to the Lodge where Mum had prepared a hearty Chicken noodle soup for us. We sat and started our meal with enough vigor. But Mum stopped eating and mused, "Do you suppose there are animals about who might eat those bodies?"

Both Dad and I stopped with spoonfuls of soup at our mouths. Dad's mouth just dropped. I said, "Oh, shit."

We all agreed that we should do something to keep the bodies from the varmints. Dad and I wanted to wait until tomorrow morning. Mum insisted that we had to do it that very night. So we turned to the question of what to do. The ground was frozen as hard as rock, so we couldn't dig a shallow grave to put them in temporarily.

Dad said, "How about the primitive cabins? They're not heated. The bodies will just sit there frozen solid. No one would know afterwards that dead bodies had sat in them for a few days."

Mum was shocked, "You can't do that. There'll be smell that we'll never get out of there!"

Dad insisted—and I agreed with him—that bodies frozen solid were not going to give off smells, but Mum wouldn't budge.

I had an idea. "I've heard that people who are camping in the wild, hang their food from limbs of trees out of the reach of bears and other animals."

Mum wasn't exactly happy with the idea, but she was willing to go with it since she didn't have a better idea. Dad raised the obvious problem, "How do we hang a body from a limb?"

We all thought about that problem. Amazingly, Mum had a decent idea. "Well, you say the bodies are frozen solid."

"Yes," we agreed.

"Then you should be able to loop rope under their armpits and pull them up that way."

God, I wish we could have thought of a better idea. But we couldn't. So, long after sunset, we all—even Mum—bundled up, and we went looking for rope. The always well-stocked tool shed had a good bit.

So, Mum held the flashlight on the bodies as we worked a sort of noose through the armpits and tied it securely. We then had to find a good tree to hang the bodies. It wasn't easy. We needed limbs that were high enough to hang bodies from and weren't easy for animals to climb up and reach the bodies.

We finally found some tall trees that had strong limbs. Later I learned that they were ironwood trees. There were a few tall ones among stands of shorter trees. We finally found one that was tall, had strong limbs, and I was able to climb them. It was miserable work. The flash that Mum had provided barely enough light to let me find footholds. I finally reached a limb that seemed good. Dad threw the rope up a couple of times before I caught it. I passed it over the limb just beyond a couple of small limbs that would hold it in place. Then Dad and Mum slowly pulled the body up. I help release snags.

When it reached a good height, they took the end of the rope and wrapped it around the trunk and tied it securely.

The next two went a bit better, but none of them were exactly easy. When we were finally done, Mum and Dad started walking off toward the Lodge. I had to shout after them, "Hey where are you two going?"

Dad answered, "To the Lodge of course. Why?"

"How about helping me down?"

They grudgingly came back, and I went down to the lowest limb. I let myself down, and Dad caught my legs and helped ease me down. We all dropped into bed without undressing. It was well after midnight, and we were all exhausted.

The next day none of us were up much before noon. We all had sore muscles and joints. At lunch, we discussed what to do next. Mum was in favor of just leaving them up in the trees for a few days. Dad wanted to come up with a plan at least. I had to agree with him, "Look, we don't know how long it's going to take to do whatever plan we hatch. We need to get a plan and figure that out at least."

So, we threw around a few ideas during lunch. We knew that we couldn't bury the bodies in the ground. It was way too hard now, and we didn't dare wait until it thawed.

Mum suggested dumping the bodies in the deepest part of the lake. Dad objected that the bodies would surface eventually, and eventually might not be that far in the future.

Mum responded, "Well, we can put weights on the bodies and sink them to the bottom."

I saw a problem with that. "With all the fishing done here in the summer, somebody will snag one of the bodies and think that they've got the catch of the century. Then, he'll find out that he's caught the mystery of the century."

Dad picked up that idea and improved it. "What if we take the bodies to another lake far away and weigh them down and sink them in the middle?"

No one could think of a problem with that idea, but Dad insisted that we sleep on it before deciding to go with it. We dragged through the day, doing our chores and grateful when supper time came. No one had thought of a problem with the idea yet, but we were waiting until tomorrow to see what kind of problems would crop up.

Breakfast the next day felt a lot better in every way. Our muscles were less sore. Our minds felt fresher. We weren't sleepy. No one had thought of any catches to our plan. So, we started working details.

The first detail was which lake we would choose. That question sent us to the office scrambling to find maps. Eventually we found detailed maps of the area in the last place any of us guessed. There was a three ring binder full of notes on fishing in the area AND maps of the area. They were Canadian Geologic Survey maps. They showed depth contours of lakes.

We poured over the maps, looking for the largest, deepest, furthest lakes in the area. We found three good candidates. It turned out that one of them was the lake that we'd gone to the day the Deatheaters attacked. That one seemed so appropriate that we chose it.

The next problem was how to transport the bodies that far. I think Dad had the idea that we would just drag them, but I reminded him how hard it had been dragging them up to the tree they were in. He agreed that we needed a better plan.

Mum thought it was obvious. "We just use a snowmobile to drag them."

That was obvious after you'd thought of it. Anyway, we started planning carefully. How long would it take us to get there? How long to drill the hole in the ice? How long to get back?

As we added things up, it was clear that it would take more than the daylight hours to get there and get back.

Then there was the problem of finding something heavy enough to hold down three bodies. We all took a little tour of the tool shed. There were funny suggestions. Mum suggested a lawnmower. I suggested a snowmobile. That didn't get much in the way of laughs.

We finally settled on an ice-borer. That had the advantage of providing its own excuse for why it was missing. We were trying our hand at ice fishing. It had gotten out of hand as we were drilling and was at the bottom of the lake.

That left only the problem of what to do with the bodies once we arrived at the lake where we would dump them. There were arguments. Dad was in favor of just leaving them there and returning the next day to finish the job. We could get there a lot faster the next day than if we were dragging bodies.

Mum was dead set against that. Her first suggestion was camping there overnight. That had the advantage of letting us dump the bodies and be rid of them before night-fall. But when she thought of what camping out in Arctic cold would be, she dropped that suggestion.

I couldn't think of dragging those bodies up another tree. No one suggested it, and I certainly didn't, so we were back to Dad's idea. Just leave them out for one night.

By this time, it was far too late to start. Besides that, we really hadn't thought about how we would drag the bodies. Mum just thought we'd let them down and tie the ropes to the snowmobile and we'd be off. Dad and I vetoed that idea right off. We'd ridden the snowmobiles there, and we knew how rough the terrain was. We needed some way to secure the bodies better and protect them from getting snagged. That question forced us to sleep on it again.

The next morning, the new day had brought a new idea. It was Mum's. She suggested that we wrap the bodies in a tarpaulin and drag them that way.

No one objected, and we decided that we'd start before sunrise the next day.

We were up early, had a quick breakfast, and were off with two snowmobiles and a big tarpaulin to the tree. We had no trouble getting the bodies down.

However, it was not that easy wrapping all three bodies securely. After doing that, we thought we were off. We were wrong. We attached the big package to a snowmobile, driven by Dad. I took the other with some tools and the ice-borer. Dad hadn't even gotten above the ridge that we'd sat on for about a year (it seemed to me) before wondering what was going on at the Lodge.

The snowmobile just wasn't powerful enough to carry Dad and three frozen bodies up that gentle hill. So, we had to think more. We went back to the Lodge dragging our awful burden.

Mum, of course, knew that something was awfully wrong. When we explained to Mum the problem, she suggested dragging two behind my snowmobile and one behind Dad's along with the tools.

Dad and I looked at each other and shook our heads forlornly. I explained, "I just think that's too much weight. We've got to either do this in two trips. . ." Mum shuddered at that and I wasn't exactly happy either. "Or use three snowmobiles."

Mum immediately objected that we didn't have a third driver. Both Dad and I looked at her. She got the idea and flat out refused. Dad didn't like it, I could tell, but he accepted it.

Mum had lots of good reasons for her not to do it. She had never driven a snowmobile. She was afraid of motorcycles, and a snowmobile was an awful lot like a motorcycle. And so on.

She finally gave up and agreed. We agreed that she'd have to have a crash course in driving snowmobiles. We started it that afternoon and continued the next day.

There was the additional problem of what to do with the bodies. We finally decided that frozen, wrapped in tarpaulin, they could rest overnight in the tool shed. It was not heated and was protected from the elements and the animals. Mum didn't like it, but she was stuck.

Dad rode with her on the third snowmobile and instructed. I unwrapped the bodies, cut up the tarpaulin, and re-wrapped them. By the time I was done, so was Mum's first snowmobile lesson. Mum was kind of happy with the way it went.

Dad insisted on another full day of lessons. He pointed out that she'd not driven at night, and she needed to have a little experience with that.

The lessons the next day went well—even the night lesson. So, we got to bed early, and again the next day we were up before dawn. This time, Mum had already fixed breakfast and lunch the night before. We had a very fast breakfast, and we were out to hook up the snowmobiles to the corpses. Dad insisted that we wait for dawn before we left.

At the first serious light of dawn, we were off. Dad led. Mum followed him, and I was last as added safety for Mum. We arrived shortly after noon. We'd not had any serious problems. We untied the corpses and looked for a good place to hide them.

We found a rock ledge that gave them cover. I couldn't believe that bears or wolves would have been fooled, but it was cheap protection for Mum's feelings.

We stopped for a quick lunch. We just had sandwiches and lukewarm coffee from thermos bottles. Then we were off on the way home. We made great time getting home. With full daylight, it was much faster than when Dad and I had come back partly in the dark.

Mum fixed a big meal for dinner, and at the same time fixed food for the next day. During dinner we just ate. We were that hungry. Afterwards, we discussed the next day.

Dad had a good idea. We would bring all the satellite phones. That way, if any of us got into trouble we could communicate with each other. I suggested that we use the same technique that we'd used at the dock on that awful night. He thought that we didn't need the hole to be that big and suggested three holes rather than four. I agreed to his proposal.

At the end of our discussion Mum threw a bombshell. "I'm going too."

Dad was up in arms against it. I wasn't all that happy about the idea either, but Mum made some good points. "Three are safer than two. I'm nearly as good a snowmobiler as you two are. If one of the snowmobiles breaks down, we're better off with having the remaining two."

Dad grimaced because he knew that she was right. I fell in with Mum and it was settled.

The next morning we were off as early as ever. I actually woke up before the alarm went off. I'd gotten that used to rising early.

We flew like the wind. Mum was better able to stay up with Dad, and we had way less weight than the day before. We arrived before noon and dragged the three corpses to the middle of the lake. That took longer than I'd hoped. Wwe had to tie them to the snowmobiles, and we couldn't go as fast on the lake as we had on the land. We didn't want to run into thin ice unawares.

We got out and set up the ice borer. The ice was not as thick as it had been at our lake. I didn't know why that was, but we didn't complain. After drilling the holes we used our pick axes to open up the space between. That was trickier than with thicker ice, but we managed to stay out of the drink.

The final step of tying the tarp-wrapped corpses to the one ice borer we had along was not as easy as we'd hoped, but we did. We tested the knots and the attachment to the tarps and pushed the ice-borer into the hole. It went down rapidly and dragged the corpses over the edge.

We watched them sink as long as we could see them. By then, it was much later than noon. We skipped lunch altogether. We made for the Lodge as fast as we could push the snowmobiles. Later, I learned that snowmobiles could do better than 70 mph. I didn't believe we got anywhere near that fast, but we were moving.

The sun was barely over the horizon when we reached the last ridge before we arrived at the Lodge. We pulled into the tool shed with only the last dim afterglow of the sunset left.

We ate lunch for dinner and headed for bed immediately.

Where's Aunt Marge?

The next day, we declared a holiday and just ate, slept, and watched satellite telly. I couldn't believe that we were free of that hideous burden that we'd been dragging along for days.

Of course, we still had problems. Dad introduced the topic the next day. "Well, do we jump ship now?"

Mum asked, "What are you talking about? We've disposed of the . . . uh . . . inconveniences. We're good to go, aren't we?"

I thought I knew what Dad was talking about, so I said, "Are there more Deatheaters out there who know that we're here?"

Mum made a sensible point, "We've been here for more than a week since those Deatheaters showed up. Surely, more would have come by now if they were going to."

Dad had to admit that she was probably right. I did too. Still, it didn't make for easy sleeping that they'd found us more than once. We'd been lucky. Maybe we ought to keep moving.

We slept on it uneasily the next couple of days. Dad brought the question to a head at dinner, "I'm not going to back arse first into a decision. This could be a life or death decision either way. We're going to have a vote."

He had brought a pad of paper with him and pencils. He tore off a page for each of us. He said, "OK. Vote. Stay or leave. Fold the paper and put them on the table."

Mum objected, "Oh, this is silly."

Dad was resolute, "This isn't silly. I want to be sure that everyone is expressing his real feelings."

We did as he said. He scooped them up and shook them in his hand. Then he opened them one at a time. Each read, "Stay."

That settled it. We all felt better. We were in it come better or worse. I think we all slept better after that. As the days and then weeks went by things got back to their natural rhythm. The days became longer, we spent more time outside as the weather got warmer.

□

One day, we were all out doing chores. Mum was checking the cabins. Dad was tuning one of the snowmobile engines. I was shoveling snow away from the entrance to the generator buildings. Mum was just coming back toward the house and Dad was bending over the snowmobile, putting the engine through its paces when a whim struck me. The recent snow had been wet and hard to shovel. However, it was easy to pack into a nice snow ball. I made one and threw it at Dad, hitting him on the back.

He got up, looked around at me, made a snowball himself, and threw at me. I ducked, and it hit Mum instead. Her face showed as much surprise as I'd ever seen. She immediately picked up some snow and started making a snowball. That was it. We were soon having a three-sided snow battle.

March flowed by, and we were fast approaching April. That was significant. We'd signed on for 6 months. We had started in late October. That meant that we ought to be done sometime after mid-April. We all knew that. No one said anything, but everyone started paying attention to the lake and the high temperature on the thermometer. We all knew that they wouldn't fly the seaplane out until the lake was ice-free.

April Fools Day came, but the high was just about reaching 32 degrees Fahrenheit. We didn't know what to expect, but we knew that the lake wouldn't melt until the temperature was a lot higher than 32.

Dad finally posted a piece of paper on the back of the door to our room. It had a table with two columns–the date and the high temperature. As the days of April went by we watched the high climb into the mid-thirties and then the upper thirties, but the temperature when we got up in the morning, was still well down in the twenties.

On April 16, the day was sunny, and we started to see some small pools of standing water on the ice. That was good, but it had to go a lot further.

On April 31, the high was 45, and the low was still about 30. There was standing water on the ice in the morning, but there was still ice.

We were beginning to become stir crazy. Dad was starting to talk about us getting a bonus for having to stay so long. Mum was wondering what the garden back in our house in England was like.

I wanted to say that I didn't think we'd ever see that garden again, but I didn't. I had my dreams too.

We weren't doomed to live the rest of lives there, though. Two weeks after that we were in the Lobby having dinner when some alarm sounded. At least, we thought it was an alarm. We'd never heard it before. We tested the smoke detectors and the CO detectors, but they didn't sound like that. We searched high and low for the source of the alarm, but couldn't find it. It wasn't long before it stopped.

Then as we were eating dinner, I thought, "I'll bet that was the satellite phone." I said as much aloud.

The next morning at breakfast the sound happened again. This time we went straight to the phones. One of them was obviously ringing. Dad gingerly picked it up and hesitantly said, "Hello?" There followed a conversation of which we only heard half:

"Hello."

"Yes. . . Yes . . . No."

A long pause. Then, "Yes, we'll check thoroughly. If there are any, we'll check each day until they're all gone."

"Yes, I understand."

When it ended, Dad gave us the story. The management company had been monitoring the ice on the lake via satellite images. They thought the lake was clear but wanted us to check the lake to be sure. We were to take a boat out on the lake and look for ice chunks. We were to report. If we found any, we were to check the next day and so on, until there weren't any left. If there were a day when there weren't any left, we'd report, and they'd send the seaplane for us in a couple of days.

We went out to the boat house to get a boat out of storage. We picked the first one that we found. It had oars, so we were in for some work. There was a cart for taking the boats down to the lake. We did that and managed to get the boat into the lake, and then there was the problem of getting in.

We tied the boat up to the dock, and one of us held it in place while the other got in. Then it was my turn. I'd never mounted a boat before. The thing shook like a bucking bronco from the West of the States. I finally did a sort of controlled leap and landed in the boat.

I started rowing. We decided to go around the edge of the lake and work our way out to deeper and deeper waters. After one circuit of the lake, I was bushed from rowing. I let Dad take over. He didn't make it around the lake even once.

On my next turn, I began to get the hang of how to use an oar. Pretty soon, we were flying around the lake, and we'd almost forgotten about looking for ice. We found a chunk. It was near the center of the lake.

We looked at each other with the same idea in our heads—for one chunk, we have to wait a day?

Then Dad asked me a question, "What do you think? Suppose this chunk sort of blew over to the side of the lake?"

I went on, "And then somebody—I don't know who—pulled it out of the lake?"

"Yes. Would that chunk count as ice on the lake?"

I laughed, and he joined me. We decided that somehow that ice chunk was going to migrate out of the lake, and then we'd make a call to the management company.

It was not as easy as we hoped. We finally fitted a loop of rope around the ice and set to rowing. The rope slipped off several times on our way to the shore. We did eventually get to the shore. The only problem was that the shore was very rocky and we didn't want to run the boat into those rocks. So, we kept rowing around the lake until we finally had reached the dock.

We did get the boat tied to the dock. However, to do that we had to untie the chunk of ice. Dad held the ice to the dock as I ran for a couple of pick axes. When I got back he was complaining about his hands freezing to the ice. I managed to drive the axe point into the ice so that we could hold onto it with that. We then tried to pull it out.

The thing was a whole lot heavier than it had seemed when it was floating, and we were dragging it behind the boat. We tried different ways to get it out. We tried tying a rope around it—no good. We tried driving two pick axes in it and lifting it together—no good.

Eventually we tried just pulling it to the edge of the lake next to the dock. We found some waders in the boat house. Dad put them on and stepped into the lake, and he pushed while I pulled. It was almost suppertime when we finally got it up onto the shore.

Then we could roll it more easily. It took us a bit, but we decided that we ought to get it out of sight of the dock when the seaplane arrived.

After dinner, we called the management company. An answering service answered. The guy on the other end asked if it was an emergency, urgent, or if it could wait for the morning. We decided it could wait, but we left the message that the lake was clear of ice.

We were sitting around the Telly in the Lobby watching reruns of the Benny Hill show when I decided that we needed to do some talking. I took the remote and muted the show. After the protests died down, I said, "We've got to think about what we're going to do after they dump us in Winnipeg."

Dad looked exasperated, "It's always some bleeding thing, isn't it." He held up his hand as I was about to protest. "Yes, yes, you're right. We have to think about it. Let's all think about it and talk about it over breakfast tomorrow." He then held out his hand, "Now, give me the remote."

The next morning after conquering our hunger we sat around the kitchen table. Dad opened the discussion. "OK. I've been telling myself that either Harry or 'You Know Who' would be killed, and we'd know which it was. Then we could decide what to do. But so far I can't tell whether anybody's been killed. Maybe someone has. Maybe not. Anybody have any ideas about that?"

Mum suggested that we call my Aunt Marge. She didn't know anything about Wizards, but she could tell us something. Had Harry shown up? Had the world gone to Hell in a Handbasket?" She added, "And we can call her right now with one of those satellite phones."

Dad was against it, "We've worked hard to keep anyone from knowing where we are. If we phone her from here, we could be traced. We'd be stuck if the seaplane didn't arrive before the Deatheaters did. No, we can call her, but not from here.

"Much better would be calling her from a phone booth in Winipeg just before we move on to a more permanent location."

That raised the question for me, "What would that more permanent location be?"

Dad was stuck. As we all were. Winipeg was a big city but it hadn't struck me as big enough to really get lost in.

We kicked various ideas around. Nobody wanted to go back to England before we knew which way the wind blew there. We ticked off the major cities of Canada. There was Vancouver, of course. We knew it well. There was Montreal. There was Toronto. They were all big cities. We even talked about American cities—Chicago, Cleveland, Columbus, Cincinnati. We seemed to have gotten stuck on "C"s. We didn't want to go out of the Empire.

Without any great hope, we picked Toronto. It was the closest, and it was also close to the States, if we wanted to go there.

The next day, the management company called. They would have the seaplane up in two or three days. We should be ready for either.

So, we started packing. We'd not acquired any new clothes here, so we knew that we could pack everything that we needed to take in the same suitcases we'd come in. We were finished by the early afternoon. Then we took a walking tour of the property. We went through the cabins—both primitive and rustic. We inspected the Lodge, the tool shed, the boat house, the generator buildings, and so on.

That inspection reminded us that we needed to have our story ready when the question arose of where one of the ice borers had gone. We polished off our story from months before and added some little decorations. We got out the maps and found a deep lake far from THE lake. We established that it was just Dad and I who went ice fishing. Why had we done it? We were bored stiff. That trip cured our boredom and any interest we had in ice fishing.

So, we faced the arrival of our replacements with mixed joy and apprehension. We had to wait three days for the arrival. Except for the week after the attack of the Deatheaters, it was the worst period of our stay at the Lodge.

Mum was perpetually scrubbing the kitchen down. I'd forgotten how particular the chef was about his kitchen. Dad was not much less concerned about the condition of all the gasoline powered engines. We changed the oil and fluids on both motor-generators in those three days.

Mum insisted that we eat all our meals in the kitchen, and she cleaned scrupulously after every meal.

We didn't know when the plane would be arriving, so every day was full of the suspenseful question: Would this be THE day?

When they arrived, it was out of the blue just before noon. Mum's jaw just dropped. She went into a tizzy trying to come up with a menu for lunch as they walked up the hill to the Lodge.

Bishop immediately noticed our improvised friction strip on the edge of the porch. To his questioning look, Dad said, "Oh, yes. That edge is dangerous when wet or icy. Dudley here almost took a nasty fall on it one rainy day. We almost had to test your satellite phone that day. I improvised this to keep us safe."

Bishop nodded and said, "Yes. I see. You're right. We'll replace that towel with a real friction pad." He seemed to reflect on it and added, "Yes, that might be worth a bonus. I'll talk with the owner about it."

Meanwhile, Mum was running to keep up with the chef. He had headed directly to the kitchen. I caught a little of her description to him of what she had in mind for lunch.

Bishop assembled the rest of us in the dining room. Apparently, the chef was going to fix something for us for lunch. In the mean time he explained about what would happen in the next couple of days.

"We're really tight for time. We would normally get into the Lodge in mid to late April. Instead, he we are in May and almost late May. There's a big American holiday coming up. You may have heard of it, Memorial Day. The owner has already had to cancel several parties, and he really doesn't want to have to cancel the Memorial Day weekend, which was fully booked.

"So, we'd like to ask your assistance in preparing for the beginning of the tourist season. If you would help tuning the engines and doing other maintenance that the summer crew finds, we would give you a bonus of 10%." He quickly added, "Of course, we don't expect you to inspect the furnace or the more involved electrical system." He finished on a hopeful note. "Do you think you would?"

Dad began to speak hesitantly, and Bishop seemed to be preparing for the worst. Who knew what sort of problems that he'd found when he and his crew arrived in previous springs. But Dad surprised him, "Well, sir, actually . . ."

"Yes?"

"Well, we've already done almost all of that in preparing for your return."

Bishop seemed stumped. He eventually said, "Well, in that case, I suppose that we would appreciate your touring the facilities with our crew, pointing out what you've already done. Usually, we do the inspection unaccompanied, but this situation seems different that normal."

Dad then plunged into the difficult area. It reminded me of the old reruns of an ancient Telly series that I'd watched as a kid. There was a robot whose main job seemed to be warning the kid on the show when danger was present. He'd shout, "Danger! Danger! Will Robinson."

This seemed to be one of those moments for our family. "Danger, Danger, Dad!" I thought.

Dad began straightforwardly, "There is one problem that I have to mention."

Bishop seemed much calmer at this, "Yes, go ahead."

Dad simply said it, "We lost one of the ice-borers." He stopped there without further explanation. I thought, "Right! Don't say anything more than you absolutely have to!"

Bishop didn't ask how it happened. He didn't complain about how stupid we were. He just said, "OK. We'll have to dock the cost of it from you salary." He hesitated and then said, "I hate to do it. You've quite possibly been the best caretakers we've ever had."

The relief was apparent on Dad's face. He was almost giddy as he said, "Oh, that's completely all right. I would expect no less."

That was the last that we ever heard about the ice-borer. After lunch, which was served by both Mum and the chef, we went with the crew conducting our tour of the facility, pointing out what we'd done and not done. We didn't go with the HVAC man. His area was beyond our expertise.

Bishop had toured the cabins with Mum. That night we had dinner prepared solely by the chef. Bishop asked us to join him at 10 AM the next morning and to be prepared to leave that afternoon shortly after lunch.

We felt pretty good about the tour of the facility, but we were still nervous about the meeting the next morning. That meeting happened an hour after breakfast finished. Mum wanted to help the chef clean up afterwards, but he wouldn't have it.

We brought our luggage down and deposited it in the Lobby before the 10 AM meeting.

At ten sharp, Bishop called us into his office. He had us sit and offered us drink. None of us was interested. Then he began:

"I normally begin this meeting with a lot of comments about the caretaker's performance, and of course, the shortcomings of that performance.

"Here I can only say that the Lodge is better than we left it last Fall. I'm authorized to pay you the 10% bonus that I spoke of. I've also strongly suggested an additional 10% bonus based on your suggestion about the potential dangers of the porch. I don't know what the owner will do about that.

"The bonus will be deposited in your bank account in Vancouver before you arrive in Winnipeg. I don't know about the additional bonus, but I will argue as strongly as I can for it.

He stopped and steepled his fingers on his desk. He seemed to be lost in thought. Then he said, "I've never done this before, but I would like you to commit right now to come back next season to be caretakers again. I'd recommend you for a ten percent increase in salary immediately."

We looked at each other. I felt an almost irresistible temptation to laugh. Dad actually did chuckle and almost gave way to full laughter. He caught himself and apologized, "I'm sorry. It's not your very generous offer. It's just that the reason that we took this job was not really too much for the money." He considered what to say and then said, "We needed to get away from it all. And believe me, we had a lot to get away from. We never dreamed that this would be a good experience—just a necessary one."

He looked at Mum and then me and then continued, "I don't think we can make that commitment right now. But we will consider it seriously. I am not kidding. We will fully consider it."

Bishop sighed and said, "Well, I had to try. I hope you will really consider returning. Just let me know any time before the Fall if you will do that. We won't even post the job."

He rose as though to dismiss us and then sat again, "There's just one thing that I'd like to know. You don't have to tell me. It's just that curiosity is killing me, and I'd appreciate it if you'd give me an answer."

Dad said, "If it's something we can tell you, of course we will."

"You never used the satellite phone a single time. Ordinarily caretakers use every last second of their allotted time and often beyond that. But you never used it. Why?"

We all looked at each other. I started to say something and Dad actually encouraged me to. So, I gave him an answer that was true, but of course, not complete.

"Well, sir. We really don't have anyone to call. Or, maybe it's that we don't have anyone that we are anxious to talk to.

"You see, Mum's pretty much an orphan." It was the truth, of course. "Her Mum and Dad died a number of years ago. She only had a sister.

That sister and her husband died in a car crash about the time that I was born. I never really got to meet them.

"They had a son, Harry. He lived with us for most of my life. But he got mixed up with a bad lot, and he disappeared almost a year ago. We haven't seen or heard from him since.

"Then there's my Dad's family. His parents died several years ago. He has a sister who never married. We're pretty close to her, but she has always been against our giving Harry a home. She always thought that his stock was bad. We've sort of had a falling out over him, so we really don't have family to talk to.

"I just graduated from prep school last year. I never had a lot of good friends among them. That sort of leaves us without people to talk to."

Dad stared at me with something like admiration for how I handled the question. He said, "I couldn't have said it better myself. I left my work back in England and sort of cut off ties there. So there you are."

Bishop nodded, seeming to accept the explanation completely. "I'm sorry that you don't have anyone close." This time he really did stand and extend his hand to shake ours. We each took turns. Then, it was time for lunch.

The chef had prepared the best lunch that I'd had since the last one on that day in the Fall when they'd left us. We took our luggage and coats down to the dock. The pilot was ready to go. We loaded up the plane, and I agreed to share the cockpit with the pilot again.

Just before we took off, Bishop came down to the dock and wished us a safe flight. He also reminded us about keeping the Lodge in our plans for the Fall.

After riding a snowmobile, the takeoff seemed tame. The flight to Winnipeg seemed slow and leisurely. Again, I felt safer than I had in a very long time.

□□

The plane arrived at the airport where a limo was waiting for us. The driver asked where we wanted to go. Dad had an answer immediately. His answer was, "What's a good old hotel that has a feel of the 19th Century?"

The driver thought a moment and said, "I think I have just what you want." He wouldn't say anything more, but just drove on.

When we arrived, what we saw was not impressive. There were storefronts and an entrance. There was a title over the main entrance, but it was not imposing. The driver helped us unload and take our things into the lobby.

There wasn't a bellhop, but the lobby was the fanciest that I'd ever been in. It wasn't fancy in a boasting way. The furniture pieces seemed like they might be antiques. There were coffee tables and sofas and armchairs around them. The lighting didn't glare, but the lobby didn't seem dim either. There were a few people sitting in the lobby reading the paper or just waiting for someone.

Dad booked a room. We dragged our stuff up in the tiny elevator. It was so small that it was actually hard to find in the lobby. We had to ask a desk clerk where it was. Once it was pointed out, it was easy to see, but it was in a corner, as though the architect hadn't wanted something so modern as an elevator to be easily seen. Our room was spacious. It had two beds that were smaller than queen size. Dad and I looked at them, and I immediately offered to sleep on the floor. There was a little argument, but it was clear that Mum and Dad couldn't share a bed. It was just too small. I insisted that I'd done it before, and I was quite used to it.

As inconvenient as that sounds, the room was very . . . very . . . something. Maybe homey was the word I was looking for. It had a small desk and table. But they seemed to be antiques. The bath was the only really modern part of the room. It was very pleasant. There was a balcony with a table and two chairs. It was small, but it looked out over a courtyard that had lots of plants and lawn furniture. It was still a little cool to sit out there, but it seemed that it would be nice in warmer weather.

Dad announced that he was going to call Aunt Marge and find out if our account had actually received our salary. We all decided to come. Dad stopped at the front desk to see if he could get change and an idea where a pay phone was.

The desk clerk suggested that he call from his room phone. She said, "I know we charge a pretty hefty fee for calling, but if it's a short call, it shouldn't be too bad."

Dad insisted on using a phone booth. The clerk suggested that a better way would be to buy a phone card. Dad had heard of them but had never used one. The clerk filled him in. "Oh, it's pretty easy, and they usually have good long distance and international rates. Our gift shop sells them, I think."

So we went into the gift shop. She was right. Dad bought a card for one hundred dollars. He thought that we might end up talking for a long time. We went across the street to a drug store. It had a phone booth inside.

Dad read the instruction on the phone card. As a matter of fact he pored over them for quite some time. Finally, he announced, "I'll need some help. Somebody hold the phone card and read the numbers off. I have to dial an 800 number. Then, I dial the phone number including the international code. Then, I have to dial this access code that seems to have about twenty digits." He chuckled, "I'm going to wear my ruddy fingers off dialing all those numbers."

We got going. I read off the numbers, and Dad dialed. He got through the 800 number OK, but then he missed one of the international phone number digits, and we had to start again. That time, we got all the way through Marge's phone number but somehow screwed up on the access code. The next time, we didn't even get the 800 number right.

Finally, we got all the digits right. There were 42 digits altogether. Dad reported that the phone rang and rang without an answer. I asked, "Couldn't you leave a message on the answering machine?"

"She doesn't use one. She thinks that anyone who wants to talk to her enough will keep at it and eventually get through."

Mum asked what time it was there. It was 9 PM. She said, "You'd think she'd be home."

Dad wasn't worried, "She's probably playing bridge with her friends. We'll try again tomorrow."

Then we looked at the phone book to find a branch of a bank. We couldn't tell which was close, but we called a cab and gave the cabbie a choice of three. He picked one that was about a mile away. We walked in, and Dad went up to a teller. He wanted to see a bank officer.

The teller claimed that she could do almost anything a bank officer could. Dad just rolled his eyes and asked, "Can you cash an out of province check for ten thousand dollars?"

She just formed an "O" with her mouth and asked us to sit on a sofa and wait for an officer to show up.

It wasn't that long. When he showed up, he invited us into his office and invited us to sit. Dad leaned forward and explained what he wanted. The officer scratched his head and said, "Do you really want ten thousand dollars in cash?"

"Yes, I do."

The officer tried a different approach, "Do you have a debit card?"

Dad nodded.

"Then you can draw out five hundred a day. Is that not enough?"

Dad shook his head.

The officer said, "OK. Here are your choices. You write your check and open an account. You deposit the check, and in a few days, the money will be available to you."

Dad shook his head again.

"You can get your bank to issue a cashier's check and overnight it to you. We'd still have to let it sit maybe two days. AND you'd have to open an account to deposit it into."

Dad shook his head again.

The officer said, "OK. The best that I can do for you is this. Write me a check for one hundred dollars, open an account, and deposit the check. Then you'll have an account number. You then call your bank right away.

If you're lucky and have a good relationship with them, they'll be willing to wire transfer the money to your account here. If we do it in a hurry, they might get it going today. The wire transfer would be available overnight, and you could come in and write a check for ten thousand at the open of business tomorrow morning."

Dad agreed readily with that, but the banker added a bit to that. "First, I can't guarantee that all that will happen overnight. You might have to wait until the next day. Secondly, the bank will probably charge you a hefty fee. Third, they might refuse to do it at all."

Dad was in a hurry and just said, "Let's just get started."

So we filled out an application. The banker didn't like using a hotel as an address, but he couldn't say it was illegal. He took Mum and Dad's passports as ID. When he'd finished, we had a temporary checkbook with an account number and a bank number. The banker said that we'd need the name that the account was made out for exactly and the address of the branch exactly for the wire transfer to work. We were careful to get that all correct.

The banker actually offered to let us use his phone to make the call to our bank in Vancouver, but Dad insisted that he wanted privacy. The banker offered us his office, but Dad refused.

We left the bank and found a phone booth. Again we worked through the 40 numbers (fewer because we were not calling internationally). This time we did it right on the second try. We got our bank and found that we needed to call the home office to set up the wire transfer. They tried to transfer our call, but it dropped.

We were back on the line with the bank, and this time before transferring, we got the direct line to the wire transfer department. Of course, the transfer worked.

Dad spent a lot of time on the phone. It seemed that they wanted all kinds of proof that we were actually THE Dursleys who owned the account. They asked for our address in Vancouver. Fortunately, Mum remembered that. They asked for the passport numbers of both Mum and Dad. Then, they made Dad give them the account information that we wanted the transfer to go to about a dozen times. Really not, but they wanted to be really, really sure about it.

When the conversation finally ended, Dad reported that they didn't know for sure whether the wire transfer would go through over night or not.

So, we went back to the hotel and decided to have dinner there. There was a restaurant in the hotel. It reminded me of the dining hall at the Lodge. There were some big differences, though. The tables all had tablecloths. The food was delivered in dishes covered by what looked like silver covers, but I suppose were stainless steel. There was a buffet but unlike any that I'd seen at a buffet in England. It had large warming trays that had metal covers that rolled back to reveal what was inside. The place settings all had three forks and two knives. The food was not delivered quickly, but you didn't seem to mind because it was such a pleasant place to sit and talk.

And talk we did. I asked Dad why he wanted ten thousand dollars in addition to whatever he was still carrying in his money belt.

He answered, "I'm now convinced that it will be quite a long time before we know for sure what's happened in England. We need money to last at least through the summer. I want to hide ourselves as best we can. That means no more jobs. We find a place to hole up, and we do it."

Mum asked, "But are we not going to try to find out what's happened?"

Dad said that until we get in touch with Marge, he didn't want to do anything else. After we talk to her, we could decide on next steps.

We left the dining room, and I paid more attention to the Lobby. Something that I hadn't noticed before was that there was a stained glass window in the ceiling of the Lobby. The Lobby was actually four stories high, and there was a walkway around the Lobby at every level. I stood there and stared up at it until Mum took my arm and dragged me along to our room.

⊞

The next morning, we were up early and ready to be packed. Our bank was open at 9 AM. So, we went to the Dining Room for breakfast. No one suggested it, but we all had enjoyed dinner the night before, and we all just assumed that we'd breakfast in the hotel. In a way the breakfast was better than dinner. It was a brunch. You could order off the menu, but it was hard to not spend as much as the brunch cost and still get a decent English breakfast. So, we all did the brunch. It included all the usual things, but in addition, there was a chef who would make waffles or pancakes or an omelet for you to your taste and deliver it to your table.

By the end of breakfast, we were secretly hoping that the wire transfer had not come through so that we could spend at least one more day there. Actually Mum and I were not so secret about it.

By the time we were finished, it was almost 9 AM. Mum talked Dad into making the call from our room. It was a local call, so it was free, and the chances that anyone would trace that call back to us before we checked out was minuscule.

It turned out that the wire transfer hadn't come through. So we were all happy—even Dad. We weren't sad about having to stay in the hotel either. We were lying low, but we could do that in style. Dad bought a newspaper in the gift shop, and we all took sections, sat in the lobby, and read. It was

211

probably not the best way to lie low, but it was so pleasant in the lobby that none of us cared.

We left the hotel to make another call to Aunt Marge. Dad let it ring for what seemed five minutes. He finally hung up and shook his head. I asked if this were bad.

Dad's face was downcast but he said, "No. No. It's not unusual. I just wish we'd get through to her."

We had had such a good breakfast and no exercise, so none of us was really interested in lunch. In the afternoon, it was warm enough that we went into the courtyard. Dad bought a deck of cards, and we played gin rummy through most of the afternoon. Toward the end of the afternoon, Mum had an idea that would have seemed silly to me, but that somehow in this hotel, seemed nice. She suggested that we "dress" for dinner. I didn't get it at first, but she explained that what she meant by dressing for dinner was dressing up.

We went out and made another call to Aunt Marge. There was still no answer. Nobody had the heart to ask Dad what he thought about it. We all were beginning to know what to think about it, though nobody wanted to say it.

Then, we went to our room, changed into our best clothes, and came down to the dining room. It was a little before 5 PM when the dining room began serving, but they would let you take a seat and wait for five.

The meal was superb again. This time, I noticed something that I'd not noticed before. The room was very quiet. Every restaurant that I'd ever eaten at was noisy enough that conversation was at least a little difficult, but this dining room was one that was almost as quiet as ours at home when we were eating. As a matter of fact, it was quieter. We often watched the Telly at home. That brought another realization to me. I hadn't watched the Telly–even for news–since we'd first arrived. That was true despite the fact that there was a Telly in our room. Then I realized another strange thing. There wasn't a Telly in any public room in the hotel.

The next day, we all were slow rising. I think that we weren't anxious to find out that the wire transfer had arrived. So we had a late breakfast and then went to the bank. We didn't arrive until almost eleven.

Before we went to the bank, we tried calling Aunt Marge again. It was mid-afternoon in England. There was no answer. Dad was still not worried. At least, he said he wasn't worried.

When we arrived, the bank officer that we'd dealt with noticed us immediately. He invited us into his office and gave us the "good" news. Our wire transfer had arrived overnight.

He said, "Now that it's arrived, it's all available to you except the hundred dollars that you deposited by check. It won't clear for another day, but you'll have to leave some money in the account anyway. It can be that amount.

"Now, this amount is too much for a teller to dispense, so I'll have to ask you to write the check in my presence, and I'll get the cash for you. Now, how do you want it?"

Dad answered for us, "I'd like 5000 dollars in five hundred dollar bills, 4500 dollars in hundreds, Four hundred in fifties, 50 in tens, and the rest in two dollar pieces."

The banker looked a little dismayed, "I'm sorry, but the largest denomination bills are one hundred dollar bills."

Dad was more than a little dismayed himself. "Nothing larger than hundreds?"

"Nothing." But he quickly added, "We can offer you American Express Travelers checks. They do have larger denominations."

Dad shook his head. I knew that he didn't want to have any money that required him to show an ID when he spent it.

So, the banker went to the tellers to collect ten thousand dollars. While he was gone.,Dad informed Mum and me that we were each going to carry one thousand dollars apiece, mostly in small denominations.

He returned with a thick envelope containing mostly hundreds and other bills plus some coins. He counted it all out carefully. We transferred the bills to our wallets. Our shares was not too bulky but his, which he kept in the envelope was. Mum and I each had five hundreds, four fifties, a couple of tens and some coins.

Our banker (we had begun to think of him as *our* banker) tried to talk us out of carrying so much cash about with us.

Dad asked if Winnipeg were a dangerous place. Our banker shifted uneasily in his chair and said "no" in a sort of whine. He added, "I feel that I should be your adviser concerning money. It's just that I worry that you might mislay it. How would you feel then?"

Dad just said, "Unlucky." I thought to myself that we'd had so much bad luck lately that we were due some good luck.

Dad rose to leave, and so did our banker. We all shook hands, and our banker wished us good luck and hoped that we'd have more business for him in the future. We all smiled, and I thought that if we were lucky we'd not see him again.

On the way back to the hotel, we first stopped our cab at a phone booth on a corner. We had the cabbie wait for us. We tried Aunt Marge. No luck.

Then we went to the train station. Dad bought tickets for us on the transcontinental for Toronto. The next departure was the following morning at 10 AM. So, we ended up having to spend another night at our hotel. No one was disappointed.

In the afternoon, we had a conference in our room. Dad brought the topic up which was on everyone's mind. "Well, it's beginning to look bad for Marge. I'm not giving up. We'll phone at every stop on the way to Toronto, but I think that we have to start considering the possibility that she's either been taken by the Deatheaters, or she's . . ." Here he stopped, and his face contorted as he tried to keep from crying. He never ended that sentence, but Mum and I knew what he couldn't bring himself to say.

The silence stretched on. I asked the question, "Dad, what can we do to find out for sure?"

Mum suggested that we try to call Aunt Marge's friends. Dad's answered, "No, frankly, I don't know many of their full names. She only talked about them by first name, but even if I did know them, I don't think I'd try calling them. If she's . . ." There was another uncomfortable pause, and then he went on, "Well, I don't want to make life any riskier for them. If it ever came out that we contacted them, they might become persons of interest for the Deatheaters."

We were all silent, and then Dad went on, "I think we need to go to a library when we get to Toronto and start going through back issues of *The Times* and the local paper in Tudley-on-the-Thames to see if there's any . . . well . . . notice of her disappearing." Again, the obvious went unsaid.

So, the afternoon went a lot slower. Dinner was excellent, but we didn't really enjoy it all that much. The evening dragged on, and we went to bed. We tried calling another time or two before we checked out and went to the train station.

The Wizard Hunt

The change of boarding the train and starting to move lifted our spirits. It seemed that in moving toward Toronto and the next phase of our attempt to reach Aunt Marge, there was more hope. I don't know why, but it seemed that way.

Shortly after we left the station, the conductor came through and announced that we were leaving Manitoba and entering Ontario. Dad commented, "We'll spend the rest of this trip in Ontario–all day and a half."

We watched the endless flat terrain pass us. At first, it seemed exciting to see closeup what we had flown over a few days before. However, that novelty only lasted for an hour or two. Then it became boring, but even that was interesting. We had had very few hours of boredom since we left home. The combination of feeling safe that travel always seemed to provide and boredom was almost intoxicating.

We stopped every few hours at stations. People came on and left, but nobody seemed threatening. Dad would go off and find a pay phone. He'd always return with the same negative report. No one answered the phone. We kept that up despite the fact that disappointment had become the norm, and we almost would have been disappointed if it were otherwise.

Night fell. We discovered that we'd not eaten yet on the train. We went to the dining car and found something to eat. The next morning we were back and were assigned to the same table.

The long miles continued to flow past. Lunch came and went. Dinner time arrived, and we ate. We knew that Toronto was close. So, we lingered in the dining car. We knew that we'd probably never ride the rails again–at least in Canada.

The conductor came through and announced that we'd be in Toronto in about half an hour. So, we reluctantly returned to our cabin and prepared to leave.

As we were preparing our luggage, Dad declared that we really had to cut down our luggage so that we would find moving easier. Mum complained about having to give up clothes that she ABSOLUTELY had to have.

I really didn't need a lot of my clothing. I basically wore two pairs of jeans, a pair of dress slacks, about half a dozen shirts–some casual, some dress–and one suit (not counting underwear and socks). I said, "Look, I don't even need all of one suitcase. Mum, you can have the space in mine that I don't need."

Dad grumbled a little and said, "I can probably find some room in my suitcase for some of your clothes."

So we came to a rough agreement that at the next convenient point, we'd slim down—at least our luggage. Actually, come to think of it, we'd slowly lost weight as we'd traveled—at least Dad and I.

We left our compartment without any of the disquiet that I felt when we arrived at Winnipeg. I only hoped that that was a good sign. We left the train and after exiting the station discovered a hotel across the street. We decided to stay the night there and then work on more permanent accommodations. We had to walk a long block to get there, not to mention crossing the wide boulevard in front of the station. By the time we'd gotten there, Mum was beginning to change her feelings about carrying two pieces of luggage each even if she were carrying the smallest.

I was a little afraid of just how bad the hotel might be, but I was pleasantly surprised when we entered the lobby. It wasn't Winnipeg, but it was pleasant, and well-maintained. It had a front desk that we could walk directly up to and not have to wait behind a long line of people. I guess it was maybe nice that there was a line of people.

Our room was again not as pleasant as the last hotel, but was more modern and had a decent bath. That's how I'd come to judge hotel rooms. How pleasant was the bath?

I really didn't get to experience the hotel much. We went to bed as quickly as we could. We were up. While Mum and I showered and shaved, Dad was using the phone book to find an extended stay hotel for us. He found one that looked like it ought to be like the one that we had in Vancouver. That one had been wonderful.

We checked out, called a cab, and arrived at the Marriott before noon. They let us have our room a little earlier than the 3 PM check-in time. We had an early lunch or maybe it was a late breakfast across the street.

While we were eating, I raised a question that had been bothering me for a while. I asked Dad, "OK. Why don't we just call one of Aunt Marge's friends and find out from them what happened?"

Dad looked exasperated, but probably not as much as I was. "I thought we went through this before."

I just shrugged and said, "I don't think we covered all the possibilities."

"OK. Here's the deal. I actually know a couple of her friends. So, we call them, and maybe they tell us what happened. On the other hand, maybe they don't know. Either way, what do they ask us?"

I wasn't expecting that, but I'd started it, so I had to keep going, "Well, I suppose they ask us where WE have been all this time."

"Right-o. What do you say?"

I thought that one over and said, "I guess 'None of your business' and hang up."

I knew the point that was coming, and Dad delivered it, "Somebody tries to trace us—either Marge, if she's actually still around or her buddies if she'd not. They can trace us back to Toronto. So what do we have to do then?"

I supplied the answer for him, "We have to move again."

But I wasn't done. I went on, "OK. I get it. What if we tried getting hold of someone who isn't so closely tied to our family. What about your friends at Grunning?"

He actually laughed. It wasn't a laugh that had much humor in it. "Oh, my! You know I didn't give Grunning's any notice. Never said a word. Friday I went to work, and I never came back in again. They probably would just as soon turn us over to the Deatheaters as talk to me."

I kept going, "Well, what about friends back on our street? What about that old biddy who lives across the street? What was her name?" It occurred to me before Dad could answer. "Oh, yeh. Mrs. Figg."

I had second thoughts about her, "Of course, she might remember that one Guy Faulks day, but she wouldn't hold that against you. Would she?"

Dad laughed at that suggestion, but it was a friendly laugh. "You know, we might as well ask her where the Irish Republican Army is going to strike next. I'm sure she doesn't know about Marge or the IRA or Deatheaters."

I wasn't done. "What about the Prime Minister or his office? They surely know about what's happening."

There was no humor in his face when he answered, "You're right. They probably do, but if we were talk to anyone there and say the word wizard, they'd trace the call so fast that the RCMP's would be breaking down the door before the phone was back on the hook."

We then prepared to go to the Toronto Reference library. I'd given up, and we were on our way. Dad decided we would be less conspicuous if we rode the bus downtown. We'd ridden plenty of buses and other public transport, so we were right at home. We arrived at the library and quickly found the periodical room. There were lots of magazines and Canadian

217

newspapers and a good number of foreign papers. There were a few major English Newspapers–*The Times of London*, the *Guardian*, and so forth.

Marge's hometown newspaper wasn't among them, so we decided to concentrate on *The Times of London*. We discovered that they kept two months of the newspaper accessible to the public. We divided up the dates and started reading. We'd arrived about 4:30 PM and spent a solid two hours reading. We'd made a pretty good dent in the stack of newspapers, but we would clearly need a good bit more time to finish going through even just those two months.

We stopped for dinner, but before we left the library, we asked a librarian how we could look at older copies. She informed us that they were on microfiche. We'd have to borrow the microfiche editions from the stacks in the basement. To do that we needed a library card. To get a library card, if you were an adult, you needed proof that you lived in Toronto, like a passport, driver's license, or so on.

But if you were a student, you just needed a grade card and a proof of residence, like a letter from your teacher.

We dropped back to think over dinner. We found a fast Chinese food place, the Lee Chan Asian Bistro, and ordered a couple of entrees that we shared. We discussed the options for getting a library card.

I had an idea that I thought would get me one. I explained it to Mum and Dad, "Here's the thing. I'm still 18 and could pass for a student. As a matter of fact, it was just a few months ago. I go in and claim hardship. I'm a student. I have to finish my final term paper. I only have a couple of days before it's due. I don't have time to get the letter from the school. So won't you, please, please just let me sign up for an in-library access card?" I used appropriate body language with just a hint of whine that I'd perfected during my years in school.

Dad laughed, "That might just work. What do you say, Pet?"

She was disgusted but admitted that it couldn't hurt to try.

I told them that I'd go back alone. It wouldn't look good if I were with my parents. I left them finishing dinner while I ambled back to the library practicing my elevator speech.

□

I came back to Lee Chan's emporium and found my parents enjoying a cup o'. I had a big smile on my face. I sat down at the table and raised a hand that was not empty but had a card in it. I did a little sign-song announcement, "I've got an access card."

We decided that it was a good time to call it a night. Dad decided to splurge and take a cab back home. It's funny how quickly you begin to think of a place as "home" when you're constantly moving.

On the way, I suggested that we do something fun for once. Mum said that one fun night would set her up for the rest of the summer. Even Dad grudgingly admitted that a fun night would be a nice change from the last year.

When we got to the hotel, we picked up the lobby copy of the paper and greedily flipped through the pages to the entertainment section. It had a listing of movies in town. Each movie had a one paragraph description. Of course, there were the big adds for movies and theaters. It had been so long since we'd seen anything about movies that we went directly to the one paragraph descriptions. Dad had me read them.

"The Mummy. A three thousand year old mummy is dug up by archaeologists in 1925. Cairo librarian awakens the Mummy which follows her back to Cairo."

Dad shook his head. "I've seen a dozen different 'Mummy' movies. I pass. What about you, Pet."

Mum wrinkled her nose, mouth, and every part of her face that she could as she said, "You know me, I hate horror movies."

Dad simply said, "Done. Go ahead."

I read the next, "*A Midsummer Night's Dream*. A romp in the woods with fairies, lovers, and fools. One of Shakespeare's best comedies."

I said, "That's out right off. No Shakespeare for me." I immediately went on to the next. "*Star Wars Episode I: The Phantom Menace*. The back story of Obie-wan Kenobe and Darth Vader with comic relief by Jar-Jar Binks. The beginning of the Star Wars Space Operas."

Dad laughed, "Jar-Jar Binks! Is that some kind of fag in drag? Any movie with a character named Jar-Jar can't be worth the money."

Mum didn't object, so I kept going. "*Notting Hill*. Romantic comedy where bookstore owner is mistaken for journalist, interviews the star of a new sci-fi film, and spends lots of time with other women before getting together with the star."

Both Dad and Mum made the face. Dad said, "Bloody hell. Romantic comedy." Mum said, "Euwe. Science Fiction."

I went on, "*Austin Powers: The Spy Who Shagged Me*. Austin Powers is married to a robot and fights Dr. Evil in Seattle."

Dad seemed interested, "It is a British film. Probably lots of buxom . . ." At that point, he happened to glance over to Mum who was giving him the evil eye that Dr. Evil could never imitate.

Dad just said, "Maybe we've had enough of Seattle."

So, I went on. I'd reached the last one, so I thought that this had better be it. "*Wild, Wild West*. American steampunk western action-comedy." I stared at it, because that was all the tiny paragraph had to say about the movie.

Dad who seemed slightly interested asked, "Go ahead. What's the rest?"

"There is no 'rest'. That's all of it."

That left us all lost for words for a minute. Both Mum and Dad walked around behind me to look over my shoulder at the page of the newspaper.

Dad seemed to be searching the display adverts to see if there were any movies that the little mini-reviews hadn't mentioned. Mum was looking at the rest of the page.

She was the first to speak. "Here! Look at this article here about a Glenn Gould."

Dad shrugged but told me to go ahead and read the article to us. I did.

> Glenn Gould, the world-renowned interpreter of J. S.
> Bach will present a rare charity concert tonight benefiting
> the United Cerebral Palsy Organization.
>
> Although a prolific recording artist and once a world-
> wide concertizer, he has not performed in public for nearly
> twenty years.
>
> He now spends his time producing and performing a
> wide variety of Baroque and Classical music. In addition,
> he produces documentaries for the Canadian Broadcast
> Corporation.
>
> Tonight's program begins at 8:15 PM. at Roy Thomas
> Hall. The program begins with The Art of Fudge.

At that point, Mum interrupted, "That can't be right, dear. They don't mean Fudge." She looked over my shoulder again and said, "No, see, it's The art of the Fugue."

I couldn't help asking, "I know what fudge is. What is a fugue?"

Mum and Dad both could only shrug, and I went on reading.

> The program begins with The Art of the Fugue, BMV
> 1080. After intermission, it will conclude with the Toronto
> Symphony Orchestra performing Bach's Italian Concerto
> and Concerto No. 1 for Keyboard and Strings. Mr. Gould
> will be the featured soloist in both works.

Mum looked from one to the other of us, "Well, what do you think? It's not every day that you get to see Glenn Gould perform on the stage."

Dad emitted a sort of low growl. He normally does that when he doesn't like one of Mum's ideas, but he couldn't think of anything to say against it.

I said, "Before right now, I'd never heard of Glenn Gould. Why do you want to see him?"

Mum stared at the two of us for a moment and said, "Didn't you hear? He's world-renowned." Dad and I looked at each other. We knew that resistance was futile. So we resigned ourselves to an evening of Bach.

Bach Strikes Back

We ran up to our room, taking the stairs rather than wait for an elevator. None of us really had a choice of clothes for a night on the town. We all wore the best clothes that we had. Dad called for a cab from the room. We took the elevator to the lobby because we knew it would be a while before a cab arrived.

When it did, we found that the cabbie was a little touch of home. He had a Cockney accent buried under what must have been years or even decades in Toronto.

"What's your pleasure, guv?"

Dad fumbled for the name of the music hall, but before we had to admit our ignorance, it came to him, "Roy Thomson Hall. And please get there as fast as you can."

The cabbie turned around and looked at us. "Yes, sir. When I first saw you, that was the last bloody place I'd have pegged you for. So, you're going to see G. G."

We were all puzzled for a minute, and then we all realized that he was talking about Glenn Gould. Dad said, "Yes. You're right. You know about the concert?"

"Bloody Hell, doesn't everyone in Toronto know about the concert? The first time G. G. has been out in public in twenty years. You're bleeding lucky to get tickets for that concert. They've been sold out for months. Must have set you back a packet I'd say."

We were all beginning to feel a little green. Of course, without tickets there wasn't a chance in hell that we'd get in. We all looked at Dad.

He turned a little red and blustered, "There are always tickets available at the last minute for these things. I'm sure we'll find someone with a few tickets that he wants to sell."

The cabbie didn't say anything.

221

Dad continued—probably trying to convince himself as much as anyone, "Well, I don't mind paying extra. Someone will be willing to give up their tickets for enough money."

I knew that Dad's money belt was bulging with cash, but I wasn't so sure. The cabbie wasn't either. He said, "I hear that balcony seats are going for more than a thousand."

Dad gulped, turned a bit green, but didn't say anything.

The driver went on, "It would be a real privilege to get to see G. G. He's not performed publicly in almost twenty years.

"As a matter of fact, there's this conspiracy theory that says that he died in the early '80's."

I asked, "If he died, why didn't people just admit it?"

The cabbie was warming to his story. "The story is that the CBC wants to keep releasing CD's of his music, and they figure they can make more if G. G. is a mystery character recording music in top secret in his hidden studio."

Mum asked, "But surely, they can't keep releasing CD's if he's not recording them."

The cabbie laughed, "That's the beauty of it. Everyone knows that he was a maniac for perfect music. He stopped performing because concert halls aren't perfect. For one thing, there are the people—coughing, whispering, sneezing, making all sorts of noises.

"The conspiracy nutsos think that he spent the last five years of his life making super recordings. CBC just pulls one or two tapes out of its super-secret vaults every year and releases them as newly made CD's."

I asked, "What do the nutsos think that he died of?"

The cabbie responded immediately, "That's the beauty of it. He was always a bit of a nut about his health–a hyperchondic as you might say.

He paused a minute and asked, "Who is it who has a fool for a patient?"

We didn't say anything and the cabbie laughing at his own joke said, "The man who doctors hisself." Without waiting for a response he went on, "That's G. G. to a T. He got all sorts of prescriptions for crazy conditions that he thinks he's got. He doses himself accordin' to his own ideas about medicine. Then one day he takes an overdose." He snapped his fingers and said, "And that's all she wrote." He seemed to reflect a minute and said, "Like a bleedin' rock star he was. At least the way they say he died."

Dad asked, "That's why this concert is such a big deal. If G. G.—I mean this Glenn Gould is really dead, he can't exactly walk out on stage and play the piano before hundreds of people."

The cabbie replied, "Bloody right! It's like that Twain guy."

Mum asked who that "Twain" guy was.

"You know, Marty or Martin Twain. Something like that. He said, 'The rumors of my death are fucking exaggerated.' Pardon Twain's French."

Dad was really glum now. I got it. Nobody was going to sell a ticket to this show.

It was a long quiet drive the rest of the way to downtown Toronto. We came in on a freeway that went along the lakefront. With the lights of the city starting to turn on as the last rays of the sun disappeared, it was a beautiful drive. I thought that even if we didn't get to see Glenn Gould, the drive was worth it.

We pulled up to the hall and the cabbie let us out. He asked Dad if he wanted him to wait to see if we got tickets. Dad just paid him and sent him away.

□

We glumly walked up to the main entrance, followed the signs to the box office, and Dad paused trying to decide which window to approach. There was one with a sign above it that said, "Future concerts", another that said, "Will Call" (whatever that meant), and a couple that didn't have a sign. We walked up to that window. He put a brave face on it and asked–just as though there would be plenty of tickets, "We'd like three tickets for tonight's concert."

The clerk, who had had a bored look, changed to solicitous, "I'm sorry. All tickets have been sold out for months, and none have been turned back in."

All Dad said was, "Oh." He seemed stumped as to what to do next, but I had an idea. I said to the young lady, "Oh, that's too bad, we came all the way from Winnipeg. As soon as we heard about the concert, we decided that we'd just come and see if we couldn't find some tickets. They could be anywhere—in the rafters, under a seat, hanging from the chandelier."

The young clerk laughed at that but still there were not tickets. We were about to walk away. I have no idea what Dad would do, but just as we were turning to go, the lady in the Will Call window said, "Mary, send them over here. I might just have something for them."

We didn't have to be asked even once. We were at her window as quickly as we could trot there. Dad said, "You said something about tickets."

She nodded and then said, "There are a set of 4 tickets here at Will Call. We're supposed to wait until the concert starts to sell them if no one shows up, but I couldn't help hearing about your story—all the way from Winnipeg and no tickets to boot. I just have to bend the rules a little for you." At that, I swear that she winked at me.

She went on, "Now here's the thing. I have to sell all of them. Would you buy all four?"

Dad was like a drowning man who had just had a life preserver thrown to him. "You bet we will."

She wrinkled her nose a little, "Well, they're not really very good tickets. They're on the right side of the orchestra in the first row. For this kind of concert, that's pretty bad, and they're pretty expensive."

Dad's smile was a mile wide, "You heard us, we don't care if they're in the rafters, we'll take them–all four."

She took a deep breath as though preparing us for a shock and said, "They're one hundred eighty dollars apiece. That'll be 720 dollars."

Dad didn't blink but said, "Good."

She asked, "Will that be VISA, American Express, Mastercharge?"

He just smiled and said, "I'll pay cash."

She stared but didn't say anything. He drew out his wallet, peeled off eight one hundred dollar bills, and said, "Keep the change. Give it to charity. Let's just say we rounded up."

Her eyes bugged out, but she took the bills, gave them a quick inspection, and handed over the tickets. "Get moving, you've not got five minutes left before the concert."

Dad had been to a few concerts. He quickly got us sorted out and found the proper entrance. We had to walk down a long sloping incline just outside the concert hall. The usher at the last door glanced at our tickets, handed us programs, and pointed us at the first row. Our tickets turned out to be next to the last four seats on the row. Just as we reached the row, someone who had come out on the stage announced "God Save the Queen". Everyone stood, and we didn't have to ask anyone to get up to let us through to our seats. The man on the stage led the singing, which we joined in.

At first, I thought he might be Glenn Gould, but as soon as he finished, he walked off the stage. The stage had a piano on it in the middle of the front. Behind it were a number of chairs and music stands, but nobody was sitting at them. I wondered if they would all walk on stage at once.

That didn't happen. What did was that everyone stood up almost at the same moment and broke into enthusiastic applause. I had no idea why. Nothing seemed to have changed on the stage, but then, I could see someone walking onto the stage from the opposite side of the stage. Our view of him was blocked by the piano, so we didn't really see him until he reached the piano.

He was clearly tall, but I couldn't tell how tall because no one else was standing near on the stage to compare him to. He had long black hair that he had combed straight back from his forehead. The hair actually had a little gray in it but no more than my Dad had. He was wearing a black tuxedo. He was well-built but not muscular. When he reached the piano, he turned toward the audience and bowed once. He then turned back to the piano, sat, and without any further warning started to play.

I opened up my program for the first time. I thought that in such a thick booklet, they must say something about the piece that he was playing. They did, but I had the devil of a time finding it. The booklet seemed to be all advertising.

The booklet said that the piece was originally written for organ. At that, I almost gagged. I can't imagine sitting through organ music. But, Gould had transcribed it (whatever transcribing is) for piano. I was very thankful that he had done that. While I was reading the program, I realized that someone was humming. I don't know a lot about classical concerts, but I'm pretty sure that people aren't supposed to talk or even hum. I looked around to see who was doing it. I didn't see anyone, so I asked Mum (very quietly), "Who's humming?"

She just kicked my shin and shushed me. It's kind of funny seeing a woman trying to use hand signals to get you to stop making noise.

I got it right away. Almost immediately, I realized where the humming was coming from. It was Gould himself. I'd never heard of anyone humming while they played music—singing, yes, but humming, no.

We were on the other side of the piano from him, but the way that he was sitting and his height made it possible for us to see his face. He was moving his face back and forth in rhythm to the music. Although he seemed to be staring in our general direction rather than at the keyboard, he seemed to be looking at something on the other side of the world.

That made me think of a movie that I'd once seen, *Apocalypse Now*. One of the characters described this fixed stare that people sometimes got in the jungle on a long march. He called it, "The Thousand Meter Stare". That seemed to be Gould.

As I listened to the music, I realized that I was kind of getting into it. It sort of helped me think. I wouldn't have ordinarily had all these ideas and thoughts while listening to music. It was strange, but the strangeness didn't bother me at all.

Then, suddenly, he stopped playing. He stood up and again the crowd leapt to their feet and wore their hands sore clapping. I was one of them.

He bowed once and walked off the stage, but the crowd just kept applauding. It went on and on. Finally, Gould walked back on the stage and bowed once. He then walked off the stage as though the crowd weren't standing and clapping and even doing some whistling. I didn't know that I loved the music that much, but it was good, and I didn't mind going along with the crowd in clapping. After a while, he walked back on stage, bowed to the crowd, and completely surprised me by saying something like this, ". . . Temper Career, Prelude Number 1." I didn't catch the first couple of words. Like I said, I was not expecting for him to say anything. He hadn't said anything so far tonight.

So, he turned back to the piano and sat. He immediately started to play a song. It seemed to me to be a song, because it just seemed to be made for words. However, other than Gould's humming, there weren't any other sounds.

That song was soft and seemed like it must be the easiest piece in the world to play. Still, I couldn't get over the feeling that it was maybe the most beautiful thing that I'd ever heard. It was short. I couldn't believe that it was already over when Gould got up from the piano, bowed to the audience, and walked off the stage.

The end had taken me by surprise, but most of the crowd knew that it was over and were already starting to stand as it ended. They were clapping till their hands were sore. I knew because I was with them, clapping as long and as loud as I could. My hands were sore, but I didn't care. If only we could have lured him back to the piano to play that one more time, I'd have paid the ticket price again just to hear it that one more time.

Listening to him play that song had made me sad and made me feel like I was in heaven all at the same time. When most of the "religious" people talk about heaven, I'm pretty sure that they don't know anything about the place—if there even is such a place. For the first time in my life, it made me want to be in the heaven that had music like that someday. I knew that that music must live in the real heaven. I then noticed that there was a stinging in my eyes. I realized that it was tears in my eyes.

Everyone seemed to be leaving the hall. That scared me for a moment. Had I somehow missed the second half of the concert, but Dad had said, "Let's go out and get something to drink."

Of course, it was a break between sets. We walked out of the hall and found the bar. Mum had a glass of wine. Dad had a glass of whiskey—a rare drink for him. I just had a bottle of water.

The lights flashed and Dad herded us back to our seats. We got there just in time to get seated before Gould came back out on the stage. This time the chairs all had musicians seated at them. They all seemed to be tuning their instruments and practicing at the same time, but when the conductor came out to the stage, they immediately stopped.

The conductor made a brief announcement. The Concerto that was originally scheduled was to be replaced by Bach's Concerto in D minor. It didn't mean anything to me at the time.

When Gould came out, everyone stood—even the musicians, and they did something strange. Everyone who had a violin tapped their bows against their violin. I guess that is applause for violinists.

Gould sat, and the conductor looked to him for the signal to begin. He gave it. Almost before the performance had begun, I was convinced that I didn't need to go to heaven. I was there already. At times the music was so soft that I was not sure that he was still playing, but it didn't matter.

Somehow, I figured out when the piece was about to end. I was on my feet on the last note, and I swear that I was the first to start the applause. The reverberations of that applause still wrung in my ears the next day.

There was still one more piece on the program. When it ended, I was stunned, realizing that I'd heard the last that I would hear for a very long time. Maybe no other audience would ever hear him perform again.

□□

We were all stunned as we left the auditorium. None of us seemed able to focus on what we should do next. However, the surprises of the evening had not come to an end.

Someone standing outside of a cab was shouting. It was for us. He seemed to be shooing people away from his cab. He waved at us, and we went to his cab. It was our cabbie from earlier in the night.

He looked us up and down and said, "I'd say you had quite a concert."

Dad just nodded. Then he came to himself and asked if the cabbie would take us home.

He said, "I'll do better than that. I'll take you home for fee! But only if you tell me what it was like."

Mum asked the sensible question, "You haven't been waiting out here for us all the way through the concert?"

He laughed as he opened the door for us. He said, "No. I did stay for about 15 minutes while I waited to see if you got tickets. When you did, I decided that I had to come back to give you a lift home so I could find out HOW you got tickets. You threatened someone didn't you?"

He drove off, and we waited until he was out of the worst traffic to answer. Mum said, "Good Heavens no. A nice young lady in the box office sold us some tickets that no one had picked up."

The cabbie winked knowingly, "I'll bet the young man has to pay in some coin other than coin of the Realm."

I was startled to hear him suggest that I had something to do with it. I defended myself, "No, sir. I made no promise either with words or winks."

He guffawed at that and said, "Well, I won't try to force your little secrets out of you. But what I want to know is this. Was it really G. G.? Was he as wonderful as everyone says he is?"

I thought about that. I'd not seen a picture of Gould–either as he was at his previous concerts or recently. There hadn't been one in the paper. How could I know?

Dad said, "I don't know if it was Gould, but I can tell you that he made you think that you'd died and gone to Heaven with his playing."

I was surprised that Dad had thought about Heaven too. I wondered if Mum would have said the same thing. I never found out though because the cabbie had another question.

"How much did you pay for the tickets?"

Dad shrugged as though it were nothing. "Oh, about two hundred apiece, I guess."

"Blimey, are you carrying a Platinum American Express card around with you?" Then he surprised us by asking, "And how did you Jew them down so low?"

Of course, the funny thing was that Dad had cut up his Gold American Express card just before we started this trek.

As the cabbie was saying that, he interrupted himself and said, "Oh, of course, the young man."

I just shook my head, refusing the idea that I'd had anything to do with that either.

We reached the hotel. He let us out and handed Dad something as Dad tried to give him some money, which the cabbie resolutely refused.

After the cabbie drove off, I asked Dad what the cabbie had given him.

"Oh, nothing much." He handed me the small card that turned out to be a business card. "He just wants the pleasure of our business. That's his card."

I glanced at it and handed it back to Dad.

In the Realm of Words

The next day, I took a little time to read the review of the concert of the previous night. The music critic was a pain in the ass. He worked hard to find something to complain about. The best he could come up with was that he didn't like the tempo of the Well Tempered Clavier, Prelude # 1. He thought it was too slow.

I thought he was crazy. I was tempted to write a letter to the newspaper complaining about the lousy level of criticism in the paper. Of course, I didn't. I just wanted to.

We finished reading the first two months of *The Times*. We were exhausted. It's hard to read for hours on end knowing that you can't let up your concentration once. You might miss something critical.

We were done for the day, but we decided to go to the basement and check out how to borrow earlier editions of *The Times* and how to use the microfiche readers. I went to a librarian for help making a request for microfiche and to learn how to use the reader. After learning, Mum, Dad, and I started working our way through the March and April editions of *The Times*. We didn't get very far. We didn't want to. We just wanted to be ready to go at it seriously the next day.

The next day came, and we almost finished March and April. I began developing headaches that forced me to stop every hour or so.

The next day we finished March and April and went on to January and February. We were all beginning to get discouraged, but we didn't have much choice but to keep going.

The next day was Sunday, and we declared a holiday. We just sat around the patio of our place except that I always worked out every day.

We were back at it on Monday. I was doing December while Mum and Dad were working the end of January and February. Around 2:30 I was reading December 28th, 1998. On the next to last page of the first section, there was a small article near the bottom of the page. It read:

Woman in Tudley on the Thames Goes Missing

On Boxing Day every year for more than twenty years, a group of ladies got together to play bridge. However, this year, when they met at the home of one Miss Margorie Dursley, she was not there. Her three partners came to her home as they had for years. They couldn't attract the attention of anyone in the house, so they used a spare key that Miss Dursley kept under her welcome mat to enter the home.

They found that there was no sign that anyone had been in the house for many days. Miss Dursley's dog, Ripper, was not there. There was dust on every surface. They found a local constable and reported Miss Dursley as a missing person. The police are treating her disappearance as another of the many disappearances that have been happening since summer.

I had found what we had been searching for. We had been looking for almost a week, and now we had what we really hoped we wouldn't find. I got up and walked to Dad's machine, tapped him on the shoulder and signaled him to follow me. We walked to Mum and got her as well.

I led them to my machine and just pointed at the screen. It took them a minute to find it. When Dad found it, he dropped into a nearby chair and buried his face in his hands. Mum put her hand on his shoulder and squeezed gently. We took the fiche to a librarian and had him print a copy of the page.

We took a bus back home. When we arrived we went to our room and really didn't know what to do. Finally, Dad said, "Let's find a pub."

A cab took us to a nice little bar and grill. We took a table, and Dad ordered a shot of whiskey for us—even me. He declared that I was old enough. He lifted his glass and proposed a toast, "To Marge. I'm sure she gave the Deatheaters a hard time."

Mum said, "She may have, but maybe Harry gave himself up to save her."

I shook my head, "You know Mum, I don't think that even Harry would do that for her. Don't you remember that day she made fun of his Mum and Dad?"

We finished our drinks and had a good meal of hamburgers and chips.

The next morning, no one got up early. We had breakfast at the extended stay and sat around on the patio trying not to think about the previous day. In the afternoon, Dad said, "We've got to keep going. What do you think we should do next?"

Mum had an answer, "What do you think about this? Maybe we should hunt for wizards?"

Both Dad and I stared at her, but she held her ground, "No, listen." She said with real force, "Canadian wizards probably don't like 'You Know Who'. If we found one, they might know what was going on in England." She hesitated, "Don't you think?"

Dad nodded. I wasn't so sure, but I thought that it wouldn't be easy to find a wizard, so I was willing to go along with her idea. I raised the obvious objection, "How do we look for one?"

We all pondered that for a while but eventually Mum had an answer, "Why don't we go back to the library and search the local newspapers for strange events?"

No one else had a better idea or any other idea, so that afternoon we were back on our way to the library. We were back in the library basement searching newspapers.

On the second day, the librarian whom I'd gotten the access card from, came over to me where I was seated at a table pouring over an edition of the *Toronto Star* from a couple of weeks before. She sat down opposite me and asked me, "What in the world are you researching? Maybe I can help."

I sighed. What could I tell her that would be a more reasonable story than that I was trying to find a wizard? I decided that maybe the truth was the best idea. "I'm researching occult happenings. Do you have any ideas?"

She suggested the paranormal shelves upstairs. I replied that I wanted current events. Then she surprised me with an interesting idea. "Did you notice that on the main floor, we have a section where local newspapers leave copies for the public? They're mostly full of advertising, but there's one that might interest you. It's called the *Quizzer* or something like that. I haven't noticed it recently, but there may be some up there still.

"It seems to be devoted to all sorts of bizarre happenings. Maybe that might help."

□

I went up to the main floor and found a stack of *Quizzers*. They were only a few pages each and didn't seem to have regular publication dates. I picked up one and took it back down to the basement to show Dad.

He read the headline on the front page aloud, "Man Turned To Frog Returns To Tell About IT." He shrugged and said, "Let's give the publisher a call and see if he's got anything real."

We collected Mum and found a phone booth on the main floor. Dad had me make the call. A woman answered the phone and said, "Goodwin residence."

I asked, "Isn't this the publishing office of the *Quizzer*."

"Oh, you mean Ronald's silly paper. I'll call him up from the basement."

I had to wait a few minutes then Ronald came on, "Can we come over to talk with you today about the *Quizzer*?"

He seemed excited but didn't want us to meet at his house. I offered to take him to dinner. He was excited about the idea and agreed. I told him we'd pick him up in an hour.

He lived in a modest single story house in a suburb nearby. He was waiting outside when we arrived. He seemed to be a little older than me. He wore large glasses that were very strong and made him look a little like an owl.

We asked him for a suggestion for dinner. He had us go to a little Italian restaurant that was only a few blocks away. We got seated and ordered. Dad came to the point while we waited for our orders to arrive.

"Well, Ronald, we're looking for wizards. We're not very particular. We just want one that we can talk to for an hour or so. We have a couple of questions that ought to be easy for him to answer."

Ronald was excited. "You bet. I know lots about wizards. Just ask me."

It looked to me like a dead end, but Dad kept going with him. "No, we don't want to talk with you about wizards. We want to talk TO a wizard."

"But I know all about them. I can answer any question you want. I once went to a dark ritual where . . ."

Dad cut him off. "OK. Here's a question. Do you know about . . ." He stopped and seemed puzzled.

I thought I knew what he was puzzled about, so I gave it a try, "There's a wizard whom everyone is afraid of. They're so afraid of him that they never say his name. They usually call him something like 'You Know Who' or even 'He Who Must Not Be Named'. What do you know about him?"

Ronald didn't hesitate a second. He started reeling off facts, "Sure, I know about him. He's from Baltimore originally, but he lives in New Orleans now. He calls himself the Crimson King, but . . ."

Dad stopped him right there. I don't know why Dad kept on at him, but he did, "OK. Do you know anywhere that wizards get together?"

Ronald said, "You really want to know one don't you?"

Dad nodded.

"Sure, I know a couple of places."

Dad nodded again, "Go ahead."

"Well, you don't expect me to take you right there do you?"

I think we could all see that this was going nowhere. Dad even admitted it later. Just then our food arrived, and we ate for a little while in peace. Then Dad ended the discussion, "Well, Ronald, it's been interesting meeting you. I wish you good luck with your paper."

Ronald was surprised, "But don't you want to meet a wizard. We can set up a meet in a couple of days."

Dad got up and held out his hand. "I think we've got all the information that we need from you. Thanks."

Dad didn't even wait for the check. He put a hundred dollar bill down on the table, confident that it would be enough to cover our bill. There was a pay phone in the restaurant that Dad used to call a cab for us.

Ronald was still trying to sell us on going to see a wizard with him, but I knew that it was hopeless. I'd seen Dad like this before. He could be polite and determined in a way that almost everyone realized was beyond changing. This fellow was the exception. He kept trying to sell Dad while we waited for the cab, while we were driving to Ronald's house, while he got out of the cab, and Dad shut the door.

When we got back home, we sat out in the cool early evening air on the patio, and Dad just shook his head. "This is hopeless."

Always hopeful, Mum suggested putting an advert in the paper. I'd ordinarily go along with her ideas, but I was with Dad on this one. We'd just get more kooks like Ronald.

The next day, we were down at the library, but our hearts weren't in it. We gave up at noon. Nothing unusual every seemed to happen in Toronto.

□□

The great thing about Mum is that she keeps trying with ideas. Sometimes she strikes out, and sometimes she has a hit. This time Dad and I had to listen. What she had to say was simple, "We need to try someplace else–maybe in the States."

That, at least, sparked a discussion of where we might go. We all agreed that it should be in the States, that it should be a large city, and that it should be east of the Mississippi. I wanted to go to New York. Dad voted for Cleveland. How he came up with Cleveland, I never had an inkling.

Mum asked for Washington D.C. Her argument was that it was the center of power for the United States, so it was an obvious place for powerful wizards to be. It made a kind of crazy sense that appealed to me, and I guess to Dad too. We were on our way to D.C.

233

What Do Georgia, Ohio, & Scotland have in Common?

The next day, we packed our bags and decided that this was the day to shed excess clothes. We ended up with several bags of clothes that we decided that we'd give to the Salvation Army. One of the desk clerks agreed to drop them off for us, and then we were off to the bus station.

At the bus station, we decided to take a bus first to Niagara Falls and stay the night. Then the next day we'd take off for Washington, D.C. The bus left at noon and arrived at 2:30 PM.

We crossed the Rainbow Bridge. Then we went through customs. It was quick. Quick was good. No one was looking for us. There were several hotels near the falls. After a try or two we found one that had a vacancy. After that we decided to act like tourists. It was the first time that we'd had the luxury to do that in a long time.

We walked to the Maid of the Mist Dock, bought a ticket, and rode through the spray of Niagara Falls. I was not much impressed. However after that we had dinner, and since there was lots of time before sunset, we decided to walk to Goat Island. It was about a 20 minute walk. Once we got onto Goat Island, it was fascinating to see the Niagara River rushing by. It flowed faster than any river I'd seen in England.

We were able to walk to the edge of the falls. I couldn't believe how close we were to the edge. I looked over at Dad and was about to ask him something, but I didn't because I didn't see Mum. Then, I heard her. She was saying something about us getting away from the edge. I guess she was bothered by how close we were to the edge.

I had to admit that it was kind of spooky. There we were one giant step away from the rushing water that was just about to go over the precipice. It was hard to believe that they'd built a way to go right up to the edge of that swirling maelstrom of destruction and not protected it with anything safer than a railing with huge gaps between the rails. How many suicides had happened right where I was standing? I stared for a minute thinking about the amazing view. There was a scary temptation to just step up on the railing and jump off. I looked over at Dad and saw the same fascination in his eyes.

He smiled and said, "I think that your Mum would like us to walk away from the edge."

As we walked away from the edge and back toward our hotel, Mum was going on and on about how she'd seen parents with young kids there! If I were a dozen years younger she wouldn't have let me within a mile of that spot.

We got back to the hotel in time for dinner, which we had across the street. We discussed the next steps. They were really pretty simple. We would take a bus to Washington, find a hotel, and start reading local newspapers. We'd start with current papers and work our way backward for a couple of weeks. If we couldn't find any clues then to local wizards and witches, we might as well pack it up and . . . There was the problem. And what? We would figure out something. We always did.

□

The next day, we were up bright and early. We found the Greyhound bus terminal and bought tickets to Washington DC. We had choices and decided to go via Harrisburg, Pennsylvania. It was the capital of that state and seemed like it should be a good place to stop for a layover.

Our bus left at 11 AM. We had to change buses at Harrisburg where there was an hour stop. Then we'd stop briefly in Baltimore. Then we'd be on to the capital. If the schedule held up, we'd arrive in Washington around 9 PM. Why was it that we always seemed to arrive at night?

Anyway, the route was interesting. We went mostly through mountains. They weren't like the Canadian Rockies that we'd ridden the train through. They seemed more accessible. There were lots of little towns that we went through. We made so many stops at little crossroads to let people on or off that I'd completely lost count before we reached Harrisburg. We'd had a good breakfast before we left, but by the time we reached Harrisburg, we were ready for a real meal. Unfortunately, we had to get what the Yanks call "fast food" at a Subway near the bus station. We noticed that there was a train station next door, but Dad insisted that we stick with the bus. After all, we'd already paid our fare for Washington.

The rest of the way to Washington was less interesting. When we arrived, there was still a good bit of light in the sky, which was a blessing. I hate being in a strange place when it's dark. We found a cab easily, and Dad told the driver what he was looking for.

"We need a reasonably priced hotel near the underground and . . ." Dad was interrupted there with a question about what he meant by "Underground".

He hemmed for a minute looking for the word and then found it, "Oh, yes. Subway."

The cabbie said, "You mean Metro. That's what you should ask for when you want to find direction to the nearest station. Ask for the Metro."

Dad went on, "I'd like to be in the suburbs, and if it is close to a bank, that would be good too."

The cabbie immediately started the cab rolling. I suppose that he must get requests like that fairly often. We'd had good success other places asking for specific hotels. I chuckled to myself. I wondered if we'd asked for a "HoJo" what the cabbie would have said?

It only took us twenty minutes to reach a hotel. On the way, the cabbie pointed out the Metro station and actually drove past a bank as well. Dad had used Canadian dollars in Niagara Falls. Everyone had accepted them after applying a pretty stiff discount to US dollars. Here was our one sticking point. The cabbie didn't like the idea of taking Canadian dollars. Dad and he did some dickering, and they ended up agreeing to double the cab fare in Canadian dollars but with no additional tip.

We went into the Lobby. I expected more trouble, but Dad and the desk clerk came to a better agreement. This time, Dad offered British pounds. The clerk agreed to take them at the official exchange rate plus 5% for the first night's stay, but Dad would have to use US dollars afterwards. The clerk started to give us directions to the nearest bank, but Dad forestalled him by reciting the directions to the bank that the cabbie had shown us. Everyone was satisfied, and we went next door to a sort of outdoor mall to find someplace that was still open to eat.

We decided to sleep in and got up rather late the next morning. By the time that we'd showered and dressed, we'd missed the breakfast that was included in the price of our stay. Dad went out, saying that he was going to the bank and would meet us at the little mall that was nearby for breakfast. By the time that he arrived, it was more like lunch.

We'd had a snack at a doughnut shop, and we had lunch at a place called the "Corner Bakery". It was good enough. I wished we'd had breakfast there.

Dad explained why it took him so long to join us. The bank had balked at changing so many Canadian dollars. They'd wanted all sorts of information. They wanted him to show them his passport. Then, they'd dickered over the exchange rate. He finally had escaped. He'd become quite grumpy about the process, but having a good meal under his belt made a difference in his attitude.

While he'd been waiting at the bank, he'd asked someone about a good library in the area. A teller had said that there wasn't a better library than the Library of Congress. Dad had asked, "Do you need to be a member of Congress to use it?"

The teller had laughed, "No, anyone—even foreigners—can use it. You just have to register, and then you can use any of the millions of books in the library."

That was good enough for Dad. We picked up a map of the Washington area in a local booksellers and quickly found the library. We discovered that it was close to a Metro station. As we stood outside the bookstore, Dad gave us each a rather thick wad of US dollars that he'd gotten at the bank.

We then went to the Metro station. Now, if there's anything I know about, it's Tube stations. I took the lead and used some of my cash to buy us three day passes on the Metro. The Metro is just about the same as the Tube in every way. We were quickly on our way to the Library of Congress.

We arrived at the Metro station and found our way to the Library. It was certainly impressive enough. There was a fairly long line outside waiting to get in. That was discouraging,, but we decided that if it was that popular, it must be pretty good. It turned out that the line was for a tour of the library. We decided that that would be a good way to learn how to use the library.

It turned out to be mostly disappointing, once we were in and took the tour. It turned out to be mostly a history lesson about when the Library was built, how many books it had, where the stacks were, and so forth. But one good piece of information did come out of the tour. The library was not a good place to go to just read newspapers.

We buttonholed the tour guide after the tour and asked him about real, useful libraries. He suggested the Martin Luther King Library. It was a little too far to walk. So we took a cab there.

We quickly found the room that had newspapers. It was pretty well stocked. It had all the major local papers–the *Washington Post*, the *Washington Times,* the *Baltimore Sun*, and some other local papers.

Before we started, Dad reminded us what we were looking for, "We're looking for suspicious things. You can't assume that it will be in any particular section of the paper. We want to check classified ads, obituaries, world news, local news—everything."

I asked, "If we're looking for local wizards, why would we look in world news?"

His answer: "You just don't know where a clue may show up. Now get to it."

We divided up the papers. I had the *Washington Times*, Dad took the *Washington Post*, Mum took the *Baltimore Sun*.

We finished the last couple of days of those and decided to take a break for dinner. We walked the neighborhood and found something called, "Chipotle Mexican Grill". It was Mexican all right. Mum almost burned out her taste buds, but Dad and I did OK.

Then, we went back to the papers. None of us had anything that looked likely. Maybe we just didn't know what to look for. Anyway, we finished before it got dark. That was important to Mum if we were going to ride the Metro. In the station, we passed a newsstand. I glanced at the papers as we went by. I noticed that the cover of the *Washington Times* didn't match any that I'd seen. I stopped and bought a *Times* and the *Post* and caught Mum and Dad up.

Dad asked, "Aren't you tired of reading newspapers?"

"Oh, I noticed that today's editions weren't out when we were in the library. I thought I'd find out what we'd missed."

Mum said, "OK. I'll take *The Times*. Maybe it's like *The Times* of London."

I took the *Post*. We boarded the train and found seats. I scanned the front page and turned to the second page. My eyes were immediately drawn to a title–Joint Military Exercise with Britain."

I started reading it, but before I'd gone very far, I interrupted Mum and Dad, "Hey, listen to this." They weren't excited about listening to more news but I insisted, "No, really. This sounds good. It's news from home."

I read.

□□

AP–Dayton, Oh. Today, the Defense Department reported that the United Kingdom and the United States had held a joint military exercise that included units of the United States Air Force based in Dayton, Ohio, an elite commando unit based in Georgia, a British task force in the North Sea, including an aircraft carrier, various aircraft, and an elite naval marine unit. It included a mock raid on a terrorist base. The operation was mostly carried out in Northern Scotland. The US forces included a B1B bomber, a C-130 transport, . . ."

I stopped reading at that moment because we were all looking at each other. We spontaneously said, "Hogwarts!"

That made the rest of our ride on the Metro completely different. We found a secluded couple of seats and talked seriously. Dad was convinced that this was "IT".

Mum said, "Well, then, why don't we go ask them?"

Dad asked, "You mean the US Defense Department? But where are they"

I asked, "This is the capital of the United States. Surely the Ministry of Defense, or whatever has to be somewhere around here."

Mum simply said, "It's at the Pentagon."

Dad pulled a Metro map out of his hip pocket and opened it. Sure enough, there was actually a Pentagon stop on the Metro! We agreed that we would go there the next day and see what more we could learn.

That was a nearly sleepless night for all of us. We dragged ourselves out of bed the next morning, not exactly refreshed but anxious to see if this were finally the end of our pilgrimage. This time, we were up too early for breakfast, but we hadn't missed it by much. We picked up a complimentary copy of USA Today in the lobby and looked through the various sections as we waited for breakfast.

I got the comic pages. I kidded Dad a little, "Maybe there's a hint to wizards in the comics."

He was not in a mood—before breakfast, before tea, before a long day with little sleep—to be kidded. He just grimaced.

It actually wasn't too long before the self-serve breakfast was ready. It was decent compared with all the other similar breakfasts we'd had over the last year. We finished quickly and were on our way to the Metro station in record time.

At the station, we had to buy a more expensive all-day pass because we were going with the commuters. The train was crowded and we couldn't even stand very close to each other. When the Pentagon stop arrived, we barely were all able to get off. It was that crowded.

We were there, and now none of us were that excited about bearding the beast in its lair. Dad led the way. It turned out that as visitors, we had to sign in and provide proof of identity. Our trusty British passports served us well. The person at the security desk asked us why we'd left our reason for visit blank.

Dad tried to answer without giving much information away. I probably could have done better, but he was running the show. He said, "Well, we're visitor here and we were reading a local newspaper and uh saw an article about a joint US-Brit operation. Since we were so close, we were . . .

uh . . . curious about it, so we . . . er . . . decided to come here and see what you lot knew."

The guard looked at him quizzically and said, "That seems like a lot of effort for simple curiosity."

I decided to help out, "You see, sir. We have a relative who lives in Northern Scotland. We were hoping to get a leg up on him when we get back to England. We'll tell him all about this little adventure in his backyard."

The guard seemed a little friendlier, "Where does he live?"

I thought for a second. What I said was the first thing that came to my mind. It was probably not the smartest thing to say, but it was out of my mouth. What can you do about it, "Oh, it's a little town called Saint Brutus."

The guard actually laughed. "That's a town that I wouldn't want to admit that I'd come from."

I had to laugh too, "You're right. We're always kidding him about it."

The guard gave us temporary badges and told us where to go, "You'll want the Public Affairs Office. It's quite close. Just go down this hall and at the crossroads turn to the right. It's just after you make that turn. Good luck with Saint Brutus."

The office had a reception area with old magazines, uncomfortable chairs, and a desk with a receptionist behind it—just like a dentist's office. The receptionist could have been pretty if she'd not been wearing an Air Force uniform, had her pale blonde hair pulled back in a tight bun at the nape of her neck and been wearing glasses. As a matter of fact, after talking with her for a few minutes, I might have liked to ask her out for a drink after work, but we were there on business.

Dad explained why we were there. She made a phone call to someone. We couldn't tell from her side of the conversation how it was going, but before she finished, she asked Dad, "Would you be available for lunch today?"

He shrugged nonchalantly, "Sure. Should we wait here?"

She was back on the phone and hung up. "No, he won't be available until nearly noon. You can go do some sight-seeing and come back to this office at noon. Keep the badge. Just come back to this office."

So, we were off for a bit, but before we left, Dad asked her what would be good to see close to here. She pursed her lips—one more good feature that she had—and said, "The Arlington Cemetery is good. Anyway, I like it." She hesitated, and her brow wrinkled, "Of course, I have a friend who's buried there."

Mum said, "We're so sorry."

She took out a Kleenix and dabbed at her eyes, "Sorry. He was killed in the Gulf War. His helicopter went down in an oil field.

240

"Of course, you may not find it that interesting. You can see Robert E. Lee's mansion there. It's the next stop on the Metro, so you can get there and come back quickly."

Dad thanked her. We left. I couldn't help looking back at her as we left. She really looked a lot better to me leaving than she had coming.

We did take her advice and spent some time in Arlington Cemetery. It was more interesting than she let on. We saw the changing of the guard—sort of like at Buckingham Palace. There was the eternal flame and all that stuff.

We got back to the Public Affairs Office about a quarter to noon and found that there was a man waiting for us. He was in a uniform and was talking to the pretty blonde. I have to admit that I was a little jealous.

We introduced ourselves. I made a point of getting the name of the blonde. The officer was a Major named Castle. He led us out of the office. As we left, I waved at the blonde and said, "See you later." She smiled.

We reached the Metro station. Castle suggested that we go to a nearby Mall that had a Metro station. He said that he usually ate lunch there. I wondered to myself if he usually ate there with the blonde. As we waited for the next train going South, I idly thought about tripping him out in front of a train—not that I'd actually do it, but it made for a pleasant time-waster as our train arrived.

We rode only four or five stops down and got off at a mall. The station was actually at an underground entrance. Castle led us in and to a Bistro. The waitresses seemed to recognize him. I was glad. That probably meant that he was playing the field. Anyway, we were seated quickly, and he confided that he tipped very well so that he would get preferential seating.

He suggested that we might like a menu item that would remind us of home. He ordered it himself—Bangers and Mash—although that was not what it was called on the menu. Dad and I had it as well, but Mum decided that she would have soup and salad. She had Tomato Basil soup and declared that it was the best that she'd had. Dad and I were satisfied with the Bangers and Mash. After we'd got our hunger under control, Castle started the conversation.

"What can I tell you about Operation Snitch?" He was smiling as though he found the name humorous.

Dad's answer was simple, "Anything you can. But we'd be especially interested in exactly where it happened."

Castle shrugged, "Well, I can't really give you a precise location. I can tell you that it's close to the sea on a fjord. There were mountains and a large forest nearby."

I asked, "Is there a town of any size nearby?"

"Not really. I think there is a town or two, but I'm sure that you'd not have heard of it."

Dad raised an eyebrow and asked, "Oh?"

"Honestly, I don't know any of the nearby towns. I guess I can tell you that it involved a special commando unit that had trained in a base in Georgia. There was a B1 bomber and a troop transport involved. You Brits had some Harrier Jump jets in the exercise and a Royal Marines unit."

Dad sighed, "I think we knew almost all of that from the newspaper reports."

Castle asked, "Do you mind telling me why you are so interested in this operation?"

Dad started to tell him about having a nephew whom we thought lived nearby, and we wondered if he might have seen any of it. We wanted to play a joke on him by knowing more about it than he did, and so on.

Dad hadn't gotten very far when I had an intuition. I tried to signal Dad that we needed to get away. He was fully attending to Castle. I looked to Mum. She was pretty engrossed to. I tried to signal to her without seeming to. Finally, I kicked her under the table. She looked over at me with a sour look, but I squeezed her forearm and I said, "Don't we have to get going?"

She must have seen the intensity in my look because she picked up on the idea. She nodded, "Yes," and then she feigned surprise. "Of course, we've got an appointment that we'll be late for if we don't leave right away."

Dad noticed and looked over at me. He too noticed my consternation. Mum continued, "We've got a . . . tickets. Yes. Tickets for the Washington Memorial. They're time-stamped and we've got to go right now!"

Mum and I stood in unison and pushed our chairs back. Dad had picked up the hint and stood as well. He did a fair job of agreeing. "Oh, yes. Of course."

Castle said, "At least, let me pick up the meal." He reached into his wallet and pulled out a card.

Dad pulled out his wallet and threw down two hundred dollar bills. "This should cover all our meals. Leave the rest for a tip. You'll really improve your service!"

We were walking fast for the entrance to the restaurant. Castle had got up and was following. I picked up my pace and saw that a train had just pulled into the station. Under my breath, I said, "We've got to catch that train."

We broke into a trot. I looked back and saw that Castle was actually running. We reached the train just as the doors were starting to close. I held the door, and Mum and Dad, huffing, ran through. I jumped in, released the door, and it closed behind me. Just then, Castle arrived. The train started to move. I sat down next to Mum.

Dad asked, "What was that all about?"

I said quickly, "First, we're getting off at the next stop. Get ready. We'll be there in a minute. We've got to get off and up to the street where we can get a cab."

Dad repeated, "Why?"

I had a bad feeling about Castle, and I'm sure I'm right. He ran after us, and he had his cell phone out and was calling someone as the train left the station. I think he's going to have people waiting for us at all the stations ahead. We've got to get off the train and away from it as quickly as we can."

So, we stood up and prepared to enter the next station. As we stood waiting for the doors to open, I began to explain a little. "I just got this feeling that Castle wasn't buying our story, and he was going to arrest us."

I expected Dad to tell me how stupid I was being, but he didn't. Instead, he asked, "Where are we going then?"

The train had stopped. The doors opened, and we were the first out. I'd never been here, but I led us up. We discovered that we were at an airport. It was great luck. There were cabs everywhere. We picked one and got in.

The cabbie, who seemed to be Middle Eastern, asked, "Where to?"

I said, "Just go."

He said, "I can't go until I know where."

Dad said, "Just start driving and we'll give you a tip as big as the fare." That got us moving.

As we drove, an idea formed in my mind about what to do. "OK. You'll get that tip, but you have to agree to do these things. One, don't tell anyone where you took us. Two, tell your dispatcher that you've got tourists who want to tour the city, you're going to be driving around, you're not sure where, but you're going to get a good tip. Three, you forget what we look like when you leave us at the final stop."

The driver was on a freeway but was cruising well within the speed limit. He said, "I don't know. Can you do more?"

Dad thought, and then said, "It'll all be cash." Of course, that was going to happen anyway, but the cabbie didn't know that.

He said, "That's good. But that's a lot of money. Show me the green."

Dad said to me, "Show him a hundred." I pulled a single bill out of my pocket. I wasn't going to show him the wad of cash that I had to draw from.

The cabbie said, "You've just got yourself a cab. Where are we going?"

Dad looked at me. I named our hotel. The cabbie said, "That's easy."

I said, "That's not all. We want you to wait for us. We'll have more destinations after that."

The cabbie left the freeway and took a surface street. Eventually, we reached our hotel. When we arrived, I started to tell Mum and Dad to check out and pack. Dad was ahead of me. He said, "I'll check out. You and Mum go up and pack."

I was the last out. Before I could leave, the cabbie said, "Wait, young man. I want to get paid."

I asked what the fare so far was. He replied that it was twenty bucks. I thought a second and said, "I'll pay you the fare so far, but no tip. You don't get a tip till the end."

He scratched his chin, "How do I know that you'll pay me a tip?"

"Easy. If we don't pay you the tip, you're free to tell anyone where we went."

He smiled, "How do you know that I'll not tell anyway?"

"We trust you."

He laughed at that and said, "Go pack."

By the time that I got to our room Dad was already there and packing. I couldn't believe Mum. She was just throwing clothes in the suitcase as though there was no tomorrow. Maybe there wasn't. I'd never seen her pack a bag without folding things carefully.

Dad had already packed my bag. He said, "We're ready. Let's go." Then he asked, "What odds do you give that the cabbie is still out there?"

I just said, "He's out there." I then grabbed Mum's bag, and I headed for the stairs. "Follow me."

We all hustled down the stairs two floors. Dad huffed, "I've checked out. Let's go."

The cab was still there. He unlocked the doors and made to open the trunk to put our bags there. I shook my head and said, "We need the bags with us."

He shrugged, helped me put the bags I was carrying in, and drove off. Now that we were driving again, I noticed that the driver hadn't asked where to. I guess he trusted that we would tell him. I did. "We're going to a souvenir shop. One that has sports caps and tee shirts and that kind of thing."

He asked, "Why not the hotel? They must have a souvenir shop."

I said, "I don't want to use that one."

The cabbie turned a corner and headed for the mall that we'd gone to the last night. I realized that and said, "Not there either."

The cabbie was a little sarcastic when he replied, "What? Do you want to go to Baltimore for a souvenir shop?"

"No, I just want one that's farther away."

The cabbie found another one. He said as we pulled up, "This is good anyway. It's my cousin's."

I told Mum and Dad, "We'll take our bags in." Dad stared at me, but the cabbie looked completely unconcerned and said, "Don't worry. I know. I'll be here." Then he turned to me, "Don't forget about the fare."

"Sure, how much?"

He said, "Thirty bucks."

"That's not the fare."

"Sure it is. Look at the meter."

I laughed, "I'm only paying the additional fare. So that would be ten." I gave him the ten spot and followed my parents in. They were standing around looking at things like the typical tourists that I suppose we still were. I walked past them and said, "Just keep looking. I know what I'm looking for, and I don't need help."

Dad just shrugged, but Mum was beginning to look a bit bothered.

I went over to a display of sports caps. I picked a Pittsburg Steelers cap, a Baltimore Orioles cap, and a Philadelphia Phillies cap. I then walked past a display of sunglasses. I picked up a pair of clunky wrap around glasses, a conventional pair, and a pair of aviators. I walked over to the counter where a guy was sitting on a stool. He looked vaguely like our cabbie, but I suppose that was just because they were from the same part of the world.

I had him ring those up, but before he was finished, I noticed that he was wearing a well-worn cap with a bear on it. When he finished, I asked him, "How much would you like for that bear cap?"

He looked surprised and then realized that he was wearing a cap. "You mean this Cubs cap?"

"Yeh, I guess so."

"That's been with me a long time." He seemed to consider it as though he were giving up a close relative. "Oh, I don't know that I'd sell it."

I was not in a bargaining mood, so I said, "I'll give you fifty for it. Take it or leave it right now."

He heard the finality in my tone of voice and just said, "Done. And it's mine, so it's not on this ticket." He finished ringing up my purchase. I paid him for it. Then I gave him the fifty for the Cubs cap.

I took out the Baltimore cap and handed it to him and said, "This is yours. Oh, yes. The fifty includes both the cap and the fact that you're going to forget that you ever saw us the moment we step out of your store."

He started to say something and then stopped and just said, "Yes."

I took the bag of my purchases and turned to Mum and Dad who had been watching the whole process in amazement. I handed the Pirates hat to Mum along with the wrap-around sunglasses. I handed the normal sunglasses and the Steeler's cap to Dad. I put on the Cubs cap and the aviator sunglasses. Then I asked the clerk, "Do you have a bathroom in the store."

He didn't say anything but just pointed us to the rear. I led Mum and Dad there and said, "Go in and change into your oldest most worn clothes and wear the glasses and cap when you come out."

They did. Then I went in and changed. I just changed my tee-shirt and added my sunglasses. I led my parents out to the cab. We walked up to it, but the cabbie didn't seem to notice us. I tapped on the glass. He rolled the window down a little and said, "Don't you see that I've got a fare."

Then he looked closer and said, "And it's you. Wow! That's a decent disguise. Well, get in and where are we off to?"

I said, "What's the first train station outside of Washington suburbs."

That made him think. He had to ask some questions. "Are you going to Pennsylvania?"

"No."

"Where are you going?"

"West."

He thought for several minutes and got a map out of his glove compartment. Then he got a cell phone out to make a call. I objected, "No dispatcher."

He nodded. "My brother-in-law."

I nodded. He made his call. They talked for some time in a language that I couldn't even identify. That made me nervous, but, he eventually hung up and said, "It's west of the Beltway. It's a long way off. I won't have a fare on the way back."

I thought about it for a few minutes and looked at Dad. He said, "We'll pay you an additional amount equal to the fare from here to the train station."

The cabbie looked prepared to say something, but my Dad was definite. "That's it." The cabbie shrugged, and we got started. It was a long drive. A lot of it was on good highways—not freeways. We arrived at the train station about 4:30. We paid the cabbie. The additional fare was forty bucks. The whole fare, including what we had already paid was 85 dollars. Double that and add in the extra tip for the fare back to DC, and the total came to a little over two hundred bucks. Dad just pulled out two one hundred dollar bills and handed it to the cabbie. He said, "Keep the change."

The cabbie was about to object, but Dad just said, "Don't forget what we've already paid you."

The cabbie smiled again and said, "Nice doing business with you."

I said, "Same to you."

We entered the train station and looked at the schedule posted on a wall. The next train through was not due till almost midnight. So, we decided to find some supper. There was the additional issue that we didn't really know where we were going.

Finally, over dinner we talked about all the topics that I'd been afraid to talk about when we were in the cab or the store. Dad opened up with the questions. "Why in the world did we leave the Metro rather than going straight to the hotel?"

"Whoever Castle was calling, they'd have been waiting at all of the stations. We had to get off and change to cab. I had done a lot of Tube Tag in my day. I know how to avoid people on the Tube."

Mum asked, "Why were we in such a hurry to get away from the hotel."

Dad answered that one, "We had to provide our real ID's at the Hexagon AND at our hotel. I was afraid that we might find somebody waiting for us there."

That left us with the real question. I asked it, "Where are we going now?"

Dad said, "I'm fresh out of ideas. Anybody?"

Mum asked, "Where was it that those airplanes came from?"

I asked, "You mean in that British-Yank 'exercise'?"

She nodded. I said, "Dayton. Some air force base. It was Right-Pat-something, wasn't it? Where is Dayton, anyway?"

Dad agreed, "Maybe we should try to look up one of the pilots. Maybe they can tell us something."

Mum was against it. "Surely they'll be ready for us, won't they?"

Dad said, "I suppose so. But, really, what have we got left? Go back to England and take our chances there?"

I laughed, "They probably think we're too smart to do that."

We went back to the train station.

We were at the train station about two hours before the train was scheduled to depart. We talked to the ticket agent about what we wanted to do. It turned out that there wasn't a train to Dayton. The closest that we could get was Cincinnati. So, Dad was about to buy tickets for Cincinnati.

I drew him aside and asked him, "Shouldn't we buy a ticket for further down the line. You know—to throw people trying to follow us off?"

He agreed. We looked at the route map. Dad wanted to buy a ticket for Indianapolis. I shook my head no to that. "Let's buy tickets for Chicago. It's a big city and makes sense for a place to lose ourselves."

He did it. We boarded the train and were off. It was scheduled to arrive in Cincinnati at 1:30 in the afternoon. Why did we always end up sleeping on trains?

This time there wasn't a sleeper car, so we had to do our best in the reasonably comfortable seats of an ordinary train car. There was nothing to see until the sun rose around 6 AM. We were in mountains. The scenery from the train was interesting, much like Pennsylvania from the bus. The seats were like bus seats too.

There was a stop where we could get out and buy fast food around breakfast time. We'd just crossed a big river. Dad guessed that it was the Ohio River. We had had a bad night's sleep. We were hungry and fast food just didn't satisfy. I think we all were beginning to wish the Deatheaters would just catch up with us and put an end to our misery.

The mountains or high hills or whatever they were gave way to mostly flat country as we neared Cincinnati. We had a snack for breakfast in the Dining Car. It was good but didn't really give us much to go on for the rest of the morning, let alone the afternoon that was still ahead of us before we arrived in Cincy as other people on the train referred to our destination. We disembarked from the train.

We left the train terminal and found a few cabs hanging about looking for fares. So we approached one of them and asked if the cabbie knew the Greyhound terminal. He just laughed and said, "Sure. It's right next to the Horseshoe Casino."

Dad shrugged and told him to take us there. We arrived at the casino, which didn't look like much from the outside except the main entrance. When we entered, we discovered more glitter than anywhere except London. We were hungry and decided to find a coffee shop or restaurant. There were several. We picked one that seemed more sedate and ordered a good meal.

When the waitress returned with our order, Dad asked her, "How far is it to Dayton?"

She laughed and said, "I had a feeling that you weren't from around here. Dayton's only about fifty miles from here. Where are you from?"

That would teach Dad to ask a question that he didn't know the answer to. He was prompt in answering, "England." I suppose it was a good idea. I don't think that we'd had time to pick up a Canadian accent.

She said, "I'll bet you're tourists."

Dad nodded, but she wouldn't let go. "Where have you been?"

There was a puzzler for him, but I decided that the truth would be the safest route. It wouldn't be strange for tourists to visit Washington DC. I immediately answered, "Washington."

But that should have taught me a lesson, because she returned with the question, "Where are you going after here?"

I was definitely stumped as to what to say, and Dad seemed to be as well, but Mum came in to the rescue, "We're going to spend a couple of days here and then we'll go on to Dayton."

When we questioned her later about being so honest, her answer was straight to the point and reasonable. "You'd already asked how far away

Dayton was. If we hadn't admitted that we were going to Dayton, she'd have been asking herself why we'd asked about Dayton." I had to grudgingly admit that she had a good point.

However, in the mean time, the waitress had gone on to another question, "I suppose you're going to see the Museum?"

Dad glanced over to Mum for a second helping of help. She had none. Dad gave the minimum answer, "Yes."

The waitress, Beth, whose name tag I'd finally read, said, "Good. Everyone likes it."

Dad just nodded.

Since the conversation seemed to be over, she left us to our meals. Mum conversationally asked, "I wonder what Museum she's talking about?"

Dad's response was, "Well, I'm sure not going to ask. Let's just finish and get out of here as quickly as we can."

That turned out to be harder than we expected. Oh, we were hungry enough that the really decent food went down quickly. When the tab came, Dad pulled a wad of bills from a pocket and just left money on the table— enough to cover the bill and a generous tip.

No, what turned out to be hard was finding our way to the Greyhound terminal. In the first place, just finding our way out wasn't that easy. There were plenty of employees around to ask, but their directions were none too clear until you actually got out of the building itself. Once you left, you turned left and walked to the corner and then turned left again. The problem was that the casino didn't seem to make it all that easy to leave once you'd entered. It reminded me of a song that I kind of liked, "Hotel California." Well, this was Hotel Cincinnati, but we eventually did leave it.

We found the Greyhound terminal and were pleasantly surprised that a bus left every hour for Dayton. We bought tickets and waited for the next departure. While we waited, we discussed what we were going to do when we arrived in Dayton, which would apparently be near normal dinner time. Of course, we were all exhausted and just wanted to find a hotel. We were too tired to discuss little details like what we would do the next day when we had to actually go to the Air Force Base and try to learn something about the military exercise of a couple of days before.

The bus had comfortable seats. we were so exhausted that when we arrived in Dayton, the driver had to come back and wake us up. We were startled that we had fallen asleep so quickly. We stumbled out of the bus with our suitcases and looked for a cab. There wasn't one in sight. We were next to a public transit station, but since we didn't know where we were going, we decided to call for a cab and let the driver help us.

The cabbie arrived about a half hour after we'd called, but we were so tired that we didn't feel like complaining. When he asked where we were going, Dad said, "A motel near Wright Patterson Air Force Base, but not expensive—you know?"

The driver knew. He nodded sagely, and we were off. Apparently, it was across town, but it didn't take that long for us to reach it. The motel—apparently named for the famous brothers—had vacancies.

Dad registered. While he was doing that, the clerk asked why we were there. Dad said hopefully, "To see the Museum."

The clerk nodded. She commented, "Yep, that's the big attraction around here."

Dad really tempted fate by asking, "How long does it take to get there from here?"

She smiled, "Well, you couldn't get much closer. It's just a couple of miles off. I've been there a couple of times. It's really big."

Dad nodded, apparently willing her to say more. She went on, "It's got just about every airplane ever used by the Air Force. It sure is big. They've got these three huge hangars, just packed from floor to ceiling—and I do mean ceiling—with all those planes!"

I could see Dad breath a sigh of relief. He asked, "What cab company would you recommend tomorrow when we go there?"

She smiled the wide smile of a queen granting a special favor, "I'll call you a cab myself tonight. What time do you want to go?"

Dad looked over at me. I answered, "What time does the museum open?"

In answer, she looked under her desk, saying, "I've got a brochure here." She seemed to rummage for a couple of minutes and then straightened up with a slick color brochure. She opened it and read, "Nine AM to 5 PM every day except Christmas and New Year's."

I experimentally asked of Mum and Dad, "What do you think of getting there when they open?"

Dad said, "I feel like I could sleep till noon, but yes, let's get an early start."

The desk clerk, Susan according to her name tag, said, "Good idea, the Museum is big. You might not be able to cover it in a full day." She shook her head, and her short blonde hair quivered slightly. Then she added, "My son's in the Air Force. I had never been to the museum until he joined up.

"He's a jet mechanic, you know."

Her good humor was infectious and I couldn't help asking, "How does he like it?"

"Oh, he loves it. He's been to Korea and Germany. He claims that he joined up to see the world. Well, he's seen a good bit of it. He's in Darmstadt Air Force base right now. In Germany, like I said.

"He hasn't been able to talk about what he does lately. There's some sort of secret hush-hush thing going on over there."

We all perked up at that and Mum asked, "Really? I read that there was some sort of training thingee going on over England a few days ago. You wouldn't know anything about that?"

Susan shook her head, "Afraid not. He has been as quiet as the grave lately. I didn't know that there was something going on in England."

Dad shook his head sadly, "I'm afraid so."

Susan had *kindly* set a seven o'clock wakeup call for us. After Dad hung up, we all looked at each other, shook our heads, and returned to our pillows for a few extra snoozes.

The next call was at 8:30. The desk reported to Dad that our cab had just arrived. Dad spluttered, rubbing the sleep out of his eyes and said, "Please tell them that we'll be down in ten, and we'll pay a good tip if the driver waits for us."

We completely forgot about shaving, showering, grooming, and almost dressing. Mum pulled a skirt and dress out of her bag and headed for the loo. Dad and I pulled on our clothes from the last night and stuffed our limbs into them as quickly as we could. We reached the Lobby in eight minutes.

The driver already knew where he was taking us, so we didn't have to say anything. He dropped us at the building, and we stumbled into the Lobby of the building—hungry, sleep still clinging to our eyes, and no plan for what we would do.

Fortunately, the lobby had an information desk. The volunteer at the desk gave us a quick review of the museum using a detailed map of the museum. I don't think any of us picked up on half of what she said, but we all heard her say that there was a help desk that would be glad to help us with any detailed questions. She handed the map that she'd been using to Dad and said, "We would appreciate a contribution to the museum for the map. The museum is completely supported by contributions, you know."

Dad nodded, pocketed the map, and reached for his wad of bills. He pulled off a fifty dollar bill and pushed it into the jar sitting on the desk. The volunteer stared at us as though we had just stepped off a space ship from Mars. After we entered the first hangar, I told Dad, "You know, I don't think they get fifty dollar bills that often for the pamphlet."

He turned to me and said, "This is a great museum. If it's all volunteer, then we ought to pay what it's worth. I think a fifty might be just about right for the three of us."

I think he might just be right. We were astounded by the vast collection of airplanes. Many were hanging from the ceiling. I could hardly believe that all of these airplanes were in one building. We finished the section on early planes and World War II planes around lunch time. There was a cafeteria in the museum, so we went up to eat there.

We found a secluded table and planned strategy. Dad told us his idea. "I think the Help Desk might be able to tell us who to contact to see if we can find someone—preferably a pilot from here who participated in that recent training mission."

Mum said, "That's probably the best thing, but I don't think that we should ask yet. I think we should wait to closer to the end of the Museum hours. That would seem more natural. So what is our story about why we want to know more about this training mission?"

We all sat and pretended to eat while we thought about that question. Then I had an idea. "How about this? I'm college age. Maybe I want to enlist in the Air Force like that Susan's son who's over at that Durmstrang Air Base or whatever it's called. I want to talk to somebody to find out what it's really like in the Air Force?"

Dad thought about it, and then we started to take the idea apart. Dad asked, "But you're British? How could you enlist in the US Air Force?"

Mum said, "Well, maybe, you're British, but I'm your American wife and Dudley," I was so happy she hadn't called me Diddy-kins like she used to, "has dual citizenship?"

I asked, "Well, we've all got British accents–even you, Mummykins."

She had an answer for that, "We got married and you were born in Britain. We all lived there from then till now. But you're trying to decide what you want to do. So we came here on a final family vacation before you leave home."

We all pondered on that and thought that we couldn't come up with a better idea. Then we re-entered the Museum proper and continued our tour. We didn't finish the Museum but managed to reach the section on modern warplanes. One of the ones that we saw was a real B1 bomber. It was huge! Maybe it wasn't quite as big as the B52 that we'd seen, but it was big and just looked like SPEED. The swept-back wings and sleek black exterior was just too awesome.

It was after three PM by then. We decided to go back to the Help Desk and see just how good they were at "help".

It turned out that they were pretty good.

Dad walked straight up to the desk and gave them our cover story– with appropriate support from Mum and me. The person at the desk was an

252

old retired Air Force staff sergeant. He had served in England and commented on how natural our British accents were.

He asked Mum where she was from. Mum was up to the task. She replied, "Seattle. I wanted to get away from all the rain and where do I end up—rainy old England."

He laughed at that and asked me, "So, why do you want to be in the Air Force?"

I smiled, and my answer was amazingly honest, "Have you seen that B1 airplane? It's totally rad! I've got to fly in one of those things."

"Yes, I have seen it. I agree. It is . . . uh . . . totally rad. I can help you find a recruiter."

I tried to shovel it thick, "Oh, I just want to talk with someone who's actually flown one of those things!"

That seemed to puzzle him for he looked up in the sky as though contemplating the wild blue yonder. Then he said, "Let's just try this." He opened a loose-leaf notebook and thumbed through the pages, stopping at one and running his index finger down the page. He stopped at a phone number and nodded.

He said, "This is the Public Affairs Office of the Tactical Air Command at this base. They should be able to put you in touch with someone."

Mum got out her little notepad that she carries in her purse. She wrote the phone number down. Dad asked if there were a public phone booth in the building. There were a couple.

Dad deposited coins and dialed. We heard his side of the conversation, which turned out to be enough to understand what was going on. Dad said:

"Is this the Tactical Air Command Public Affairs Office? . . ."

"I'm visiting the Museum. My son has just graduated from . . . high school, is it? Yes. He's interested in the Air Force and would like to meet a real pilot—preferably a B1 pilot to find out what the Air Force is like. . ."

There was a long wait. Then, Dad said, "Thank you Major. I know it's late today, but we'll be visiting the Museum again tomorrow. We hope to finish about noon. Maybe you could send someone over for lunch? . . ."

There was another long gap, then Dad said, "Well, I can't give you our phone number because we just got into town and went straight to the museum. We haven't register in a hotel yet."

The gap was short this time and Dad said, "Thanks for the recommendation. I'm sure the Beaver Creek Hilton is wonderful, but we normally depend on our cabbie to suggest a good spot. We'll give you a call tomorrow to let you know our phone number."

There was another long gap. At the end of it, Dad just said, "Thanks, Major. We'll talk to you tomorrow." Then he hung up.

All the way through the conversation, a bad feeling had been growing in my gut. I wasn't the only one either. Dad said, "I'm calling a cab. Let's go."

He dialed a cab company and asked for a cab. There must be a lot of people around the base that use cabs because one showed up in less than five minutes. We got in and drove off the base. I think we all released a sigh of relief.

We arrived at our motel. Dad told Mum, "Wait here for us. I'm checking out and we're going to the airport." He turned to me and said, "Let's go." As we walked toward the office, he said, "You pack everything. I don't care what goes in whose suitcase. Just get us and our luggage out by the time I've checked out."

Fortunately, we'd not really unpacked when we'd arrived. We'd been that tired. I just threw the few items of clothes into the suitcase with the most room, snapped them shut, took one last quick survey for overlooked items, and carried all three bags out. I went directly to the cab and tossed the suitcases in the trunk. Dad was close behind.

We got in and Dad told the cabbie to go to the airport. The cabbie took off.

Of course, Mum and I were confused but Dad hadn't steered us badly wrong yet, so we kept our mouths shut and waited for developments. As we approached the airport, the cabbie asked which airlines we wanted.

That made him pause, but he came up with an answer that seemed to satisfy, "American."

Dayton's airport is small and not particularly close to town. The cabbie dropped us in front of the American sign and took his fare. As he drove off, Mum asked, "Where are we going?"

Dad said, "Back to town."

Mum and I looked at each other but didn't say anything. There was a shuttle service to downtown Dayton. Dad paid for us, and the driver helped us get our bags on the shuttle although I think I could have done it faster and easier than he could. There were a couple of other riders who boarded before we left. They were dressed in suits and had briefcases in addition to their suitcases. They were talking about some technical computer thing while we rode.

As we left the airport, the driver asked the van in general where we were going. The suits immediately said they were going to the Wingate Fairborn. Dad said, "The Hilton."

The driver asked, "You mean the Beaver Creek Hilton?"

Dad quickly said "No," but he didn't add anything more.

That didn't bother the driver. He replied, "You mean the Garden Hilton, then?"

Dad agreed.

Unfortunately that was not the end of the subject. One of the suits asked if we were going to the Wright State conference. He immediately clarified why he'd asked the question. He was going to the conference. He wondered if Dad were going to the conference.

Dad assured him that we were strictly in Dayton on pleasure. His son, I, was touring universities in the States to choose which ones that I'd apply to. That, of course, brought the question, "Is Wright State one of them?"

I think that Dad hadn't considered the possibility that Wright State might be a University. I stepped up to bat by saying, "No. I'm . . . uh . . . considering the other school here."

One of the suits saved me by saying, "Oh, UD?"

I temporized by agreeing while I worked out that UD must be University of Dayton. The suit who'd asked the question said that it was too bad that we couldn't carpool to Wright State. Both Mum and Dad agreed solicitously.

It was terribly frustrating that the three of us couldn't discuss what kind of crazy plan Dad had for us, shuttling us all over Dayton. I was itching to talk, but we were stuck in this shuttle with strangers, who were talking about NOSQL databases, whatever they are.

The unending trip finally ended, and we were let off at the Hilton. Almost immediately, a doorman ran up to help us with our bags. No help was required, but we didn't want the other passengers to think that we didn't intend to stay there, so the doorman rushed our bags to the front desk. At least the shuttle was gone by the time that we got there.

Dad rose to the occasion when the desk clerk asked if we had a reservation. "No, ma'am. And to tell you the truth, we're so hungry," by now the time was well past seven PM, "that we really just want to go to the coffee shop or restaurant and eat before registering."

The clerk offered to keep our bags behind the desk while we ate. Dad was funny to see. He drew out his "No" so long that I began to wonder if he'd ever finish it. He also screwed up his eyes as though it cost him a lot of effort to get the word out. He did finish the word and said, "I'm just kind of nervous about leaving our bags with anyone."

The desk clerk smiled, said that she understood, and directed us to the coffee shop and the bar which featured a full service menu.

We went directly to the coffee shop. There we were seated. I don't think that any of us were in a big hurry to order, but the Hilton staff was prompt to a fault. A waitress came by our table to give us menus, take drink orders, and greet us.

She was back amazingly quickly with hot water and tea bags for all of us. When he thought she was going to give us a few minutes rest, Dad said, "I'm out of ideas. I just don't know what we can do next. Do either of you?"

Mum shook her head. I didn't even bother to do that. I just stared numbly at the menu. None of us had any ideas. The waitress returned to see if we had decided on what to eat.

I don't think any of us had really studied the menu. But Mum ordered her standard whenever she's out without any ideas—soup and a sandwich. There were some negotiations about what kind of soup and what kind of sandwich. It gave Dad and me some time to think.

She turned to me next. I stuttered, and what came out was, "a a a hammmmburger and fries." I figured that every restaurant in the States must have that. I was right.

Dad had the most time, and he made it count. He'd noticed an item on the menu that he always is up for—steak and potatoes. We figured that those orders would give us some time to talk undisturbed. Mum did. "What in the world have we been doing going from pillar to post around Dayton?"

Dad shrugged, "Well, you had to hear both sides of my conversation with the Major. I had the impression that he wanted to send a car over for us right then and there." He added, "I'm not so sure he didn't."

"I thought that we had to get away as fast as we could and not leave any trail behind us. So, we checked out, took a cab to the airport as though we were flying somewhere, took a shuttle back here. I hope it takes them some time to figure that all out." He paused again, "Now, we're stuck with nowhere to go."

Mum is usually an optimist, and that trait came to her aid at that moment, "What do you mean, 'Nowhere to go?' We could go almost anywhere in this country."

Dad shook his head. "Yeh. Anywhere. But we've no idea what we're doing."

Then an idea struck me, and I blurted it out without thinking, "What about Jennifer?"

Mum asked, "Is that a girlfriend of yours back in England?"

I then realized that I'd spoken the question out loud. I answered, "No. No. You know Jennifer." Both Mum and Dad seemed confused and then Mum got it.

"You mean Jennifer on the ship?"

"Certainly!"

Dad asked reasonably, "But she didn't know as much about wizards as we do. How could she be a help?"

"No. Not Jennifer, but Jennifer's boyfriend or lover or whatever he was. He was at Hogwarts, and he seemed to know what was going on with 'He Who Must Not Be Named.' We should try to get in touch with him."

Dad nodded and said, "That's not a half-assed idea. Now for the other, hard half. How do we get in touch with him?"

Mum had an answer for that, "Isn't he a Yank?"

Dad nodded again, "But you don't think he's in this country now do you?"

I shrugged, "He might be, but even if he's not, he probably has family here who might know how to get in touch with him."

Mum agreed.

I smiled, "So, all we have to do is find one man in 300 million people here in the States."

Dad said, "Well, let's get started. How do we find him?"

I said, "Well, his name is something like Went, isn't it."

Mum replied, "His name is Wendt, James Wendt." She spelled his last name.

Dad took that as a positive thing. "Wendt can't be a common name. There probably aren't lots of them in the States—and probably a lot of them are all closely related. So if we find one, we've got a good chance of finding him."

Mum said, "That can't be hard. All we have to do is look in the phone book."

I said, "I don't think there's a national phone book. We have to look in the phone books of a lot of towns. Maybe, they're in some dinky little town in the middle of Kansas."

Dad agreed, "We can't travel around all the towns in the States looking at their phone books. I know libraries have some phone books. Maybe a big library would have lots."

I agreed. "You know the reference library in Toronto had whole shelves of phone books in the basement. What we need is a really big library."

About this time, our waitress started delivering our meals. We continued talking as she placed the plates. I was going on, "A big university is what we need."

The waitress had been listening to our conversation and made a suggestion, "The biggest schools around here are Wright State and the University of Dayton."

I looked up at her directly for the first time. I had to admit to myself that she had nice dimples. I said, "No, we want bigger. What are the nearest really big schools?"

"Easy," the wrinkles disappeared from her face and her dimples really stood out, "that would be either the University of Cincinnati or The Ohio State University."

Dad was decisive, "Cincinnati's out." We all knew why that was true. "Where is this Ohio State University."

She giggled, "That's THE Ohio State University to you. All the graduates make a big deal about the THE."

Dad was losing his temper, although I didn't mind it if she had to spend a little extra time talking to us. As a matter of fact, that was just perfect for me. "And WHERE is it?"

She came back to Earth and said, "In Klumbus."

We were all confused by the name. We'd not ever heard of a Klumbus. Dad asked, "Where is that?"

She laughed again—really charmingly, "It's the capital of the state, don't you know."

Mum got it. But to be sure, she asked, "You mean, Columbus, Ohio, right?"

The waitress nodded. "Anything else I can help you with?"

I had several things that she could help ME with, but I had to shake my head. We had real business. Dad did have a question, "How far away is that?"

She shrugged—again, really charmingly, "I don't know. Maybe a hundred miles."

That was really the end of the discussion.

Dad said definitely, "Then, we've got our next destination."

We finished dinner hurriedly. Dad wanted us to try to catch a bus for Columbus before the night was over. We got the check, and I decided that I needed the waitress's phone number. So, I asked her, "You are such a good source of information that we might need to get in touch again. What's your phone number?"

She blinked her eyes and asked, "Are you staying here? Because I can't fraternize with Hotel clientel."

I answered before Dad could get his mouth open, "I guarantee that we're not staying here, and I'll never stay here."

She touched herself on the cheek and said, "Well, understand that I don't give this out to just anyone. It's . . . "

I interrupted and looked to Mum, "Mum you've always got a pen. Can I borrow it?"

She frowned at me but got a pen out of her purse and handed it to me. I said, "Go ahead."

She said, "615," followed by a string of digits that I wrote on the palm of my hand.

Dad paid her. We gathered our bags and left the Garden Hilton never to return. Mum demanded, "Why did you get that phone number? Do you think you're going to come back, enlist in the Air Force, and date that girl?"

I just shrugged and said, "I'm just saying . . ."

Before we left, I actually did have to go back and ask the waitress one last question. I found her in the kitchen. She asked, "Want a date already?"

"No. I need to know how to get to the Northwest Transit center of the bus line."

She was apparently a regular on the bus line, "Oh, that's easy. You just go to the bus stop outside the hotel, and when a bus comes, ask the driver. It should be easy. Lots of bus lines must go there."

We followed her directions and found that it was easy, if by easy, you meant transferring three times. The drivers were all helpful, though. Each told us where to get off for the next transfer. We arrived at the Transfer station just barely before ten PM. We ran to the nearby Greyhound station. I carried two bags and Dad one. We ran in the station just as the ticket clerk was closing down.

Dad asked, "When is the next bus to Columbus?"

The clerk said, "That's it out there. I'm closed, but if you run, you can get on and buy a ticket from the driver."

We did run, and the driver did sell us tickets. He asked us which stop in Columbus we wanted. Dad replied, "Whatever is closest to Ohio State."

He nodded and said, "No problem. We actually stop close to the University at the Blackwell Hotel on the edge of the campus. It's supposed to be pretty nice."

So we were on our way to Ohio State. On the way we stopped at about half a dozen towns. We pulled into The Ohio State University a little after one AM. Thank God! There was a vacancy. We told the clerk we'd be there for a week and paid in advance for a week.

It looked like a dorm on the outside, but the inside was swank with wood paneling, a nice restaurant, and comfortable beds. The boring exterior and the quiet interior gave me a feeling of safety that I'd not had in quite a while—maybe since Winnipeg. The next day, we were up around ten and ambled down to the front desk, where we discovered that there was no place to eat until we walked several blocks to the High Street.

We accepted our fate and walked there. There were lots of fast food places along the High Street. We finally settled for MacDonald's breakfast pancakes and juice. It wasn't great, but I think that we all had the feeling that we could be on the verge of a breakthrough. So we were in good spirits.

There was another long walk to the main library. It was a pretty campus—nothing like Cambridge, but some of the buildings around the vast "Oval" reminded me of that town—slightly.

The librarians were helpful, and we soon found ourselves in a large room with shelf after shelf of telephone directories. One set of shelves was devoted to Ohio directories, but the rest were alphabetical by city name.

Mum smiled as she looked over the Ohio shelf and said, "Why don't we start here? We could get lucky, and our Wendt could be an Ohioan."

Dad grimaced and said, "But I bet he's not."

As before, I took the Z end of the alphabet, Mum started with the A's and Dad started in the middle. We had bought small notebooks at the Student Union on the way to the library. The plan was to go through all the Ohio directories, noting names, addresses, and phone numbers. When we'd gone through them all, we'd compare notes and start phoning—assuming there were any Wendts in Ohio with telephones.

We'd agreed that we'd note all the numbers for the exact spelling that we had plus make a separate list of close-sounding names like Windt, Wand, Wend, and so forth. We got started a little before eleven AM. We agreed to break for lunch mid-afternoon if we hadn't finished the Ohio directories by then.

We were dismayed when mid-afternoon arrived, and we'd only gone through a little over two hundred directories. There must have been over a thousand.

We decided to go back to High Street for a late lunch. The walk actually did us some good. As we walked, we did a little calculation. Dad figured that it would take us three solid days to go through all the directories—just for Ohio.

We strategized the rest of the day. We would work until seven PM, get a quick bite to eat and start making calls. When we reached the pizzeria, we opened our notebooks and compared counts. We had found a total of seven Wendt phone numbers in all those directories. There were also seventeen variations on Wendt. We didn't want to look at those yet. The idea of cold calling just seven people or maybe three apiece was as much as I wanted to tackle this night. I knew though that we'd find more.

We went back to the Library and struggled on. By the time that we called it a day, we had ten phone numbers. Dad graciously agreed to call four. He handed out quarters to everyone, and we went in search of phone booths.

The library had several phone booths in their little cafeteria. We settled in for a night of bad news. Bad news was what we got. By the end of the evening, we'd discovered that two Wendts had children by the name of Jamie or James. Both were still in school—at home.

That day had exhausted us, and we speculated on how many days it would take for us to work our way through the entire U. S. Dad asked, "There are something like fifty states, aren't there."

Mum optimistically pointed out that Ohio was a large population state. Maybe the rest of the States had only twenty times as many people.

I did the math and announced, "Then I guess it will only take us about sixty days to go through them all."

Mum replied, "But, if we don't have bad luck, it will probably take only thirty days before we find him."

Dad shook his head, "Unless he doesn't have living relatives still in the States."

On that pleasant note, we went to bed.

The next day, we were up a little earlier and got started sooner. We now had a routine and went through the directories so fast that by the end of the day, we'd added another four hundred directories and had a dozen phone numbers.

Back in the library we were calling. On my second call, I got a woman. I asked my usual question, "Ma'am. I'm doing a survey. We're trying to reach a James Wendt. Can you help me?"

There was a little gasp on the other end of the line, and my heart skipped a couple of beats. Then she said, "I'm sorry. There isn't a James Wendt here." My heart skipped another couple of beats.

I forced myself to say, "Well, even if he doesn't live there or is not even related to you, do you know of a James Wendt."

This time, there were actually tears—more skipped heartbeats. She sobbed and said, "We had a son James but we've not heard of him for nearly a year, and we think he must be dead."

I asked the critical question, "He didn't happen to live in England, did he?"

The sobs were open now, but through them, I heard her say, "Yes."

By this time, Mum and Dad had come over to my booth. They looked expectantly at me. I nodded. Then the woman asked me if I'd known him.

I started to say, "Not exactly. But . . ."

With that Mum grabbed the phone out of my hands. She immediately started talking, "Mrs. Wendt, this is Mrs. Dursley. . . We're so sorry for your loss . . . Yes, we'd be glad to come and visit you." Dad had started shaking his head "no." It became more violent the longer the conversation went on. Finally he started pacing up and down shaking his head violently when she said, "We're in Columbus. I think we can get to you sometime tomorrow."

When the conversation ended, Dad almost screamed, "What are you thinking of! You practically told her who we are and where we are!"

Mum was unperturbed. She simply said, "She's deep in grief. She probably didn't hear half of what I said."

Well, we were done far sooner than any of us expected. It seemed to me to be just one more dead end—in this case literally dead.

Before we left the campus, Dad made a call to Greyhound to find out about the schedule of buses to Circleville, Ohio where the Wendt's lived. It turned out that a bus left from the downtown station at ten AM and arrived about 11:30 AM.

The next morning, Dad insisted on calling the Wendt's and telling them that we would arrive at the Greyhound station in Circleville. Would it be convenient for them to meet us there?

There apparently ensued a battle over how we would travel to Circleville. Mr. Wendt insisted on picking us up in Columbus. Dad insisted that we would make our way to Circleville. I knew why Dad wanted us to get there on our own. It must have seemed crazy to Mr. Wendt. It wasn't an hour's drive to Columbus from Circleville.

Dad, of course, won in the end. He was bargaining for our safety and even our lives, while Mr. Wendt was just bargaining for politeness.

The next morning, we took a city bus down the High Street to the Greyhound station. We bought tickets and boarded. We'd brought our luggage just in case somehow we were traced and had to escape from Circleville. Dad wanted to have clothes with us. He assured the desk clerk at the Blackwell that we would be back and added under his breath, "I hope."

We had done so much traveling by bus lately that we immediately settled into our favorite seats and were on our way. It was the shortest bus ride that we'd had so far in our travels. The low rolling hills along the roadway were pretty. There was supposed to be a river that we were running near, but I never had a glimpse of it. The town was like very many small towns in the US that we'd seen. We pulled up at what seemed to be the town square.

We got out and looked around the square to try to find the Wendts. It didn't take long. There was a couple walking directly toward the bus. The man looked to be a little taller than Dad. He had dark brown hair. He was thin and seemed to be generally fit but not what I'd call muscular. He wore a pair of brown slacks and a light green dress shirt. The woman had shoulder length light hair—not blonde, but barely brown. She wore glasses. She wore a white blouse and black skirt. Her shoes might have had heels, but I'd have said they were flats. I'd barely had time to notice these details when they arrived.

262

The man said, "Mr. Dudley, I presume." Dad had decided that we'd go by that last name while we were with the Wendts as a safety precaution–for them and us.

Dad held out his right hand, and they shook. Mum took Mrs. Wendt by her arm and said, "I'm sorry to have to meet you under these circumstances."

Mr. Wendt said, "Oh, please let's go by first names. I'm Ed and this is Jane. And you are . . . ."

Dad gave our fake names. He was John, Mum was Janet, and I was Vernon.

The Wendts led us to their car—a large minivan. Mr. Wendt was talking as we walked, "We're close to home. Let's just go there before we talk. Jane has fixed us a nice casserole and salad for lunch."

He was right. We were less than three blocks away from their home. We entered the home. It had a small entryway with a closet on one side. Nobody was wearing a coat, so we didn't get to see the inside of it. The living room was very light and airy. It wasn't large, but it had four large windows. To the left of the living room was the dining room.

Mrs. Wendt got the casserole and salads from the kitchen, and we all served ourselves. Mr. Wendt started some small talk that didn't get very far—how was the bus trip, how long have you been in Ohio, and so on.

It wasn't long before we turned to the real topic. Mrs. Wendt went straight to it. "What can you tell us about James?"

Mr. Wendt quickly asked his own question, "Maybe it would be good if you told us about how you got to know James."

Mum started to answer Mrs. Wendt's question. Of course, her answer was itself a question, "I'm sorry, Mrs. Wendt. I'm afraid that was exactly the question that we wanted to ask you."

Mrs. Wendt hadn't shown much emotion until now. She compressed her lips and was apparently trying to hold back tears, "I was so hoping that you could tell me about him."

Dad took Mr. Wendt's question. It was funny. It was almost like the two women were talking to each other, and the two men were talking to each other as well. However, Dad named the elephant in the room. "I really think that we should start by telling you how we know about your son.

"I guess that you'd say that we . . . uh . . . met him through Jennifer Waters." That brought a sob from Mrs. Wendt. Dad started to go on, but he was interrupted by Mrs. Wendt.

"Oh, can you tell me what she's like?"

Mum, Dad, and I all stared at her. She explained, "Oh, we never met Ms. Waters. She was James' girlfriend the first year that he was in England. I had really hoped that she might be The One for James, but it never worked out. He never even sent us a photo of her. What does she look like?"

Dad looked over at me. I guess I'd been elected to talk about her, so I started in, "Well, she's very attractive. She has short brown hair—not so different from yours, Mrs. Wendt." At that she sobbed again. "She's a couple of inches shorter than I am. We only saw her in uniform so I can't tell you much about what kind of clothes she wears."

Mrs. Wendt interrupted, "So, she's in the military?"

I waved my hands trying to reinforce the negative, "Oh, no. She's the purser on a cruise ship. Anyway, she struck me as a very appealing woman. If she were younger, I would find her really attractive myself."

Apparently I'd broken some rule because everyone instantly frowned, and I added, "But she really is much older than me." That didn't seem to help very much, so I gave up. I'd told her everything that I could anyway.

Mrs. Wendt asked, "She was his girlfriend seven years ago. You must have known James for a long time."

Dad opened his mouth to say something, but nothing came out. He looked at Mum who clearly didn't want to handle this one, but she gritted her teeth and started in on our story. "Well, actually, we've known her less than a year ourselves. We met her on a re-something cruise to the Caribbean."

Mr. Wendt interrupted, "You mean a re-positioning cruise? From England, I suppose?"

Dad nodded and Mum went on, "It was last summer. So we really haven't known her long, and really, we didn't meet him then."

Mrs. Wendt said, "I suppose she still is carrying a torch for him after all these years if she talked to you about him so recently."

Dad opened his mouth again and said, "It's not exactly that. . ." He paused to think about what he would say, and then he went on. "You see, we thought that he was on the cruise."

Mr. Wendt broke in then, "What do you mean, 'You thought he was on the cruise?'"

I picked up the story, "Well, you see, the cabin next to us was assigned to James Wendt. We met Jennifer on the first day of the cruise. She was assigned to our table as a sort of hostess. Anyway, he was also assigned to our table, but he never showed up."

"We got into a conversation with Jennifer when we were both interested in the fact that he'd not showed up for the meal." A thought occurred to me, "I guess it wasn't that much of a coincidence that he was assigned to the same table as Jennifer. We were there by luck, I guess."

Mrs. Wendt leaned over the table, "But he wasn't on the cruise?"

Mr. Wendt added the question, "Why were you interested in him?"

I looked over at Dad, unsure just how much to reveal about our problem. He just nodded at me. I guess he wanted me to open the bag and let the cat out, so to speak. So, I did, "Well, you see, we were kind of in trouble with some . . . oh, I guess you'd call them. . ." I was about to say "terrorists."

However, Mr. Wendt filled in the blank for me, "Deatheaters."

Mum, Dad, and I all felt our jaws drop. Mr. Wendt went on, "Oh, yes. We know about Deatheaters. Do you suppose that James told us NOTHING about what was happening in England among the wizards?"

Dad shrugged, "I guess that should have occurred to us. You see, our nephew, his cousin," Dad pointed at me at that point, "Harry Potter, was kind of the leader of the anti-Deatheater group, the Order of the Arizona or something like that." He laughed, "Looking back on it, it was kind of ironic. We were afraid that your son was a Deatheater."

Mr. Wendt was not happy. He said, "Yeah, ironic. So, do you know why he wasn't on the ship?"

I said, "We don't know why he wasn't on the ship, but we can tell you that we sneaked into his stateroom. There were clothes and everything that he might have brought onboard."

Mr. Wendt said, "I suppose the Deatheaters got him after the ship sailed."

I smiled, "I don't think so."

Mrs. Wendt jumped on that quickly, "Why not?"

Dad said, "He was never on the ship. We learned from the Captain that MI6 had brought his things onboard. Apparently, they wanted people to think that he'd actually sailed."

Mr. Wendt shook his head convulsively as though trying to shake a fly away, "You don't say. Why would they care about that?"

Dad said, "We never learned. I don't think the Captain did either."

Mr. Wendt went on, "But I can't believe that you came all this way to ask us about our son just because he didn't board a ship that you were on. Why are you here. . . really?"

Dad answered that too, "We have been trying to get away from the Deatheaters ever since last summer. Harry thought that they might try to snatch us so that they would be able to blackmail him."

Mrs. Wendt took Mum's arm, "Oh, Mrs. Dudley, you've been a refugee all that time?"

She nodded and said, "It's been hard, but what was our choice? They almost caught up with us a couple of times."

I was really scared that she might say something about the Deatheaters who actually did catch up with us. I was shaking my head trying to communicate with her. I finally kicked her in the shin. She did pretty well not to show signs of that.

Dad went on, "There was this rumor that our Harry and 'You Know Who' couldn't both survive long. One would have to kill the other. I thought that it would have happened long ago."

Mr. Wendt asked, "And you were hoping that we could tell you if IT had happened yet?"

Dad nodded. Mr. Wendt said, "I'm afraid that we can't help you. We may know less than you do." That sort of ended another hope that we'd had.

Mrs. Wendt asked us if we would like to see the house. Mum agreed. Dad and I rolled our eyes and went along. Mrs. Wendt started in the living room. She led us over to the mantle of the fireplace. There were a couple of pictures on it. One was of a boy with a baseball bat over his right shoulder. Another showed a young man in a cap and gown. There was a Lucite plaque with some sort of award inscribed on it. It was James Wendt, of course at a younger age. As we looked at this sort of shrine, Mrs. Wendt talked about her son. I didn't catch much of it. I thought he probably was dead and we were seeing the last momentos of a nice guy. I was lucky that it wasn't me.

We took a tour of the rest of the house. There was James' bedroom— left just as it had been the last time that he'd been there. There was a banner hung on the wall. It said, "Hogwarts Forever!" There was a dress shirt hung over the back of a chair at a desk. I prayed silently that we wouldn't hear about when that shirt was last worn by JAMES. We didn't.

At the end of the tour, Dad was preparing for us to leave. He said, "It's been nice meeting you, but if we want to catch a bus back to Columbus, we've got to get on our way."

Mr. Wendt said, "You really should stay for dinner. We don't have anything prepared, but we could go to one of our many nice restaurants, namely Chili's."

Dad tried to back out, but Mr. Wendt wouldn't be convinced. He argued that he could give us a ride up to Columbus and drop us off anywhere we liked—even if it were only a bus stop.

Mum took Dad's arm, "Oh, we should have dinner with them." That settled it.

I discovered that Chili's was a Mexican restaurant. I never learned why Americans like spicy food so much. All three of us were drinking water by the gallon that night.

After dinner, Mrs. Wendt insisted that we stay the night. Dad really didn't want to, but Mum was for it again. It turned out there was just one problem. Where would we all sleep. The Wendts had just one Guest Room. That was fine for Mum and Dad but what about me. There was James' room, of course, but I had a feeling that it was out of bounds.

Nothing was said about it. No one mentioned it. So, I said, "Well, I'd like to sleep on the couch in the family room."

Mrs. Wendt was against it, but somehow she didn't have an different idea for me.

I was determined, "Oh, don't be concerned. I've slept in lots of worse places the last year. The couch is just great!"

Mr. Wendt went to the couch and started pulling the cushions off it, revealing a cloth handle. He pulled it up, and I realized that there was a mattress hidden in the couch. I went over and grabbed the mattress to prevent it from being pulled further out. I said, "Oh, no. No. I really like sleeping on the couch as a couch. Just give me a couple of sheets, and I'll be just fine."

Mrs. Wendt had a pained look on her face but she didn't say anything. I repeated my words, "No. Really. I'll be just fine. Don't worry for a second. I can even use one of the cushions as a pillow. I've done it loads of times."

Thank goodness we didn't have to argue about that any more. Mrs. Wendt got out some sheets and a real pillow, and I was set.

However, it was still early. Mr. Wendt suggested that we play cards. I looked over at the Telly with hope in my eyes, but a funny thing happened. I began to realize that I wasn't all that excited about watching the tube. So, I didn't object to cards. He taught us a game that he called Back Alley Bridge.

Apparently, it was a game that was popular in the US military. Mr. Wendt had learned it while he was in the military at the beginning of the Vietnam War. He'd been stationed in Korea and had never gotten closer to Vietnam than that. But he'd learned this game, and he'd loved playing it ever since. He had a hard time finding people to play with.

Mrs. Wendt would play with him as a partner when there was no other choice. It could be played with four or six players. There were five of us. Mrs. Wendt took that as a sign that she would sit out, but Mr. Wendt wouldn't have it. He said, "We never get to play with six. Why don't you invite your sister over? She likes to play it. We could have six!"

Mrs. Wendt sighed and got on the phone. Apparently everyone lives close to everyone else in Circleville. The sister, Nan, arrived almost before Mrs. Wendt had hung up the phone.

Mr. Wendt called her Aunt Nan even though she was his sister-in-law. She was the tallest of the ladies in the room and had short black hair shot with silver. She wore a purple dress and had horn-rimmed glasses. She looked a good bit older than Mrs. Wendt.

Mr. Wendt introduced us. Nan was very polite, but when it came to me, she shook my hand for quite a long time. When she eventually unclasp our hands, she said, "You're related to that Potter boy, aren't you?"

267

I gaped but didn't say anything. Dad asked, "How'd you know that?"

Mr. Wendt echoed, "How do you know about Potter?" putting the emphasis on "do".

Nan answered Mr. Wendt, "Oh, your son told me about Harry Potter. I think that he was a little afraid to tell you and Janie much about the wizards." She turned to Mrs. Wendt, "Oh, Janie, it's all right. He hardly told me anything—just that there was trouble coming and that this unlucky Potter boy was going to be part of it."

She turned back to me and continued to stare at me. Finally she said, "You are so like him. I can see it in your eyes." That was weird—really weird.

Anyway, it turned out that Back Alley Bridge for six was played with two teams of three each. Ordinarily, you draw cards from the deck to decide who will team with whom. However, Nan suggested that since we had three boys and three girls that we play boys against girls.

It was a strange game with all sorts of strange rules, but it was an exciting night.

The next morning, Mum and Mrs. Wendt fixed a proper English breakfast for us—ham, eggs, fried potatoes, English muffins, and a few other things. We packed and were preparing to leave for the bus station. We'd just finished putting our bags in the van and were climbing in when we heard a phone ring in the house.

Mr. Wendt said, "Oh, just let the voice mail pick it up, Janie."

However, Mrs. Wendt went back in the house. In about a minute there was a scream from inside the house. We all got out of the car and ran in. Mr. Wendt was easily the first in.

We found Mrs. Wendt standing transfixed with the telephone at her ear, facing away from us. Even so, we could hear her loud tears. Mr. Wendt grabbed her by the shoulders and whirled her around while he asked, "What is it?"

She just kept crying and said something like, "It's HIM."

Mr. Wendt took the phone from her hand and put it to his ear. Then he shouted for joy. Just one word escaped his lips, "Boy!"

The three of us all stared at each other and wondered to ourselves if that were James Wendt. We soon found out. Mr. Wendt turned to us and said, "James, there are some people here who want to talk to you almost as much as I do."

After a pause, he said, "They're the Dudley's."

A look of consternation came over his face and he said, "The Dudley's. The Dudley's. You know that Potter boy's family."

Finally, he handed the phone to my Dad, who took it and asked urgently, "Does He live?"

Immediately after that question, Dad shouted, "Hurrah!" Then he was silent for a long time. He then said, "Yes, I understand. Let me give Mrs. Wendt the phone now. Good bye. Thanks so very, very much for the good news."

He then drew us aside and took us outside. He said, "Well, 'You Know Who' is dead. Potter's alive. We can go back to England."

Both Mum and I stared at him in disbelief. After so much time trying to run from England, it was almost too much to believe that we could return.

Dad had cautionary words though, "There's one little thing."

Both Mum and I frowned. I just knew there would be something.

Dad noticed our downcast faces and said, "Oh, it's not bad, really. Apparently, most of the Deatheaters are captured or killed, and they're just cleaning up, but Wendt suggests that we stay over here for another week or so while they mop up.

"We don't have to hide. As a matter of fact, we can do some real sightseeing without having to look behind our backs all the time."

We stood around for quite some time while we waited for the Wendts to come back outside. As a matter of fact, I'd begun to think that they'd forgotten that we were here. They did come out. Mrs. Wendt insisted that we stay with them one more night at least to celebrate all of our good fortunes. I could tell that Dad didn't want to, but even I thought it would be bad Karma to run off without celebrating with the Wendts.

Mum and Mrs. Wendt planned a great celebration dinner. They invited all their relatives that lived near. In the end, it was just Nan and Mr. Wendt's uncle Jonathan. The ladies were in the kitchen working on dinner while we guys sat around. Dad and I told stories of our travels.

We got to repeat them for the ladies when we ate dinner. The table had been designed for eight but it was a crowded eight. There was an eighth place set at one end of the table. I asked who it was for.

Aunt Nan, as I'd begun to think of her, answered, "Why, of course, it's for James. We look forward to the time that he's back to visit."

That night, Mrs. Wendt decided that it would be alright if I slept in James' room. We had a little argument. I still insisted on sleeping on the couch. I won.

The next morning, was actually pretty sad. We had the same breakfast that we had the previous day. Somehow, it was not as happy.

Mr. Wendt asked what we were going to do. He added, "I suppose you're going straight to Port Columbus to fly back to England."

Dad thought about it and said something that surprised me, "No. We want to do some proper sightseeing now that it's safe to do so. I don't

269

know. I'm sure that we'll go to New York City. Maybe we'll go to Boston. Anywhere else you'd suggest?"

Mrs. Wendt asked, "Have you been to Washington?"

I said that we had.

Mr. Wendt pressed on, "But you'll want to fly. My offer to take you to the airport stands."

Dad declined with thanks. "I think we'll go back to our hotel and do a little planning before we leave. We've still got most of a week left there, but, I will let you drive us directly there."

That was agreed. After breakfast was finished and cleaned up, we all got back in the van and left Circleville. We arrived at our hotel where Mr. Wendt repeated his offer to take us to the airport whenever we wanted to go.

Dad declined with thanks again.

After they'd left, I asked why he was so insistent on not letting Mr. Wendt take us to the airport.

Dad smiled, "I thought that we might like to continue our sightseeing by bus."

We all laughed. Dad insisted that he was serious. You get a lot better idea of the country from a bus than you do from an airplane. So, we decided to go by bus from Columbus to New York City. We'd get off where we wanted to. If some small town beckoned to us, we'd stop, spend a night, and move on.

Diamonds Are Forever

The trip from Columbus to New York City took us four days. We decided to take a little side-trip to Gettysburg. We saw the great battlefield and the museum. We'd not had a real war fought in our country for hundreds of years. Oh, there'd been World War II, but that was different than having armies swarming over you home and thousands killed before noon on a fine July day almost exactly one hundred thirty-six years before.

We spent a day in Philadelphia and saw the Liberty Bell and the Franklin Institute. Then, it was on to New York.

New York was overwhelming. There was the Empire State Building, Central Park, the Twin Towers, the Subway, the department stores that Mum was so anxious to visit. I wanted to run in Central Park, but Mum absolutely forbade me to. She was afraid of muggers.

We spent several days there. Toward the end, Dad made airline reservations for us to return to England for the next day. On that next to last day, he told us that after lunch we would go to a department store in the afternoon.

He called a cab after lunch. He gave the cabbie an address, 727 5th Ave. We fought our way through mid-day traffic, and the cab stopped at the corner of 5th Ave. and 57th Street.

Mum was behaving strangely. She started to gasp as we drove down 5th Ave. The gasps became louder and louder as we approached the end of the block. When we stopped, and the cabbie opened the door, she suppressed a scream. "Oh, Vernie, are we going into . . . into . . . "

Dad was as cool as a cucumber as he said, "Are you trying to say Tiffany's?"

"Oh, YESSSS!"

He simply said, "Yes."

He took her hand, led her up to the door, and opened it for her. I just trailed behind them. He led her through the store. It was filled with display cases with jewelry and other very expensive things. We reached a display case that had a variety of bracelets—mostly diamond bracelets. He pointed to one simple one and said, "What do you think of that bauble?"

Mum's mouth opened and closed several times, but no words came out. Finally, she said, "Oh, that's too much."

I had to agree. I didn't see a price tag anywhere, but I knew it was way too much.

A clerk who had been hanging back came forward. You know, somehow calling such a person as that in a store like this a "clerk" just didn't seem right. Anyway, he approached and asked, "Has Madame settled on something?"

Mum was still mainly speechless. Dad wasn't. He said, "Yes, that bracelet will do."

"Thank you sir. I'll have it wrapped, if you'll just accompany me."

Apparently, no one mentioned a word like "pay" or "credit card" in such a place. Mum kept staring at the display case. I watched Dad and the "clerk."

They had reached a table. I saw something then that is pretty rare in a place like that. Dad reached in a pocket and pulled out a thick roll of bills and started peeling them off. The "clerk's" eyes actually bugged out as Dad handed him the stack of bills.

Then they returned to where we were standing. The clerk told Mum, "I hope that you enjoy your purchase." She was still speechless, but she did take the small, flashy, plastic bag that had Tiffany's written on it in letters that I was pretty sure were real gold.

Dad and Mum kissed then. Now, I've seen them kiss, and I've seen Tony Malicki kiss his girl friend. Those two kisses are nothing alike, but this kiss was so, well, intimate that I had to turn my head.

It was a good thing that I did. I noticed a couple of men outside the main entrance. They were dressed in cloaks despite the warm day. As they entered the building, they drew something long and thin from pockets inside their cloaks. In an instant I knew what they were doing.

I grabbed Mum and Dad and pulled them down, shouting, "Down!" Luckily, there was a display case between us and them. A display case behind us shattered, and I saw green glints off the larger shards that flew over our heads.

Then, all hell broke loose. There were red flares over our heads coming from some other directions. There were cases exploding everywhere, but somehow the one that we were behind didn't explode.

It was suddenly over, and we were still breathing. Someone in a black flak vest came up to us. It had letters A, U, R, O, R printed on it. He told us to come with him. We were led along with a few customers and some clerks into a back room.

One of the people in flak vests addressed us, "O.K. We just need to ask you all a few questions, and then you can go home. If you cooperate, you'll be on your way as soon as possible."

Somebody asked, "You're not NYPD?"

The man who had been talking said, "We're a special unit of law enforcement." With that they did start taking people into another back room. They seemed to be coming for people every five minutes or so. It seemed awfully quickly to me.

When our turn came, the man in the AUROR suit just asked us one question, "OK. What did you see happen?"

I answered. I'm not sure why I did, but it just seemed so obvious that I didn't hesitate. And besides, I'd been the one who had seen the Deatheaters enter the store.

"Well, sir, I happened to be watching the entrance when these two . . . uh . . ." I was a little afraid to say what they were.

The AUROR coaxed me a little, "Yes, what did you think they were."

So, I just took a deep breath and said, "Well, these two Deatheaters came into the store, drew wands, and started to . . . ."

Again, he interrupted me, "Did you say, 'Deatheaters'?"

I shrugged and said more definitely, "Yes, Deatheaters. At least I'm pretty sure that's what they were."

Again the AUROR interrupted me, "Just a minute young man. I need to talk to my partner." He walked to the door and talked in rapid whispers with his partner. Then, they both came back to us.

The first AUROR asked, "You're not wizards, but you know about Deatheaters?"

Dad spoke now. "Sure, we do. They've been chasing us for almost a year now. I thought 'You Know Who' was dead!"

The AUROR agreed, "Yes, but he has a few followers that are still on the loose. I don't know if these two actually are Deatheaters, but it fits the M.O. You haven't told me how you know about Deatheaters."

Dad said, "Well, I'm Harry Potter's uncle, she's Harry Potter's aunt, and he is Harry Potter's cousin."

The Auror nodded and said, "Well, you're in luck. Ordinarily, we would obliviate your memory of this incident and then send you on your way, but I think there are a couple of problems with that approach."

Dad interrupted, "Obliviate our memories! What happened to civil rights in this country!"

The Auror was unperturbed and went on, "It's not at all bad. It happens all the time, and people are none the worse for it."

Mum chimed in, "None the worse! How would you like to have your memory obviated?" I'd not often seen Mum this intense on an issue. It was entertaining. As long as they were around, I wouldn't have to do the heavy lifting on this issue.

The Auror went on, "No, I said we weren't going to obliviate your memories, and, for your information, all Aurors have some memory obliviated as part of their training. So we do know what it's like."

Dad muttered under his breath, "I think they obliviated your compassion by mistake."

Anyway, the Auror set his jaw and worked on to the points that he wanted to make, "There are three reasons that we're not going to obliviate your memories:

"One, you are witnesses to a crime, and we don't have enough evidence to know who's done it. Can any of you identify the suspects?"

To their credit, neither Mum nor Dad could see our attackers, and they admitted as much. On the other hand I could see them. I sort of overemphasized my ability to identify them, but I did see them.

The Auror went on, "OK. Two, you already know about the existence of magic, wizards, Deatheaters, and all of those things. So we'd really have to do a major memory job to do away with all that.

"The third reason is that you are relatives of Harry Potter."

I thought to myself, "You just can't get away from that, can you?"

By this time, everyone had been processed through. The Auror, whose name was Jake Everdine, led us out through the room where we'd been attacked. There were a couple of Aurors reassembling the room. It was astounding to see all the broken glass and shards of metal and fragments of inlaid wood swooping up into the air and fitting together like some giant three dimensional puzzle. We reached the center of the room. The Auror held out his hands toward us. He said, "Take a hand, each of you, we're going to disapparate to the Auror Office in Boston, where I'm based. We'll have you give a formal statement, and then we'll discuss options."

It seemed like that was a reasonable thing to do, so we took Jake's hands. We spun through the air and were turned inside out. It was pretty awful but I guess wizard ways always are.

At the Auror Office, we were taken into an interrogation room, and a police stenographer took our statement with what they called a spell-check quill. Each of us told our story, correcting each other where necessary. I knew that was not standard procedure in police investigations in England, but maybe the States are more lax about the niceties of getting independent statements.

We read over the statement and agreed that it was good enough. Then, we signed it. Having had the little run-in with the law from time to time, I knew there would be more, but Mum and Dad seemed to think that we could just leave. Auror Jake had other ideas.

He asked us to stay in New York until further notice. We all objected to that. Dad put it in words, "Look, we have no intention of hanging around until those coo coos pick us off. We want to go back to England immediately."

Jake grimaced, "I can understand, but we need to have you be available for lineups to identify the suspects and then to testify. You were the only witnesses."

Mum grumbled, "Maybe we wouldn't be if you hadn't obliviated the memories of the rest of the people in Tiffany's."

Jake was reasonable. "We interviewed them all, and none claimed to have had a view of the suspects."

Dad rolled his eyes, "Of course, they didn't. They didn't want to be targets for mad Deatheaters."

Jake said ominously, "We have ways to know if people are telling the truth."

I said, "Well, then, you'll give us special protection, right. You don't want your star witness to be vaporized or whatever before the trial."

Jake sighed, and I knew that we were in for trouble. "I'm afraid I don't have the manpower to put you on 24 hour surveillance."

Dad said, "Well, twelve hour surveillance, then."

Jake shook his head. I said, "I've got a feeling that you can't have us on surveillance at all, right?"

Jake didn't say anything. Mum immediately said, "I want to see the British Ambassador."

Jake tried another tack, "Look, even if you went home, do you think that they couldn't follow you back there? Your best chance is stay here and see this out."

Dad asked, very reasonably I thought, "Well, what about Muggle police? Can't you get them to provide us some protection?"

Jake paced back and forth for a while. He finally said, "Yes, but I don't think it would do you any good. The Muggle police would not be any more protection than nothing."

Before any of us could say anything, he went on, "BUT, I have an idea that might actually help you. We'll go see the New York homicide department, and maybe something can be worked out."

Mum made the obvious objection, "But, I thought you said Police would not be any help?"

Jake just nodded and said, "Yes, but. . . but . . . just wait and we'll see."

I figured this was better than a stick in the eye, so I shrugged and said, "What could it hurt?"

275

A few minutes later we were standing in an alley. Jake led us around to the street, and we saw that we were in front of a police department building. Jake led us in and walked up to the metal detector. He showed something like a business card to a guard there who motioned us to walk around the metal detector. I don't know about Mum and Dad, but I was impressed. We then went to an information desk. Jake flashed his card again and asked for visitor badges. We got them promptly. I still didn't get a real look at the card, but I did see the sign-in sheet where Jake had written our names and his. His title was Detective Inspector Everdine. I didn't catch who we were there to see. We put our badges on, and Jake led us to the elevator.

Once inside he selected a floor that had a label that said, "Homicide West." He led us down a dingy corridor to a room with only a room number. He opened the door and led us in. We marched across the room which was filled with cubicles with very low walls so that anyone could see everyone else. We entered the cubicle that had a name plaque that read, "Lieutenant Stebbins". Apparently Lieutenant Stebbins was in his chair behind his desk.

He smiled and said, "Well, well, well. If it isn't Jake the Snake. What do you have for me?"

Jake gave a quick report of the crime that we'd witnessed and the fact that we needed to be protected.

Stebbins said, "Doesn't everyone in New York City? What do you expect me to do about it, since you apparently don't want to, and we can't really protect them from your buddies."

Jake was not put off. He said, "Well, Purly, I know you can't do much for these good Muggles, but I thought that we both know a civilian who might be able to help."

Purly smiled broadly. "You're talking about Mr. N, right?"

Jake just nodded. Stebbins said, "Well, you know that I don't have a lot of pull with Mr. N, but maybe my boss does."

Jake said, "That's what I was hoping."

"Well, then, let's go see him."

We all stood up, and Stebbins led us out of the big office and down the hall to a private office that said in gold letters on the door, "Albert Cramer, Department Head, Homicide". Stebbins opened the door and stuck his head in. He asked, "You got a few minutes for me?"

A voice from inside said, "Purly, is this really important?"

Stebbins didn't really answer the question, but just said, "I think you should see who I've got out here."

The voice said, "Oh, all right, come on in."

We entered the room. It was much larger than Stebbins cubicle, had walls that went to the ceiling, and even had a window that looked out on a city park. He had several hard wooden chairs. Cramer's chair was a red leather swivel chair. He must have known Jake because as he cleared the door, Cramer said, "Oh, cheese and rice."

He motioned to chairs and pulled a cigar out of an inside pocket of his suit. He pulled a pocket knife out of a pants pocket and started to cut the end off of the cigar. I was so surprised that I exclaimed, "They let you smoke in this building?"

Purly provided the answer, "You're right, this is a non-smoking facility, but Mr. Cramer doesn't smoke them."

He was right. After cutting off the end and licking the end, he put the cigar in his mouth. There was no sign of match or cigarette lighter or anything that could set a cigar on fire the whole time we were there. He just chewed on the cigar and rolled it around in his cheek, and sometimes took it out of his mouth to point at someone while he was making a point.

The first thing he said was something like, "Damn that wolf." Or something like it. Then he asked Stebbins, "What do we have here?"

Stebbins introduced us and explained about the assault in Tiffany's and how we needed protection from "those people."

Cramer took the cigar out of his mouth and pointed it at Jake like a gun. "I suppose you think that we should try to get wolf to help with this problem of YOURS." He made it very clear that it was not his problem. How a wolf could be a help, I had no idea.

Then he turned to Dad with the cigar gun and asked, "Do you have lots of money? Because that's what you need to get wolf to help you."

Dad shrugged, "What do you mean by lots of money?"

Cramer put the cigar back in his mouth and said around it, "Well, to start with, these days, wolf always insists on a retainer of at least five thousand. And if it looks like real work, he will usually ask for up to ten thousand. That's just a start. When he delivers the final bill, it could be substantially more than that."

Dad asked, "I suppose you are talking in U.S. dollars?"

Cramer laughed, "Sure, did you think I was talking Mexican pesos?"

Dad squirmed a little, "Most of our money is in Canadian dollars at the moment. I don't think that we'd have any trouble converting that to U.S. dollars. That should be plenty."

Cramer rubbed his hands together with the cigar between them and said, "This should be interesting." Then he added, "Don't think that I bring wolf business every week. That fat genius has his buddy Archie to do that, but this is clearly a special case."

I was tired of talking around the elephant in the room. I asked, "What is this wolf that you keep talking about?"

Cramer laughed and Stebbins chuckled, "It isn't a wolf. It's a man whose name is Nero Wolfe. He thinks he's the greatest detective in the world."

Dad asked, "Is he?"

No one answered.

Cramer then asked Stebbins to get him on the phone. Stebbins reached across Cramer's desk for the phone. He punched in the numbers as though they were the ones he dialed most. The phone apparently rang several times before there was an answer.

Archie's Story

It had been a slow week. As a matter of fact, it had been a slow month. At the beginning it had looked promising. The very first case was the Winslow embezzlement. Wolfe had identified the man who was embezzling money from the Winslow Frontier Trust company. The only tough part was negotiating the finder's fee for recovering most of the embezzled funds. The Board of Directors of Winslow thought that the fee agreed on for solving the case included any finder's fee for recovering the two million that had been embezzled. We, of course, maintained that the retainer had been for just determining who the guilty party was. The normally iron-clad contract that Wolfe writes would normally have spelled that out. Everyone was convinced that there was no chance of recovering any money. So when Wolfe had gotten the criminal to actually bring the whole amount into his office except for a few miscellaneous thousand, there was a difference of opinion about finder's fee.

Wolfe had managed to squeeze a measly two percent out of the Board by reminding them that the next time they needed help, it would be a very different story unless they were minimally reasonable in this case. That had turned the trick. We got almost 40,000 dollars out of them.

But after that, the month was absolutely dead. Not even the teeniest hint of a case had walked through the door. I was thinking of polishing up my resume when the phone rang.

I lifted the phone receiver and said in my usual urbane tones, "Nero Wolfe's residence. Archie Goodwin speaking."

The voice on the other end was that of Lieutenant Purlie Stebbins of Homicide West. "Hello, Goodwin. Is the boss available?"

I never liked to give Purlie an easy time, so I looked over at Wolfe and said, "Let me check. I think he went off to the kitchen for a minute."

Purlie wasn't fooled. He just said, "I know you're eyeballing him right now. Just put me on with him."

"Just a minute, Purlie."

I said to Wolfe, "Purlie Stebbins on the line. Do you want to take it?"

Wolfe gave a little shudder. I covered the mouthpiece and said, "Look, under normal circumstances, I like to string Purlie along as much as the next guy, but we could really use a fee. Why don't you just humor him?"

Wolfe wrinkled his nose and said, "I suppose." He lifted his receiver and signaled me to stay on the line.

Purlie said, "Mr. Wolfe, Mr. Cramer would like to talk with you a moment."

Wolfe said, "Is this really important?"

Purlie answered, "I think you'll find it interesting."

Then I heard Cramer come on the line. I could tell that he had a cigar in his mouth by the way he talked. This didn't look good if he'd resorted to a cigar already. Cramer said, "Well, Wolfe. I'm prepared to do you a little favor."

Wolfe's eyebrows rose a fraction of an inch and he said, "Really. What is it?"

"I don't think I can describe it adequately on the phone. When can we come by to talk?"

"I'll have to check with Archie to see what's on our calendar." He covered his mouthpiece and looked a question at me.

I shrugged. I didn't know any more than he did. Wolfe uncovered the mouthpiece and said, "You know when I come down from the Plant Rooms in the afternoon. Be here then, Aad are you bringing someone other than Stebbins along with you?"

I could tell that Cramer had taken the cigar out of his mouth. "You bet I'm bringing some people—potential clients."

Wolfe asked, "You know my fee structure. Can these people afford it?"

Cramer said, "Oh, yes. I think they can. The wife is wearing a diamond bracelet that looks like it came from Cartier's." Then he wrung off.

Now, we'd had women come into this office who could easily afford to wear jewelry from Cartiers, but there had been very few occasions when they actually had. I thought that this might be just the shot in the arm that our bank account could use.

□

Wolfe had just come down from the Plant Room when the doorbell rang. I got up and went to the door, checking through the one-way glass as usual to make sure that it was not college kids peddling magazines. I saw the face that I knew second best in the world. It always seemed to be apoplectic—even when its owner was happy. I could see that there were

280

several other people on the stairs. I opened the door, gave Cramer a big smile, and said, "Welcome, one and all." All turned out to be half a dozen people. It was a hot summer day and very few men wore hats these days, so I had no hatcheck duties. The one woman was not wearing a hat. However, she was wearing a diamond bracelet that very well might have come from Cartier's. I had a problem that I had to deal with right away. Normally, Cramer got the red leather chair when he was in the room, but there were potential clients present. Who got The Chair? I decided on Cramer. Cramer was leading our guests, so it was easy to seat him in The Chair.

When they were seated, Wolfe asked for names, "I recognize Mr. Cramer, Mr. Stebbins, and Mr. Everdine. But who are our other guests."

Cramer smiled. That was ominous. He said, "These are the Dursleys— Petunia, Vernon, and Dudley." They were a strange group. They were all tanned—not as you might expect a wealthy family to be from spending time at the spa, but the deep tan that comes from spending lots of time outdoors. They all seemed to be fit, but again, not as though they went to the gym every day, but as though they worked hard every day.

But then, there was that Cartier bracelet and the fact that they were here at all. Cramer knows the kind of wealth it takes to hire Wolfe. He wouldn't have sent them here, let alone come with them if he didn't think that they could afford Wolfe.

Mrs. Dursely in particular was a puzzle to me. She was obviously in her forties. She had a grown son, after all, but there was something about her that was intriguing. Like the others, she was clearly fit and tan. She wore a khaki miniskirt that did nothing to conceal legs that were worth looking at. She was wearing a black blouse that had almost no cleavage. That was a problem—the cleavage that was almost not there. Her hair was short, brown, and simply coiffed. She was a real problem for me. Despite the fact that I knew several striking beauties—Lily Rowan for one—who were clearly better looking than Mrs. Dursley, I still had a hard time keeping my attention on the discussion that was going on. My eyes kept wandering to Mrs. Dursley's knees, which were demurely locked together at an angle.

Wolfe had asked who the spokesperson for the group was. Mr. Dursley had volunteered and began telling us about his problem. "There are some Deatheaters who are trying to kill us. Do you know about Deatheaters?"

Wolfe waved it aside with a brief assent, "Yes, I've had dealings with some of those disciples of Tom Riddle in the past."

Mr. Dursley was surprised, "Who is Tom Riddle?"

Wolfe was irritated, "Oh, you maybe know him as 'You Know Who' or 'He Who Must Not Be Named'."

Mr. Dursley nodded and went on, "They've been following us for almost a year, and they caught up with us in Tiffany's. They almost killed us there."

Wolfe nodded his head slightly, "Yes, I notice that Mrs. Dursley has a bracelet from there. Why didn't they kill you?"

That had Dursley flustered. Everdine answered, "We were alerted to the use of an unforgivable curse and arrived in time to prevent that."

Wolfe went on, "Well, Mr. Dursley, what do you expect me to do? You are in the presence of representatives of two efficient law enforcement organizations. I know that Mr. Cramer probably can't help you much."

At this Cramer's smile that he'd been wearing since he arrived disappeared, and he said, "Now wait one minute Wolfe. This is not exactly the kind of case that we can . . ."

Wolfe said, "I know that you are working under a great disadvantage in this case, but surely Mr. Everdine can help you Mr. Dursley."

Everdine compressed his lips, took a breath, and said, "Well, We in the Auror Department are pursuing this case, but I really can't assign Aurors to protect the Dursleys."

Wolfe rarely expressed surprise, but this made him actually raise his eyebrows. "Can't, Mr. Everdine or won't? Surely, if these were wizards and witches, you'd provide them with protection."

Everdine was clearly uncomfortable with the way the conversation was trending. "Look, Mr. Wolfe, our staff is overextended as it is and well, we don't really have the freedom to extend protection to people who are not in our jurisdiction."

Wolfe exclaimed, "You bigot! I think you would be sure to have Aurors available if the Dursleys were wizards!"

Everdine looked at the floor and said, "My superiors wouldn't approve it if I did, and I would be disciplined."

Cramer's smile had been widening as this conversation had been going on. He was apparently not bothered that Everdine was uncomfortable.

Wolfe turned back to the Dursleys, 'What do you want me to do? I can't defend you any more than Mr. Cramer with his army of minions can."

Mr. Dursley said, "Maybe you can find the Deatheaters and turn them over to the Aurors."

Wolfe leaned back and closed his eyes. The Dursleys were surprised, but the public employees had seen this before and knew that it was normal. After a minute or two, he opened his eyes and said, "What you've asked for is something that I might be able to do."

I gave a sigh of relief. Our bank account could certainly use a shot in the arm, and this might just do it.

Wolfe was going on, "You must understand that this could take some time, and my services are not cheap. I would require a retainer of five thousand dollars. That might cover our services, but I doubt it. They might go well beyond that amount. Are you prepared to pay that kind of fee?"

Dursley shrugged and said, "If we have to. I was rather hoping it might be less."

Wolfe said, "Yes, we all have our hopes. I was hoping to finish the Isaacson biography of Einstein today, but I too was disappointed."

Dursley went into a huddle with his wife and son. I didn't catch all that they said, but I'm pretty sure that he asked if each of them had fifteen hundred dollars with them.

Wolfe was getting impatient, "Come now, Mr. Weasley, can you pay my retainer or not? You can use a credit card. We're equipped with a card reader, aren't we, Archie?"

I thought that Cramer's smile was going to break his face.

I answered, "Yes, sir. We've never had to use it except for a couple of tests, but it should work."

Dursley said, "Well, we left all credit cards behind when we fled England. We didn't want to leave a trail that could be traced. Of course, we'll pay you now." He pulled from his pocket a check-fold and started to write out a check. But before he finished, he asked, "This check is good for Canadian dollars. It's drawn against a bank in Vancouver."

This was the first time that we'd been offered payment in foreign currency. Wolfe turned to me and asked, "Archie, what's the conversion rate of Canadian dollars into US dollars?"

I shrugged, "I don't know the precise current exchange rate, but I suppose it favors US dollars by thirty or forty cents on the dollar."

Wolfe nodded and said, "Just make it out for seven thousand dollars." Then he turned back to me, "Print off our standard client contract. Specify that the service to be rendered is discovering the identity of the assailant or assailants of Mr. Dursley at Tiffany's and seeing them delivered to the relevant authorities."

He then turned to Cramer and said, "We may want some small assistance from the police in this investigation. Considering that we are rendering the Police Department a substantial service that it isn't able to take on itself, I think it's not unreasonable."

Cramer's beaming smile dimmed somewhat, "Well, it depends on what you think is a small service. But, yes, if it's small."

Wolfe asked, "Should we contact you through Lieutenant Stebbins? And what about you, Mr. Everdine? If we need to contact you, how should we do it?"

Cramer grunted, "Yeh, Purlie's OK to get in touch, and, he can contact the Aurors too." Everdine nodded.

The client agreement was printing by now, but I saw one problem, and I addressed it to Wolfe. "Uh, sir. There's just one thing. You'll remember that in the past, we've had a client stay here when she was in some danger of being killed and that she actually was murdered after she left us. I was thinking that maybe. . . "

Wolfe's brow wrinkled, and he repressed the temptation to make a face with difficulty. "Yes, I suppose we might learn from experience." He turned to our clients. "Mr. Goodwin is suggesting that you might like to stay with us until the conclusion of our agreement. I offer that additional service to you."

Mr. Dursley's face showed considerable relief as he accepted the offer. Cramer's face resumed the beaming smile as he said, "Well, we'll be seeing you Wolfe. Enjoy your company."

Wolfe simply said, "Pfui!" as the public employees left the office. I accompanied them to the door to be sure that none of them repeated the mistake that someone had once made of closing the front door and finding himself on the inside of our house.

I returned to the Office and found that Wolfe had summoned Fritz. He was telling Fritz that we were going to be having company for the near future and that all meals would have to accommodate five. He turned to me and asked, "Archie, how will we accommodate our guests?"

I said, "Certainly, Mr. And Mrs. Dursley should have the Guest Room. As to Mr. Dudley Dursley, I suppose he could have my room, and I can take the sofa in the Rec Room downstairs."

Dudley immediately rose and said very forcefully, "No. I would really like the sofa. I've slept on sofa's and worse loads of times lately."

Wolfe said, "There you are. Now, we've got to get the Dursley's luggage here." He turned to me and went on, "We'll need Saul and Fred at least. Get in touch with them. In the mean time, have Mr. Dursley authorize the . . ." He turned to the Dursley's and asked what hotel they were staying in. They mentioned a nice midtown hotel. "Good, have them pack the Dursley's room and take it down to the Security Office for Fred to pick up.

"Tell Fred to be extremely careful. Remind him of the McGonagall case last year."

Then he turned back to the Dursleys, "Mr. Goodwin will have you call your hotel. You heard what I want you to ask them to do. We'll have to settle your bill whatever is left."

Dursley said, "We were going to check out tomorrow and return to England. We paid the bill in advance. I don't think there'd be any additional charges. I suppose that we should cancel our airline tickets."

Wolfe shook his head. "It would be better if no one knew that you were not returning to England on schedule. The airlines will know, of course, but that will only be after the fact."

Dursley objected, "But won't the Deatheaters assume that I'm returning to England and go there? That doesn't help us find them."

Wolfe wagged a finger at them, "They either know that you have airline tickets or they don't. If they don't, which is more likely, they will not assume that you've left the country. If they do, then they'll be waiting for you at the airport and will know immediately that you've not gone—at least on that flight. If the airlines know nothing of you, such as the phone number that you called from, the better."

So, I gave a call to the boys to check on their availability and to get Fred set up to collect the luggage. He would pick them up that evening. I took Mr. Dursley out to find a phone. I didn't use our usual drugstore—just in case. We went to a department store and found a pay phone.

That evening, after dinner, Fred, Saul, and Orrie joined us in the office to plot strategy. I suggested that the Dursleys could go down to the basement and watch TV. They went down but when they discovered that there was a pool table, they started a game. I heard that Fritz joined them later in the evening.

□□

When the boys arrived, Wolfe had me outline the situation. No one was happy about the idea of tangling with Deatheaters again, but they were all game. Wolfe outlined his strategy and assignments for them all. "It seems to me that the Deatheaters found the Dursleys either by magical means or by plain detective work. We need to tackle both possibilities.

"First plain detective work. I think it's likely that they'd hire a local detective agency. So, we need to start making the rounds to see if anyone has.

"Now, they would have to take photos of the Dursleys to the detective agencies. So Archie will take a photo of the Dursleys and send it by text message to each of you. You can show it to them and see if there's a reaction."

Here Saul interrupted, "Sure, that will work with the smaller agencies that don't have great ethics, but what about the firms that protect their clients like you do?"

Wolfe said, "We'll also try to get a photo of their clients to send along as well. If you show them that photo first, you may get a reaction even if they won't answer your questions. You could even suggest that you want to find these people, and you'd be willing to hire them to look for them."

I asked, "We can get a photo of the Deatheaters?" That was news to me.

Wolfe said, "Yes, we know that they were in Tiffany's and we even have a pretty good idea of the time. Their security cameras may have gotten a decent image of them."

Orrie said, "Well, if you get a photo of them that way, aren't we done?"

Wolfe sighed, "If only it were true. It doesn't give us what we really need, which is where they are located. If they've hired an agency, we have a strong lead to them if anyone recognizes the photo. There's also the possibility that the photo won't be good enough for a positive identification but good enough for someone in an office to recognize."

Saul went back to what Wolfe had said at the beginning, "But what if they used some kind of magical means to find the Dursleys?"

Wolfe nodded, "I think that's more likely. I have an idea for that. We don't need you to pursue that idea. Archie can do that."

I smiled at Saul. I rarely got a leg up on him, but this seemed to be an exception. I asked how we were going to get Tiffany's to give up photos of potential clientele.

Wolfe smiled. You could tell when Wolfe smiled. The corners of his mouth inflected slightly. "That will be another task for you."

He turned to the others who were sitting on yellow chairs in the office. "That's it for now. Archie will get in touch with you when he either has photos of the suspects or knows that he can't get them. Then you can begin. Now, let's divide up the agencies among you."

We did that, and then the boys left for the night.

⌗

The next morning, we faced the problem of breakfast. I usually ate breakfast in the kitchen. Wolfe ordinarily had it in his room. Guests were very rare. I suggested to Fritz that our guests and I would have breakfast in the formal dining room. He agreed that it was probably the best option. We weren't through discussing it when the guests arrived. They liked the idea. It was about 8 AM. The menu for breakfast was set by Wolfe. This morning it would be French toast, fruit, and blueberry muffins. They would be ready at 8:30 AM.The guests enjoyed breakfast. Mr. Dursley declared, "We've dined in quite a lot of places over the last year, but breakfast here is superior to anywhere that we've stayed with the possible exception of that hotel in Toronto."

Young Dursley agreed and added, "The blueberry muffins make me think that I might actually like blueberries."

Mrs. Dursley agreed with the general approval of Fritz's cuisine. She wore a white blouse today that showed a little more cleavage than the one yesterday. I thanked God that at least I couldn't see her legs. What I did see was too much for me to keep my neutral stance as an observer.

Fortunately, Mr. Dursley brought up a subject that caused some conversation when he asked, "What are you doing today."

I grimaced. This was the problem with living with your clients. You were always available for questions. So, I talked about Client-Detective communications, "Well, you see, sir, we find it works a lot better for everyone if the client doesn't see much of the details of detecting. There's this temptation—that everyone succumbs to—to want to run the show. It's understandable because you're providing the working fluid for detection."

At this point, I was interrupted by Petunia. That is by Mrs. Dursley, "What is that working fluid?"

I bit my tongue and said, "Well, mostly money, although other fluids sometimes grease the wheels."

She set her chin resting on her hand and asked, "Really. What other fluids are there?"

I simply said, "I'm not at liberty to discuss that," and wished that I hadn't said anything. I went on, "You see if the client sees the detecting, it's like seeing inside the sausage factory. You never want to eat sausage again." I kept finding ways to put my foot in my mouth, but I swore that this was it. So, I finished my breakfast and said, "I have to go into conference with Mr. Wolfe right now to get my marching orders for the day."

Mrs. Dursley said, "Or is it how you should grind the sausage?"

I was up and out without further comment. I met Wolfe in his bedroom just before he was set to go up to the Plant Rooms. When I entered his room, he asked, "Well? You know what to do. Get Stebbins to go with you to Tiffany's and convince them to let you see their security tapes. Get a couple of photos if there's anything to see."

All I could say was, "Yes, sir."

I went down to the office, called Homicide West, and asked for Stebbins. He answered after five rings with, "Hello Goodwin, what a surprise."

I answered, "Yeh, I figured you'd be out on the street somewhere. You must have been waiting for my call on the edge of your seat."

"OK. Cut the comedy. What is it that Wolfe wants."

I decided that it was way too serious in a lot of ways to waste time, so I just gave it to him straight, "I'm going to give you a break today. We want to have a look at the Tiffany security tapes from the day of the incident.'"

Stebbins asked, "What incident? Tiffany says nothing happened that day. We haven't heard a peep from them."

"I'll meet you there. When are you leaving?"

"Right now."

I walked out to the sidewalk and called my favorite cabbie, Hank, on my cell phone. By luck he was available and was fairly close. He arrived within ten minutes, and we were off. He asked, "Where are we off to?"

"Tiffany's."

He looked back at me and asked, "Did some lady finally get her hooks in you?"

I grimaced to avoid smiling, "No. This is strictly business."

The cabbie shrugged, and we pulled away from the curb. This was the end of rush hour, but it was a slow ride. He dropped me off at the corner of 57th and 5th. I glanced at myself as I left the cab. I was wearing a nice hand-tailored tan suit with my next favorite tie. I should look fine for Tiffany's.

I walked in through the main entrance and was greeted by a clerk before I could reach a display case. "May I help you?" The clerk was dressed as impeccably as I.

I got straight to the point, "Has Lieutenant Stebbins of the NYPD arrived yet?"

"Not that I'm aware. I could check with the Manager, but in the mean time is there anything you'd like to look at?"

I glanced around and still didn't see Purlie, so I told the clerk, "No, I'll just wait." He turned to go, and then I did think of something. "Wait a minute, I am interested in looking at diamond bracelets—something simple—a narrow band with say one tenth of a caret stones."

He turned and said, "Follow me, We have a display case of nice ones."

The display case was close. I saw one that looked pretty close to Mrs. Dursley's. I pointed at it and asked, "How much is that one?"

The clerk gave the obligatory answer, "Ah, yes. That is nice." He walked behind the display and looked for a couple of seconds and answered, "That one is $9,990."

I mumbled under my breath, "Price point."

He looked up from the display case and asked if I wanted to see it.

"No, just check with the Manager for me."

He left, and I stared at the thing. I guess the Dursleys could afford us if they paid for that with cash as they must have done. I couldn't imagine this establishment accepting a check on a Canadian bank from across the continent.

Just then I heard a voice that I instantly recognized, "Goodwin, you have someone in mind for that bobble?"

I turned to see Purlie's face which almost never has a smile on it. Today was no exception. I answered, "I thought you might need something for evening attire."

He grimaced and said, "We're burning sunlight, Goodwin. Let's go find the Manager."

Just then the clerk returned with the Manager and said, "Here's the Manager."

He said, "A Lieutenant Stebbins has not arrived yet."

Stebbins commented, "Now he has." He then took his ID card out of an inside pocket and displayed it to the manager. Then he said, "We're making a little discreet inquiry. Could we go to your office?"

The Manager agreed. He led us back to his office. It was rather small considering that it belonged to the Manager of Tiffanys, New York. There were three guest chairs. Purlie and I sat. The Manager did as well. I let Purlie do the talking.

Purlie said, "We are investigating a report that a group of known criminals have been researching your store for possible criminal activity."

The Manager assured us that he was protected by a famous, large protective service with a mostly well-deserved reputation.

I have to admit that Purlie was fairly smooth. He nodded and said, "Still, it wouldn't hurt to have some professional help from the New York Police Department, would it?"

The Manager warily asked, "What do you want to do?"

Purlie replied, "We've received a report that representatives of that group were casing your establishment yesterday afternoon. We'd like to review your security tape from that period to see if we recognize anyone."

The Manager asked, "Do you have a warrant?"

Purlie smiled and said, "Do you really want me to have to go to a judge and get that warrant?"

The manager looked glum, "I suppose not." He stared down and to the left for a while and then said, "You see, the thing is that we had a system failure yesterday, and we had to close the store early. Nothing was missing. No one was hurt. It's just that I don't like this incident to get publicized."

I decided that I ought to give Purlie a little hand here, so I said, "Did it occur to you that that system failure might have been a dry run for the real thing?"

Purlie almost growled at me, but the Manager took it differently. He said, "Well, I almost wondered that myself." Then he said more definitely, "Yes, let's go look at the tape." Then the manager turned to me and asked, "By the way, who are you?"

Purlie grimaced again and said, "This is a Mr. Goodwin. He's a consultant that we use on rare occasions."

I smiled and briefly displayed my investigator's license. The Manager then led us deeper into the store. He reached a locked door. There was a phone beside the door and a video camera above the door. He picked up the receiver and dialed two numbers. He looked up at the camera and said, "I have Lieutenant Stebbins of the New York Police Department and a consultant by the name of Goodwin. We need to review some security video from yesterday."

We heard the click of the door unlocking, and the Manager opened the door slowly. We entered. I saw an old acquaintance at one of the consoles. I walked over and said, "Well, I didn't know that they'd transferred you to pushing electrons, Sam?"

Sam smiled, "For about six months. Have you joined the NYPD?"

I shook my head, but Purlie answered for me, "No, he's still working for that obese egomaniac." Then he turned to me and said, "See Goodwin, I can use big words too."

If we had time for banter, I might have responded, but I was in a hurry. Purlie asked the supervisor in the room when the system had gone down the previous day. The answer was 2:13:59.

Purlie asked, "Well, back the tape up to 2 PM even and play it forward."

I contributed, "No, just the Main Entrance, please."

The Supervisor took us to his corner of the room. He had a desk with two computer monitors. One was quite large. The other was normal size. He worked the keyboard and mouse, and in a few minutes, the large screen showed four video views frozen in time at 2:00:00. One was a straight-on view of the door. Another was a view that included the entrance in the upper left corner. The other two video views were somewhere in the store and another door. He said, "OK. I'm going to start the view at normal speed."

After about a minute, a pretty much normal couple entered the main door. They looked like middle-aged rich. We continued to watch for the next ten minutes.

Then, another couple walked in, but you could never call them normal customers of Tiffany's. They were both wearing something that vaguely looked like dark hoodies, but they extended to floor length. It was difficult seeing much of their faces. They stopped just inside the store and looked around. Then, they both reached inside their hoodies and pulled something out. In the process, one of them lifted his head slightly, and I got a partial, poorly-lit view of his face. Then, the signal broke up, and in a couple of seconds, it was just video noise.

Both Purlie and I said simultaneously, "That's them."

The Supervisor was as shocked as we. He said, "I don't remember that."

290

Purlie looked at me and said, "The Aurors have a neat way of cleaning up after their messes. No memory."

I commented back, "Yeh, you can only wish that you could do that."

Purlie asked for stills to be made of a couple of frames of the video. We re-played them in slow motion and Purlie picked two spots. I asked for another—where the Deatheaters pulled out their wands. It wasn't as clear as the others, but I wanted one where it was clear that they were using wands.

After the Security Supervisor had created the stills that we wanted, Purlie asked him to email them to him. He gave the Supervisor one of his cards that had his email and phone number on it.

We were done and left together. Outside Tiffany's Purlie told me that as soon as he got to the office, he'd download the photos to his phone and send me a text with the photos attached. I thanked him and thought about calling my favorite cabbie, but decided to walk to the bank.

At the bank, I looked up my favorite banker. He was finishing up with another customer, so I had to wait a little. When he was finished, he called me into his office and asked why I'd stayed away so long.

I answered, "Well, business is slow. As a matter of fact, it's so slow that we're now taking overseas business paid for with foreign currency." I handed the check over to him.

He looked at it and commented, "Canadian, eh?"

I asked the obvious question, "How quickly can you find out if this is good?"

The banker steepled his hands and said, "Well, it will take several days to clear through the network."

It had been a while since we'd talked last, "You know Mr. Wolfe and his business. His business is time sensitive. We need to know if we can spend money with the expectation that we're actually going to be paid." I leaned forward conspiratorially, "You've got back channel ways of checking on this check and these people."

He laughed. "You know, I sometimes wonder if I'm going to get paid back for spending my back channel capitol."

I laughed too, "Come on, you know Wolfe. We've hit a dry spot. We'll hit dry spots in the future, but we always have our flush times. This could be the beginning of a really good one."

The banker scratched his chin. I knew that meant that he was going to do it. He just needed to figure out how to justify it to himself. After a pause, he said, "I'll get you an answer by tomorrow. Is that soon enough?"

I nodded. As I left the bank, I realized that it was well into the afternoon. I'd stop at a drugstore to have something to eat. It would not be Fritz's cooking, but under the circumstances, it might just be better for my health to eat as much away from the office as possible.

I was just starting in on my apple pie and coffee when my phone beeped. There was a message from Purlie. It had three photos attached. I downloaded the pictures, added them and the photo I'd take of the Dursleys, and sent them by text to the boys. My message was simple, "Here are the Dursleys and the Deatheaters. Guess which is which and start searching for an agency that knows one or the other of them."I quickly got responses from all of them. They were on duty. That left the other possibility. Wolfe had an idea, and I needed to find out what it was. So, I needed to finish my pie and get back to the brownstone before he left for the Plant Room. For that I called a cab and arrived a little before 2:30 PM. Wolfe was reading *The Virtuous Burglars*.

When I walked into the room, he asked about Tiffany's. I replied by opening my phone and pulling up the best of the three images. I said, "We got the crooks."

Wolfe will never touch a cell phone. I think that he's afraid that he'll acquire the texting addiction. He claims that he just doesn't see a use for them. So, I had to hold the small screen of the phone near his head so that he could see the photo. His comment was, "Satisfactory. I don't think that that could be used in a court of law—even those kangaroo courts that the Magicals think are halls of justice.

"However, it's good enough to create a reaction in anyone who's seen one of them."

I showed him the other photos. He shrugged. For him, one was as good as several.

He then took up the point that I'd come back for. He said, "Now we must handle the likely probability that they aren't using an agency to find the Dursleys. We'll put ads in *The Times*, the *Post*, and the *News*. We'll use twelve column inches on page four. Let's run this for three days and see how we do. What will that cost?"

I asked, "Not the *Wall Street Journal* as well?"

He snorted, "Pfui. Deatheaters watching the stock market?"

"Well, I think that would cost about $1000. That still leaves a lot of money to pay the boys."

He nodded and said, "Your notebook." When I had it ready, he went on, "Title at 20 point font. 'Have you seen this family?' Then use the photo we have, print it at the width of the ad. Below that in 14 point font. 'Contact', our number full stop. 'Leads resulting in the discovery of this family will receive $1000 reward' full stop."

I said, "Neat. Since we already have the family, we don't have to pay anybody. I suppose you hope that we can entice our Deatheaters to try to freeload on our mystery client."

"That would be good. I don't expect it, but like most investigation, there is lots of hit and miss. This is just part of it. Now, do you think you can get that ad in the papers tomorrow morning."

I glanced at my wrist. "The *Post* and the *News*, certainly. With our special relationship with Lon, we have a shot at getting it in *The Times* in the evening edition."

"Good. Do it if possible."

I picked up the phone receiver and dialed Lon's direct number.

He answered, "Well, Archie, what's up? Do you have an exclusive for me?"

I asked him, "How do you know it's me."

"Oh, Archie, you've got to keep up with the times. Don't you have Caller ID on the office phone?"

I was in a hurry, so I just said, "Can you get an ad into tonight's paper?"

There was a pause, and then Lon was back on the line, "What page?"

"Page 4 of section A. Twelve column inches."

"Color or black and white?"

"Black and white is OK if it gets us in tonight."

There was another hesitation. Then he said, "I think I can do it. Do you owe me or do I owe you?"

I hated to admit it, but we were in his debt, and I said so.

Lon said, "That's what I thought. Is there an exclusive in it for me?"

I thought a minute. What could we publish out of this case? Nothing. I said, "Sorry, Lon, not only is there no exclusive, there isn't a story that anyone can publish either."

Lon shot back, "Well, hell. I'm just going to have to do it because we are friends. Give it to me."

I did and wondered what I'd owe him the next time.

A little after five PM we got a call from the "teers". They called in separately, but we combined their calls in one conference call.

As it turns out, one of them could have called in for all. Each of them had the same story. Saul, not surprisingly, told it best. Here's his part of the conversation:

Wolfe asked for a report. Saul started by saying, "I've been to 20 % of the agencies on my list. I started by asking to see someone about hiring a detective.

"The receptionist asked what kind of job it was. I said that I had missing persons that I wanted to find. She asked me the standard sort of things—how long have they been missing, did I have photos and so on."

"I gave the standard gold answers that would guarantee that someone would talk to me who could actually be hired to do the job. You know—the person has been missing for fifteen days. I've approached the police. They have not been helpful. And so forth.

"She had me talk to one of their senior investigators. I made sure that it was not one who knew me. We talked about fees and so on. I told him a sad story about my cousin Vernon coming with his family to visit from England. He got off the plane and started sight-seeing before coming to visit. After the third day, we didn't hear from him.

"I showed him the photo, and he didn't react in the least. Mr. Wolfe, you can lie about that kind of thing, but there aren't many people–even in the business—who won't show any reaction if they see someone that they've been hired to find recently.

"So, I finished by suggesting that I was going to see another agency or two before deciding which one to hire."

Wolfe nodded, "Satisfactory. You had absolutely no nibbles?"

"No sir, no one was especially interested in the case other than as a possible job."

Wolfe persisted, "No one asked you where they had been last seen?"

Saul smiled, "No, that would have been a real giveaway. If they'd wanted to know that, they might well know someone who would find that information useful."

Wolfe went through the drill with the rest of the "teers". Nobody had anything worth talking about. Wolfe told them to keep up the work.

Orrie reported that he had seen 30% of his list. Wolfe asked him, "Are you sure you've given them all thorough consideration? We don't want to miss a lead because of being in a hurry to work through the list."

Orrie said, "Mr. Wolfe, almost all of my agencies are one or two man shows. They would have jumped for the chance to get a second fee for doing the same job twice."

Wolfe pursed his lips, which only I could see, but said, "Very well. Just be sure to be thorough."

By then it was almost dinner time. We adjourned to the Dining Room. We arrived and found that the guests weren't keeping up with the rules of the establishment. Dinner starts promptly at 7 PM. The guests arrived by 7:05. The first to arrive was Mrs. Dursley who sat across from me. I was sitting near the opposite end of the table from Wolfe. She was wearing a flowery print dress and a simple gold chain necklace along with the Tiffany stunner.

Mr. Dursley was next. He was wearing a grey suit, judging from the luggage that they brought probably his only one with him. Dudley Dursley was last but close behind his dad. They were talking heatedly when they entered the room but promptly stowed the discussion to be resumed later presumably. Mr. Dursley sat next to his wife, and Dudley opposite him.

Dining with Wolfe is like entering an informal seminar. You never know what subjects will strike Wolfe's fancy any particular night. The one thing that you can be sure of is that it will not be work-related.

That night Wolfe chose to talk about Shakespeare. Wolfe contended that Shakespeare was the weakest spinner of plots in the history of the English language. He gave numerous examples from the plays both well-known and obscure.

One play in particular that he talked about was "A Winter's Tale." The plot was preposterous and full of pointless death. It was, however, enough for the Bard to write numerous memorable speeches for that play to secure its fame.

While Wolfe holds conversational sway, it's difficult and perilous to enter the fray. He will skewer anyone with facts and sharp commentary. Consequently, most guests let Wolfe's fancy roll on, which is what he wants. And really, it is entertaining listening to him even if you know little about the subject.

The next morning, I was up early. We might start getting responses to our ads quickly. I went to the bathroom on Wolfe's floor. I found a line waiting to get in. Mrs. Dudley was standing there. She was wearing a rose terricloth robe and matching slippers, and as far as I could tell, nothing else. The bath robe was drawn tight, and it was very obvious from the lines that she had nothing else on.

Hers was such a striking figure, even though I could see hardly anything other than her ankles and her head, that I was struck dumb. She glanced over me. I was wearing a bath robe as well, but I had boxer shorts on under it. She said, "If you're thinking of going downstairs to the basement, Vernon, Dudley, and Fritz are working there.

I regained my voice and said, "Oh, I may just go back up to my room and wait for you to be done."

She smiled, "Good idea. I'll run up to your room and let you know just as soon as I'm done."

Suddenly, that didn't seem like such a wonderful idea. I said so. She said, "Good. I'll have someone to talk to while I wait."

At that point, Wolfe opened the door, glanced at the two of us, and grunted his disapproval. I again had nothing to say. That was becoming a bad habit.

She went in, and I could hear the shower start almost immediately. I figured her for the long, hot shower type. Instead, the shower turned off after four or five minutes. She did spend another ten minutes or so. Then, the door opened, and she came out.

She smelled as fresh as new-mown grass. Her robe revealed the same lines as before, but now she was finishing drying her hair. She was working on the hair at the back of her head. She worked the towel with both hands. Her uplifted arms brought her breasts into sharper contrast under the robe than even it had before.

I was struck speechless as before. This time her eyes drilled mine, and she said, "You'd better get in there while it's still hot."

I tried to walk around her without brushing the least strand of her robe, but one of her hands working the towel brushed my cheek as I passed her. Then, I was safely in and locked the door behind me.

I had to shower and shave quickly so that I could eat breakfast and be on duty quickly.

Fritz had made buttermilk buckwheat pancakes, my favorite. He served them with crispy bacon and fruit. I would ordinarily linger over them with coffee and the newspaper. Today, Mrs. Dursley appeared wearing a black dress that barely approached her knees. I decided that I had to finish quickly and get to my post.

Before I left, she asked, "Can I watch a hard-boiled detective at work today?"

I wagged a finger at her and said, "That would break more rules of the house than have ever been broken. Remember what I said about the sausage factory."

She didn't reply, but pouted the smallest pout that I'd seen. I was off to the office.

When I arrived, Wolfe said, "Archie, that witch has you flummoxed."

"I am not flummoxed."

But Wolfe continued to stare at me, and I admitted, "Well, perhaps a little."

"That woman has you ensorcelled. We have to finish this case as soon as possible."

I agreed. "Perhaps you should apply your massive intellect to a better way to finish it."

All that Wolfe would say was, "Pfui."

Shortly after that, the phone calls started streaming in. There were calls from people at the hotel that the Dudleys had used, of course. There were a scattering of other calls, including someone from Tiffanys.

Our standard response was, "Sorry, we've found the Dudleys." The stream was steady through the morning. Wolfe went up to the Plant Room, and I found no call worthy of troubling him.

I think that Fritz might have been a little flummoxed himself. That lunch and all the meals we had while the Dudleys were here seemed above the normal superlative standard that Fritz sets.

Wolfe gradually became ever testier at meals. He maintained that it was undoubtedly due to the disruption that women in the house caused.

Then one afternoon, just after 4 PM, the doorbell rang. I went to answer it, looked through the one-way glass, and recognized the ringer. It was Cramer. I didn't take the chain off the door but opened the door as far as that would allow.

I said, "Well, we've got all the subscriptions that we need. Come back in a year or two."

Cramer growled, "Cut the comedy, Goodwin. I want to talk with Wolfe. I know he's down from the Plant Room."

As a matter of fact, I heard the elevator door close on the way up to the Plant Room just then. Wolfe must have just called it. I didn't feel like he ought to have to walk into his Office and be greeted by the unpleasant view of Cramer sitting in the red leather chair. So I said, "I'm pretty sure that he's not down yet. I'll let you in if you'll be polite and wait in the Front Room until I've talked with Wolfe."

Cramer growled again but agreed. I released the chain and led him into the Front Room. I then went to the Office and resumed my seat at my desk. Shortly after, Wolfe came in. He walked to his desk. I didn't want him to get started on his latest book before I warned him about Cramer. So just as his ample rear touched his made-to-order chair, the only one in creation that he's really comfortable in, I said, "Ah-hem. Mr. Wolfe, we have a visitor in the Front Room."

He growled. "Do I have to see him?"

I said, "I think so. It's Cramer."

Wolfe made a face and said, "Bring him."

I went to the Front Room and found Cramer pacing with a newspaper rolled up in his hand. He muttered something like, "Finally!" and followed me to the Office.

Rather than walking straight to the red leather chair, he strode directly to Wolfe's desk and threw the newspaper down on the desk. It was *The Times*, open to the 4th page where our ad was. He practically roared, "What is this?"

Wolfe glanced down at the paper and then looked up at Cramer. "You know I like eyes at a level. Please sit, and we'll discuss this rationally."

Cramer did take a seat and sneered, "Rationally! Are you trying to get those people killed?"

Wolfe showed good restraint. "Why do you think they are in danger?"

Cramer said, "Well, for one thing, this pretty much confirms that you think they're still in the city. You might as well say, Deatheaters, come and get them."

Wolfe smiled, "They're as safe as they would be anywhere in the world."

Cramer looked at Wolfe suspiciously. Then he laughed. Between gasps for air, he asked, "You don't mean to say. . . ha ha. . . that you've got them here . . . ho ho. . . Even the woman? Under your roof?" He then stood half up, and his laughter was so violent that it had reached inaudibility."

Wolfe looked disappointed, "Well, yes. It seemed the only reasonable thing to do."

Cramer had resumed control of himself and said, "Well, I take back what I say about you. You do have a smidgen of compassion in you."

He then turned serious, "Any bites?"

Wolfe turned to me, "I'm afraid not Mr. Cramer. There are plenty of legitimate responses from people who you'd expect—hotel employees, Tiffany employees, and so forth. No responses that look hopeful."

Cramer asked, "Is that the only idea you've had?"

Wolfe said, "No. But I'm reserving others to myself for now."

Cramer got up, briefly glanced inside his suit coat, as though wishing he had a reason to get a cigar out, but didn't. He said, "Good luck, Wolfe. I've got a feeling you'll need it." He then left the room. I made sure that he was on the right side of the door before he closed it. Then, I returned to my post.

A little later the "teers" reported in. There was no progress other than shortening their lists of agencies to contact. They would exhaust them in a day at most.

Dinner was superb again. Fritz had tried a new dish that he'd never done for Wolfe before. After the dinner, Wolfe accompanied him to the kitchen to discuss it.

Dudley challenged me to a game of pool. The Dursleys and I adjourned to the basement. Mr. Dursley watched as we set up for the game. Then he said, "I'm going up to read the newspaper. Where is it, Goodwin?"

I said, "I have a copy on my desk in the Office. Just stay away from the windows. I think we left the blinds up on one of them." He left.

Mrs. Dursley sat on a stool that swiveled. She was wearing that damn black dress again. Both the gold of her necklace and that Tiffany bracelet stood out against it when she rested a hand on her legs, which were crossed primly.

We lagged for the break, and Dursley won. His shot broke the formation nicely but didn't put anything in. As I lined up my shot, I couldn't help noticing that she swiveled her seat so that I couldn't help aiming the ball in the general direction of her crossed knees. She was leaning back slightly, and my line of sight also carried on to her breasts and necklace.

I did my best to concentrate on the target. I managed to put the ball into a corner pocket with a good bit of reverberation back and forth. As I lined up my next shot, I saw her adjust her seat again. Again, I had a darned good view of her legs as I shot. I purposely put some backspin so that my next shot would be out of the line of sight to her.

Somehow avoiding looking at her didn't help. As a matter of fact, I missed. Dursley took over and began a run of a couple of balls. Mrs. Dursley pursed her lips as if to ask a question, but then didn't. That left me staring at those lips. Then she said, "Have a question Mr. Goodwin?"

I growled, "Not one that I can ask."

The rest of the game went that way. I lost but it was close. I decided that I'd better not ask for a re-match. She commented, "Not coming back for revenge, Mr. Goodwin?"

I frowned, "No, I think I'd better get to bed. Tomorrow may be a busy day."

She said, "I think that's a good idea—going to bed." Her eyes didn't leave mine during the whole conversation. It was a case of copulative gaze if I'd ever seen one. The trouble was that I was returning the gaze. I trotted up the stairs. I glanced back at the last moment, expecting her to be following, but I found that she was playing a game with Dudley.

The next morning, I had set my alarm really early. I was the first one in the bathroom. I set a record, showering shaving, etc. Even so, As I left, Petunia was coming down the stairs in her rose bathrobe. It was so dangerous trying to pass on the stairs that I waited for her to arrive at the bottom of the stairs before I ascended. Breakfast was brilliant as usual, but I stuffed it down as though it were my last meal. Fritz noted. He called me into the kitchen. "Archie, is there something wrong with my potato pancakes?"

I said, "No, Fritz. It's just that I'm expecting an important call soon, and I need to be in the Office."

"Oh, Archie, you should not let Mrs. Dursley disturb you."

All I could say was, "Yea."

In the office, I took up my station at the phone and waited for the important call. There were calls that came. They were all false alarms. There weren't as many as the day before, but there were still several.

After the torture of another lunch, I took up my post. Mrs. Dursley had nudged my calf during the lunch. I had all that I could do to pretend that

I'd gotten some food down my windpipe to cover my gasp when that happened. I excused myself from the table shortly after that and wondered if I could make up an excuse to go eat at Rusterman's.

The call came in at 3 PM. They obviously didn't know the rules here. The voice at the other end of the phone asked for an appointment to meet with us about a possible case.

I tried to get as much information as possible about the caller without scaring them off. All I could get came down to the fact that they wanted to hire us to find a missing person. I made an appointment for them to come after dinner. I broke a rule by calling Wolfe on the house phone while he was with the orchids. He answered, "What is it?" in his surliest.

"We've got a bite. They're going to come at 8:30 tonight. I'm going to get in contact with Purlie."

He grunted, "Yes. Have him bring the Auror as soon after I come down from the Plant Room as you can manage. Call Saul and have him come as well."

"Yes, sir."

I got Purlie on the phone. I decided that I could use his personal phone because this was urgent. He answered, "This had better be important Goodwin."

"We have some Deatheaters visiting us tonight. Is that important?"

Nonsensically, he asked, "Why didn't you say that at first. I'll get hold of Everdine. What time are they arriving?"

"Wolfe wants you all here as soon as possible after he comes down from the Plant Rooms."

I could hear the edge in Purlie's voice. "I'll do my best. When are they actually showing up?"

"8:30."

Purlie just said, "OK." and hung up.

Wolfe was down shortly. He looked the question at me, "Purlie and Everdine are going to be here as soon as they can manage."

He closed his eyes for several minutes and said, "Better bring the Dursleys here now. It won't hurt to fill them in on details before officialdom arrives."

I scoured the brownstone. Vernon was in the kitchen reading the paper and talking with Fritz. I told Fritz, "Better put some more on. We might have more guests for dinner."

Fritz threw his hands up in the air and said, "I only have so many squabs. How do you expect me to feed . . . how many is it?"

"Probably two more."

Fritz looked glum and shrugged, "We'll do what we can do."

I found Dudley in his parents' room reading a copy of *The Adventures of Sherlock Holmes*. He asked if I'd read it.

"Yes, He didn't have to deal with Fritz."

I sent him down to the Office. That only left the Plant Rooms. I found Mrs. Dursley with Horst. He was showing her the Hot Room. I asked her to come downstairs.

She asked, "You mean to your room?" And then she added, "Just kidding."

When they were all assembled in the Office, Wolfe explained the situation. "We have candidates for the Deatheaters that attacked you. They're going to come here this evening. Archie and I will deal with them.

"The Auror, Everdine, will be here as will Lieutenant Stebbins of the police force. We will have at least one of our operatives who have been working on this case. We have done everything that we can to insure your safety.

"However, we want someone to identify these people if they are indeed the Deatheaters. From your account, I think that only Mr. Dudley Dursley could. Do you agree?"

All of the Dursleys looked at each other. Dudley answered, "That's right. What do you want me to do?"

"I would like your mother and father to go with Fritz to his room. You will be stationed in a small adjoining alcove where you can see the people in this room, but they cannot see you. One of my operatives, Saul Panzer will be with you. If you make a positive identification, you are to let him know. Then, the Auror will take them into custody."

"They are scheduled to arrive at 8:30, so we will have our meal as usual. We will be joined by the people who have . . ."

Just then the doorbell rang. I went to answer it. I saw Saul. I felt a little better because he would be involved with the operation tonight. I brought him into the Office.

Mr. Wolfe made introductions and went over the part of the plan that Saul had missed. Saul was satisfied and only asked, "If things get out of hand, I assume that I will be shooting to kill?"

Wolfe nodded. Then he turned to our clients for reaction. None of us saw any. Wolfe spoke, "You aren't surprised by this?"

Petunia answered, "We've been hunted by Deatheaters for so long that I don't think we expected anything else."

The casualness with which they accepted and adjusted to it surprised everyone in the room, I think. I began to see her in a different light. Maybe living with death constantly hounding you made you willing to do things that seem foolhardy. I actually wanted to take her hand and assure her that we wouldn't let that happen to her, but of course, no one could assure that.

Wolfe dismissed everyone to the Living Room or their rooms to wait for dinner.

A while after that, the doorbell rang again, and I found Purlie, Everdine, and someone else wearing a black jacket with "Auror" stenciled on it. I brought them through to the Office. Wolfe was back to his book.

I gave Purlie the red leather chair, and the rest got yellow chairs. The only person who needed introductions was the Auror that Everdine brought around.

Wolfe went through the plan in detail. The suspects were to arrive at 8:30. They would be brought to the Office and Dudley would examine them from the alcove through the hidden peephole. If he could identify them, Saul would signal Purlie and the Aurors waiting in the Front Room. They would take the Deatheaters by surprise, stun them, and transport them to the Auror Office.

The second Auror whose name was Sam asked, "What if they aren't the Deatheaters or we don't get a positive ID?"

Wolfe assured them that he was quite sure that they were the Deatheaters. Everdine wasn't quite so sure. He said, "You'll have to maintain a way of getting in touch with them. We'll devise a way to prove they are the guilty parties or aren't."

Wolfe agreed. He then invited them to dine with us. They accepted. It was almost time for dinner, so I conducted them all to the Dining Room, and we had a little tutorial on conduct at dinner in chez-Wolfe.

"All right. There are only a couple of rules for dining here. However, they are very strict. You can find yourselves dining in the kitchen with Fritz the Cook if you break them.

"First, no business talk during dinner. Second, courtesy is the rule for conversation. Finally, respect the Cook. Any questions?"

No one had any, and in a few minutes, Wolfe entered the dining room . Shortly after him came Fritz with the first course. Fritz's response to having lots of extra guests was to lay on more courses—none of them was large. We had cheese and olives, salad (not a lot for anyone), a cup of soup, then the main course, followed by nuts, and a desert, crème brulee.

Toward the end of the meal, Purlie tempted fate by remarking to Fritz, "I now understand why Archie puts up with the f . . . that is, the foibles of your boss. This meal is scrumptious."

It didn't quite cross the line of discussing business, but I was poised for Wolfe to break in.

As the meal went on, I was thinking about the fact that I'd not cleaned my Marley recently. Whenever we're on a case like this, I always wear my holster and the Marley on my person.

We finished dinner. Everyone took their assigned places, and we waited. Wolfe was clearly nervous. He asked me every two minutes what time it was. All he had to do was incline his head to the digital clock on his desk that had been given him by a Russian oil magnate, but he had to ask me. At 8:35 just before Wolfe's next time check, the doorbell rang. I rose from my desk where I was pretending to work on germination records. I patted the Marley. I walked to the front door, and I looked through the one-way glass. The two people in the twilight looked like the grainy photos that we had from Tiffanys.

I released the breath that I'd been holding and opened the door. They both took a step forward into the brownstone. I asked them what I could do for them.

Number 1 said, "We made an appointment with Mr. Wolfe."

I smiled, "Certainly. Come this way. Can I take your cloaks?"

Both declined without thanks, and I led them carefully to the Office. I seated the one that I referred to as Number 1 in the red leather chair. Number 2 got a yellow chair that I pulled up close.

Wolfe didn't rise, of course, when they entered. He said, "I understand that you'd like to hire us to do a job."

Number 1 said, "Yes. We are looking for a family much like the photo that you published in the newspaper. Can you help us?"

Wolfe played it cool, "Well, as you must realize, I already have a client. Didn't Mr. Goodwin tell you that?" He turned to me, "Why didn't you tell them that?"

I shrugged, "The conversation didn't proceed that far."

Wolfe went on, "Well, you see, it wouldn't really be ethical for us to accept a fee for doing the job that we've already been hired to do. Would it?"

Number 1 said, "I don't see the problem. Someone hires you to find this family. You find them. They pay you. You inform us when that happens, and we pay you for being informed. What is unethical about that?"

Wolfe smiled foxily, "I see that you folks are lawyers." He added swiftly, "I mean no offense. I just mean that you know your way around the law and ethics." He then seemed distracted and said, "Archie, would you mind checking with Fritz? What happened to the English pudding we were supposed to have for dessert?"

I got up and said, "Of course, sir. I wondered about that myself."

I walked out and to the alcove where Saul and Dudley were supposed to be. I gently pulled back the drape a bit and looked in. Saul shook his head. I nodded, returned the drape, and went back to the office.

I said, "Fritz reports that the pudding was underdone, and he decided not to serve it."

Wolfe nodded and said, "I was afraid of that." Then he turned back to the Deatheaters. "Well, I think that you have proved your point. We will be willing to report to you on the completion of our commission and where you can find the family for a fee.

"My standard fee for these things is ten thousand dollars. Are you prepared to pay that."

Number 2 pulled on the sleeve of Number 1 and they conferred briefly. Number 2 spoke, "Yes, we accept your offer."

Wolfe said, "Good. We normally require a retainer. It needn't be a lot. Clients customarily give us 10% of the final fee."

Number 2 gritted his teeth but said, "Of course. We mostly have our own currency, but we can pay the one thousand."

Wolfe smiled. "Good. Mr. Goodwin will print up a contract. You can sign it, and be on your way."

Number 2 drew a purse from inside his cloak and counted out one thousand dollars. Number 1 said, "We can sign the contract when you deliver. We trust you with the retainer."

Wolfe said, "I'd like to protect you, but that is acceptable. How will we get in touch when we're ready to deliver your order?"

Number 1 brought out something that looked like a business card and handed it to Wolfe, "Contact us at that number. The one who answers can set an appointment for us."

Wolfe glanced at it and said, "Very well. Mr. Goodwin will see you to the door."

I was extra careful that these visitors ended up on the right side of the door before I locked, bolted, and chained the door. As I approached the office, Wolfe came out and said in a fairly loud voice, "Archie, let's go down to the basement and play some pool."

I answered in a normal voice, "sure," and then louder, "I'll go downstairs with you to play pool."

We went down and were followed by everyone else on the main floor. When we got down, Wolfe went directly to the one chair in the basement that he actually liked. He asked everyone to find a chair and sit. We had to bring three chairs in from Fritz's rooms, add the four swivel stools that were already there, Wolfe's armchair, and have one on the sofa to accommodate everyone.

Wolfe began. "You'll allow me to provide a quick overview of what happened today for everyone before we discuss our options.

"First, the two Deatheaters who came tonight." Everdine seemed about to speak. Wolfe forestalled him, "Hold your piece Mr. Everdine, while I complete my statement. I am convinced that they are the Deatheaters that

304

we're looking for. I realize that you don't have evidence that proves it to the satisfaction of the law–even your feeble attempt at law.

"So, the purpose of this meeting is to decide how to provide that evidence.

"Let me continue. The main reason that we couldn't prove that they were the guilty party was that the only witness, Mr. Dudley Dursley, couldn't be sure that they were the Deatheaters that attacked them in Tiffany's. Is that right, Mr. Dursley."

Dudley nodded.

"Good. Now, we need to maintain contact with these Deatheaters until we devise a means of proving their guilt. To that end, I promised them that they could hire me to notify them when I found the Dursleys.

"So, we need suggestions of how we can prove their guilt."

Vernon Dursley asked, "Isn't there a way to know what . . uh . . spells have been used by the Deatheaters?"

Everdine said, "Yes, but. But you have to have the wand that the criminal actually used. Nowadays, it's pretty common to have 'drop' wands —stolen wands that are used one time and then either thrown away or destroyed."

Saul suggested, "How about finding some lesser crime that they're guilty of. Maybe they've entered the U.S. illegally?"

Purlie liked that idea. However, Everdine saw a problem. "Yes, they probably have entered the US illegally, but the only thing that we can do under wizarding law is extradite them. They could still return or just look up the Dursleys in England."

There was a long silence. I wanted very badly to come up with an idea, but the only thing that I could think of was so dangerous that I didn't even want to suggest it. In the end, I didn't have to.

Wolfe said, "I can only think of one possibility. It will require the approval and co-operation of the Dursleys.

"If we were to confront the Deatheaters with the Dursleys in this office, what do you think would happen?"

We went around the room, starting with the Aurors and Purlie, proceeding to the operatives in the room and ending with the Dursleys. Around the room, each person spoke:

"Try to kill them."

"Try to kill them."

And so on. Each of the detectives agreed. Finally, the Dursleys said, "Try to kill us."

Wolfe went on, "With that many witnesses, it would be a no-brainer to get them for attempted murder."

He turned to the Aurors and asked, "Do you think you could stop them?"

They looked at each other and Everdine said, "If they didn't know that we were present, we could probably stun them before they got a spell off." He turned to the Dursleys. "I sure couldn't guarantee it though."

Wolfe said, "that was what I thought." He now turned to the Dursleys. "This is your decision. We can sneak you out of the country easily enough. You could go to some distant land—say, Australia for example. We could give you a false identity that would fool almost all Muggles. I don't know if it would fool Deatheaters. You have to make the choice. You can take your time. We have a day or two that we can stall them before we have to decide on a stategy. We'll let you sleep on it at least."

No one said anything. Then Wolfe said, "I suggest that the authorities and Saul leave by the rear."

Everdine said, "No, it's better if we disapparate. That way, even if the Deatheaters are watching the front and back, they'll not know that we were here. We'll come back that way as well, to this room." The three of them disappeared with Purlie in tow.

I started putting back the furniture. When I left Fritz's apartment, Dudley and Petunia were still there. Petunia was staring at me. I guessed that she wanted advice. I was doubly out of advice. In the first place, I wouldn't advise anybody about that decision. Secondly, of all people, I didn't want her blood to stain anything. For a minute, I had a vision of Petunia in that rose bath robe stained a deeper red. At that moment, I'd have advised her to run to Australia and not ever return here. But I wouldn't do that either.

The next morning, I couldn't bring myself to take a chance of seeing her in that rose bath robe. I decided to shave in my room and not shower at all. I didn't go down for breakfast. Instead I slipped into the kitchen and had breakfast the way I used to at the kitchen table with Fritz making hot cakes. I read the newspaper. The big front page article was about the Republican Presidential candidates.

When I got to the Office, I found that the Dursleys were already there. Wolfe spoke, "They wanted to wait until you arrived to give their decision." Then he turned to them.

Mr. Dursley was in the red leather chair. He said simply, "We're going to end this now."

I couldn't help looked at Petunia. She noticed and nodded. They'd all agreed to it.

So, Wolfe and I started planning. We called in Saul and Fred Durkin. We left Orrie out there continuing the fiction that we were looking for the

Dursleys. We settled the plan pretty well before calling in Purlie and the Aurors.

No one was perfectly happy with it, but no one had a better idea. The timing would depend on the Deatheaters, but we tried to make it adjustable to any timing the Deatheaters imposed on us.

The plan started in the late afternoon. I called the number on the card that Number 1 had given us. The voice on the other end of the line said, "Yes."

"We've located the Dursleys."

"When will you turn them over?"

I hesitated as though I were calculating. "Well, it depends, but I think that we'll bring them into the office around 5 PM tomorrow."

The voice on the other end said, "We'll come at 3 PM."

I said, "Don't do that. You won't be admitted. Mr. Wolfe doesn't come down from the Plant Room until at least 4 PM. You could come then."

The phone hung up.

That night I showered before going to bed. On the way back to my room, I ran into Petunia. It was certainly not by accident. She said, "Do you think we're doing the right thing?"

I said, "You certainly did. You made the decision yourself. That is always the right decision." I went on, "Mr. Wolfe is smart. Saul Panzer is the best operative this side of the North Pole. I kid Purlie Stebbins a lot, but there's not any policeman I'd rather have here. The Auror Everdine is one we've worked with before. He's good."

She asked, "What about you?"

"There isn't anyone who wants you to come out of this whole more than I do."

She nodded. Then she seemed to make a decision. She asked me, "I've never seen you drink anything but milk. Do you drink?"

"On very special occasions–yes."

Then she took a deep breath and asked, "Have a drink with me." At least, I thought it was a question. Maybe it was a request.

"Sure. Let's go down to the Dining Room."

I led the way down. When we arrived, I went to the liquor cabinet and asked, "What do you want?"

"Do you have some Johnny Walker Black?"

I opened the cabinet door and said, "Let's see." I rummaged around through the bottles and found one.

"Here we are. An unopened bottle."

She said, "You don't have to open it. We could do . . ."

However, I opened the bottle and said, "This is a special occasion, isn't it."

Her smile was wan. "Yes, I guess it is."

I asked, "Ice?"

"Just one cube."

I opened the little refrigerator that was built in. There was ice in the ice catcher. I picked up two pieces and deposited them in two small tumblers. I wedged them between two fingers and carried the bottle in my other hand to the dinner table.

We sat down. I asked, "How much?"

"To the rim."

"Good enough."

She took a glass and took a healthy sip. Then she asked, "Did you go to college?"

It was a strange question, but I went along with it. "No."

She took that in and asked, "Where would you have gone to college if you had."

"Well, I grew up in a small farming community in Ohio. The closest town of any size to me was Chillicothe."

A quizzical look came over her face. I explained, "It's one that not many people have heard of it. It's an Indian name.

"Anyway, I'd have gone to Ohio State, I suppose."

She closed her eyes and took another sip. "If I'd gone to school at Ohio State, and we'd been in a class together, would you have asked me out?"

It was the kind of question that I'd been fearing for several days, but I answered straight up, "Yes, I would."

She nodded, still with her eyes closed. Then she asked, "Why didn't you go to college?"

I smiled at that. "Well, where I came from, at that time, you just didn't go to college."

"What did you do?"

"Oh, I'd gotten interested in photography in high school. I was in the Photography Club. I decided to go to the big city to seek my fortune. The big city being New York.

"I went to work for the *Gazette* as a photographer. I worked with several different reporters, but eventually, I teamed up with a young reporter named Lon Cohen.

"We got our big break after I'd been there about six months. There was a murder case that had been around for almost that long. It would have been a cold case by then except that the victim was a young British socialite. She had come to the US to visit her aunt. One night, she was standing on the porch of the home she was visiting, and she dropped to the ground.

"The people who were with her had no idea what had happened. They turned her over and discovered a bullet hole over her heart that was gushing blood. However, no one had heard a shot. A witness who had been out on the street thought he'd heard a car backfire somewhere in the distance.

"The police investigated thoroughly. They never found a lead. No one could supply a motive. The young lady had been well-liked. There had been no death threats. The gun was never found.

"The *Gazette* sometimes revisits old stories like this to find out what had happened. Lon and I were assigned to do the follow-up. We went back and interviewed family in the U.S. and sent cables to family in England.

"I did some photos of the murder scene and the people who'd been present at the time. We'd pick one of them for the Sunday supplement article that Lon was writing.

"After the article was published, a young private detective approached us. He had not been hired by anyone to investigate the case, but he had a theory. He told us that he knew who the murderer was."

Petunia asked, "I suppose it was Mr. Wolfe."

I smiled, "Yes, it was. He presented his theory to us. He was the laziest guy I'd ever met. He wanted us to do some leg work to help him get the evidence that would get the murderer convicted. He could have done it himself, but he thought that since we were doing the article, we'd want to be part of cracking the case."

She asked, "Why was he doing it at all?"

"He was just getting started. His problem was that he was too lazy to do any real leg work that's required in the detective business. He thought cracking a big case that the police had worked on for months and failed at would give him a reputation that would bring him real business. He was right. He was also right that we'd benefit from helping him and getting an exclusive for the *Gazette*.

"That was the beginning of Wolfe's string of successes. It was the beginning of Lon's rise to the point that he had an office next to the publisher of the *Gazette*."

I paused and added, "And it was the beginning of my job with Wolfe. After we broke the case, he offered me a job. I would be his leg man. He would do the hard work of thinking. He couldn't pay me yet, but he was so sure that we'd be successful that he offered me the job anyway.

"He impressed me so much that I decided to take the job for a week or two and see what happened.

"We did start getting jobs. Though we've had dry spells like the one that we were in when you landed on our doorstep, we've mostly done very well."

She opened her eyes and took another big sip. I did as well. She asked, "Who was the murderer?"

I smiled, "Wolfe had learned that the socialite had recently inherited a lot of money, an estate, and a title from her father. She was the only child in the family of the man. However, there was a cousin, a boy, who had grown up and fought in World War I. He'd been lost on the battlefield and presumed dead.

"What actually happened was that he had been wounded and gassed. He had scars that made his face unrecognizable. His parents had died during the Great War, and he ended up staying in France.

"Years later, he was reading an article about the heiress's trip to the United States. It occurred to him that if she were dead, he would be the nearest kin and would inherit, money, land, and title.

"He'd been trained as a sniper in the military. He bought a ticket for the US. Over here, he bought a war surplus sniper's rifle on the black market and investigated the neighborhood of the heiress's aunt. He found a public library with a clear sight of the front porch of the aunt. For several nights in a row, he hid in the library and went up to the roof where he waited for the heiress to provide a good target.

"One night she did. Then he waited. His plan was to let a year pass after her death and then present himself as the rightful heir."

Petunia was leaning on her hands as she listened with rapt attention. She asked, "How did Wolfe get the evidence to convict him?"

I laughed, "He had Lon and me find the black market gun merchant. He then used a trick that he's used many times since. He invited the killer to his home on the pretext that he'd discovered that he had inherited the dead heiress's fortune. He, Wolfe, wanted a finders fee. He'd also invited the police.

"He presented the killer's story to him, and the police provided the name of the gun merchant. He claimed that the police could get the merchant to testify against him. Wolfe took one of his lucky leaps of faith that the killer had not disposed of the gun. He told the police where the killer lived so that a search could be made. Then, he added the *coup de grace*. He simply informed the killer that under British law, a murderer cannot benefit from his crime. Even if he were not convicted here, he would never be able to inherit, and if he inherited, he would be a pariah.

"The accumulated pressure of all that caused the killer to snap and confess. The police did discover the gun at the killer's apartment. The man was tried and convicted."

She finished the last of her drink and got up to go to her room. I rose and said, "I've got a what-if for you."

She stopped and turned, "Yes."

"What if we graduated the same year from Ohio State, and I asked you to marry me?"

She looked exhausted, but she said, "Yes." Then she turned again and left the room.

The next day when I woke up after a troubled night of sleep, I reflected that we'd never actually come closer to putting anyone in deadly peril at any of these parties that Wolfe had thrown as we were this time. People had been in deadly peril and even died, but we'd never planned for that being a possibility. The main players started assembling shortly after Wolfe returned from the morning Plant Room session.

There were the Aurors. Everdine brought two additional Aurors. Fred Durkin showed up. Then, Saul arrived. We had lunch. The table was full to capacity. We'd never had exactly the number of people for lunch before to fill the table.

Wolfe had his usual seminar on a variety of topics. Today, he wanted to talk about astronomy. He talked about the roots of astronomy in time-keeping. I might have enjoyed it if I weren't on edge about the little party we were throwing. Eventually, the lunch ended, and we got down to work.

Everyone went to the Office, and we rehearsed our parts. The timing was going to be critical, so we went through a complete dress rehearsal with accurate timings.

This was a day for breaking rules. One of them was the afternoon session with the orchids. Wolfe eliminated that from the agenda.

The one thing that bothered me was that Purlie hadn't arrived yet. It was 2:30 when the doorbell rang. I went to the door and had a shock when I looked through the one-way glass. I opened the door and brought our visitors to the office.

Wolfe looked up and said, "Well, Mr. Cramer have a seat. This is an unexpected pleasure."

Cramer kicked Everdine, who happened to be seated there, out of the red leather chair, and Purlie pulled up two yellow chairs—one for Everdine and one for himself. Cramer said, "When I heard what was on the program for the day, I decided that I had to see this."

Wolfe cracked a smile—a barely discernable uplifting of the corners of his mouth. "Of course, you're welcome. However, I'm afraid that you can't have your accustomed seat. That's reserved for someone else."

Cramer smiled, "That's OK. I'll take the alcove then. The view is actually better from there."

Wolfe frowned, "I'm afraid that is reserved as well. You'll have to wait in the Front Room."

Cramer started to object but Wolfe added quickly, "We've set up a closed circuit camera in here. You'll be able to watch what goes on in the Office, and since the room is sound-proofed, you'll be able to hear on the TV what goes on as well."

Cramer apparently was mollified somewhat by that possibility, but he intended to keep the red leather chair until he was forced from it. Wolfe

311

gave him a quick resume of the show. Cramer's frown turned into a smile as it went on.

By the end, he commented, "Good. We'll show them that they can't try to kill people in my town."

All that was left was the waiting. Fritz had brought a variety of beverages out and offered one and all something to drink. No one wanted anything alcoholic, which pleased me. Some people asked for bottled water. There were several coffee takers. Having something in your hand was a welcome distraction from the slow tick of the clock.

Four o'clock arrived. No one glanced at their watches, but I could tell that everyone knew it. Wolfe shooed people off to their posts. There was no place for me to go. I was already seated at my post. The minutes wore on. Just when I'd forced myself to stop looking down at my watch, the doorbell rang. I was up, checked my holster under my armpit and was out to the front door. A glance through the one-way glass showed that our favorite Deatheaters were there. I opened the door and carefully led them to the Office.

Wolfe greeted them. "We wondered if you were going to arrive. Quickly, we must make plans."

Number 1 took the red leather chair. "Why do we need plans?"

Wolfe looked like an exasperated stage manager, "Well, not for you. You know everything, but our other client can't get a whiff of your presence. If he thinks that we've been double dealing with him, he might bolt and then we'd have lost the fee, and maybe you'd lose you chance to find the Dursleys."

Number 1 wasn't happy but he went along with us. "All right. What do we have to do?"

Wolfe smiled, "It's really quite easy. We have a little spot where you can hide and see everything that goes on in the Office. You just take that position and watch what happens. When the critical point comes, you come out, and everyone gets what they want. Go with Archie. He'll show you where to hide."

I got up and led them to the alcove. This was another rule broken. We never showed any but real clients the alcove. I showed them the little hole that would let them look through the picture of the Richenbach. I urged them to stay quiet. Of course, everyone knew where they were going to be, so that instruction wasn't necessary except to maintain appearances.

I returned to the Office, and Wolfe asked me about the latest germination records. It was hard to answer his questions totally seriously, but I'd had a certain amount of practice holding fake conversations with guests in the house, so I did all right.

The doorbell rang on schedule. I went to the door, found Fred on the other side, and let him in. I greeted him as I would a normal client. We went to the Office. He got the red leather chair. There was another break in protocol. Operatives never got the red leather chair when real clients were expected imminently.

Wolfe greeted Fred, "It's good to see you're on time, Mr. Durkin. We'll have your people here shortly. I trust that you have the final payment?"

Fred was a little wooden in saying his lines, but he wasn't awful. That question surprised him a little, but he recovered, "Oh, yes. Yes! Here it is." He pulled a small manila envelope from an inside suit pocket. It was a good thing that he didn't have many more lines.

Wolfe glanced at it and said, "Yes, thanks. As I said, your people ought to be here shortly. If you don't mind, I'm going to talk with my assistant, Mr. Goodwin about some hybridizing issues while we wait."

Fred just said, "No problem." He leaned back and smiled a wide smile as he surveyed the view from the red leather chair, which I don't think he'd ever have seen before.

This went on for about ten minutes. It was getting close to 5 PM. I wondered what was going on with Saul and the Dursleys. They were in the basement. They were supposed to go out the back way, walk around the block and ring the doorbell. They should have done that by now.

Wolfe kept prattling on about seeing Mr. Hewitt to get cuttings from a new hybrid that he'd developed. The doorbell finally rung. I got up as naturally as I could. I had to struggle to keep myself from patting the little lump where the Marley was. I reached the front door. I looked through the one-way glass. It was indeed Saul and the 'fugitives'. I opened the door.

Saul winked at me. I've got to cure him of that. Then, I led the party back to the office. They stood there, a rather nice tableau. Saul had them lined up. I noticed that he had a gun—as planned. The gun was one that I'd not seen him use before. It was a Glock 10 mm. He had certainly come loaded for bear. He was apparently holding it negligently, not pointed toward the real clients.

I was almost afraid that Fred had forgotten his lines, but he stood and said, "Well, Mr. Dursley, you and your family thought that you could cheat me, did you. You thought you could run out on your debt. Well, it may cost me more than you owe me, but I will not let anyone get away with cheating Big Fred Durkin."

He actually didn't do too badly with his lines, except for improvising the "Big" part of his name. He too had pulled his gun and had it loosely held, pointing toward the floor.

It was at that point that we expected the Deatheaters to rush around the corner and some nice juicy conversation to ensue with them moving to kidnap the Dursleys.

Instead, there was a silence that stretched on for a long minute. Saul stepped up to the plate. He said, "Mr. Wolfe, I've filled my part of the deal. How about just paying me, and I'll be off."

Wolfe picked up the thread, "Well, I have to be paid by Mr. Durkin first before I can pay you." They all turned to Fred.

Saul kept up the improvisational play, "Well, if I'm not going to be paid, no one is. I'll take these good people away and drop them someplace no one will find them."

With those words, all hell broke loose. Two figures, the Deatheaters, disapparated into the room. They had hardly solidified when they both raised wands. What happened then was so quick that I didn't realize everything that had happened until we had a postmortem with Wolfe and the "teers" later.

Saul is quick. He had his gun up and put a 10 mm. slug into the wand arm of one of the Deatheaters. His wand went flying and his body spun around. I had gotten up when Saul had talked about leaving just to support the general idea that we didn't want anyone leaving.

I realized that the other wizard was trying to point his wand at Petunia. I really think that my intention had been to match Saul by drawing my gun and firing at that Deatheater, but that wasn't what happened. Instead, I leaped in front of the Dursleys like a soccer goalie trying to block a shot.

I did. I felt an intense pain in my left side, and I dropped. I lost consciousness for some amount of time. The next thing I remember was feeling hands cradling my face and hearing, "Archie, don't die!" I was still mostly stunned, but I blinked as I tried to regain control of my body.

I heard Wolfe shout, "Does he live?" I realized then that it was Petunia who was holding my head up because I felt her kiss on my lips and heard her say, "He's alive!"

I had regained clear vision and some control of my body. I looked around and saw the mayhem that had ensued. Apparently, the Aurors had broken the door to the front room open. There must have been a brief battle of wands between them and the one remaining Deatheater. Both appeared to be immobilized on the floor.

There must have been several wand-blasts that went astray. Books were scattered everywhere, and the great globe had a big gash in it. It was then that I began to be aware that I might have a gash in me. The left side of my torso had begun to hurt like the dickens.

Cramer with his giant 45 handgun was standing over the two Deatheaters saying, "Goddamit. I want to plug one of them!" He turned to me and said, "Goodwin, if you die on me, I'll never forgive you!"

Petunia was still kneeling beside me, and I heard her say, "Oh my GOD! He's bleeding." The Auror came over and reassured me by saying. "It looks like you are seeping a little. Let's take a look. He used his wand to rip off my good hand-tailored shirt. There was a Kevlar vest underneath.

When Petunia saw it, she gasped but didn't say anything. I was glad that I couldn't see it.

Everdine made a first-aid kit appear out of thin air. He took a stainless steel surgical pair of scissors and said, "This may sting a little."

Yea. It stung a little. As a matter of fact, it also stung quite a lot as he cut through the vest. He pulled it away, but I was expecting the pain that I felt, so I managed to limit myself to a gasp.

Everdine said, "Good. As a matter of fact, really good. I expected much, much worse. I could have sworn that was the Avada Kedavra spell that he used on you. You should be dead now."

Petunia sobbed. I don't know why. It looked like I was going to live.

Everdine had a small bottle stoppered with what looked like a medicine dropper. He unscrewed it and drew a little of the fluid into the dropper. He then poised it over my side and said, "Goodwin, this is going to hurt. On the count of three." He reached two, and a drop of the stuff hit my skin. I shouted.

Petunia took Everdine's hand and said, "Let me." He looked at her skeptically but handed her the dropper. She reached into the medicine kit and pulled out a roll of gauze. She cut off a length and rapped it around the palm of her hand. She put two drops of the stuff on the gauze in the palm of her hand.

She then dabbed it on my side. It still hurt like hell, but it wasn't as intense as when Everdine had simply put a drop on it. She asked Everdine if that were enough. He agreed.

She took a sterile pad and pressed it against my side. Amazingly, it didn't hurt that much. Then she wrapped adhesive gauze around my body and cinched it tight.

At that point, she asked me, "How are you doing? Are you going to faint on us."

I shook my head. It was painful to do, but I couldn't say anything yet. About then, I heard a siren. Then two EMT's came into the room and asked the usual stupid question, "Is this the victim?"

Everyone nodded. They took my vital signs. They declared that I'd probably be OK. Then they put me on a stretcher and immobilized me. They wanted to replace the dressing but Everdine warned them not to do that until a doctor saw me.

They carried me out to the ambulance. They got in with me, and I found that Petunia had come along. The EMT who appeared to be in charge asked, "What's your relation to the patient?"

She simply said, "We're engaged."

He looked at me and then at her and shrugged, "OK."

She sat next to me and took my right hand in hers. She didn't say anything on the whole ride. The siren was going, and we made good time. I went directly into an examination room in the ER.

It wasn't long before a nurse came in and checked my vitals. She was about to cut off Petunia's bandage when Petunia said, "No. There was a doctor on the spot who said that only a doctor should remove that."

She looked doubtfully at me and asked, "Is that right?"

I nodded.

The nurse asked Petunia, "And you are?"

Her answer was direct, "I'm his fiance." The nurse nodded and left the examination room.

About an hour later, a doctor came in and sat beside me. He extended a hand and said, "I'm Dr. Kelsey. And you are, Archibald Goodwin?"

I said, "People call me Archie."

"OK. Archie. Tell me what happened to you."

I explained that I worked with the famous detective, Nero Wolfe. We were investigating an attempted murder. One of the perpetrators had shot me. Luckily, I was wearing a Kevlar vest. Still I was badly . . . bruised?

Kelsey nodded and asked Petunia if she could verify that. She never released my hand and agreed. Then he said, "OK. I'm going to remove this dressing, which by the way is pretty good. Did the EMT do it?"

Petunia admitted that she had.

"Nice job—especially considering it was your dad that you were working on."

She corrected him, "Not my dad. My fiance."

He raised his eyebrows and then took a pair of surgical scissors and started to say, "Now, this is going to sting . . ."

But I finished what he was saying for him, "I know. It's going to sting some. I've been here before. Go ahead."

He gingerly cut the adhesive and then pulled away the pad slowly as he observed what he found. Amazingly, I hardly felt it.

He asked, "Didn't this hurt some?"

"Not too much."

He gingerly felt the area, "Any pain?"

I honestly answered, "Not much."

He just stared at it for a while. Then he said, "If I didn't know better, I'd say that you had some minor bruising from a minor trauma—like being hit by a car door slamming shut. As a matter of fact, if that were what you told me had happened, I'd release you right now. But since I know what happened, I'm going to send you down for an X-ray and have you admitted. We'll observe you through the night and have the resident look at you in the morning. If nothing shows up on the X-ray, and you look OK in the morning, I think you can go."

I was pleasantly surprised. I didn't want to say it, but I was expecting to have serious internal injuries.

He smiled and shook hands. "Good luck, Mr. Goodwin."

A little later, an orderly came and gave me a ride in a wheelchair to the radiation department where they took several X-rays. Then they took me up to a room. Petunia didn't leave my side the whole time, except when I was getting X-rayed.

When they left me in the room, I told her, "I think I'm going to be just fine. You can go home now."

She just shook her head and sat beside the bed.

I said, "Well, I've got to change into my embarrassing hospital pajamas."

She didn't take the hint but said, "Go right ahead."

I limped over to the bathroom and went in. When I came out, I was in the pajamas and got into bed. She looked up from the newspaper that had been in the room when we arrived.

I asked her, "Please turn off the light on your way out."

She turned off the lights, came back to the guest chair, sat beside my bed, and patted my right arm. "Goodnight, Archibald."

I said, "I don't know how I'll get any sleep with you here."

She smiled, "You won't get any sleep anyway with the nurses monitoring you every hour or two."

Of course, she was right.

The next day, they brought me breakfast. It wasn't awful. It was so far from brownstone standards that I almost didn't eat it. The resident came in around nine and had me get up. He cut off the dressing and looked at it. He then looked at the X-rays. He then poked my side.

Finally, he said something to me, "Well, are you sure you're the same man who came in last night."

I rolled my eyes and said, "I'm pretty sure. Right, Petunia."

She shrugged and nodded.

"Well, you are the most amazing case of healing that I've ever seen. If I hadn't read your chart, I'd have sworn that you were faking to get pain meds.

"You look good. I'll send for an orderly to take you down to admitting to check out." Finally, for the first time, he extended a hand to shake. He said, "Good luck." He then left the room.

Petunia smiled at me, the broadest smile I'd ever seen on her face, and said, "Feel pretty good about yourself, don't you."

I had to admit that I did.

In Admitting they asked how I was getting home. Petunia said, "I've got a cab." We got in. Petunia told the cabbie, "I pick up the fare."

I shrugged and sat back. She gave the address that I could recite in my sleep, and we were off. She gave the cabbie a fifty to pay for the ride that couldn't have cost more than thirty.

The traffic was light, and we arrived quickly. The chain was on the door, so I couldn't use my key to get us in. Petunia rang the doorbell and shortly Wolfe himself showed up.

He had a broad smile on his face. Something I'd rarely seen. He looked me over a moment and said, "We're behind on the germination records, get going."

Back in the office, I saw that people were preparing to travel. All of the luggage was lined up in the Office along with their owners. It didn't surprise me, but it was not exactly a welcome home from the hospital that I wanted.

Vernon Dersley announced, "We're ready to go. We're long overdue to get home. Let's go." Dudley seemed anxious to be off as well. I could only smile

Wolfe said, "Come on Archie, we need to get going."

At that point I noticed what I ordinarily would have noticed instantly. Orrie Cather was sitting at my desk in my chair. I glared at him. He mildly announced, "I've just finished the bill for the Dursleys. It's here, completely itemized." He turned to them and handed Vernon the bill as he announced, "Two thousand, three hundred, fifty-seven and fifty-nine cents."

I grabbed the bill and gave it a quick once-over. I announced, "It looks complete. Thank you very much Orrie. I suppose you were hoping that I'd have a longer stay in the hospital." I turned to Wolfe, "It looks complete, but . . ."

He said, "I went over it. I think it's fine."

I grimaced and handed it to Mr. Dursley. He glanced at it and said, "I don't have that much American cash, but I can pay that amount in pounds Sterling."

With that he had a fat wallet out and counted out fifty pound notes. When he reached forty-eight, he said, "I know this is a little over, but I insist that you keep it. It's worth far more for my family to be free of threat.

"Now, Mr. Cather, if you'd just call us a cab, we'll be off to the airport."

This was the final indignity. I said, "Orrie, you will not call for a cab if you know what's good for you. I'm getting the Lincoln out, and I'm driving the Dursleys myself to the airport."

Orrie was very solicitous, "Are you sure you should do that so soon after being released from the hospital?"

I had a grimace on my face as I said, "Yes!" Wolfe knows me ,and he knows that when I am determined, there's no putting me off. He made no comment.

I turned to the Dursleys and said, "I'll be back with the Lincoln in ten minutes. Don't let Orrie foist a cab on you. I'll see you soon."

On the way down, I called the garage and had the Lincoln brought up for me. I was back to the brownstone in hardly more than five minutes.

Vernon and Dudley had already brought the luggage down to the curb. I opened the trunk and got out to make sure that it went in correctly. I held the door for them, and Petunia said as she got in, "Thanks, Archie."

I drove away from the curb and realized I didn't know what airport. Vernon told me that they had tickets on British Airways at LaGuardia.

I commented, "Good choice. It's close in and is pretty easy to get to."

We drove without further conversation until we reached the terminal. I pulled up to the curb. I released the trunk and got out to help them get the luggage out. By the time I got there, the two male Dursleys were on their way with all the luggage toward curbside check-in. Petunia was standing next to me.

She came close to me and put her arms around me. "I'll not see you again, will I?"

I shook my head. She lowered hers and started to pull away. Then she grabbed me, pulled me closer, and all in one motion, lifted her head swiftly and kissed me. I don't know how long that kiss lasted. I only knew it was too short. Then she was away headed for the family. I lowered the trunk lid. It occurred to me that she'd stolen two kisses from me, and I'd not stolen a single one back. I must be getting old.

When I straightened up, a city employee came up to me. "She's gone. Now you need to move the Lincoln."

"Yes, sir, officer." I'm always polite to city employees who are reasonable. I got in the Lincoln, started the engine, and pulled away from the curb carefully. I looked back in the rear view mirror to see if she were still there, watching me go. There was no sign of her.

Britannia Rules the Waves

I watched Mum with that American and said to Dad, "How can you let her get away with all that flirting and snogging with him." I pointed at them for emphasis.

Dad said, "Look, Dudley, have you completely forgotten what I did to your Mum? What I told the both of you about on the cruise?"

I was still boiling, "But this is different!"

He shook his head, "Yeh, it's different. It's me getting the short end. Just lighten up."

I knew he was right, but I just couldn't stand the thought of him snogging me Mum. In disgust, I said, "The two of you deserve each other!"

Dad smiled, "Yes, son, we certainly do and we're going to have each other. That kiss was goodbye. Forever."

Mum left his arms and started walking briskly toward us. We'd already checked our luggage and gotten our boarding passes. So as soon as she arrived, we could enter the terminal and get to our gate.

When she was in easy talking distance, she said, "It's good to be back."

Dad said, "It's good to have you back."

I said nothing, but I supposed that Dad was right.

We went through security and waited next the gate. We boarded the jet, and I was pleasantly surprised that we were in first class. Dad explained that we'd traveled so much lately by last class that we deserved at least once to have first class accommodations.

I'd never flown first class before, and I enjoyed all the little surprises that were in store. The most important thing, though was that we were on British soil again—in a way.

We had everything! The hot towels. An actual choice of menu. The pretty stewardesses. The one that I saw the most was really hot. She had bright platinum blonde hair pulled up in some sort of bun or something.

Her shape was super! I was beginning to be full of myself and thought about how I could ask her out.

Then I noticed the ring on the third finger of her left hand. I though about Mum for a second. That sort of ruined her for me. It was a fun flight though.

We landed at Heathrow. It was night. We went through customs. The only things that excited any interest was Mum's bracelet and our visa stamps in our passports. One customs man asked me, "It looks like you've been out of the country for almost a year. Is that true."

I shrugged, "Yes."

He asked, "What in the world were you doing all that time? Especially all that time in Canada."

I opened my mouth to answer, but nothing would come out. Then I said, "I could spend a week telling you or I could not say a word. I can't say anything between."

He stamped my entry visa, and I was stepping into Britain in less than a minute—almost exactly a year after having left it. What would we do?

Dad's first act was to go to a kiosk where he bought a cell phone. He gathered us around a quiet corner of the terminal and said, "I'm going to try to get Marge on the phone. We'll talk to her on speaker if she answers."

He dialed the number. It rang four times and then we got her standard message, "Leave a message. I'll be back with you or not."

That was not surprising, but it was one more disappointment. We really hadn't done a plan. I guess the relief of getting back on home territory had us lulled. So, we found the Starbucks in Heathrow, ordered coffee and rolls, and sat down to think it through.

Mum said, "We should have been thinking this through on the plane. What are we going to do?"

Dad shrugged, "Well, it's not that hard. We've got a home. We can't just go there now because it's not got any furniture in it, but we've got that in storage, and we'll get it delivered, maybe as early as the day after tomorrow.

"We'll stay at a hotel near the airport tonight. I'm sure there's a Marriott somewhere around the airport. We'll go there.

"Tomorrow, we'll hire a car. We don't want to use a hire car forever, but we've got time to deal with getting a new car."

"We'll arrange to get our furniture delivered. I think we should go visit Marge's house."

Mum interrupted. "That makes me think of something. Who's paying the phone bill?"

Dad was surprised by the question. Then it dawned on him. We had called Marge's phone a number of times. We'd always gotten an answering machine. It hadn't said that the number was disconnected. We didn't get somebody else's phone. It was Marge's. Who was paying the phone bill?

Dad shrugged and said that we'd find out. He went on, "We should go to our house before the day is over and assess it. There may have been damage. Petty vandalism. Weather damage. We might have to have repairs before we move back in."

That seemed to cover the main points. There was a Marriott near the airport. Dad called them and had them send a shuttle to pick us up. We arrived at the lobby looking pretty bedraggled. Mum hadn't changed her clothes since the day before yesterday—it was after midnight when we arrived. Dad and I at least was wearing fresh clothes, but our luggage had been through a lot. They were dented, scraped, hinges were loose, latches looked like they might pop open at any minute.

The night clerk was surprised that we paid with cash. He insisted on seeing ID. We displayed our wear-worn passports. In the end we got a room. They were nearly full. We had to take a wedding suite. None of us cared.

□

The next morning, we were up none too soon. We showered and put on fresh clothes. Breakfast was not what we'd had at Wolfe's brownstone, but no breakfast we'd ever had was quite like that. Dad wanted to hire a car first thing, so he got Sixt Car Hire to send a car over for us.

Getting that car hired took longer than I thought was possible. They did accept a cash deposit as a guarantee against damages, and we were eventually off the car park with a small car.

We went directly to Aunt Marge's house. We had no idea what to expect. From the exterior, it looked normal. We walked up to the front door and rang the door bell. Of course, there was no answer.

Dad looked around and said, 'I know where Marge keeps a backup key." We went through the gate to the back yard, and Dad walked over to the slat fence at the back of the yard. His hand ran along the slats for several feet, and then he stopped. He pulled something from between the slats and walked over to us.

It was a small plastic bag with a rubber band around it. He removed the rubber band and opened the plastic bag. Inside the bag was a key. We went to the back door and opened it. Inside we found the kitchen left pretty much as it had been the last time I'd been there.

We opened cabinets, the pantry, and the refrigerator. The refrigerator was empty—absolutely. It had been emptied systematically. There wasn't even the box of open baking soda that she always kept there. The pantry had lots of dry goods. We looked at the "use by" dates. Most of them were in the past or about to expire.

Mum said, "Nobody's been here for months."

I asked, "Who did all this? Who cleaned out the refrigerator? Who's paying the phone bill, the light bill?"

No one had an answer.

Dad said, "Well, there's nothing more we can do here. We've got to get to the storage facility and get our furniture schedule to return to our house."

He looked up their phone number and made a call. They reminded him that he had only paid for six months storage. We'd have to come to the office and settle the past due payments before we could arrange delivery.

He called the public utilities bureau and arranged to have the power, gas, and water turned on effective tomorrow. They too required us to make a visit to pay a deposit to have them turned on.

Any of them would have let us pay with a credit card, but of course, we didn't have credit cards. Luckily, we still had lots of cash.

We locked up Marge's house and began our driving tour of Greater London. We went to the storage facility. We paid our debts and were able to schedule a delivery in two days.

We ate somewhere in that time, but I don't remember where. The public utilities office was the worst. We had to wait in queue for hour after hour, but we finally reached the end and paid our deposit. Dinner was late.

Dad wanted us to go visit the house. It was a very long time since we were there last. We knew that there wouldn't be much to see, but we all wanted to go anyway.

By the time we arrived, it was late twi-light. We went to the front door. We stopped a minute. All of us remember the last time we'd been here. We remembered Harry urging us to leave. We remembered the wizard couple who took us in. Mum wondered out loud what had happened to them.

Then Dad slipped his key into the front door and turned it. He opened the door, and we all looked in. It was pitch dark in there, but we all took a few steps in. This was finally it. We were finally home. There was nothing to see. Even if we'd had power and lights, we'd only see bare walls, but that would have been all right.

As it was, Dad just closed the door and locked up. He knew of a couple of hotels not far off. We found a spot.

The next day we kept re-building our life. We went to the bank and Dad wrote a Canadian check to transfer most of the money to that account. We knew the money wouldn't arrive for days and days, but we had to start somewhere.

We had a little fun. We went car shopping. We went to a Ford dealership near our home and looked at new models. I was wandering around the car park and found an old used car. I thought Dad would get a laugh out of it. "Hey, Dad, come over here."

He did and stared at the car with as much amazement as I did. Dad identified it, "This is an old Ford Anglia. How long has it been since they made this model?"

The car salesman had trailed along. "Oh, that's old OK, but those old Anglia really held up over the years. We got this in trade within the last couple of weeks. It took some work, but it's not in bad shape." He glanced over at me, "It would be a super starter car for the young lad."

Both Dad and I laughed. Dad said, "We'll think about it. We're just looking for a family car at the moment."

Dad even called Grunnings. He talked with one of his friends. I heard one half of the conversation:

"Is Ted Baxter still there?"

. . .

"Oh, tell him it's Vern. He'll know me."

. . .

"Hi Ted. Yes, it is Vernon Dursley. . . . "
"I know. I'll bet everyone thought I'd died."

. . .

"Listen, can I meet you for lunch next week? I'd like to get the lay of the land and see if there's any point in trying to come back to Grunnings."

. . .

"Good. It's Tuesday next for lunch at the usual place. You're a pal! Say 'Hi' to the wife and kids for us."

We had had a long day. We went back to the hotel for dinner. When we finished, there was plenty of light in the sky. Mum said, "Don't you think we could go back to the house while it's still light? Maybe the power's back on. We could turn on the lights and take a look around the place."

Dad and I were agreeable to the idea, so we drove to the old neighborhood. In the better light, we took our time to drive around the neighborhood a bit before coming to our house. Mum noted that the Gundersons had new drapes, and the Finchs had put up a new fence.

The sun was close to the horizon when we reached our house. The old house looked a little worse for wear and tear, but none of us cared.

After parking, we walked up to the house. Dad unlocked the door. This time when he opened it, there was sunlight streaming through the door and filtering through the windows in the rooms. Dad flipped the light switch. THERE WAS LIGHT!

We began walking through the house. Mum went back to the kitchen. I walked past the cupboard under the stairs. I could barely remember that cupboard from when we left the house a year ago, let alone remember it when Harry lived there. I opened the door. There was a string operated light switch. I pulled the string and the little room filled with glaring light. I noticed that there was a tin soldier on one of the shelves. I supposed that it had been Harry's.

Dad had gone into the living room. He gave a shout, "What the bloody . . . has been going on here?"

We all gathered in the living room. We could immediately see what had Dad bothered. The carpet was stained, discolored, and even ripped in places.

Mum said, "Somebody's been messing about in the kitchen. As a matter of fact, it's a right mess."

Just at that moment, there was a crash at the front door. It was a rending of wood, screws ripped from holes, and heavy equipment hitting the floor. Almost immediately, there was a deafening shout, "Thames Valley Police. Everyone on the floor."

I didn't know what it was all about, but I knew that the safest place was on the floor. I dropped to the floor. Mum and Dad were frozen in shock. I grabbed Mum and pulled her down beside me. A policeman knocked Dad to the floor. Meanwhile, the police were shouting, "Hands on top of your heads."

Other police were streaming in the front door and fanning out through the house. Someone pulled my hands behind my back and handcuffed me. I could see that the same was happening to Mum and Dad.

Dad shouted, "What's going on here?"

A policeman who seemed to be in charge said, "Mr. Vernon Dursley, I'm taking you into custody under the charge of running a crack cocaine production organization. Your associates are also being taken into custody on that charge.

"You have the right to remain silent. You have the right to legal representation. If you can't afford legal counsel, a solicitor will be appointed. Everything that you say will be taken down and may be used in evidence against you."

I relaxed. I knew there was nothing that I or my parents could do for the moment. I said to Mum and Dad as much. Dad was still angry, but he would see how far it got him in the next day or two.

We were put in a police car. It took us half an hour to get to the police station. Once there, we were relieved of all our personal possessions. They were carefully inventoried, written up, and signed for by us.

Each of us had a good bit of money on us—of varying countries. The officer who did the inventory was surprised to find that I had US dollars,

Panamanian dollars, Canadian dollars, even some Mexican Pesos (I had no idea how they got there), and of course, lots of pounds sterling.

We were taken to separate cells. About an hour after we arrived, I was taken to an interrogation room. A tall, thin, dark-haired Inspector came in with a Sergeant. The Inspector introduced himself and his Sergeant.

There was a tape recorder. The Inspector started the tape machine and said, "It is 10:43 PM on July 7, 1999. This interview with Mr. Dudley Dursley is being conducted by Inspector Robert Lewis and Sergeant James Hathaway. The interviewee has been cautioned as to his rights.

"Mr Dursley, can you tell us why you were present in . . ."

Here I interrupted. "Inspector Lewis, I refuse to answer questions without the presence of legal counsel."

Lewis nodded and noted the fact and turned off the recorder. He turned to me and said, "So have your parents. We'll arrange for legal counsel, and there will be a preliminary hearing to set bail tomorrow morning. Sergeant Hathaway will return you to your cell."

I shrugged and said, "Let's go."

I actually slept fairly well. I was up, had breakfastm and was waiting in my cell when Hathaway came for me. I was taken to a courtroom where I joined my parents. We waited for about two hours for our turn to come.

Dad had found a solicitor that I'd never heard of before. Our brief appearance before the judge cleared up a question that I'd been wondering about all night—why the police thought we were drug traffickers.

Our house had been discovered to be a center for processing raw cocaine into crack for more than four months. The police had been watching it almost half of that time hoping to find the higher levels running the drug ring. They knew that the owners had been staying hidden and evading international law for longer than that.

We had finally showed up, and though we didn't have any drugs, we were carrying large quantities of cash from various countries in the Western Hemisphere.

We had a long history of fleeing from international law and were a real threat to flee. Therefore the bail should be set very high.

Our solicitor argued that there was no evidence that we had any history of illegal activity. We had been touring the world, and the appearance of fleeing authorities was an unhappy coincidence.

The judge agreed with the state and our bond was set at 300,000 pounds apiece. Dad went ballistic. He said, "300,000 bloody pounds. We've done nothing. We should sue for false arrest." Etc. etc. etc.

Lewis and Hathaway interrogated us one at a time. Lewis was actually rather nice. One of the questions he asked was why we'd been away from home for so long.

I said, "We were touring the world."

326

Lewis asked, "You had lived in one house for almost twenty years. THEN you suddenly decided to pull up stakes and travel the world."

I shrugged.

Hathaway asked, "You had a great deal of money in your pockets when you were arrested. Where did it come from?"

My solicitor said, "You don't have to answer that."

I smiled. I wanted to. "I worked. I had a couple of jobs while we were traveling."

The solicitor shook his head, but Hathaway wanted to keep asking, and I wanted to keep answering. He asked, "What jobs did you have?"

I smiled. Hathaway blanched. "I worked as a janitor's apprentice in Vancouver, British Columbia. I worked with my parents as caretakers for a fishing Lodge in Manitoba."

Lewis was interested, "That doesn't sound like you could make a lot of money at those jobs."

"Oh, yeah. The janitor job was low wage, but the caretaker job was big. We were there for almost eight months. We got lots of overtime for that. We were on duty twenty-four by seven."

Hathaway persisted, "Tell me about that."

So, I did. I went into detail about our duties, about how remote the location was, about the long, bitter, cold winters. I talked about keeping generators working so that we could survive. I told about cleaning rooms and cabins. I got so excited that I almost told him about our guests. I guess that's why the solicitor was so unhappy about my talking so much.

At the end, Lewis dismissed me, and I went back to the cell.

□□

The next morning, our jailers let us have breakfast together. We talked about our separate interrogations. I said, "I think they've decided that our stories are close enough together that there isn't any chance of our lining up our stories further."We were enjoying the instant fried eggs and soggy toast with tepid tea when a guard came up to us and told us to come with him.

Dad objected, "But, I've not finished my nutritious egg and toast, not to mention this piping hot tea."

The guard just urged us to get up and get going again. We had a rather long walk. We ended up in the office of Inspector Lewis. Apparently, Hathaway was elsewhere. He was talking with a woman in a chair facing him. There was something that seemed familiar about herm but I couldn't place it until she spoke.

I spoke too. "Aunt Marge! What are you doing here? They don't think that you're part of this crack cocaine gang, do they?

She rose, turned, and looked us up and down. "I should say not! I was just explaining to this gentleman how wrong he was about you."

She stared at us for a second, "Although I can understand how he might get the wrong idea from your appearance."

After two nights in jail without a change of clothes, I don't know how she could think we wouldn't look rather scruffy, but she was running on.

"I think I've straightened out this misunderstanding, and we can all be on our way." She turned to Lewis, "You're lucky if they don't sue you for false arrest."

Lewis said, "Well, you can certainly be on your way any time that you want,, but the Dursleys will want to collect their belongings before they go."

Aunt Marge make a sound with her mouth and said, "I suppose so. Well, come by my house for lunch today, and we'll get caught up." Then she had a thought, "Do you need a ride? Of course, you do. I'll wait down below for you." Then, she bustled out of the office.

Lewis released what I'm sure was a sigh of relief. He pointed at chairs and said, "Why don't you sit down. I've sent Sergeant Hathaway for you items."

We were all mystified by the change in attitude. I know that Aunt Marge can be a real pest, but I couldn't quite believe that she could pull that switch in attitude off.

Lewis looked at us in some puzzlement, "You look surprised. Do you mean to say that you weren't expecting this release?"

Dad tried to bluster through it, "Well, I was sure that once our real position came clear, you'd let us go."

Lewis seemed a bit surprised himself, but he went on, "Well, a Major from the SAS showed up at my office with Ms. Dursley. He made it abundantly clear that you folks should be accorded every courtesy and even deference. It appears that you were working for the government in some official capacity. Perhaps it was MI5 or SAS or something else.

"Anyway there was even mention of a possible knighthood. You were to be released immediately if not sooner, and all record of you expunged from our files.

"I didn't inquire for more details, and I don't expect you to provide them. I just want to get you on your way with a promise to me that I'll never have to deal with that woman again."

Dad chuckled, "Yes, she can be something of a pill, can't she? Well. Don't worry, we'll do our best to keep her out of your hair."

While we were discussing this, Sergeant Hathaway appeared with several large manila envelopes. Each had one of our names on them. He opened them one at a time, withdrew the inventory list inside, and read them off, assuring that we agreed that all items had been returned intact. We each had to sign a receipt, and we were free to go.

We walked out to the street and found Marge's car. Dad mentioned that we'd not had much breakfast. Marge reacted immediately, "Well, we need to have a proper breakfast in place of lunch."

She drove us to her favorite restaurant. After we were seated she immediately ordered breakfast for all of us. That is what she's like. Really, she knows our tastes in breakfasts pretty well, so no one objected.

Mum said, "Well, no one was more surprised than we were when you showed up this morning to get us out of jail."

Aunt Marge needed no more urging. She picked up her spoon and pointed it around at us and said, "Let me tell you about that." I knew we were in for a story.

She began.

꙳

"When you disappeared a year ago, I was disturbed and worried about you, but I didn't have any idea at first how to find out what had happened to you. But I didn't give up. I had an idea. You know that Ripper is a great tracker. I decided to use that skill to find you. I went to your house. I looked for something that one of you wore frequently to give Ripper the scent. I found a sock on the floor. Ripper really got into the hunt.

"I followed the path to the Tube station. We got on. Now you might think this was the end of the trail, but I stopped at each stop. Ripper and I looked for the trail. We found it after many stops. We followed a very clear trail into the warehouse district. Ripper led me straight to one warehouse and to one door in that warehouse. Before I had a chance to knock on the door, two ruffians grabbed me and Ripper and dragged us into the warehouse.

"They put us in a little cell. We waited and waited. Finally, a man and woman came. He talked with me. He said his name was something like Wandt or Wand or Wen or something like that."

Mum asked, "Could it have been Wendt?"

"Yes, yes. I think that was it."

I shook my head and thought, "We just can't get away from that guy, whoever he is."

She continued, "When he was done, he took us to a courtyard where a helicopter was waiting. Ripper and I were hustled into the helicopter. It took off. The pilot was a madman. He flew just above the rooftops. We flew out over the North Sea. I could almost feel the spray from the waves hitting the helicopter.

"We flew over Germany and landed at an Air Force base. The Nazi's! They hustled into a concentration camp."

Dad said, "Nazi concentration camp, really Marge!"

She was insistent. "Sure. We were in Germany. We were in a hangar that was full of cells. People were constantly flowing through there. There were armed guards. They were Americans.

"There was an Exercise Room and they sometimes let us go outside the hangar to run or walk.

"I heard the name of the base once. It was something like Durmstrang or Darmstrang or Durmstadt or something like that.

"Anyway, we were there for a long time. Then two days ago, we were rescued.

"The door to our cell opened, and a British commando came through. He urged me to pack quickly. It was easy, I didn't have clothes to mention. A couple of other commandos were outside. I don't know what happened to the guards—how they got rid of them, but they were gone.

"They rushed me to an RAF helicopter that was revving on the tarmac. They hustled me in, and we were in the air. This pilot was not a madman. We got up to a good altitude, and we flew to an RAF base. When I got out, there was a Hum-Zee or whatever they call those things waiting. It drove me straight to my house.

"The house was in amazingly good shape. The refrigerator was empty but that was lucky. Someone had been there recently. They must have used the emergency key that I keep in the back yard to get into the house."

Dad said, "That was us. I know where the key was." He put his hand into his trouser pocket. It came out with a key. "This is yours."

Aunt Marge went on, "I had hardly got back in the house when early this next morning an SAS Major showed up at the front door. He said that he wanted my help to get you out of jail."

"I wasn't going to hesitate. He took me to that police station.

"Well, I tell you, he gave that Inspector a proper prangning. He told him that he should have done a proper investigation before arresting anyone.

"He should know that you lot were working for the government on some sort of hush-hush project.

"That sergeant Half-baked or whoever he is tried to defend the Inspector. The Major put him in his place. He said that he'd better have you released immediately and treated proper.

"More than that. They'd better put everything to right for you. Get your name off the police records and so on. He was hopping mad!

"He said that he had to go, but that I would be here to make sure that everything went right. If it weren't, he'd hear about it, and there'd be Hell to pay."

330

She had gotten more and more worked up as she went on. Then she returned to calm and finished, "So, here we are."

While she was going on, our food had arrived, and we'd finished eating. There was a little battle about who would pay for lunch. Dad won that battle, one of the few that he'd ever won over Aunt Marge.

She offered to take us home, which we accepted gladly. As we turned onto our street, I could see a crowd a couple of blocks down the street. As a matter of fact, it was in OUR block.

When we reached our block, we saw that the small crowd was in front of our house! Dad thumped himself on the head and said, "I completely forgot that our furniture was being delivered yesterday."

When we parked we discovered that all of the furniture was on the yard in front of the house. The small crowd was around a man who was standing on a packing crate. He seemed to be an auctioneer.

Marge was out of the car before any of us. She was running to the crowd shouting, "You, there! Yes! You! Stop that now! You can't sell these things!"

I was right behind her and actually passed her by the time we reached the crate. The fake auctioneer and a friend had taken off running as soon as we got close. I pursued them. All that running had done me some good. I quickly caught up with the auctioneer and pulled him down. I pointed a finger at him and said, "Stay. Or I'll break your arm."

Then I took off after his accomplice who had picked up a good lead. It wouldn't have been a race if he didn't have such a lead. I caught him as he was about to jump a fence. He said, "Shit. I almost was gone."

My only comment was, "In your dreams. Come on. If you give me any trouble, I'll do the same thing I threatened your mate with. I'll break your arm."

We got back to the house and found that most of the crowd had dispersed. Marge had apparently convinced them that there wasn't a sale going on.

I picked up the "auctioneer" on the way back, and we had a little discussion. Marge was all for calling the police. Dad wanted to negotiate with them. I agreed. As a matter of fact, I started negotiating without Dad's concurrence.

"OK. Here's the deal: we don't call the police. In return you give us all the money that you collected. You help us move this furniture into the house. If I ever see you hanging around our house again, you'll regret it."

They agreed. We got the pittance that they'd collected. Aunt Marge stood guard and directed traffic. She seemed to know our house as well as we did. She always seemed to send the right piece of furniture to the right room.

Dad helped me move the biggest pieces. Mum carried boxes in.

I asked Dad why the deliverers didn't take the furniture in at least. His answer was, "I found a note on our door. Because no one was home, they would not try to guess where pieces went. They offered to come back and take everything back into storage–for a fee.

"We were in jail at the time."

After a while, some people who had bought things came back and returned their purchases. They all seemed too embarrassed to take a refund on their money. A couple actually stayed to help us move in.

About mid-afternoon, a step van pulled up outside the house. Two men got out and came up to the only man standing there at the moment—me.

One held out a piece of paper to me and said, "We've been hired by the Thames Valley Police to repair or replace your door at your option."

The paper essentially was a work order to do that. There were no prices on the invoice. I said, "Well, the door is pretty much matchsticks at the moment, I think we'll have to take the replace option, but let me get my Dad who is the actual owner."

I found him upstairs with the "auctioneer" and his mate carrying a dresser up to my bedroom. I explained the situation. He came down and thanked them. He then said, "Of course, replace it. Do we have a choice?"

The leader of the installers took us back to the step van. There were a couple of doors of different sizes and designs. Apparently, one of them had measured the door-frame while I was up getting Dad. The leader pointed to three candidates. Once had glass in it and was natural wood. Another was steel and had a peephole, the third was solid wood with a peephole. Dad picked that one.

The leader then asked, "Do you want us to keep your current lock if we can get it to work?"

Dad asked, "Would we have to replace the lock in the back if we went with a new lock?"

"No. We can re-key the lock in the back if the key is compatible with the new lock."

Dad thought about it and said, "Let's stick with the current lock if you can manage."

That settled it. They went to work.

By the time that they finished, the last of our belongings were back in the house. Almost all the furniture was in the right room. There were boxes of clothes and tools and toys and food and every other imaginable thing everywhere.

There were lots of little things missing: lamps, pillows, a dinner tray set, lots of games and toys, and so forth. We didn't expect to get any of them back.

The door installers finished. We tested all the keys that we had. They all worked in all doors. They insisted that Dad sign the work order acknowledging that the work had been completed.

We all went inside except for the installers and the thieves. We turned on all the lights in all the rooms and gazed on the bewildering mess.

Mum said, "I think it will take a week for us to set all this right."

Dad laughed, "A week. You are such an optimist! We'll be lucky if we can do it in a month."

Aunt Marge said, "I'm starving. You lot must be too. Let's go get something to eat. You won't be able to cook in that kitchen in days."

We agreed but we couldn't agree on who would pay. Aunt Marge was determined to pay. You can only win so many battles with her, so Dad graciously gave in. He did get the concession that from now on, he and she would alternate picking up the check.

We went to our favorite Italian restaurant. This time we got to sing or actually recite for our supper. We told her about our adventures on the road. We didn't include everything of course. We have never told anyone anything about the Deatheaters who came to visit us in Canada.

We got home, dropped into bed with the intent that it would be the return to things as normal the next day.

The next day was pretty normal if you think that unpacking boxes and trying to organize a total mess is normal. It was not as long as Dad thought before we had the house pretty well restored to normal.

I never picked up any of the electronic games that I'd played before our little adventure. They all seemed so boring compared to the reality that our lives had become.

Things didn't stay normal for as long as any of us expected, but before things changed again, I took the chance to ask Mum about Goodwin.

She said, "That was another world. There are a million IF's in that world. IF I met Archie before I met your Dad, IF I lived in the States, IF he didn't work for Mr. Wolfe, and on and on. If all those IF's were true, I might not be your Mum, but I am and always will be. Never forget that."

THE END

About the Author

William Wilkin lived in a small Southern Ohio town until he began his college career. He has a Bachelor's degree in Physics from The Ohio State University and a Master's degree in Physics from The University of Chicago. He had a career in corporate Information Technology and currently lives in Nashville, TN..

He enjoys music, both "serious" and "classic Rock". He reads classic Detective fiction and Science Fiction & Fantasy as well as trying to stay current in Physics.

He began writing seriously about 2005. He has a blog, in-mid-world, where he writes about Science Fiction & Fantasy and remotely related topics.

www.ingramcontent.com/pod-product-compliance
Lightning Source LLC
Chambersburg PA
CBHW072124250626
47159CB00007B/2554